In The Forest

EDNA O'BRIEN

First published in Great Britain in 2002
by Weidenfeld & Nicolson

This promotional edition published by Paperview U.K. Ltd. in association with
the Irish Independent and with acknowledgement to Orion Books Ltd.
and Edna O'brien
www.paperviewgroup.com
www.independent.ie

Cloosh Wood

Woodland straddling two counties and several town-lands, a drowsy corpus of green, broken only where the odd pine has struck up on its own, spindly, freakish, the stray twigs on either side branched, cruciform wise. In the interior the trapped wind gives off the rustle of a distant sea and the tall slender trunks of the spruces are so close together that the barks are a sable-brown, the light becoming darker and darker into the chamber of non-light. At the farthest entrance under the sweep of a brooding mountain there is a wooden hut choked with briars and brambles where a dead goat decomposed and stank during those frantic, suspended and sorrowing days. It was then the wood lost its old name and its old innocence in the hearts of the people.

Ellen, the widow woman, did not join in the search when the men and women set out with their dogs and their sticks, clinging to the last vestiges of hope. Yet she dreams of it, dreams she is in Cloosh Wood, running back and forth, calling, calling to those search parties whom she cannot reach, the tall trees no longer static but moving like giants, giants on their grotesque and shaggy roots, their green needly paws reaching out to scratch her, and she wakens in a sweat, unable to scream the scream that has been growing in her. Then she gets up and goes into her kitchen to boil milk. She looks at the sheen of dark beyond her picture window, the plants, geraniums and cacti limp in their sleepiness, looks at her big new brass lock, bright as a casket, and then she comes fully awake, and as she tells it again and again, Eily, the dead woman with her long hair walks towards her and says, 'Why, why didn't you help me?'

'The Kinderschreck,' she answers back. 'The Kinderschreck,' and with her raised arm tries to blot out the woman's gaze, the light of the eyes a broken gold, like candles puttering out.

KINDERSCHRECK

The Kinderschreck. That's what the German man called him when he stole the gun. Before that he was Michen, after a saint, and then Mich, his mother's pet, and then Boy, when he went to the place, and then Child, when Father Damien had him helping with the flowers and the cruets in the sacristy, and then K, short for O'Kane, when his hoodlum times began.

He had been a child of ten and eleven and twelve years, and then he was not a child because he had learnt the cruel things that they taught him in the places named after the saints.

He was ten when he took the gun. He took it so as not to feel afraid. They put him away for it. It was his first feel of a gun, his first whiff of power. It felt heavy. When he stood it up it was taller than himself. He did not know if he would have the guts to fire it. His hands shook when he loaded it, yet he loaded it out of a knowledge he did not know he had. Then he cuddled it to himself and gave it a name, he called it Rod. *I didn't mean to kill, only to frighten one man.* He wanted to say that, but he was not able to say it because they were beating him and shouting at him and dragging him off. There was the guard, the sergeant, his father and Joe Mangan, the bad man that threw the shovel at him and blamed him for cycling over his wet concrete and destroying it. It was not him that cycled over it, it was Joe Mangan's own son Paud, but they blamed him. No matter what was done wrong they blamed him, and there was no one to stand up for him because his mother was dead. They said she was dead but she wasn't, they buried her alive, suffocated her. They brought him up flights of stone stairs and into a cold room to show her lying on a slab with no colour in her cheeks and no breath. It was snowing outside. It was the snow that made her white and made the world white. She was not dead. They only told him that so as to trick him because he was her pet. They were jealous, they were. They put her in a coffin and buried her. He stole out at night and went and talked to her, and she talked back. He crept out through the window and ran across the fields to the grave at the edge of the lake. He was a cross country runner and had won a medal for it. He scraped the earth back and made a hole where he could talk down to his mother and where she could hear. She promised to come back and save him when she was less tired. His plan was that he would run away until then, live in the forest and eat nuts and berries and in the winter go from house to house to beg for food. He would give himself a secret name, Caoilte, the name of the forests.

The first time he spent nearly a night there he was dead scared and dead excited. There were spots before his eyes and shimmers, different colours. He got on his hands and knees and broke sticks, building a sentence around the totem words—'God hates me, Father hates me, I am hated.' In the wood that night he saw things no one else saw, not Joe Mangan's sons, not anybody's sons, only him. He climbed into a tree and hid. A fox, a she fox, let out a sound that scared him. It was like a woman having her throat slit, only worse. The vixen was calling for her mate, her husband. She was in a bad way and so were the pheasants that were letting out cluck-cluck sounds to warn each other of the danger. He heard a badger barking and he ducked well into the branches because he knew a man that a badger bit and the man said it was worse than any dog bite. He swore then to live in the wood, to make a log cabin up in the trees, with a floor and chairs and a rope ladder leading up to it. He and his mother would live there away from his father and everyone else. While he was thinking it, a princess floated by, flying. She was wearing a long white coat and had very long hair down to her ankles. She was carrying slippers. His mother was still in the house, his father attacking her with a poker. She shouted at him to run out, to run off to the woods, and she stayed behind to take the blows. He'd got one blow. There was blood at the side of his mouth that had run down from his ear and he put a fob of a pine branch on it to stop it. The thing was to keep awake, no matter what. There were noises and there was silence. The louder the silence, the scarier the noise to come. A cock pheasant was warning all other pheasants of an imminent attack. He was waiting for his mother to come but he was afraid she might be dead.

There was a full moon and it was walking across the sky and in places the light spilt onto the ground, where there were no trees. That was called a glade. He knew that from school.

When his mother came he was fast asleep. Mich Mich Mich.

He wouldn't let on he heard her and wouldn't let on when he came awake. She lifted him down and tweaked his nose and said, 'Sleepy head sleepy head.' One of her front teeth was gone and she didn't look nearly as nice. He put his finger into the hole and felt the damp of the blood and tasted it and it was warm. His mother and he were not two people, only one.

'I saw a beautiful lady.'

'Go on.'

'She was on her way to her wedding.'

'How do you know?'

'She had silver slippers.'

His mother carried him back to Glebe House, through the scrub and the moon was a lamp to show the way. She said he was a brave boy to stay all alone in the forest and not scream like that silly vixen. She said he was a true son of the forest. Next day he wrote that in the front of his copy book at school—*I am a true son of the forest*. They jeered at him, called him a liar, a bluffer, said that he'd run scared from his own shadow, he that had to have his mammy walking him to school and waiting for him out in the cloakroom and sometimes having to sit in the back of the classroom because of him bawling. A mammy's boy, a patsy, a pandy, a sissy and a ninny.

Soon after that, they had to leave Glebe House and went to live in a cottage, far from the woods.

His father and the guard and the sergeant and his sister Aileen and Joe Mangan and Mrs Joe Mangan are all in the court, and the judge is sitting at a big brown desk, higher up. The sergeant is telling the judge the terrible thing he'd done. The German man is on the other side, nodding about the terrible thing he'd done. His sister Aileen is beside him, holding his hand. His nose is streaming and his eyes and he has no hanky. The sergeant is describing how he stole a bicycle from the doctor's shed then rode it over the wet cement that Joe Mangan had just put down and did it on purpose and then rode and got the groceries for his sister and left them on the window sill and ran off in search of an empty house where he could find a gun. The sergeant got very wound up when he came to the bit about breaking into the German man's house and finding the shotgun and the belt of cartridges, and then painted the picture of him creeping back towards his own house, hiding in a ditch at the end of the garden and waiting for the opportunity to shoot. The sergeant told how he himself and the boy's father were behind that very door that had been shot at and were lucky to be still alive. There was more and more about his aggressive behaviour from a very young age, from the innocence of stealing apples to the non-innocence, the evil, the knowing evil of stealing a gun. He was listening to it all but he was not allowed to speak. He had not cycled over wet cement, another boy did that, Joe Mangan's son Paud did that, but he got the blame and they called him dirty names at the time and told him what they would do to him. They would carry him off to the Shannon and drown him and he'd never be found. He ran to his own house to tell his sister that, but she wouldn't let him in because she had a friend of hers there and she was ashamed of him. When he asked for a glass of orange, she poured it and put it out on the window sill and told him to drink it there. That was when he ran away because no one wanted him and no one believed him and he had no friend.

When the judge gave the sentence he didn't understand it. A detention centre. What did that mean? The judge's voice was very low but his face was very red. The sergeant thanked the judge and they trooped out. His sister told him outside the court that he was going to be going away to St Malachi's and it was lucky that there was a vacancy as it was a very nice place. He cried and screamed and ran down the street, but they caught him in a car park and lugged him back.

'If ever you try to escape, I'll hunt you down like a dog until I find you,' Sergeant Wiley said to him, and there was hate in his eyes and in his spit.

His sister said that it was only for a little while and that it was a nice place and had a swimming pool, just like a holiday camp. He would be let home at Christmas and he could write letters, so he mustn't cry. '*I didn't mean to kill, only to frighten one man.*' She told him to shush it or they'd murder him for thinking such a thing and anyhow they had to hurry home to start washing and ironing and packing his things. She borrowed a suitcase from Mrs Joe Mangan.

When they arrived there he wouldn't get out of the motor car but clung to his granny's knee. She was the one nicest to him, along with his mother and his sister. The car drove past iron gates into a yard with big high walls. The sergeant sat in front and he

7

in the back, refusing to get out because the place was not a holiday camp but a big dark creepy castle. His granny kept telling him to be a good boy and do as he was told and walk in there like a man. The sergeant lugged him out by the ear and led him past a whole lot of boys, boys his own age and boys younger and boys older, gawking and jeering. The sergeant passed him over to Brother Finbar and Brother Finbar took him in and shut the door and bolted it. Brother Finbar had a long brown robe on him and a pair of rosary beads that swung in and out. They walked fast, with Brother Finbar telling him they would put manners into him. He was brought to a cloakroom to be fitted with clothes. He and Brother Finbar fought over his jumper, the one his mother had knit for him when she was sick in the hospital. It was purple and red, with navy cuffs and a multicoloured tassel at the end of a zip. It smelt of his mother and when he wore it he could feel her soft hands and her kiss. He would not part with it. He would not raise his arms to have it pulled off. Brother Finbar dragged and dragged, then found a loose thread in the waistband and started ripping it. He could see the colours breaking up, navy blue and purple and red; it was like his mother was being ripped up, and the threads were in wormy coils on the flagged floor. He was fitted with short pants, a jacket three times too big for him, and nailed boots. 'You will wear our clothing whilst here,' Brother Finbar kept shouting. Whilst here. Whilst here. Whilst here.

Out in the yard, boys cuffing and roughing each other. He stood apart with a group of boys studying him, making a ring around him. Where's he from. Ask him. Ask 'im. Down the country. Where's that. Where's down the country. Ha. Ha. Ha. A Bogger. Has he got a cigarette? Hey, Rambo, got a fag. He doesn't smoke. Eejit. Bogger. Give him a hook. Test his mettle. Show your mettle, Bogger. Clinging to his mammy's knee. By the time the bell went they had him down on the ground kicking him until a boy called Bertie pulled them off. The tea was in mugs and the thick slices of bread were streaked with lard. Brother Finbar stood at the head of the table like he was an iron figure with iron rosary beads and an iron beard.

'Eat your tea, boy.'

'I'm not hungry.'

'The boot is on the other foot now ... there's no guns here to scare people.'

'I want to go home …'

'You'll go home when the boldness is gone out of you, however long that takes.'

For two weeks he was assessed so as to be sent off to the other place. The Castle it was called, and it was run by the same order of Brothers and was miles from anywhere. The woman that assessed him sat him at a table and asked him questions, asked him if he had three wishes what they would be. He said he wanted to go home. Other boys told him he'd better get rid of the notion of going home. They said that once a person went to the Castle over yonder, they never got home. No use hoping. No use.

The Castle had the same big gates and the same rules and the same cabbagy smell. The boys were older, rougher. On the first evening he was late being brought over in the van and he had his tea alone with a young Brother. He couldn't swallow.

'I have stomach cramps,' he told the young Brother.

'Drink a drop of hot tea, 'twill help you,' the Brother said. He was a nice Brother and one side of his face was a raw red and he said that was called a strawberry face. He took different pieces of cutlery to draw a map of the country and then he put the sugar bowl down to show where he came from, a scenic place with mountains and a famous lake. He missed it. He said he was very young when he joined the order but they were a family of fourteen and with his face and everything there were no other chances for him.

'How long will I be here?'

'Years.'

Brother Anthony ran off then, saying he had something for him. He thought it was a slice of cake but it wasn't. It was a prayer that Brother Anthony had copied and that he read out to him—

'Jesus said to them, when you make the two one and when you make the inner as the outer and the outer as the inner you shall enter the Kingdom.'

'A child and his mother are one.'

'Ah, yes … but that's secular and I am talking of being with God.'

'Will I not be going home for Christmas?'

'It's not for me to say. Who's at home?'

'My sister and my pet fox … I didn't get to say goodbye to it.'

'No use crying over these things … these losses.'

The rain was sliding down the window and plopping onto the flat roof.

He tried. He tried to keep awake so as not to wet the bed, but he always fell asleep and he always wet the bed and he wakened with the smell of ugly wet and Brother Jude putting his hand in under the blanket and dragging him out by his mickey. You dirty thing, you dirty thing you. He brought him to a room that led off the dormitory. The strap was kept in a refrigerator there, to keep it cold and hard. It was a leather strap with studs down both sides of it. He was beaten on both cheeks of his bottom and on his legs and on his arms, but not his face. He was just punched on his face. When he got back to the dormitory boys came around his bed to know what happened, asking if Jude did any bit of fly-fishing, or fiddled with his yoke. Lazlo led the interrogation. Lazlo was leader and they were all afraid of him because he was a schizophrenic. A schizophrenic meant that he heard voices and he could attack any boy if the voices told him to. Lazlo said that Jude was a wiggledy wiggledy wanker. Lazlo trained boys to be tough. He took them into the lavatory and made cuts on their wrists with a flick knife so they'd get used to the pain. Lazlo said a boy had to teach himself one thing, to hate *them* with a worse hate than they had for him. The flick knife had a wooden handle with a picture of a labrador on it.

In the morning he got another beating from the prefect on account of the plastic sheet being wet and smelly. That beating was with the back of a lavatory brush. At Christmas his granny would come for him and bring him home and he would tell her everything and he would never have to come back. In the letters to his granny he had to say that he was a good boy and learning his lessons and getting a star for his subjects. The Brothers made them say that, made all the boys say it. He would not tell her about the beatings in the car when she came to fetch him, he would tell her at night when she tucked him up in bed.

A psychiatrist saw him twice a week and asked him what he was afraid of. He said that he was afraid his grandmother would die because he had dreamt it. He had dreamt that his mother would die and she did. He didn't say that he was afraid of Brother Jude or Lazlo because that would get him into a big mess. He was given the same three pretend wishes. He wished that his mother didn't die and that he could go home and that he would never use a gun again. Other times he wouldn't talk at all. Or he'd say funny things. He said, 'Big fish eat little fish and little fish eat littler fish. Kangaroos have their own courts.' Out in the fields where he and other boys worked digging potatoes, or pitting potatoes he ate them raw to show how tough he was.

One morning it was a priest that rang a bell for breakfast. Father Damien. Boys said that Jude had gone crackers, had gone into the fields and stripped himself naked and ran off. His brown habit was found in the field and his beads and his sandals.

Father Damien was home from Africa and had a tan from all the sunshine. He was not cross over the wet bed and called him Child—'What is it, Child, what is it, Child?' Father Damien gave him a toffee. It was a white toffee with ground nuts in it. Lazlo and the other boys made fun of him. 'Lick arse' they called him for playing up to the priest.

Father Damien told him one day that he was a lucky boy, he was going to be let help in the sacristy. He wouldn't be an altar boy yet but he would train to be. He would fill the glass cruets with wine and with water and get the vases ready for the flowers. They were the first flowers he smelt in months. They were white with bits of yellow, the colour of egg yolk, and they grew wild at home. At home they were called bog-lilies.

One evening after Benediction they were in the sacristy and Father Damien was wearing a white garment, like a gown, with big pockets in it. 'Put your hand in my pocket, Child.' There was a sweet in the pocket. Father Damien told him to keep his hand there until he was told not to. He felt the swellings, his own and the Father's, and his cheeks got very red and he was hot and damp between his legs and Father Damien clung to him until he was finished. Then he said, 'Good Child, good Child,' and warned him not to tell.

Davey was his new friend. Davey was older but not like Lazlo. Davey was fourteen, nearly fifteen. He ran the disco. They had discos one Saturday a month and Davey danced with the best-

11

looking girls, 'motts' he called them, and he steered them down to the back of the hall where it was dark. The girls were delinquents like them, they came in a bus from a convent ten miles away and two nuns stood up on the platform next to the player so as to keep an eye on what went on. They couldn't see into the back of the hall where Davey and the big boys were lifting up girls' jumpers and blouses. He danced with the small girls. Boys danced with girls their own age. The girls knew the steps better than he did. The big girls were motts and they had lipstick and fishnet stockings. Davey went in for the slow dancing and said he went through the girls like butter. 'This is me new mott,' he'd say of whatever girl he was dancing with. Once Davey had kissed a girl it was on to the next, because the more girls a lad had the greater his status. Status was a new word. Davey was his mentor. He said that. Davey said learning in class was only a small part of a man's education, fiddlesticks. The other thing Davey said was to drop a girl like a hot cake once she showed interest, got clingy. Hot cakes and hot crumpets were two different things, all part of girls' pussies.

The night of the Hallowe'en dance he got his first drink, cider. A lot of the boys were dead drunk and gassing outside in the yard. Two boys broke into a factory not far from the school and siphoned cider from vats into lemonade bottles. It tasted of apples. Davey called him aside, he had a plan and it was thus. Davey said that every Saturday there were games in the grounds, hurley and football and handball, priests and brothers and boys, all running in all directions, pandemonium. Davey said that young Mich would go into the chapel the next Saturday and open the back door that led out into a field and on down to the river. He wouldn't be playing hurley that particular day because he would have a nose bleed. Davey would pay a rough Jackeen with a cigarette to give him a few punches and a humping nose bleed, dead easy. Davey said that they would probably find a boat or a canoe down by the river and they would drift out for miles and miles until they came to the city. Then they could be stowaways in a ship or go into town, whichever. He seemed to favour the town on account of having mates there, criminally minded like himself. He said it was brilliant crashing a car, either doing it alone or with a crowd, it gave a great buzz. Best of all was doing it with girls in a car because they lost their marbles on account of having such a big fright.

He left the games field with a handkerchief to his nose and went into the chapel and no one paid any attention to him. He unbolted the back door and then hid in a confessional box until Davey came.

Once out that door they ran helter skelter, down the fields to the river and along the river and over gates and fences and across fields, all the time hoping there'd be a boat moored at the next bend or the next but there wasn't. He was proud of how fast he ran in the nailed boots. By the time it was dark they had come to an estate with a whole lot of houses and ponies in a paddock. There was a bonfire with kids around it. Davey said that they'd best chat up the kids. They were smoking and having a sing song. They were enjoying themselves and then a boy said 'Jesus. Look.' A car was coming into the field, the headlights full on. Someone had grassed. It was the white van from the Castle. The head Brother and two other Brothers and Lazlo and a boy jumped out. He ran to the river and jumped in clothes and all and he could feel the current pulling him along and he was happy because he was going to drown and he would never be going back to the Castle again. The boy that caught him was Lazlo, who got his own back on him for having dropped out of his gang and joined Davey's. Lazlo held him under the water until he nearly drowned and brought him up and shook the water off him. Then he put him down again and held him and he was smothering and his head and his brain were all water and Lazlo wouldn't let him up until he nearly died. 'Lick arse, lick arse.'

He was put in solitary and had to write down how bad he was. He had to write it hundreds of times. Christmas would be soon but he would not be going home. He didn't cry much any more. And he could take the beatings. He stoppered the tears up, like putting a cork in a bottle. It got that it was just as bad between the beatings, waiting for the beatings. He never knew when they were coming for him. He was due a hundred lashes. He only cried when it came to Christmas because he was not let home. Most of the boys were let home, even Lazlo. His sister sent him a card with silver salt on it and he licked it and it tasted gritty. She said the family hoped he was well and that they missed him. They had been told about his running away and his aggressive behaviour and they were all praying that he would turn over a new leaf. She put kisses at the end. He cried at midnight mass because of the singing. A woman sang but he couldn't see her because it was on tape. It was like hearing his mother singing in the kitchen, hearing her, but not seeing her. Father Damien called him aside after mass and asked him what he would like for Christmas. He said he would like a guitar. Father Damien gave him a teeny box of chocolates and a holy picture. He ate the chocolates on a garden seat and wondered if it would snow. The plants were all lying down, like someone had beaten them and they had no strength to get up.

He was put working in the fields, after school, as a punishment. He and other boys were taking potatoes out of pits and putting them into sacks. Lazlo was in charge. When they'd finished they told him that they had some business with him and they went to the opposite end of the field away from the school where there was an old plough with a car cushion on it. They knew what he'd done with Father Damien and they said they were going to cut it off. He screamed and held onto it and begged and Lazlo said, 'OK OK, off with a caution.' They put him face down on the cushion and pulled his overalls off and they took turns.

He could hardly walk back because he was so sore. And he was bleeding.

He dreamt about running away because if he dreamt it it would happen. Himself and another boy were sent to the top gate every other morning to collect the milk. One morning, the other boy was sick so he went down alone. The routine was always the same; the driver got out the full crates, took the empty ones, and set off. When he was found out in the next big town, the driver said, 'Holy heck.' He told the driver that he'd been kept prisoner there and his grandmother and himself made a pact that he would run away when the opportunity came up. The driver didn't believe him, but he knew the bastards they were, so he let him go.

He ran towards home but he was not going home. Three nights on, soaked and scared, he was knocking on the door of Mr Cleary, a man he knew. The man couldn't believe it, but he let him in and they dried him and gave him hot cocoa and he slept in the room with two of their sons, who were afraid of him. He knew they were afraid because when one went to the toilet the other went as well, so as not to be alone with him. The man had gone to the guards because there was a warrant out for him to go back to the place he ran away from. He got a reprieve for seven days. Then he got sick and the doctor came and he was going to be allowed fourteen days in all. He helped the man bring in the cows and do odd jobs in the fields.

One evening the man was milking the cows and he stood beside him in the cow house and he told him the things that happened to him in the place and the man asked him several times if it was true. 'God's honour,' he said, and the man hugged him and stopped milking and the dribbles of milk went over the floor. The man said he would talk to his wife and that they would take it up with the authorities. He was in their house then, part of their family. They had their dinner in the evening and the woman ladled out meat and vegetables into soup plates. They had apple pie or jelly after. Then the man opened the door and made some sort of cluck sound and his pet rabbits came out of their hutch and into the kitchen and ran around. The favourite, Dustin, climbed onto the man, onto his knee and then up onto his shoulders and nibbled at his ears. The others perched on the tiled kerb around the fire. Everyone laughed. He laughed too. This was home, a dinner, apple cake, a calendar on the wall, and a record put on for the rabbits to waltz to. In bed, the sons would try to get him to talk, to tell what it was like in the Castle, but he wouldn't. He knew things that they didn't know. Then one night he boasted about getting a blade and slitting his wrist and being in the ambulance, hopping along the dark road to Casualty and the twenty stitches he had. He told them how he bit the stitches and spat them out. He told them he was a head case and that Lazlo and the gang were scared to death of him. They knew he was sent away because of trying to shoot his father and the sergeant, everyone knew it. There was a hole in the panel of the door for everyone to see, for proof.

One day after planting cabbages the man sat him down on a wooden seat in the front garden, to have a talk with him. He thought it was about going back, but it wasn't. The man asked him if he would like to be part of their family, one of them, a son. He said he didn't know.

'Would you like me to adopt you,' the man asked.

'I don't know.'

'Legally adopt you.'

'Can you?'

The man said it would take time, that he would have to go

through all the correct channels, but he felt confident. His father had given the permission. His father didn't want him back and his sister was gone away. She was gone to live with her granny. He'd seen her on a bus; she'd waved to him from the bus window and he waved back but the bus was moving. It was evening. The man asked him if he'd like a different name and he said he would, he would like to be called Caoilte, the name of the forest.

It was about a month later that it came over him. He began to hate the rabbits and the attention they got, the fussing over them, the cluck cluck and oats put down on the kitchen floor for them, their supper. He hated other things too, the sons, pretending he was their brother when he wasn't. He knew the movement of the rabbits, the time of evening they came out and frisked around the fields and nibbled at grass, same time as when the crows cawed and then the cluck cluck cluck and their trooping in to be petted. He went out to the field that bit earlier and took oats in a bit of cardboard and funnelled it out in little heaps. Several came across but there was one in particular that he decided he would like to kill. A namby pamby. A weakling. He struck the shovel down on the nape of its furry neck and it fell sideways like a glove. No one saw him. Next morning the dog brought the carcass and flung it on the steps. No one said anything.

It was only after he killed the kittens that there was trouble. One of the sons saw him, was peeping from behind the hay shed, a peeping tom. There were six kittens in all, cleaved together in their sleep so it was easy; it was just like killing a mat except for the squeal that came out of them and the blood. The son ran into the house yelling and the mother came out and blessed herself and asked him why in the name of God had he done such a wicked thing. She stood above the kittens and asked him what harm had they ever done to him. He said it wasn't him that did it, it was someone else, a boy that came on a motorbike and then scooted.

The father broke the news to him in the dining room. There was the father and him and a big jug of artificial flowers. The father held up papers, the documents about the adoption, and said it would have to wait. He would have to go back to the Castle for a while because his head was all scrambled up. He got on the floor and clung to the man's trousers, but the man said it was out of his hands now, it was in the hands of the state and the social workers and the people experienced in these matters.

They drove to another place, to where the local doctor had made arrangements for him to go. They'd made a special case of him. He was not going back to the Castle. A secretary took down the particulars and signed him in. The man told him to shake hands with her and say thank you and he did.

'We've been trying to get him to eat for days but he wouldn't … he's very weak,' the man said.

'We can't have that,' she said, and went off to see what she could raid from the kitchen.

When she was gone a head doctor with a red puffy face came and looked at them and the man handed him a sealed letter.

'Hang on, hang on … we might have a problem here,' the doctor said, and went off to make a phone call. He came back and said they couldn't keep the boy, but that there was a place for young offenders about twenty miles away and he would be placed there.

'Can you make an exception?' the man asked him.

'I can't … he's under age … someone got their knickers in a twist,' he kept saying that and a Latin phrase—'*inter alia, inter alia*'.

'So what do we do?' the man's wife pleaded.

'St Sebastian's … that's the place for young offenders and it's not far. The only snag is his father will have to meet you there to sign the admission forms.'

'His father won't,' the man said.

'I'll go and phone him and make sure that he does. He'll be there to meet ye … I'll tell him exactly where it is.' He went off to telephone his father and came back telling them to drive nice and slow but to keep their eyes out for a big white notice board that said St Sebastian's, two miles this side of the town.

They drove, the man, his wife, and himself, without saying much, and when the town lights winked the man started asking the way. One person said, 'Straight on' and the next person said, 'You've passed it.' The man had to get out and make a phone call. The woman asked him was he cold and he said no. Then she asked was he sorry for the things he'd done wrong and he said yes. Yes.

Two nurses saw him. One took his pulse and another put a stethoscope on his heart because he was shaking and twitching. Then one of them asked him why he killed the kittens. He said,

17

'I forget.' The other asked him why he ran away from the Castle. He said he hated it. The nurse said hate was not a good emotion, especially in a growing boy.

His father had not arrived so they sat in the outer hall and waited and waited, but he never came. Two more phone calls were made, and then a nurse and a doctor came out and had a piece of paper that was a dossier on him. The man and the woman stood with them and he was standing nearby, next to a big green plant, and he could hear what they were saying. The doctor was telling the woman that it was not advisable to have him around other children.

'Why not … why not?' she kept asking. He held up the dossier again and showed it to the husband and the husband said 'Jesus' and said he would rather not show it to his wife. The doctor insisted. He held up the piece of paper for the woman to see, and when she saw it she screamed and said it out loud for everyone to hear—*This boy could kill.*

The man and his wife shook their heads at one another and then the man came across to him and said that there was no room at the inn and that they would be taking him back to the Castle.

'Don't send me back, don't send me back.' He got down on his knees and shouted it to strangers sitting in armchairs. It was visiting Sunday. A woman came forward with a biscuit and he refused it and shouted louder, louder, 'Don't send me back there … I'll do away with myself.'

He said it to himself when they drove through the night in the rain. He thought if he said it often enough that his prayer would be answered, but it was not. They drove along dark country roads, where there were hardly any cars, and now and then came on a dead fox or a dead cat, outstretched, its fur and its guts strewn there, a pitifulness to it, as if there was something that cat or that fox badly needed to say.

EILY RYAN

I would come here for the mornings alone. Everything fresh, sparkling, the fields washed after rain, the whole world washed. Daisies and clover and blue borage springing up, and the young cattle on the other side of the fence, frisking, kicking their hind legs and their tails, as if they have taken leave of their senses. The apple and crab-apple trees are coming into flower, apparitions of white, cloaked in green.

I went up the lane very early to give an eye to the ewes in Dessie's field, like I promised him I would. They are due to lamb. There was a fox padding over the far field, out for its breakfast, and I wondered what I would do if it attacked the ewes. First it drank out of the stream and then crossed over, lifting its leg every other minute, and came at a trot to where I was. Its pupils are vertical like a cat's. It's the nearest I have ever been to a fox. A big heavy ewe was cropping the grass and it stole up to her like it was invisible. It was sniffing, sniffing, when our Smokey came and charged it and chased it back over the stream and up the opposite hill, the pair of them ferocious, a chestnut coat and a grey coat savaging one another, then the fox vanishing into a burrow, and Smokey coming back frothing.

The nights can be long. My sister, Cassandra, says we won't stick it in the winter, Maddie and me. We'll have coughs and colds. We will stick it. We'll wear loads of jumpers and thick socks, and anyhow we have the summer to acclimatise. I leave the door open for the clean, fresh smells to come in. The house has had no one in it for years, so it smells mouldy, a reek of lime and damp mortar. Apple Tree House it was named.

Up in Denny's pub they said that a cobbler lived here once and most likely I will come upon odd shoes. I did find a bracelet in an old coal scuttle where someone must have hidden it. It polished up nicely. And I have Maddie gabbling away nonstop. He says the daftest things. He says this house is 'yucky' and that we should go back to the 'apportments'. That is his new big word. I say, 'Wait until we have a bathroom and a tiled stove and a birdcage and a barbecue,' just as in the garden of the 'apportment'. People think I spoil him, carrying him everywhere, little hulk that he is, but the field to the road is a swamp. I bought a lorry load of chips to make a path and just stood there and watched them being swallowed into the mud as fast as they rolled out. The driver kept telling me I should have put big stones, rocks in there first—'Ah don't let it get to you missus.'

Denny's pub is two miles away. He keeps a roaring fire no matter what the season. He did all the smithy work himself, the fire grate, the fire irons and the ornamental eagles on his piers. He has two wash basins that are a feature for tourists. The pedestal of one is a lady's white porcelain legs moulded into black porcelain court shoes, and the other, in the gents, features a lady's plastered protruding buttocks. He escorted me in to have a look at both. I wonder what they make of me. Anyhow they're all smiles. Once he got a bit fresh and said that if I came at night I was to bring a change of underwear. Then to make amends he said he'd save me the sawn-off language some of them used.

The townland is named after goats, except that there are only a few around. There is a herd of cattle and a reigning red bull. In the evening they all come to the fence and bawl and bawl and Maddie bawls back. He pretends to be thwacking them with his stick and shouts some important new word. He's the cop and they are the robbers. The 'apportment' is a place we rented before getting in here. More scenic than here, a lake, reeds, water birds, and cruisers that docked in the evening. Two city slickers invited Cassandra and me over for cocktails. The one with designs on her wore a ridiculous T-shirt and mine took me on a tour of the inside, pointing to the amenities, the bunk beds, en suite, the cocktail cabinet and the Scandinavian shower. He suggested that he and I motor over to Dromineer for a bite. Cassandra was miffed at being left outside and came in and said how naff that he served Martinis from a plastic glass, then stormed off in her very high heels. She says it's the Mars in her.

Apple Tree House was waiting for me, or so Billy said. He had it on his books for nearly a year but kept it for someone special and that someone turned out to be me. He had to bring a slash hook to fight his way through the briars and the brambles across the field, the house itself and the chimneys smothered in ivy and different trees. He put a crowbar to the door and pushed it in, and as it heaved and creaked back, a startled bird flew out at us, a blackbird, a she. We'd scared it. It was then Billy said he would help me to find a loan and he did. Cassandra always says that I was born with a silver spoon in my mouth.

The day we moved in Billy helped us, brought things in his van, and Maddie and me drove on ahead in my little daffodil-coloured Beetle, hooting to let the world know. We had to park the car where the three grassy roads meet and walk across, lugging stuff. Billy brought an old sofa, pink velvet, with the nap worn down. I had cups and saucers and cutlery in a bucket. Maddie carried a lump of bog oak that Cassandra found for us. As we came around the house, there was our visitor, a dog on its haunches, a grey coat, the grey of steel wool, and the most pitiful expression in its eyes. It as good as spoke to us. Its coat had been burnt in places. It isn't a frisky dog, it's a thinking dog, and its hind leg is buckled so that it hops like a kangaroo. It took to us, jumped on us, yelped to make us welcome and followed us up and down the lane while we got our bric-a-brac. Billy said it had been through fire so we called it Smokey. It goes off nights and isn't often back until noon, but back it comes because it wants to be here, guarding us.

We broke a bottle of red wine to launch our arrival. Billy only conked its neck and then strained it through a bit of muslin Brigit had left me to put over the milk. It's a little muslin cap with coloured beads dangling from the edges. Billy knew all the history of the house, told us how a shopkeeper in a market town owned it and thought he would retire here but found it too isolated, too run down. At times he believed that people had broken into it on account of finding ashes in the grate and a mattress and an old torch. We sat outside on a broken wicker seat, Maddie hugging his new friend Smokey and us drinking and the light of the sky changing from one deep blue to another, like paint on a palette. Billy made me promise that I would get a 'phone, said a woman alone would need it, shouted me down when I said I had an army of spirits protecting me. He won.

'Jaysus,' Billy said when he spotted an old coal scuttle with jewellery in it. It was a silverish bracelet showing through the black dust, and he took it out and wiped it in the grass.

'Jaysus ... it's the crock of gold,' he said, spitting on it.

'Jaysus' Maddie said, and we laughed and laughed and it was

21

the beginning of everything, the buds on the trees, the birds scudding about in some sort of spring daftness, in the occasional gusts of wind, falling blossom, the very same as if someone had emptied confetti from a packet.

Twice I went indoors just to look at the letter again, to look at the words, to drink them in—*Thinking of you across two seas. Should one be upside down because of a beautiful crazy red haired girlfriend. I guess yes. Your Sven.*

Homecoming

Sergeant Wiley is fixing up his hedge to keep McCarthy's bloody bullocks out. It is a straggledy hedge, hawthorn, privet, and different kinds of greenery tangled in together and sprouting with a will of its own. McCarthy's bloody cattle have made big holes in it and keep coming in, time and time again, and trampling on his wife's lawn and his wife's flowerbeds. With a slash hook he loops down the high branched bits, and with his hands knits them together and packs them into where the gaps are.

Coming across from the graveyard he sees a youth in a bomber jacket carrying a rucksack, but he pays no attention, thinking him a hitchhiker on his way to the hostel. He has knelt to drive a peg into the ground when suddenly there is a face peering at him from the other side of the gap, the tongue forking in and out in obscene and apish mockery. The two faces are level, the one laughing, the other rigid with surprise, realising it is O'Kane, who should be in England, doing time for mugging an old lady.

'On maternity leave are you?' O'Kane says chuckling.

'Sure now, I retired from the force over eighteen months ago … I potter … I'm fixing my hedge because it's necessary to keep stock in or keep stock out.'

'How far is the town?'

'You're looking across at it … you can see the smoke from the factory chimney.'

'Didn't expect to see me, did you?'

'So you're home for a bit.'

'For keeps. They were shit scared of me … my negativism. Define negativism,' he asks, then answers in a gallop, 'an act of striving against all attempts at contact, ergo, when a hand is offered I withdraw … give me your hand.'

The sergeant puts his hand through the gap and the grasp is deadly, rage emanating and pulsing from it. Their faces are so close he can smell onions off O'Kane's breath, and him raving—
The inmate's behaviour is not likely to attract much publicity because of relatively minor offences, although it should be noted

he is Irish. Reasons for refusing food, wants to die. Has no one to double up with. Sister, father, stepmother, staff all cunts. Fifteen minutes surveillance on wings C and D necessary. Shat in cell. Refused mass visit. In padded cell for management purposes. Blood potassium fell. Laughs abnormally. Resents changing milieu. Changing milieu … you're the bastard that had me put away … that started it all.'

'It was for your own good. You were wild.'

'Jail made me a man.'

'I expect it did.'

'And a monster. It's a mismatch between us now and it'll all end here,' he says with a fiendish laughter, then vanished sprite-like.

The sergeant still kneeling on the ground, feels not the damp grass but the sweat pouring through his vest and the corkscrew vein on his temple throbbing.

'It'll all end here.' He keeps repeating it as he gets up and goes into the house to phone the barracks, to warn them that the Kinderschreck is back, to gall them.

DRUIDESS

Declan has come to do the roof for Eily. Eager, rake thin, a cigarette at the side of his mouth, he is carrying something precious in a piece of cloth which he lays on the table with a certain ceremony. His sculptures. They are polished figures in black wood, embracing couples, a goddess with pendulous breasts and a warring goddess holding a sceptre.

'Someone said you'd be interested … hope it's not cheeky. Bog oak … very ancient, over five thousand years old, petrified I think they call it. It's how coal is made … what d'you think missus?'

'They're lovely.'

'Say hello to them. This is Druid at Dawn, this is Morrigan the Bloodthirsty, and that's Diarmuid and Grainne, lovers that died together.'

'And who is this?' Eily asks, picking out a figure whose hands are folded chastely across her chest.

'Ah now … she's my favourite … little Lena. She must be the loneliest child that ever lived. Came from a bog five thousand years old. You don't mind that I brought them to meet you.'

'Not in the least. What's your name?'

'Declan … but I changed it to Shiva after I went to India,' and he winks and fiddles with an assortment of silver earrings in his left ear.

'What was India like?'

'Most intense experience of my whole life … great soul … great dignity … and the dancers, Jesus, their whole personality dances.'

'Well, we'll have to do a bit of dancing up on the roof, Declan.'

'Jaysus the roof, the roof. I'll tell you what missus, miss, I went up there yesterday evening. I got the loan of a ladder, and I tell you there are piles of slates missing. That's not the worst bit, it's the joists … they're like pulp, sawdust. You could puff them away in your hand.'

'Oh no.'

'It's an old house, you've got to remember that. Empty for years … rotting.'

'I can't have a whole new roof, not this year anyhow.'

'I'll tell you what we'll do. We'll patch it up, we'll put tarpaulin inside and we'll paint it with pitch and we'll get some new slates and tuck them in under the old slates, seal them with a bit of lead for the time being.'

'Will that keep the rain out?'

'Well there's always buckets, I'll bring a good supply of buckets. One question … what made you settle here?'

'Back to nature,' she says with a hoot of laughter.

'Mystical … gorgeous.' He grips her hand, apologises for the dirt but says it's on account of being a carpenter, a stonemason, a barman, a sculptor, and a small time farmer.

'A barman!'

'I do weddings … me and my friend. We bring the barrels and we draw pints all night. I love weddings … I'm mad for them. Great craic, great singing … so if you're thinking of tying the knot, give us a shout.'

'Have you a girlfriend, Declan?'

'Not exactly. There is a girl that kind of showed interest … Muriel.'

As they are talking Maddie comes whizzing in, puts down his big stick and stands and stoops like an old farmer, one elbow on the table, looking at his visitor, sizing him up.

'So what do you do?' Declan says.

'I'm kept going … I make walls, I make lakes, I dig drains, I'm run off my feet,' Maddie says, affecting a worn voice.

'That's terrible altogether,' Declan says.

'But wait till I tell you … I met a man up at the ash tree and I'm after buying a tractor from him. I gave him ten pounds for it. I sat up on it and I drove it home.'

'Go away.'

'Yep. I have it up by the crossroads. D'you want to see it?'

'I'll see it in a minute … I'll have my tay first. Why don't you have a cup.'

'No time … I have to get my potatoes in … I'm always first with the spuds … June the twenty-ninth,' and he goes out running, shouting, 'Duncan, Duncan.'

'Who's Duncan?' Declan asks.

'Someone he's made up ... they have battles.'

'Great little lad.'

'He's dying to be five ... that's his big agenda.'

'What's your big agenda missus?'

'To cut this bloody hair, to shave it all off. The plumbing here ... well, it's primitive, a tap outside in the yard.'

'That's kinda exotic though ...'

'When will you be able to start the roof Declan?'

'It's like this ... I'm freelance. I work for a fecker over in the mills and he's a right bastard, but the long evenings are coming in and I'll be home while it's bright and I'll be down here ... Mr Fixit. Do me a favour, don't cut that hair.'

DUSK

Dusk, and the figure on the roadside barely visible. He is thumbing. What with the baby and being late, Moira Tuohey thinks not to stop, but suddenly O'Kane throws himself in front of the car and she has to pull on the brakes so as not to run him over. 'God almighty, I could have killed you,' she says through the window. He is a young fellow in a bomber jacket with a rucksack and he is holding an apple and an orange in either hand.

'Let me in,' he says in a tough voice.

'I'm only going a mile down the road.'

''Twill do.'

She feels nervous but realises she has no choice. She has to get out on account of it being a two-door car and the baby is strapped in the front seat. As he jumps in the back she notices a wooden handle jutting from inside his jacket.

'I hope you're not going to hit me with that,' she says.

'Hardly … a nice lady like you.' Something about his speech along with his stare unnerves her. His speech is too slow, too clumsy, like he has not spoken to anybody in a long time.

'I'm only going to the next town,' she says, determined to be breezy, businesslike.

'Is that baby teething?' he says and leans forward and tickles the baby under the chin.

'Don't wake him, he's only just gone off.'

She notices how fidgety the passenger is, tapping on the back of the seat, looking out one window, then another, continuously wiping the mist off them and muttering to himself.

'What's worrying you?'

'The guards are after me,' he says quite flatly.

'For what?'

'Robbery … I have to find somewhere to live. Do you have a sofa?'

'Oh I don't live around here at all, I'm just back for a visit. Tell you what … there's a caravan site about two miles from here. It's supposed to be very nice, very clean.'

'I'm a loner.'

'What's your name?'

'O'Kane, Mich.'

'Ah. My mother knew your mother,' she says, determined now to get on friendly terms.

'Bastards. They said my mother was treated for depression … she was never depressed. She loved me, she knit me a jumper.'

'You've been, away?'

'I was in jail in England … they wire you … they put wires on you and then they prod you the way they prod cattle.'

'That's terrible.'

'That's why my fucking head is not good … they wanted my brain for experiments.'

'Are you on your way home?'

'Pigs. It makes me mad the things they say around here about my mother.'

'Don't mind them … they gossip. That's why I moved … my husband and I we have a little business further west.'

'Do you sell helmets?'

'No.'

'Pity. A helmet is good cover for the face. I'm thinking of going to France for the summer … after I've done a few people.'

Her driving is reckless because all she wants is to get to the town and stop outside the chemist and pretend she has to get medicines urgently for the child. She has already rehearsed exactly what she will say, rehearsed unstrapping the harness, and in her mind has lifted the child out and run to safety. She won't even put up a fight if he insists on taking the keys. It's an old car and Jason will understand when she describes the look in the man's eyes, the fidgeting, the crazy talk.

'I'll get out here, it's the cow walk,' he says suddenly and pounds her shoulder. The car comes to a screech and she places her hand across the child's chest to protect it. As he goes to get out he drops the orange into the child's lap.

'No, you keep it yourself, you'll need it …'

'He'll need it … he's teething,' he says.

As she stands to let him out he gives her an unbearable look of reproach. 'You were afraid of me … that hurt me … I wanted so little … I asked so little.'

'What's in the cow walk?' she says, as a kind of apology.

'The true answer,' he says, and looks up into the rainy distance with something like longing.

As she drives away he is standing under a cover of young trees, motionless, half hidden, as if he is planning something spiteful.

STONES

O'Kane sits on a tree stump behind a high ornamental wall with crenellations along the top. Three men are filling potholes on a stretch of road at the outskirts of the town. His father is one of them. His father sweeps the dirt out of the hole with a yardstick, rooting and poking until every bit of dirt is nosed out, lifts it and scatters the debris into the kerb. Then he scoops the stone chips into the potholes, packs them down with a shovel while a second man sprays tar over them from a hose affixed to a tanker on the lorry. When his father has flattened the stones with the paddle of the shovel, patted them in, he adds a second heap which in turn are tarred and so on, in silent, sweating, unbroken tedium.

'I'm nearer than he thinks … I'm within striking distance of him,' O'Kane thinks as he watches through a chink in the wall, sees his father, the black sleeve, the braced arm, the thick hand holding the shovel, the face determined and gruff like it always was. The lorry trundles on as the next hole is filled and the next and the patches of tar are like black flowers, splashed on a blue road.

O'Kane decides to give his father a bit of a turn and lets out a hoot, half man, half donkey, his prison hoot and his father looks around sharp, baffled and then runs his hand down his neck as if flies have landed on it. He'd got fatter. The devil's work. The devil done that.

At lunchtime the lorry is driven onto a by-road and the three men go up the street to Nellie's Café for their grub. O'Kane leaps the wall and begins to take shovel loads of chips and throw them willy nilly onto the road and onto passing cars shouting 'Fucking provos … fucking provos.'

Walking her dog, Mrs Vaughan sees this and runs back into her house to hide. She draws her blind, drags a gas cylinder and puts it against the hall door and goes upstairs to peer through a window, to wait for him to move on.

His task done he decides to call on the parish priest. Going up the short drive towards the pink two storey house with its green shutters he recalled things he had nicked there—altar wine, nail scissors, money and hair gel. He recalls His Holiness like a big white owl in his fleece long johns, gagging for it.

'Oh Enda … nice to see you,' the priest says in as level a voice as he can muster.

'Not Enda …'

'Of course. Michen. I heard you were home … still on the road, day and night … always on the road … it will be time for you to settle down … nothing in those woods for anyone … there aren't even birds up there … I was talking to Cian Logan the other day, he's retiring, he's done his three score and ten and I said to him, *"Cian, tell me what was wonderful about being a forester"* and I had to laugh at his reply: *"Damn all … midges eating you alive in the summer and rainwater drenching you in the winter every time you sawed off a branch."'*

'You had me there,' O'Kane says, standing by a low bed with a red cover and a white linen antimacassar over the pillow.

'Yes, everyone thinks his or her own calling the most taxing,' the priest says, pretending not to be unnerved.

'I want money.'

'Now why would I give you money?'

'Because I could have you disgraced … I could go to the bishops.'

'It's you yourself that might be disgraced … nevertheless I will give you money if it means a hot meal or a decent pullover,' the priest says and looks towards the hall, reluctant to leave him alone in the kitchen and disguising his fears by muttering to himself, wondering where his overcoat could be.

'Shitting your pants?' O'Kane says with a grin.

'England has done you no good.'

'Plenty of fist fucking in the English lavs.'

'No good whatsoever.'

The priest returns, separating the new clean notes with his dampened thumb—'Today was my day for visiting the poor.' He counts them studiously then hands them over.

'Dirty money,' O'Kane says and pockets it.

'You should go on down home and make peace with your father.'

'I'm not wanted there.'

'Where are you wanted?'

'Nowhere,' he says and sits down at the end of the table as if he is about to be given food, staring out, his eyes like holes filled with vistas of nowhere. 'I might go to the Low countries … they have lots of woods there and caves,' he says with a sudden spurt of excitement.

'Well, please God you'll find your niche,' the priest says and holds the door open for him to go out, then lifts his hand in some baleful mimicry of a farewell blessing. He stands dismayed for a long while.

> *A curse on the man who puts his trust in man,*
> *Who relies on things of the flesh,*
> *Whose heart turns from the Lord,*
> *He is like dry scrub in the wastelands:*
> *If good comes he has no eyes for it,*
> *He settles in the parched places of the wilderness,*
> *A salt land, uninhabited.*

FATHER

On Friday, 15 April at approximately four o'clock, I was working on the road down from the hotel. I was accompanied by Michael Burke. We saw a car, a fairly big family car, maroon coloured, driving very fast. It was driven by my son. He was wearing dark glasses and had on a fisherman's hat. It swung around in a hand brake turn and backed up the same way as it had come. The driver did this a few times and then he drew towards the digger where we were working at high speed and got through us. I am convinced that he was trying to drive through me and knock me down. I would have been thrown to the ground only for Michael Burke pulling me back towards the wall. He drove so close by me that a button came off my jacket. There is no doubt but that he was trying to get me. Two days later he drove the same car up and down the harbour front yelling, 'Fucking provos, fucking provos.' There was damage on the left rear wing of the car. Also he was growing a moustache. The next time I saw him was when I was in my own car and stopped at the bottom of the hill outside the bank. While I was there, a silver coloured car approached from the opposite direction. When he saw me he picked up speed and tore off, shouting some 'f' words through the window.

AILEEN

There's word going around that my brother is back from England, that he was spotted in the north drinking champagne and then in Dundalk arguing in a car park, and then nearer home, thumbing a lift. He's beginning to be a bit of a legend but I hope he isn't around and if he is I'm glad I've moved away from Cloosh and made my own life here. This world is not his world and frankly I don't know what his world is and he doesn't know either, shuttled from one place to another down the years. No sooner would he be let out than he'd be caught again for some fresh crime, burglary or aggravated burglary, whatever that means. A wild young man. They couldn't tie him down, he'd escape through windows or police vans and one day he ran away when he was out for a walk with a prison officer. He'd show up around home and ask to be hidden. It even got that I was afraid of him, I that reared him. You could be talking to him and all of a sudden he'd be looking through you like you were glass and he was going to smash his way into you.

He walked in here one day and demanded a sandwich. I was changing my little boy's nappies, my little Ben, only a few months old, on a table. My brother jumping up and down wielding the bread knife and I said to him, 'Will you put that thing down Mich, what kind of fooling are you up to?' He wanted a sandwich but wanted it there and then and I changing nappies and Mich yelling and roaring at me and saying, 'Give it to me now' and I am saying, 'Pipe down or people will hear' and I wrap up the child in a duvet and walk off towards the bedroom and doesn't he follow me down with the knife aimed at me and says, 'I'm going to cut your throat' and I say, 'You're absolutely crazy but I'll make the sandwich if you put the knife down' and he says, 'I don't want your fecking food, it's poisoned and I'm going to leave a permanent mark on your face, so's every time you look in the mirror you'll think of me' and I try fighting him and he lunges the knife into my knee and blood starts gushing out. Next thing he produces a flick knife and digs it down into the duvet with Ben under it. The luck of God

35

he didn't harm him. My leg is going from under me and I let on to him that I hear the landlady and that he better get out before he's sent back to one of them detention centres. I get him out the front door and he starts kicking it and calling me every name under the sun. Then everything goes silent, even the child is stunned and there's blood pumping out of my knee and I shout out the window, 'Somebody come and help me.' I shout it oodles of times and the landlady calls up from below and I says to her, 'Would you come up and help me, my brother is after throwing a fit and I'm bleeding.' She comes up and she says we have to report it to the guards and I say I don't want to, that I want to go to the doctor and we leave Ben with a neighbour and we go out together. Up he hops from behind an oil tank with a hatchet and I tell him to go away, that I'm only going to the doctor and he says, 'You're going to the pigs.' That's what he called the guards. We try ignoring him, us going down the road and he on the opposite side with the hatchet cursing and blinding us. He sees that I've gone into the doctor's and the woman with me and he scarpers. They bandage me up and then the woman insists that we have to go to the guards and I say, 'That's betrayal' and she says, 'Betrayal or not, he assaulted you' and I say that they'll send him back to one of them places and she says that if I don't she will and we go out the lane and she heads towards home and I go on up to the barracks and I report it. Because it's gone dark I ask can they drive me back home because I'm afraid to walk and they say there isn't a car available and I walk up home lame and scared out of my wits. When I get in home I call to the landlady and she comes up with a poker in her hand and says there's no sign of him and that he's probably gone to stab someone else. We're having a cup of tea when there's a knock on my door and it's him nice as pie asking would I have a drop of washing up liquid, so I lift up my knee and show him the big bandage and I say, 'Look what you did' and he says he didn't mean to do it, it was them that told him to do it. I said who was them and he said the voices, the commands. That was the first I ever heard about them voices and I was puzzled and I felt a bit sorry for him because he looked so lonely, a loner in life. I took his hand then and I said I did something awful, 'I went to the pigs' and he got up then and went out.

I heard he was over in a caravan site by the lake for a few months and next thing he stole a priest's clothes and a priest's collar and made his way to England. He wasn't long there before he struck again. There was a picture of him in the paper, with the priest's outfit, mugging an old woman at a bus stop. After that, the odd letter was from places with Her Majesty's name on the top of the stationery. That was the first time I heard mention of voices, voices telling him to be a desperado, to earn for himself the name and state of outlaw.

FROIDEUR

They are in Otto's studio, a loft full of clutter, old floor lamps, picture frames, cane chairs waiting to be restrung, sofas to be upholstered and a motor cycle from his tearaway days. A collection of china dolls on a high ledge look out at them with beady, unblinking, compassionless eyes and from the rafters old pots and pans, ceramic jugs and the pink baby chair with its abacus of beads from Otto's babyhood. Witnesses to his wayward and wandering life.

Otto is carpenter, stonemason, weaver, ladies' man and bohemian all in one.

Each week Eily comes to paint with him and over time she has heard fragments of his peripatetic life, born in a bunker in Berlin as the city was about to fall, an adoring mother who worked in a night club to rear him, weaned on whiskey, gaudy cellars, the bittersweet songs of love and disillusion, a world of women, bonbons, prostitutes and later on, actresses to whom he gave fans or shawls, waking up next to a ravaged face each morning and always inside his head and in his urgent hands the powerful painting that was waiting to get painted. But he had deferred it and put it into life instead. Many a morning, he has paced and with a childlike simplicity spoken to her of his torment, but on this morning he is in a sulk and has not yet saluted her.

'Say it.'

'I do not wish my little woman to go away.'

'It's only a few miles down the road.'

'You shouldn't have left here …this is our valley … our Montmartre.'

'I had to … my lease was up …'

'Your house is not happy … it's gloomy.'

'Don't say that … it's costing me all I have and haven't.'

'For your whippersnapper, Sven … Prince Hamlet of the byways.'

'The local people like him, they respect him, they call him the Scholar.'

'You are a free soul.'

'So is he.'

'Not like you … you give off an aura … even the dogs in the street know that.'

'We'll still be friends Otto … always.'

'Always. What is always … go … go to your shack with its no bath and no lavatory and no Otto to come across the fields to of an evening and smoke and have a drink and conjure Chagall's floating angels circling above our valley …'

'I'm happy … don't you want me to be happy?'

'No, nein, niet.'

'What can I do?'

'Let me paint you.'

'OK.'

'Nude.'

'OK.'

'A triptych … first nude, the young Eily, vibrant, hungry, her burning hair … next she is older … a little belly on her … mother of three in a chemise and last a pilgrim woman going up a winding road.'

'Why are you so against him?'

'Question … how come Otto has not been allowed to make love to the little Madonna?'

'Because … it … wasn't … the right chemistry.'

'I see. You will tell me next that you have discovered love … you will tell me there is no other love like it … never was, never will be … the stroke of his hand and you are electrified … you think a thought and he finishes it … you will tell me you have just discovered love and I will tell you you have just discovered disappointment. It is all illusion, fantasy, chimera.'

'Why are you so against him?'

'Because he is young and nothing else matters in this crooked, lousy, beautiful world.'

He kicked a few things out of the way and went down the ladder stairs and she followed, a bit crest-fallen.

PARTING

Madge is hanging out a double sheet, mustard coloured. There is something amiss about her wave to Eily, something tentative, embarrassed. In that moment Eily thinks she should reverse up the lane, but then she thinks that would be hasty, unfriendly.

Madge and Eily have been friends since they met that warm day the previous spring when Eily had gone into the craft shop where Madge worked, to see if she might display some of the postcard drawings she had done. They were all of nudes and many were pregnant with proud voluptuous bellies.

'How about putting some clothes on them,' Madge said and they laughed, both knowing how the local people viewed them, with their long skirts and their wellingtons, their sloppy knitwear and their ethnic jewellery. 'Blow ins' they were called, a name that had originated from the flotsam of wrecked vessels that had blown in from the sea. Blow ins.

They went outside and sat on the window ledge watching the dilatory life of the street—a dog chewing a flat ball, young girls teetering in absurdly high platform shoes walking up and down, expecting a group of boys to appear.

'I hate men,' Madge said but without conviction. She had separated from her third partner, had two kids, no money, lived in a leaky caravan and had just set her cap at another heart throb. They discovered that they both had a penchant for the Jesus types, men with long, straggly, unwashed hair, woodsmen appearing at dusk like shadow men. Madge had noticed her latest on the upper road delivering oil, and many a morning since, was to be seen wandering up there, drooling.

'What hooked you?' Eily had asked.

'A silent bugger … I have this dappy notion that if they're silent they're deep. What about you? Are you solo?'

'I am now. I lived in England … I worked in an arts centre, fell for someone, got pregnant … the old story. But I have a bonny boy.'

'The old story,' Madge said wistfully.

It transpired that they lived within a couple of miles of each other, Madge in her buckled caravan and Eily in a rented apartment surrounded by rolling hills and the landlord's thoroughbred horses.

When Madge visited for the first time she marvelled at this harem, this Aladdin's cave, bright walls, oriental rugs, shawls and throws, flung around like props on a stage.

'I can see men enslaved here … Homer with the sirens,' she had said walking around, scrutinising the various treasures, little perfume bottles, tortoiseshell combs, donning a feather boa and green with envy, as she put it.

In the month of the bluebells Madge asked if she could do a portrait of Eily and sat her on a kitchen chair in the middle of Allendara Wood. The bluebells everywhere, along the ground and between the rocks and up the tree trunks and even wreathed around the skulls of two dead horses that lay there perfectly preserved in a greenish mould. There was a harmony to it, the rich myriad life of the wood all about, the deft strokes of the brush along the canvas, little shadows that danced skew-wise across her face, under the brim of a lilac straw hat. It was Madge's hat and it was made of a silken straw. They jumped when a pack of lurchers ran through chasing their leader who had a hunk of raw dripping meat hanging from his mouth.

'You're to keep the hat,' Madge said as they walked back in that filtered sunlight, stopping and starting, picking the odd flower, and concocting big dreams about buying land and selling it for a packet. That was the day they pledged to be always there for one another, but then Sven came and came between them somewhat. Farmers referred to him as the Scholar because he was so knowledgeable, knew so much about different types of land, diversified farming, lecturing them at length and sometimes a little boringly about environment, the pollution in their rivers and streams. The need for cosmic consciousness.

Madge had first sighted him in the hall dancing with an elderly woman, looking into her face and dancing the slow sedate steps that she knew, oblivious of the tempo around them. 'I bet that boy loves his mum,' Madge had said and remarked on his arms that were a little too long for his body. It was Madge that spotted him and it was Madge that eventually threw them together. How inevitable it seemed once it happened, yet before that, Eily scarcely noticed him, had given him a lift the odd time, had once seen him in the landlord's grounds, the pair of them walking up and down the avenue debating heatedly. And then, that spell, that flounder, then an instant of capitulation and not a word uttered. It was his birthday and while everybody was celebrating Madge had sent them into the kitchen to make a pot of tea. Suddenly they were kissing and he was kicking a nearby door for them to avoid the inevitable guffaws from the other room. Accidentally they bumped into and overturned a heater and as he told her afterwards in his confiding way, he left it overturned to prolong the sweetness of the moment.

Kilcash became their haunt, the oldest of all the woods, a timelessness in its rustle, in its vastness, in twig and leaf and bole, moss a thick bouclé of velvet on tree trunks, herds of wild goats fleeing at the first sight of an intruder. Their wood. Sven had fixed up a hammock inside a fort of trees and covered it with a canopy of green tarpaulin. Nearby was a well which he insisted was a magic well and where someone, other lovers perhaps, had left a little pewter egg cup for passers by to drink from. On their third or fourth visit she brought a medal and threw it into the well and they wished, jointly wished, then watched the silver sparkle down there, the medal settling itself on a bed of fawn silt ...

'Hi stranger,' Madge said, fixing the last peg to the sheet with a snapping sound.

'I haven't been because I'm working on the place day and night.'

'When is the housewarming?'

'Soon ... I want to borrow that dream book from you ... I had the oddest dream last night.'

'What?'

'Monkeys. They were swinging inside my skull ... frantic to get out.'

'Sven borrowed it.'

'Oh he's back,' Eily said, trying to sound casual.

'Yes he got back last night ... he called here ... he crashed out, but before you erupt let me explain, he was tired, we talked, we smoked a joint, I made a bit of supper and presto, it's midnight.'

'I see,' Eily said, but what she saw was a sheet hung up, water dripping from it in little piddles, a sheet as she believed that they had slept on.

'Get a grip … you sulked when he left for Dublin, now you're sulking because he's back … he's a kid … he'll go off you.'

'What makes you say that?'

'Well his family think it's all wrong … an older woman, solo with a child … they have bigger things in mind for him.'

'He told you that?'

'He trusts me, he confides in me, he runs to me, then you run to me … tea and sympathy … you're like children the pair of you … sometimes I wish I'd never flung you together.'

Eily had been sitting sideways, half in and half out of the car, bantams like little ballerinas pecking at the canvas of her shoe, when suddenly she swings her feet back in, trembling, but adamant.

'Why are you doing this. Why are you so suspicious?'

'I love him, Madge.'

'Oh Jesus. Love! All I meant was don't be such a Princess,' and with that she reached in and tried to snatch the keys and they bickered, Madge insisting, 'I only want to be his friend, I want to do a painting of him, I don't want to make babies with him.'

Eily reversed the car, startled some hens in the dust baths and trampled over a new flower-bed to get on to the rutted avenue, Madge hitting at the bonnet and pleading with her not to go—'I'm a blatherer … I know I'm a blatherer but I love you.' The car shot away, Madge, waving a tea cloth and then shaking the garments on the line, imploring her to turn round.

When Eily saw Sven outside Jacko's, sitting on the pavement, she almost melted. He seemed so young, so vulnerable, eating a choc ice, a punishing hair cut, his tongue licking the drips of cream, beside him a bundle that was his few belongings.

She did not want to, yet she crossed towards him and handed him the tape that contained the storybook words they whispered when they were alone.

'What's this,' he asked as he stood up. He had just read her eyes, the seething within them.

'I've decided that it's best you go away now … not in a month or two as we said.'

'I can't. I've told my parents … I've written to my professor … I've told them I'm staying on here.'

'We always knew that you were going to go home … we knew

43

it from that very first day in the Kilcash Wood … but we blocked it, because we're … simpletons.'

He broke into his own tongue then, believing that the depth and truth of what he said would be evident and she, for her part, kept lolling her head idly as if she was about to yield to him. A little girl who was skipping stationed herself in front of him, wildly inquisitive.

'Trying to find the right words,' he said.

'For what?' the little girl asked and he described seeing a beautiful princess on a dance floor, wearing a sailor suit and then suddenly she was gone and he had to bribe one of the locals to drive him over fields and bogs and eventually arriving underneath her window and serenading her with bits of grass and loose pebbles.

'Don't, Sven,' she said.

'Is it our age difference, then?'

'That … and … everything. There will always be people who will try to split us up.'

'Let's go to a new place … let's drive further and further west until we find, maybe an island with a few cows … me and my gypsy girl.'

'Your gypsy girl's mind is made up,' she said.

They are facing each other now, both shaking, each with a hand raised either to mediate or remonstrate. The black hairs on his knuckles are like jet.

'This is some kind of false proudness,' he says.

'It isn't … I've put down roots here and I've put them down alone,' she says.

'To be honest I don't know you now … I am looking at a woman I thought I knew … who has turned into a stranger.'

'I don't trust you Sven.'

'I didn't fuck anybody in Dublin … if that's what you're thinking.'

'You got back last evening.'

'I hitched … it was raining. I walked the last bloody umpteen miles and I called to Madge … you're just jealous.'

'Yes, just jealous.'

'Explain to me please, why you are making me go.'

'I'll write it to you.'

'So you really mean that you want me to pull out.'

'Yes, I really mean that I want you to pull out.'

'What do I do with all my feelings?' he asks boyishly.

'When we're sixty or seventy, we'll understand all about our feelings,' she answers.

'I guess you're right … everybody moves on,' he shrugged then said, 'Hey … let's make it bittersweet … let's kiss here on the street in front of all the busybodies' and his full lips, the wine red of loganberries, sought hers.

She did something other. She took off the chain and blue amulet that she was wearing and put it round his neck and tied it with infinite care.

'I'm in a rocket,' he said, her hands so stealthy, so caressing.

'I'm gone,' she whispered.

'Stay just one more minute,' but she was lifting the latch of the pub door, tall and tawny, disappearing with the abruptness of a sunset.

THE TAVERN

She sat silently and drank slowly but deliberately. She thought *I am seeing this place through different eyes.* She had been in Jacko's dozens of times, yet never before took it all in so acutely. She thought *I've drunk with him here, I've danced with him here, I've flirted with him here and now I am staring into the almost empty bar wondering why I sent him away.*

What she stared at were the high stools with their red plastic covers held down with regimented rows of brass studding, the one wall with a strip of embossed velveteen from Jacko's mother's time, the other walls white, the globes of light with segments of imitation fruits and a dented St Anthony's box. Two men are further over by the fire, arguing, grasping each other's coat collars, in an altercation. She knows them, Denny, a bachelor, small with a grizzled goatee beard and Huw, the swank, in a green corduroy jacket, with leather elbow patching.

'I'm not telling you and that's that,' Denny says.

'All I'm asking is, have you a site to sell?'

'I wouldn't let you within miles of my place … with your women and your greyhounds.'

'At least hear me out.'

'I know what you want … you want it cheap and then sell it off to another fecking foreigner.'

'How many acres have you, a hundred, two hundred?' Huw says, baiting him now.

'More.'

'Water frontage?'

'Water frontage, water views, water works … you're wasting your throttle boy.'

'I'll pay the asking price.'

'I'm not selling … I told you last week and the week before and the week before that.'

'What do you want with all that land and you an old bachelor.'

'How many illegitimate kids have you now … is it five or six?

… the state paying for them … our poor little country bled from the likes of ye …'

'You haven't done too badly with your water frontage.'

'It was my father's before me.'

'Look, half an acre is all I ask … I'm living with a Norse woman and she's mad to be by water … she misses the sea.'

'Asleep on the job, are you?' Denny says and winks to where Eily is sitting.

'And how is the Princess,' Huw calls across to her. She had thought him attractive for a few minutes one night in another pub and she always regretted that she had let him see it, because he took sneering advantage of it.

'Fine fine,' she says distantly.

'Didn't poor Mrs Burke go quick,' Denny calls across to her in a friendly voice.

'And how are you, Denny?' she calls back.

'I'm getting old and foolish,' he says laughing.

'He's sitting on a fortune,' Huw says and suddenly Denny goes towards the door cursing, 'Feck off, you and your foreign woman and them naked children, running wild.'

'Oh … a major alcoholic,' Huw shouts to him as he goes through the door.

Standing above Eily he begins to read aloud what she has just written—'*Go up to the village and turn left at the village hall. Go on not too far and take the first left turning and you come to a little road that goes over a tract of bog, you pass a derelict house on the left and further on down there's ponies, piebald ponies in a field, after that there's an old red caravan with a curtain in the window and you go on down until you come to a view of the lake way beneath you and you will come to a forked track where there is a rusted cattle feeder and you'll take the centre fork and see the house in among the trees. By the way, you'll have to walk the last bit of your journey.*' He looked at her, looked to the copy book again and whistled and said, 'Jesus you're a number one gypsy, plonking yourself like that in the middle of wilds. No one will go to a party down there.'

'Look Huw, cut it out' and she snatches the notebook back and nettled by the rejection he takes off his green scarf, dosses it with a spurious and condescending sarcasm and says, 'You're all candidates for Valium here.'

She is unnerved when he has gone and orders another pint. Jacko says nothing. That is his way. He stands in the yellow artificial light, like a figure in a frieze, stands as he has done for years, drawing pints, never once remarking on his customers or entering into any conversation with them. The wall clock seems both loud and slurpish.

'It's not like you to have a third pint' he says and she knows that that is his way of being friendly.

She thinks she will sit a while longer, then drive out to the lake road and Sven will be under a tree sheltering from the summer rain and she will stop and he will get in. At first he will be quite formal, talking with a kind of evangelism of some new theory of his and in time taking her hand, holding it, and then they will park the car and go in their little lost road, the trees all in bud, catkins like feathered tapers, the blossom in mazed and snowy whiteness, thralling in the moonlight, bridal trees in the brief ravishment of springtime.

But he was not there and she wept at her rashness, her false pride and her grandiloquent speech about being alone. Alone alone alone, the word galled her, like the hungry cry of some cormorant, far out at sea.

Cissy's new car is outside her front door, a chocolate coloured ornament, the sheer metal a mirror in which passers-by can glance at themselves. Cissy doubles as sacristan and hackney driver, is run off her feet and has gone in to grab a cup of coffee before taking a French man to the airport. From the windscreen an ivory virgin dangles down, a relic to protect her, and her rosary beads are in the glove box along with a bag of peppermints and a map.

O'Kane, sporting a new growth of moustache, jaunts down the tow path and stops to admire it, reaches in and as he turns the key the engine comes to life and he thrills to it. Within seconds he is tearing down the street and sees her in the rear mirror, a grey haired harridan, flapping like a turkey. Dogs and children scatter before him and two older men on a street bench stand up and gape after him. He drives towards the next town but bypasses it and goes on up towards the mountain, over the bumpy roads where he can give her a good ride. Ursula he named her, after that cow in the jail. She is full of juice. She bounces and rocks and sways and swags as if there is no ground, as if he is flying it. Wild horses and wild ponies appear in speckled splashes, leaping and whirling into the air, the needle jigging, the engine racing and a high that he hasn't had in over two years. Yelling with excitement he talks to himself—'Ride her cowboy … yonder yonder.'

It is evening before he makes his way over the rim of the mountain and down a rough ravine to the edge of the wood that is his favourite, the wood where he hid as a kid, before the scumbags got him and with a squealing and sprawling suddenness the car comes to a stop and he knows why it is that he has come here. He gets out. 'Welcome home son … you did us proud … didn't let the bastards get to you.' It is the wood talking to him, the trees thicker now, the trees where he hid and where his mother came and found him, the spot where he kept old cushions, the mass of cover dark even in daylight. He searches in his pocket for a rag and finding none he tears a strip from the tail of his shirt, unscrews the nozzle and dunks the cloth in it, then lays it on the front seat, about to witness his first glorious spectacular. No sooner had he struck the match than the seat caught, like it had been waiting for it, the flames breaking free and spreading, sheets of flame, flags of flame, orange, crimson, roaring and crackling. The tyres starting to burst, their bursts like priests farting, the windows beginning to crack, beads of glass falling onto the ground, flame flitting across his face and he sucking big scoops of air, flouting his importance, Davey and Lazlo and fuckers all cheering him on.

He decides to make a party of it, ask people up. He puts his arm out to catch a burning lady, an Ursula, a cunt. He's high, he's the devil's favourite son and they will never lock him up again or beat the shit out of him and into him. He's a man. He has grown to manhood in spite of the bastards and bastardesses. Better than eating, better than drinking, better than dope or screwing or anything. He hasn't screwed a woman yet. All he knows of women is from the juicy pictures in the magazines, passed from cell to cell, girls with their backs in suspender belts, one leg hoisted to show the pleat of their arses, or frontwise slung back over a table to show the pleat of their cunts, their throats waiting to be slit.

Soon he is smoochy and he wants to kiss a woman and get kissed. He debates about a name. He'll call her Veronica, no he won't, he'll call her Trish. He wants to hear a woman say, 'I like your moustache.' He feels her feeling the hard blunt hairs, up there in the dark, in the painted flame and him feeling her back, up there on the edge of the empty forgotten woods.

When the fire had died down completely he sat trying to figure out where he would go next.

Cissy's friends have foregathered to sympathise and to wait with her for the guard to come. They sit around the kitchen table lamenting that beautiful car that she had saved for, her chocolate ornament, her child, her joy.

'I even called it Cadbury,' she says and again she weeps, wondering aloud where it is and when it will be returned to her and in what state it will be.

'It'll be found … they always find them,' one says.

'He's evil, I know he's evil,' Agnes says, Agnes whose mother asked her to pop in on her way home to see if Cissy was all right.

At the mention of that word they shudder.

'I'll tell you something I didn't even tell my own mother,' Agnes says and in a hushed voice describes how she and a group of girls were practising Camougie one evening in the sports field and O'Kane stood there watching them and his eyes met hers and the queer look from him sent shivers down her spine.

'Shivers,' Oona said darkly, because they were all women and they knew what Agnes meant.

'Weren't you lucky you weren't in the car ... or where would you be now Cissy?'

'Tied up somewhere.'

'Your throat slit ...'

'I heard that he can make himself invisible ... you can go up into your bedroom and find him there and not even know how he got in.'

'Oh Immaculate Heart of Mary.'

'If the guards did their job we'd be safe and Cadbury would be outside the door.'

'It's not the guards' fault ... it's the government's ... cuts cuts cuts everywhere.'

'Tell you what,' Oona says, 'why don't we get down on our knees and pray ... pray for two things, that Cadbury will be brought back safe and that Michen O'Kane will be sent back to one of them institutions.'

HOODLUMS

O'Kane is alone in an empty chapel, white walls, the red flame of the lamp, a bare altar, by the holy water font a poster of Jesus in white with a gold halo around him.

He had gone in hoping to find some Holy Mary on her knees, to get a bit of money. He hasn't eaten for two days and his feet and his socks are soaking wet. Empty. Fucking empty. Nothing for it but to raid the box where the money for the candles is put. He finds a screwdriver round the back, in a shed, where they kept tools and a lawnmower and begins to prise the metal mouth open, bit by bit, tongues of twisted brass curling out like an opened cunt. He keeps hacking at it until the hole is big enough to put his hand in. He rummages. The metal teeth snarl at him and he snarls back. Fucking nothing. Two coins, one of them foreign. He goes pitch and toss with them on the tiles of the floor when in walks a kid, a kid not unlike himself, younger and with rosy cheeks.

'Howdie, Gunner,' the kid says.

'Who're you?'

'Not telling.'

'Little gick … got a fag?'

'They're all shit scared of you … they're locking their doors since you hit town.'

'Why aren't you shit scared of me?'

''Cause I'm a hobo like you … I can hot-wire a car … I haven't done hold ups yet but I'm planning … Did you know that Jesus is also called Emmanuel?'

'Who says?'

'It's written on the poster—*Dear Jesus alone in every tabernacle … poor Jesus.*'

'Could you get me chips or a bun.'

'I'm skint … but tell you what, there's a cure for hunger … the priest read it out on Sunday' and picking up a leaflet he hop-scotches to the altar and reads in a manly voice—'*Elijah went into the wilderness, a day's journey and sitting under a fir's bush wished he were dead. Lord, he said, I have had enough, I am no*

better than my ancestors, take my life. Then he lay down and went
to sleep. But an angel touched him and said, "Get up and eat."
He looked around and there at his head were scones baked on hot
stones and a jar of water. He ate and drank and then lay down
again. But the angel of the Lord came back a second time and
touched him and said, "Get up and eat or the journey will be too
long for you." So he got up and ate and drank and strengthened
by that food he walked for forty days and forty nights until he
reached Horeb, the mountain of God.'

'Would you come to the woods with me,' O'Kane asks.

'Which woods?'

'Any woods. We can track game and shoot and have barbe-
cues … I'll get a guitar.'

'Ah now … me mammy would die if I wasn't home for me tea'
and at that he has run into the sacristy whistling and out the door,
then off under the yew trees, over a stile towards home.

O'Kane went out wet, sullen and lonesome. He crossed fields
and back yards shouting and kicking dogs that accosted him.

It was a shop called The Wren owned by the newcomers, the
blow ins as they were called. In the doorway there were sacks of
potatoes and vegetables caked in thick brown muck. He stood
outside and looked in at the plates of scones and small pots of jam
and honey. There were women in there, talking and laughing,
with their backs to him. One of them went behind the counter as
soon as he came in and looked at him, suspicious. He was holding
the single coin in his hand.

'How much is a scone?'

'Thirty pence,' she said, then shook her head because he had
only five. Her eyes were mean looking and her hair was scraped
back in a bun.

'Go on Maggie … give him the scone,' a second woman said
and rooted in her shoulder bag for the money. She was tall, hair
all the way down her back, red hair, the ribs of it standing out,
like there was electricity in it and when she turned her eyes were
gold spots, like the beam of his torch in the wood at night.

As he is given the bun he bows to her and blurts it out—'Elijah
fasted for forty days and forty nights until he reached the mountain of God.'

Maggie comes from behind the counter and holds the door
open for him, then pulling the bolt angrily turns to Eily, 'He's off

his trolley … you shouldn't encourage freaks like that.'

'Mother Margaret,' Eily says, allowing a wisp of cigarette smoke to float in her direction.

PLAYTIME

She was in a cream, rackety little motor car with a child in the back seat. O'Kane thought it was someone else's child that she was dropping off because she looked too young to be a mother. Her hair was all hidden under a black beret and she was smoking and laughing. He tailed her in a stolen car, but kept a sensible distance.

She turned around a lot to talk to the child and on a bend nearly crashed into a haulage lorry. Suddenly she shot up a side road to where there was the new school. He put on his sunglasses and a knitted cap and he followed on foot. The school was a huddle of single storey wooden houses, some old and shook looking, some very new. There were trees and flowerbeds and ornamental rocks. There was a sandpit with buckets and spades for the kids. In the windows there were paintings and mobiles; stars, dinosaurs and fishes. He could hear singing.

Just by the vegetable garden a young fellow was emptying horse manure from a trailer and dumping it onto a pile.

'Howya,' he said as he passed him.

'Shovelling shit,' the fella said and laughed.

He followed her to the very end building and then went around to the back to have a view through a side window. They were infants and they were all in little wooden armchairs around a table, like they were grown ups eating their breakfast. When she went in they jumped up and ran to her. The child she was carrying thumped her at being put down and then lay on the floor kicking.

From a cupboard she took out things that were not school things at all, mats and bits of coloured rope and sun umbrellas. Then she took off her shoes and started clowning and they clowned with her. She walked a tightrope holding the umbrella and when she fell they cheered and started clambering over her. Then they took turns walking the tightrope and they fell.

Eamonn, the fellow shovelling shit was standing beside him laughing as well. 'It's a new kind of school … no curriculum, no beatings, no punishment.'

'You want a hand shovelling that shit?' he asked and picked up a spare shovel and the two of them worked and whistled.

'Don't put the fork through it when you lift it … it stirs up the gas … gives out a rotten aul smell,' Eamonn says.

'I'll split your skull,' he says aiming the shovel at him.

'Sorry sorry.'

'Are you local?'

'I'm not … I work with a man that owns the equestrian centre … I muck out …'

'Spend your life shovelling shit.'

'Nearly. He's going to bring me to the horse show in Dublin in August … Jesus don't put the fork through it … sorry sorry.'

'What do they do with this shit?'

'It's great for rhubarb … they make a rhubarb bed…'

A tall grey-haired woman came as they were talking, carrying a tiny mug of coffee. She was surprised to find that there were two workmen, but at once said she was glad of the extra help, as many hands make light work. She went on to praise the manure and the generosity of the man who gave it to them for free. She said that it did wonders for the rhubarb bed, the fruit trees and the little birches that were growing apace. She liked all trees but the rowan tree was her favourite because of the bright red berries. Suddenly she became very girlish and put a strand of hair behind her ear and told them—'When I was a little girl in the Forest, my mother told me that the rowan-berries were poison, but they are not … they are bitter but they are not poison … you will get a wonderful dinner with *Rönnbärsgéle*, perhaps you have had it sometimes with game or venison … no?'

'Game or venison,' O'Kane said when she left, and they sniggered and shared the mug of coffee. The rim of it was white with white dribbles leaking onto the earth-brown glaze. They had a few slugs each.

When he looked again the young, red-haired woman was wearing an apron over her jeans and carrying a skillet on which there were little loaves of bread.

'Hi Eamonn,' she said as she passed them. The children followed in a drove, behind her, their faces painted every colour and streaks of paint in their hair.

'They love you Missus,' Eamonn says.

'They love anyone that lets them play and make bread.'

She carried the tray of loaves to a clay oven that was built on bricks and shaped like an igloo. She used a toasting fork to open the slide door and a big blaze of fire leapt out and lit her face and it was all ruddy like she was blushing.

'What's her name,' O'Kane asked.

'Catherine I think.'

'You think.'

'Maybe I'm mixing her up … bewitching isn't she?'

'What the fuck would you know about bewitching.'

Soon the smell of warm dough drifted across to them and the children flopped around and the woman talked to them in a husky singing voice. She knew all their names.

It was a week before he followed her and when he saw where she lived he went wild. It was his house, his lair that summer before he went to England. He had slept upstairs in the attic room, he knew the foxes that came around there in the mornings, mothers and fathers and cubs, foxes that drank from the trough where he washed himself. He'd put the wind up the man that owned it. Left death threats. He loved sleeping there. Left an old mattress and things, an axe; souvenirs of his mother, her hairbrush and a pink bed jacket. His hidey hole. The owner, a shopkeeper from Limerick, got afraid to come, complained to a neighbour about being burgled, his tinned food eaten and his stocks of paraffin oil used up. Now she was in it, her and the child. A sadness came over him, then rage, and he thought of hurling stones through the windows but a voice said, 'All you've got to do is make friends with her, son.' It was a good voice and his heart leapt to it and he felt something like hope, he felt he was coming home for her.

From then on he watched her. He watched her eat her breakfast, watched her bathe, watched her bring out a mug of coffee to Declan Tierney, up on the roof, and whistle him down. She had a powerful whistle for a woman and a powerful laugh. She flirted. She carried furniture and bags of groceries and she carried the child back and forth to the car, the two of them always gassing— 'Hi Ho, Hi Ho, it's off to work we go.' In his daydream there was no child, there was only him and her.

He got to know her exact movements, the days when she taught in the school, the places she shopped in, the pubs she drank in, and the day at the Post Office she queued to get her child's allowance. He was about ten behind her in the queue and the people on either side of him kept nudging and edging away from him.

'Hello Michen … you're back,' a bitch said.

'Piss off,' he told her.

Eily turned and laughed and then on her way out admired his jumper. It was a green jumper with berries on it that he'd stolen from a caravan. With his dole money he would buy her a present. When his turn came a cow behind the counter told him he wasn't eligible for twenty-eight days, being as he was only recently returned.

'Eligible, what the fuck is eligible,' he roared it as he went out.

In a window across the street, there were knitted things, shawls the colour of heather and belts with tassels on them. He went in, looked around and picked up a flat grey stone with a sickle carved in it.

'Excuse me,' a girl called out.

'Excuse me,' he called back.

Later that evening he left the stone outside her door and hid in the field on the far side of the wall. The door was closed on account of it raining. He hid for hours and watched the turf smoke going up and breaking into shreds. There weren't many stars. There were clothes stooped in a big aluminium pan on the stove. The child was writing at the kitchen table. She sat next to him and from time to time went across and pounded the clothes with a wooden mallet and then took a drag out of a cigarette and inhaled it.

When she came out to hang the clothes she was so close to him that he thought she would smell him the way he smelt her. She had a clean smell like the smell of the clothes and the white flakes she had washed them in. He could have reached out and grabbed her but he didn't. She had trained the tilly lamp towards the line and the beams ran down one side of her face and neck and down the leg of the trousers that she wore. They were scarlet trousers, not the denim ones that she wore over in the school.

'Eily, where are you?' the kid called from the house. So she was not a Catherine, she was Eily and he was within a few feet of her, imagining the scream she would let out if he sprung her. Nothing was the same from then on. It was as if by some subtle unspoken signal she had let him in.

The next night, she was standing up in the aluminium bath, blood running down her thighs, blood the bright red of fuchsia, blood like he had seen on his mother once and cried thinking she was going to die. It gushed. She poured the water from a jug and the blood and the water got mixed in together and streamed down her legs, less ruddy, the rest of her body white as milk. She went up to bed early that night, the child in her arms, already asleep. In his mind he went up the stairs behind them. He knew that stairs well, knew the missing step at the bottom and the steps that creaked. He knew the rafters where the thrushes nested in the spring. He saw a mother thrush sit there day after day and night after night, her eyes like glass beads. Once when she went off to get food he took the eggs and mashed them in his hands. The shells were a light blue.

In the mornings, she washed outdoors in a big white bath, one that the Declan fellow carried across the field with three of his mates. It filled up with rainwater and sometimes the kid played boats in it. The kid got on his nerves, the way she pandered to it, the way she kissed it for no reason, made chips for it and tumbled them in a wire basket like a lady in a chip shop. When they got into the bath together she had a long brush to scrub her back and scrub the child's. She had a nail brush with a frog handle. Before she washed the child's hair she undid the knots in it, picked them out one by one and then combed it and poured a jug of water on it and Maddie rebelled when she poured on the shampoo and scrunched his eyes and kicked her.

One night she did something odd. She came back downstairs in the dark and lit a candle, then crossed to a wooden press and turned the long thin key and opened the flap doors. There was a golden figure inside it, cross legged. She sat in front of it, the same way as the figure sat and began to pray. She folded her hands and bowed her head. She was praying for something very important, he could tell. It made him cry. When he cried he could not stop, it was like when he laughed he could not stop, except that it was crying and it went on and on. She was a sad woman that night, not laughing and not smoking a cigarette. She had a book that she read from, like a prayer book and she kissed the page when she had finished.

He crossed the fields, climbed gates and walls and then went along by the shore and past the empty summer houses to where his mother's grave was. He had not been to it for over a year, since he went to England, and he lay down on the mound crying and explaining. His mother heard him but she did not talk back to him, probably on account of his having gone away and got put in jail for wrong things. Flowers and wreaths on a new grave caught his eye. He picked them all up in his arms and heaped them onto his mother's grave. He slept a bit. When he wakened it was light and he decided to go back and visit the woman and bring some of the flowers and ask for a cup of tea and say he was lonely.

When he got there he ranted because she had gone out. He tore up the flowers, tore the petals, tore the stalks and flung them everywhere. He knew where she kept the key under a flower pot and let himself in. Even before he pushed it he knew the creak of that door. Breakfast things were on the table. He ate cereal from a packet, held the packet above his mouth and funnelled it in. On the wall there was a calendar with a picture of a woman and a child, a golden child inside her chest. Underneath there was writing. He made out the odd word—ocean, deity, water, fire. The woman was all them things. Her folded tights were on a chair and he picked them up and examined them and took them for company.

The following Sunday there was a session in the pub and she was there. Her hair was in small plaits, all over her head, like snakes tapping her. Surrounded by blokes. Blokes with earrings and leather jackets and guitars. She lapped it up. The blokes made much of themselves, getting out their instruments, setting them up, testing them, big pints placed down in front of them and in front of her too. She was wearing the scarlet trousers that she wore the night he saw her hanging the clothes. She had a matching jacket with some of the buttons open down the front. She had a necklace. A pouffe was set down for her to sit on. He stood outside the pub window, his eyes burning into her, burning into her smile and the open buttons and the necklace. She swayed in time with the music. The blokes reached over, whispering things to her. When she had drunk most of the pint one of them picked up the bodhrán and laid it into her lap. After a lot of coaxing she began to beat on the goatskin, bringing every dead hair, every fibre alive. She beat it like a mad woman, like an African woman that he had seen in a picture. He banged on the window, making the same sound, believing that she would look up and see him and bring him in and say, 'This is my friend.' He would bring her up to the woods, to his hideaway and he would ride her there and she would ride him back because she had already made eyes at him in the school and in the post office, had given him scones to eat, like Elijah got. He drew nearer and nearer, his nose puttied to the window until a woman saw him and whispered to Gussie the owner.

'You bastard … you pup you, get out of here … don't ever let me catch you here again.' It was Gussie the cripple with a beer mug in his hand and a posse of men behind him.

'Fuck you all,' he said and he turned but he did not run. They were afraid of him. No one of them man enough to come out alone but in a herd. He would have to act fast because one of the earring bastards fancied her, his thigh smack up against hers for the session, his skin-tight leather thigh against her pleated satiny folds.

EASTER

It is a warm night, the sounds and smells coming through the open door, the smell of grass, pigeons cooing in the trees and a donkey that has been moved to a nearby field whining to be let back home. Her friend, Brigit's voice on the tape sounds so near, so intimate, as if she is there in the kitchen with them. On the table, the dozen eggs, the two needles, a big white bowl and a whisk, all in preparation. Maddie is on her lap and they lean in like school children to hear it.

More and more people here in Holland make an Easter branch. It is a custom that has been revived. First we empty the eggs and then paint and varnish them and display them on a branch. It can be Pussy Willow or Forsythia or any branch. To empty the egg I take a needle to the top and to the bottom, pierce a hole and then place one of the holes to my lips. Then I blow with all my strength until the white and the yellow comes out completely through the bottom hole. It's nicer to keep the hole really small but it makes blowing the eggs harder. Ever tried to blow a big balloon? This is the same. I use water paints, marker or glue glitter, cotton for hair and beards and sometimes paper hats to make a funny impression. I looked up in my symbol book and found this: 'Eggs have been a symbol of spring since ancient times. Rabbits too are associated with the fertility of spring because of their ability to produce so many young. The lamb is an important Easter symbol. It represents Jesus and relates his death to that of the lamb sacrificed on the first Passover.' Blow blow blow, dearest friends.

'Come on now, we've got to blow.'

At first Maddie loved it, puffed his cheeks out and giggled at the splutter of the yukky egg coming out of the little hole and the puddle in the bottom of the white bowl. Yukky. Yukky. Yukky. He dipped his finger in the yukky and tasted it and ran into the yard to spit it out.

'I'm having a rest.'

'I won't let you paint unless you blow.'

'Eily can blow.'

'Mr Yukky can blow … he has lungs.'

'Mr Yukky's gone on strike … Mr Yukky's on his bike …'

By the time he has come back all the eggs are empty and she has got out the paint, the markers, the glitter, the cotton to decorate them with.

'Guess what … I think there's a robber out there.'

'Really.'

'I heard him … I chased him.'

'How did you hear him …'

'I heard him running over sticks … the demon.'

'Good thing I have you as a guard dog … Smokey is dozy.'

'Is Sven coming?' he said over-quickly.

'You are a nosey one … I don't know. Why?'

'I like Sven … me and him have good chats … but I like Eily the most, then Cass, then Smokey, then Declan …'

'Then bed,' she said and had to chase him before she got hold of him.

The painted eggs hanging from the swaying branches are like jewels, scarlet and turquoise, wreathed in glitter and even as she steps across the kitchen floor, they begin to tinkle, their shells so light, so airy, as if they might shatter into smithereens.

CASSANDRA

I was Master of Ceremonies for the Easter Egg Hunt on account of my years in puppeteering, knowing how to play a crowd, how to work them into a dither, terrify them and bring them back down.

Eily had bought the prizes in the pound shop—balloons, cheap little dolls, cars and colouring books. When the guests arrived she had already set up a bowl of hard boiled eggs and jam jars of water and paint brushes. Every child was invited to decorate an egg. They did squiggles and dots and we hawed on them to dry them fast. Eily went to hide them in the orchard and when she hollered and they were let out, they charged like barbarians, roughing each other, everyone wanting to be first. Screams which meant an egg had been found and another and another. Then a big lamentation from Maddie because he'd stood on his egg and broke it. He went in for one of his fits, turned blue in the gills and had to be laid down on the grass for his mammy to stroke his tummy and tell him he was the best boy. Two other children couldn't find eggs at all, so two extra eggs had to be scrawled with a red marker and hid in a prominent place so that we could get on with the big attraction, the prize giving. They formed a line outside the kitchen door and each child in turn got a marzipan chicken, a chocolate egg and a little prize. None were satisfied. Everyone coveted the top prize which was a Transformer Robot and which Eily stupidly had put up on the mantelpiece. I knew it would lead to ructions. Me me me. Two boys tried to knock it over with a walking stick.

In the end the grown ups had to have a secret ballot and the prize went to a little chap with black curly hair who never spoke. It turned out he was a mute. Then they stuffed themselves with sweets and chocolate cake, then they fought, rival gangs, *Bang bang, you're dead, I'm not dead*, up and down the wobbly stairs, into the garden, up in the trees, peeing on one another, Kevin squirting the girls from his water pistol and mothers walking around the garden, admiring it, out of politeness.

It was evening when we got ready to leave, the grown ups

drooping, the children more feisty than ever. Two daddies came to pick up their brood and it was amazing the welcome they got. Kids descending on them, kids hugging them, kids jumping onto the running board of a vintage car that one of them drove. It was like the largest toy they'd ever seen and the daddy basked in their admiration of it.

Eily didn't want the day to end. 'Let's go to the pub,' she said. Several of the ladies gave her that look as if she was a dipso.

'We can't take children to the pub,' I told her.

'Denny knows me … he knows Maddie. We're regulars … we go for a pint at six.'

'They're tired … they'll moan.'

'A girls' night out,' she said with that soft pleading look in her eyes and the lashes fluttering a mile a minute and her saying *Please please* and me saying *Another time*.

When I drove off I could see her in my mirror waving good-bye and in that wave I saw that she was facing isolation and I thought, *Why did I ever let her bury herself in that strange old house with its haunted vibes?*

Blow Lady Blow ...

From behind a tall iron gate, patched with sheets of aluminium and looped with wire of every description, Lalla, the little girl is running as though she is shaped out of thin air, running between the snarling, yellow eyed Alsatians, in and out between the several caravans and among the men who are engaged in their sullen tasks, welding and hammering and soldering, men renowned for their cussed manners and their fights outside pubs on Saturday nights. Lalla is wearing a tartan skirt and dainty turquoise slippers with fluffy pom poms. She runs, indifferent to the men who are cursing her for making the dogs so excited, runs for the sake of running with a lightness of a bright steamer and when Eily and Maddie arrive outside the gate she calls out bossily, 'You're late, you're late.' The dogs converge on the gate and begin to leap up, their yellow eyes unblinking; hurling themselves against the wire, dropping back and hurling again, barking with a fierce and lusty malevolence and Lalla ordering one of the men to come and chain these savages up.

Inside the cramped and curtained space of the caravan, four mothers sit in a quiet inertia, smoking, staring at the television as brightly coloured balloons drift through the stale air with a randomness. Lalla's mother, Dell, cleans in the school where Eily teaches and they have been invited to make it a special birthday party for Lalla who is four.

A small table has been laid with mugs and an iced cake and the room smells of cigarette smoke and a sickly sweet air spray.

'I saw you a long time ago,' Lally says touching Eily's hair, the blue braid of her jacket and then her hand.

'Where did you see me a long time ago?'

'In heaven.'

'She's lying ... she tells lies,' her brother Shane says and ignoring him she holds up her best present, a plastic wristwatch the colour of raspberry cordial and she licks it to show how much she loves it. Maddie is tugging Eily's hair at the other side, jealous, suspicious and whinging to go home.

'We only just got here.'

'Come,' Lalla says and takes Eily's hand and leads her to a smaller room crammed with bedding and boxes and two bunk beds where herself and her gran sleep. 'Every morning we wake up at the same time and I say "Hello Gran" and she says "Hello Lalla" and it's always eight o'clock on my watch and it's eight o'clock at school and it's eight o'clock for the cows out in the fields.'

'She can't count and she can't read,' Shane says.

'I'll spit at you,' Lalla says and they have a spitting match and her mother calls in that they are to behave themselves and remember they are not alone now, there are visitors.

'I like silver and gold and I like light blue,' Lalla says, studying Eily's mouth now in which there is one gold filling at the back.

'Where do you see silver?'

'Money.'

'Where do you see gold?'

'Teeth.'

'Where do you see light blue, Lalla?'

'In the sky. I like Mrs Quilligan because she has no kids.'

'Who's Mrs Quilligan?'

'Teacher ... she lets me play football.'

'No, she doesn't,' Shane says. 'She's too scared to play football ... she plays with Hilda' and from a cradle under the bed he takes out Hilda, a china creature in a pink fur attire from head to toe. Lalla snatches it from him.

'Watch this ... she can smile ... watch this ... she can walk' and Hilda takes a few stalled steps and flops back onto the mat.

'Watch this ... she's hungry' and as she presses on her Hilda's mouth opens, her fawn tongue glides out and with a little dropper Hilda is given some milk.

'Watch this ... she needs to burp' and Hilda burps and Hilda says a croaky 'Ta' and Hilda yawns so Hilda has to be put down because Hilda needs lots of rest and Hilda is put into her cradle and brought off to her dormitory. Lalla returns with pictures of her favourite toys and boasts of the many things they can do; play football, go to war, go to hospital, get married, have babies and sometimes have twins.

'I gave her a scary spider book and she got goose pimples,'

Shane says.

'What's goose pimples?' she asks haughtily.

'Goose pimples are this,' he says and starts pinching her and as she screams, 'I hate you, I hate you' a startled mother comes in, dazed, wondering how she could have begot such unruly children. It is while they are fighting and their mother failing to keep them apart that Maddie comes in from the other room, holding something as if it is a trophy. In the one hand he has Hilda's fur outfit which he has peeled off and in the other the magic bakelite box which enabled Hilda to walk and talk and eat and burp and yawn as she went to sleep. Lalla and Shane round on him as he is the enemy now, the baddie that hacked Hilda.

'Let's chop his head off.'

'Let's lock him up in the shed with the dogs.'

'Let's put him down the well.'

'Nah, let's fry him' and as they band together to pick him up, he retaliates with vicious thumps and seeing that they will not be reconciled, Eily picks him up and apologises to the mother who runs on ahead to get the dogs chained up once again and all the while the balloons are drifting idly and harmlessly through the air.

'I want to go home … I want to go home,' Maddie says, thumping her now though in his temper he is still thumping them.

'We're going home.'

'It wasn't a party.'

'It wasn't a party because you mauled poor Hilda.'

'Were you flabbergasted?'

'No. Annoyed.'

'I'll never do it again … I swear.'

Once outside the gate she looked around in dismay. Her car was gone. She found it further up, driven off the road, hidden with over-hanging branches, a fall of yellow pollen on the roof. It looked shaken to her. There was a note on the seat and picking it up she saw a mawkish scrawl on a torn billhead from one of the shops. She read it twice—'Blow lady blow through the hole in your big fat duck egg.'

'I've goose pimples,' she said and looked around and Maddie rubbed her arms to do his magic, to rub the goose pimples away.

A Weapon

Jeremiah Keogh talks to his rifle, except that it is not there; O'Kane has just sped off with it in the night. He keeps going over its life, him and it together and the day he bought it from the firearms dealer in Limerick forty odd years ago when he could scarcely afford it. A single shot bolt action to it and the dealer bringing him into the back room where there was a sort of rifle range for beginners to practise. Giving him little tips on how to use it. He memorised the certificate number, in his head, the very same as a prayer, or a recitation, in case it should get lost. And now O'Kane has sped off with it in the night. His legs still hurt where O'Kane bound them with twine. He recalls dreaming of being in China or somewhere Far East and having his hands and feet bound by men, pickaninnies with ponytails and he wakened with the pain and found he was in his own room and there was Michen O'Kane, the returned native with a mask over his face, his eyes wild, shouting, 'Where's your fucking gun where's your fucking gun' and him defying him and telling him what a pup he was to break into a house like that. Yes he did defy him. He will tell that to his sister Geraldine when she starts to complain. When she sees the mud marks on the carpet and on the window sill that she cleaned, she will ask how he gained entry and weren't windows supposed to be locked and why was he let get away with it, why was he let run off with a weapon to threaten others with.

He recalls the times with it, going out at dusk to shoot rabbits and hares, shooting weasels and stoats and time and time again the magpies in the cornfield. One for sorrow, two for joy, three for a wedding and four for a boy. Half his life stolen, with that rifle. He has only to show Geraldine the wardrobe with its front door smashed in for her to know the blackguarding that went on. He is lucky to be alive, his shins and his feet bound and the hooligan with an axe, holding it above his head, swinging it, then smashing the lovely walnut panel of the wardrobe and him saying, 'You could at least have opened it, the key is in the door' and the vile language of the pup, every other word feck and the lunatic, flinty eyes glinting in the knitted balaclava. Geraldine will say, 'Go to the guards' and he'll say, 'No' because if he goes to the guards O'Kane will be back to finish him off. Between two stools, the law and the outlaw, O'Kane's parting words, 'You go to the guards and you're a dead man.'

If he had a woman beside him now she would bring in a basin of hot water to bathe his feet, but he has no woman, his Helena gone ten years, his rifle gone too, and the ammunition, the live rounds of bullets, at least eighty, kept in the tin that used to have floor polish and that imparted to them such a clean, housewifely smell. O'Kane with enough ammunition to do his raids and his rounds and his housebreaking. He recalls the impudence of the pup as he lifted the weapon out of the wardrobe, wrapped in its bolster case, said, 'It's as old as yourself,' then wiping the cobwebs off it and cocking it and sighting him and him trying to plead with the bugger, 'I need that gun … it's my only protection … what else have I against marauders like you' and O'Kane digging him in the ribs like it was child's play. His torch taken too, his blue torch that saw him home nights from the pub.

He has a good mind not to tell Geraldine at all, except for the fact that she will see the muddy footprints on the window sill and on the fawn bit of carpet and see the ravaged wardrobe, the lovely walnut panel in bits, splinters on the floor and the top lintel hanging off where O'Kane found his money, his last little bit of security for the rainy day. 'Where's your fucking money' and him saying, 'I've no money … I'm a pauper … I've only a pension' and he'll tell Geraldine that, how he stood up to the bugger and O'Kane repeating it and him saying, 'I forget, I forget where I hide things' and then the bolt pulled back and the bullets put into the magazine, the chill of it and O'Kane panting with excitement, the hunter in his blood coming out and him pointing to the top of the wardrobe, to the money in a leather purse that Helena had made and thonged herself when she went to night school in the technical college and studied leatherwork as a hobby.

He can just see Geraldine, one hand in her apron pocket, wagging a finger, fuming 'Go to the guards' and him saying, 'The guards are no friend of mine and never were' and not telling her, because it would scare her, of O'Kane's parting shot, 'Go to the guards and you're a dead man.' He can't tell that to the guards, can't tell it to Helena, can't tell it, has to keep it to himself, alone in his room and his faithful weapon gone.

CHASE

It is dark as the patrol car comes tearing down the lane and swings into Cooney's back yard, stones hopping off the kitchen window and Kim, their little terrier, yapping. They storm into the kitchen shouting abuse at Cooney and his wife for harbouring a felon. Children who have been around the table back off and huddle on the stairs, nervous at the sight of two men in uniform. 'Bring him down,' Corbett the senior guard says.

'The hell I will ... you come in here like cowboys ... scare the wits out of my kids ...'

'We know he was here ... we have proof.'

'Look, Rambo ... I'd agreed with Guard Tulley that if O'Kane came in here again, I'd feed him, talk to him and Rita my wife would telephone the barracks and ye'd park the car up on the road and walk in the back door and I'd express surprise ... instead of that ye burst in ...'

'So why didn't you telephone the barracks when he got here?'

'He stayed two minutes ... he wanted a sleeping bag that he left here before he went to England ... and at this very moment he could be on the other side of that ditch resolving to kill me and my family for talking to scumbags like you.'

'We have to bring him in,' Corbett says.

'Ye took your time over it,' Cooney says with a sneer.

'We had nothing on him ... until Cissy's car was found.'

'A pile of ash ... you won't get his dabs on it.'

'Is he armed?'

'He says he has an axe and an iron bar.'

'Where did he go?' Corbett does not so much ask, as fling the question from the doorway.

'Off.'

'For feck's sake, cut out the fascism, Jim.'

'Look, cut out your own fascism ... he goes one direction, then he turns round and comes back the same way ... there is no method ... there's only chaos, madness.'

'What's his mental state?' O'Heirlihy asks.

'Hyper.'

'So where might he be?'

'I'd try the Congo … he often calls to Minogue in a caravan up there.'

'You hide him on us again and you're done,' Corbett says and goes out.

They are on the mountain road by the cow walk where Moira Tuohey had reported dropping him off. Desolate country. The odd light from a window only emphasising the long and tedious distances, neither dog nor man in sight. Sometimes they slow down to peer out at a bit of plastic or a torn coat on the wayside, both hoping and not hoping that they will find traces of him.

'I wonder what brought him back.'

'To hurt the father … nothing more and nothing less.'

As they veer off the road over a bed of rocks into a field, O'Heirlihy whistles to give himself pluck. In the thick, sightless, mountain darkness the weak light from the caravan gives the appearance of a ship far out at sea, receding from them. Next to it is a second caravan, sunk into the ground, saplings forking out of the roof.

'Oh, state of the art,' O'Heirlihy says, then, 'We'll park the car so that the headlights shine directly on the door.'

They trip and stumble on stones and various bits of machinery, greeted by a growling dog and hens huddled under the adjoining caravan.

'Do we knock or do we call?'

'We shout.'

Minogue opens the door of the caravan and extends his arms in mock crucifixion. He is in his shirt sleeves and wearing rubber waders up to his thighs.

'Have you seen O'Kane?'

'As a matter of fact I have.'

'Bring him out.'

'Come in yourselves and get him.'

Then O'Kane appears. It was as if he didn't walk out of the back room, but flew, abrupt and raving, holding something and shouting, 'Get back or I'll blow your fucking heads away.'

The light from inside the caravan gives a puny feeble glare so that it is impossible to say what he is holding, whether it is a gun, a hurley stick or an iron bar. 'Put that weapon down,' O'Heirlihy says edging forward in a youthful show of bravura.

'You young eejit, I'll put you in a bog hole,' O'Kane says, leaping in a transport of joy and fury, wielding the thing with long swinging thrusts.

'Come back … we're not going to die for that fucker,' Corbett says and the two of them take cover behind the car, watching as he races back and forth, the caravan bouncing, calling them cowards, assholes, threatening them and all belonging to them. Then, as if he has wings, he floats from the caravan over barbed wire and into and beyond a copse of young evergreen trees. They move from where they have been crouching, vexed and confounded, listening for, but not hearing the sound of his feet running through the dark. Corbett massages his stiff knee with a kind of weary fatalism. He is still going through the motions of following the fucker, of catching him, but he is not following. Instead he yells at Minogue to come out and account for himself.

'You are harbouring a criminal, you pup.'

'He called for a cup of tea … I was pouring it when you boys dropped by.'

'We could arrest you, you know.'

'You weren't fuck able to arrest him.'

'There was a serious danger to guard O'Heirlihy and myself … his language, his movements, his stance … were all threatening.'

'That wasn't a gun, that was a broomstick,' Minogue says and he picks it up and rides it and starts crooning—'Gee up old gal, for we've got to get home … to … night.'

In the car they do everything to reassure one another.

'To have run after him would have been craziness.'

'Oh mad. The fight in him,' O'Heirlihy says.

'It looked like a gun, did it not?'

'You'd need to be a genius in that light to say it wasn't.'

'We won't find him tonight … he's in some hole … but find him we will … the Rat.'

As they get back towards the town they are quiet, constrained. Outside the station they stand to stretch their legs. The same stars, a few dogs, the quenched string of fairy lights around the pub, not a sound and yet an unease. He could be anywhere, behind the stack of porter barrels, beyond the high wall of the youth hostel, up in the ash tree, anywhere and fucking nowhere.

'I feel kinda bad,' O'Heirlihy says.

Corbett does not answer. A sentence seems to grind repeatedly inside his head. *We let him go … we let the little fugitive go.*

A LETTER

'Queasy in the head queasy in the tum tums too much diddly diddly dee … queasy in the head queasy in the tum tums too much
diddly diddly dee.'

Maddie goes around the kitchen, half singing it, then opens
the door and shouts it out to the cows and the stocky red bull.
Eily sits on the stairs drinking a mug of coffee summoning the
strength to go to the village. There will be a letter from Sven. She
is sure of it. Her hair is all knotted from the reckless midnight
swim and she has not the will to draw a comb through it. Snatches
of the previous evening make her laugh, make her groan. The
singing, the barbecue by the lake with Otto as head bottlewasher
and too much diddly diddly dee. Her head is splitting. She takes
a scarf off the back of a chair and winds it around until she is
slathered in it like a mummy.

'Eily's a mummy,' she says wanly.

'Eily's a mummy,' he says and opens the door again to an-
nounce it to the herd, then slams it shut. He is jocular because
there are no lessons. Every morning there is a lesson. He puts dots
on a word in his colouring book and writes a name in English and
in French. The French is on account of Elmer the elephant being a
French boy. Elmer is watching from the dresser, Elmer in his harlequin suit and his cloth eyes, who doesn't miss a trick, making
sure that they don't go without him. Elmer is no fool. His droopy
ears are all agog. He has a squeak box inside his belly. Eily loves
bellies. Eily paints women with bellies. Bellies bellies bellies. He
came out of Eily's belly and he was a giant.

Since she feels too queasy to carry him he takes one of the big
sticks from behind the door and they set out across the mud field,
him jabbering non stop. If only he would shut up. If only the birds
would stop singing. If only a cold breeze would circulate through
her head. Bits of the previous evening keep coming back, the excitement, the banter, the jokes the men made, the ice cold swim,
the way it felt like getting born down there, then the warmth from
the barbecue, their heated faces, a young boy singing a love song,

keening it out to the lonely fields and the distant lilac mountain. Too much diddly diddly dee like there was no tomorrow. Tommy, the soberest of the group, landing the van in a ditch and their having to walk to the house of the young accountant and his coming out in his striped underpants and everyone getting the giggles. Much cajoling to get admitted and then seven of them packed into a room, like children, unable to restrain themselves, still laughing, still intoxicated. The young accountant coming back in every few minutes and threatening to turf them out on the road if they didn't stop their malarking. No tomorrow.

When she held the letter up her eyes brimmed with emotion. She knew it would be there and it was. But for her own stubbornness he could be there himself, talking away and they would be crossing the road to Ownies for toasties and coffee and Maddie plying Sven with pompous little questions about farming. It was a pale blue envelope with wavelets of paler blue and it had a lot of stamps. She walked to the bench under the tree, saw how damp it was but sat there anyhow.

'Can Elmer and me go for a walk?'

'Don't go far.'

It was as if Sven were there talking to her, she could hear his voice, that soft bedtime voice reassuring her:

So I am back in my old room in my parents' house in the eastern part of the country, close to the German border. From my window I have a view of a church steeple and a water colour sky. It has been raining the whole week.

Because I got to know you so much through our listening to music together it is now very important to me. There was an old keyboard in the room here that I got tuned and I play on it, songs we played if you remember. I am also getting on with my studies. I plan to be a bit more intensive on that part of my life as it's a good way of forgetting. How is your place coming along? Does the roof still leak? Maybe not, maybe Declan came. My strongest memory is our going out that night just to make certain no one had squatted in it and playing the car tape very loud and the music went off outside and down to the lake and we made us a dance in the dark under the stars—'You can get it if you really want, you can get it if you really want, but you must try, try and try, try and try.'

I meet vibrant, red haired, attractive, husky voiced women every time I go down the street. Hahaha. That's not true. It's a shame people can't express themselves better. Listen to the tapes I guess. Of course I'm thinking about all things small and big.

She decides to write two letters, the safe and the unsafe and would ponder over which one she should send:

The other morning I went up the track to give an eye to the ewes in Dessie's field because they are about to lamb. There was a fox coming across the opposite field, lifting its leg every other minute and then it crossed a stream and I wondered if it saw me or if it would attack the ewes. Smokey our stray dog spotted it and chased it, the two of them flying like mad over the fields, barking, their coats a mirage of red and grey, rounding on each other and then the fox disappearing into a hole and Smokey hurrying back, panting, waiting for his reward, the big, dozy, pregnant ewes oblivious of his valour …

She put it down and began her second letter:

Believe me I did not want wedding bells, I hoped for something to happen between us that would be permanent and maybe it has. Life is a roller coaster and we never know, do we?

A scream broke in on her thoughts and then the crunch of brakes and someone running and her turning to look. What she saw was a car veering onto the pavement to avoid an oncoming Jeep and Maddie thrown up into the air like a ball, then coming down again and dropping under the Jeep, then a deathly silence and as she runs, the driver of the Jeep, a woman wearing a man's hat, has her head out the window perplexed. Fred from the garage comes running, shouting, 'Don't move the car … don't move it … the fan is under there … it'll cut the hands off him' and as he grips the front wheels he mimes to the woman that he is going to push them back slowly, slowly. Eily and those who have foregathered watch aghast.

'Hello there … hello there' they hear Fred say as he stoops down.

'Is he alive … is he alive?' the women shout and Eily drops to her knees, her hand reaching in to him.

As the Jeep is pushed back she sees Maddie like a trapped

animal, curled up, his knees to his chest, his face a stark white and then as he opens his eyes and blinks and reblinks a litany of thanksgiving goes up—'It's a miracle … it's a miracle … he's alive.'

As she reaches in, he begins to shake, his whole body convulsing and lifting him out he feels broken, like a vessel that has been smashed. The onlookers say that he must be left there, that she must not pick him up, that she could injure him even more.

'Leave me alone … leave me alone,' she says, gathering him up in her arms, feeling his bones through his clothes, holding him tight, tighter, the onlookers urging her to bring him to the doctor and she refusing and just staring down at him, incredulous, her little mite, her parcel of infinity.

'It's all Elmer's fault … he ran out,' Maddie says, basking in the sympathy all around him and there in the middle of the road is Elmer, unscathed, strangely comic and plucky in his harlequin outfit.

A WILL

In the outer office of the solicitor, Eily can hear him having an argument over the phone, saying intemperate things, then laughing at his own gall. His secretary who is typing at the nearby desk seems to ignore it and a couple seated on a stool are so shy and so fearful they do not even look up, the young woman just staring down at the tattered magazines on the glass-top table.

Edward the solicitor comes out laughing, rubbing his hands as if all the invective has cheered him up.

'I want you to act for Colm as well as me,' the shy woman says, half standing.

'How the feck can I act for Colm if I'm defending you, Cora.'

'He says he won't do it again … he won't harm me.'

'I want to hear it from his own lips,' Edward says, turning to Colm who is wringing the sleeve of his jacket, mortified, unable to speak.

'All right then … whisper it … imagine you're in the confessional and making an act of perfect contrition … if that's not too hard for you to imagine … and you're saying, "*I will not go with that painted Dublin woman in her Mercedes again … I will not be her odd job man … and I will not come home four nights a week dead drunk and I will not beat up Cora.*"'

'He means it … he bought me this ring,' and she holds up a silver ring with lovers entwined. Edward glances at it, then at her, then shakes his head. 'There's a stone seat under the bridge where the pair of you can sit and watch the ducks going quack quack quack and stop wasting my fucking time.'

The first thing Eily notices is a vast unfinished jigsaw, occupying most of the table and his papers and documents on the floor.

'For the ulcer,' he says ruefully.

'I'd like to make a will,' she says, a little constrained.

'Are you single?'

'Sort of … I have a child. There is a daddy, but I'm by myself now.'

'Fancy free,' he says and then less jocularly, 'Are you worried about something?'

'I'm probably imagining things …'

'Well whatever … you're doing the sensible thing. I'm always recommending it to people … the trouble I've had about wills … fisticuffs. You see that door there? Well, they broke it down one night … the sons or daughters of a certain farmer … I know it was them but I could never prove it. They got the door down, ransacked the files … they didn't touch the kitty money … all they wanted was to get their hands on that document.'

'I wonder what made her make a will … usually it's when people have the wind up,' Edward says to Maeve who is still typing.

'She left this,' she says holding up a diary with a cloth cover patterned with dainty rosebuds.

'Oh we can't read her diary.'

'I have,' she says and unprompted begins to read aloud: '*When they are all here, Declan and Cassandra and Ming and Otto and we are smoking and drinking and propounding our tinpot ideas I am full of fun and even showing off a bit, and then after a few hours a shutter comes down inside me and I want them to be gone. I want my life back, my aloneness. It is the same when I fall in love. I fall in love and I become the creature that the man requires. I allow myself to be overruled but already the love has cracks in it like cracks in a mirror. The hard experience of married life has made me afraid. Yet I tell myself that it will be different with Sven, free love, free thinkers, free everything.*'

Flinging it down, Maeve is suddenly petulant, as if something in it irks her—'These artists, these would-be artists … they're all haywire, full of complexes … if you ask me they need to do a proper job and respectable work …'

'A beautiful lady … but her feet are not on the ground,' Edward says roguishly to himself.

FIESTA

It was a Pagan feast on the mountain, old recitation, old lusts, debauchery and division between men and women amplified to the brazen beat of fiddle and penny whistle.

Since noon they had been blaring, cordant and discordant. Calling the country people, saying, 'Come, come and hear the old story, the hedge-master's recital of the Women of Munster upbraiding their pusillanimous menfolk.' The barren field with its coarse grasses and weepy reeds had been transformed into a Mecca, the marquee like a pale temple set down there, torch flame, candle flame and red and yellow fairy lights plump as tulips in the trees and along the hedges, revellers sloshing their drinks, a jig in their old bones at the novelty of it all.

They came, to marvel at the audacity of the girls, the imperiousness of the Ruling Queen—Queen Euvul of the Grey Rock, draped with dead squirrels, leaves and the accoutrements of the forest—and the benighted husbands in their hob-nailed boots with hoary beards and torn waistcoats, side by side on a long stool having to endure the taunts of these gaudy girls. There was Winnie in harlequin suit, Cindy in black corset and fishnet stockings, May in nun's habit, Agatha a dairy maid, Peg a scrubber with her battered bucket and Eily the Princess poured into a lamé dress with a white fur stole and a silver handbag dangling from her wrist.

Harry, the Master of Ceremonies, told the audience how a poet who was also a hedge-schoolmaster fell asleep one day by the lake that was within spitting distance and had the most outlandish dream concerning the arguments between the sexes.

O'Kane was there too, at one with the dark, squatting outside, quiet as a cat, the canvas flap uplifted on this sight of her in a purple dress and purple gloves up to her elbows, tears streaming down her face and that Harry spiv skimming them onto his finger like they were pearls and asking the audience to behold 'her tearful eyes red and hot, her passions burning as in a pot'.

The fiddlers outdid one another accompanying her verse:

Heart sick, bitter, dour and wan
Unable to sleep for want of a man
But how can I lie in a luke warm bed
With all the thoughts that come into my head.

The disgruntled husbands, loath to listen to these tirades, had to be held back from attacking her.

There you have it. It has me melted
And makes me feel that the world's demented
A boy in the blush of his youthful vigour
With a gracious flush and a passable figure
Finds a fortune the best attraction
And sires himself off on some bitter extraction
Some fretful old maid with her heels in the dung
Pious airs and venomous tongue.

Dissenting old maids, hoisted on wires poked her with broomsticks, but she mocked them.

Couldn't some man love me as well
Aren't I plump and sound as a bell
Lips for kissing and teeth for smiling
Blossomy skin and forehead shining
Look at my waist.
My legs are long
Limber as willows and light and strong
There's bottom and belly that claim attention
And the best concealed that I needn't mention.

Then one of the husbands rose, tottered and staggered onto the rostrum to have his say. He decried the baseness of womankind, asked what were they but scratching posts outside public houses, tramps naked to the skies in empty bogs, turf cutters astride them. Pointing to the painted jezebels he said he could guess at the layers of dirt under their petticoats, singled out Winnie, his wife, with her brazen hips and her bullock's hide, who tricked him into marriage and who made him realise on that very first night when he saw her stripped that he was a father before he had even started.

The Queen pooh poohed his gripes, egged on the mutiny, as with shouts and hisses he was sent back to his stool, to sulk.

The girls became more daring, did headstands and somersaults, flirted with the fiddlers, lampooned the husbands and cheered at the secrets Eily admitted to.

Every night when I went to bed
I'd a stocking of apples beneath my head;
I fasted three canonical hours
To try and come round the heavenly powers;
I washed my shift where the stream was deep
To hear a lover's voice in sleep;
Often I swept the woodstack bare,
Burned bits of my frock, my nails, my hair,
Up the chimney stuck the flail,
Slept with a spade without avail;
Hid my wool in the lime-kiln late
And my distaff behind the churchyard gate;
I had flax on the road to halt coach or carriage
And haycocks stuffed with heads of cabbage,
And night and day on the proper occasions
Invoked Old Nick and all his legions.

O'Kane on his belly, midges eating him, bats in eerie whirl, seemed to lose contact with the earth as the compere cross-examined her, on her vices.

'Are you a witch, Eileen Ryan?'

'Maybe.'

'Do you dabble in the black arts?'

'Maybe.'

'Are you friends with Old Nick?'

She drew her stole down and Harry gasped in mock terror and marched her around for everyone to see and be horrified by the devil's hoof marks on her breast bone, skewered in a vivid indigo colour. To the crowd it was all fun, make-believe, but to O'Kane it was real, she had stepped out of her own world into his, into his transmogrified dream of her, all-mothering, all-sinning. She-devil.

Then it was the duty of the Queen to give judgement as to which side was the most deserving and she sided with the woman, decreed that the mettlesome young Whelps of Munster be brought into the Chapel Yard and tied with chains until they distinguished themselves in the bedchamber—'Mix and mash in nature's can, the tinker and the gentleman.'

The crowd applauded, stood on chairs, whistled, clapped, finding in the beat of their hands a waiting wildness, their pagan impulses brought to life in this heady carnival.

By the Queen's divination, the hoary old husbands tore off their beards, flung down their waistcoats and became the mettlesome whelps, partnering the women in a violent instantaneous dance, to avenge the slurs and insults that had been hurled. The nun came on stage, riding a donkey, whacking it with her rosary beads and when it lifted its tail, misbehaved and brayed, the crowd laughed until they cried, tears and laughter all one. Outside O'Kane rolled around on the grass in a frenzy for it to end. By the time the crowd spilt out, the moon had risen and he stood, a raving shadow, to one side of the exit, knowing that she would come out and she did, spivs congratulating her and jockeying to light her cigarette. She and them went on down to the lake, smoking and laughing and he waited until people had scattered and the lights of the cars crawled along the road on the far side of the lake.

'Chase me chase me,' she taunted them and suddenly she was running, running out of her clothes towards the water, the men chasing her and lifting her up, her half naked body blanched under moonlight, a laughing queen being escorted on her litter.

'Isn't she plump and sound as a bell.'

'There's bottom and belly that claim attention.'

'And the best concealed that we needn't mention.'

'Shame on her.'

'Shame on you.'

'She's a water baby.'

'Let's throw her in.' A shanty song started up as they swung her back and forth and then O'Kane could hear the big splash of water and her scream, half terror, half delight as she was thrown in, her voice gasping, 'It's freezing, it's freezing, lads.' The men were stripping and leaping in after her, snorting, currents of water being churned up. He ran with wild eyes and wild teeth, pulling his shirt off, ran to the water's edge and put his face down into it, peering to catch a sight of her, her white body, her trailing hair. They had stopped laughing and there was a silence down there. Six men and her. He couldn't swim so he put his face to the water and drank it and spat it out, and the shore line sucked the water too and burped it back and he called urgently but none answered.

All was quiet, their bodies gliding together down there, through the orgies of the deep.

IN THE FOREST

O'Kane canters across the several fields. O'Kane's reflection in the sheets of standing water, scummed in weed and dock seed. O'Kane's shadow, dark and furtive scaling the lime capped walls, in a jacket he has fecked from a shop. Flying it. The lull hour. Kids packed off to school, mammies and daddies gone their separate ways. Empty world except for her and the youngster and the smoke from her chimney. He knows the days she teaches and the days she doesn't. Fields and roads drying off after a night of rain. In a pool of brown rainwater he dunks his face and in another pool studies his smart new moustache. Suits him. Then he hears a car hoot and leaps jumping Jesus, onto a gateway to catch a glimpse of her going off, except that it is not her, not her creamy jalopy. It is a sports car with a fall of rain on the canvas roof and a fucker skimming it off with a bit of a branch. Feck shit. An all night visitor while he dossed in a hay shed because of the fucking rain. Clean shaven, not the bearded bastard he'd seen her with in a pub having a bit of a to do. Her window pane with a sheet pinned to it. Private. Keep out. Fuck shit. He is waving his arms in wild rotary fury.

'Top o' the morning to you.' He is in the kitchen as Eily comes down the stairs half dressed, her top through her white slip, busty.

When she realises that she has a visitor she reaches back to the loft room, takes a sweater and pulls it on over her head. Seeing the stranger, his movements manic, his eyes agog, she looks down, then looks back to think if they could escape through the skylight. Her hair is plaited and she is barefoot.

'Want to watch that last step ... the bastard should have fixed it,' he says and dances across to confront her, wags his tongue because she doesn't remember him—'What's this? Don't tell me you don't remember me ... we're old friends. Maybe it's the moustache ... d'you like it? Goes with my mustard trim ... so you forgot me, tough shit.' The words come in a welter as if his thinking is going too fast for him, pell mell, bubbles of foam on his lip and his eyes rolling.

'Who are you?' she asks with as much composure as she can manage. She hears Maddie getting out of bed and coming to the top step of the landing to peer down.

'Put the kettle on … that's what a woman of the house does,' he says, then turning to Maddie—'What's his name … Ben … Caimin?'

'No … his name is Matthew but he's called Maddie.'

'Maddie Baddie Daddie and you're Eily.'

'What's your name?'

'Never ask a man in my profession what's his name. As a special favour you can call me Iggy, short for Ignatius … you got the fireplace fixed I see.'

'So you've been here in the past.'

'In the past!' He is walking here, there, everywhere, looking at things, his talk fast, furious, he picks a pair of stones from her collection in a basket and rubbing them, chuckles at the sparks which fly out. The sparks are of his own imagining. While he is doing this Maddie runs out and comes back with a handsaw, to attack him.

'We're not cutting wood now, darling … that's for later,' she says, snatching the saw and putting it to one side.

Her visitor stands then in front of the wall calendar that has a picture of a goddess, a flame infant, like a golden crocus inside her torso.

'That you?'

'Of course not.'

'Read me what it says.'

'Read it yourself.'

'Haven't brought my bifocals.'

He stands dreadfully close behind her as she reads—'*Thetis was one of fifty sisters and an ocean deity. Reluctant to marry a mortal Peleus she changed her form to a wave, then a fish, then a burning flame. Chiron, a centaur, advised Peleus how to win her heart. She gave birth to Achilles and in attempting to avert his fate tempered his body with magical fire and water.*'

'Won her heart,' he says and laughs a laugh that is bizarre.

'I'll make you a cup of coffee and then I'll drop you off in the town. We have an appointment there,' she says.

Without once looking in his direction she can feel his eyes following her, his mad curious eyes watching as she reaches for a mug and a sugar bowl. Then he gives a little tug to her plait as she crosses.

'Now now now,' she says chastisingly.

'I was fucked up and lonesome and who walked in but long red hair.'

'Look, there's a child here,' she says.

'OK … OK … point taken. You won't see me losing the plot. Poor Jesus, poor fucker he lost the plot. Number one bloke. Him and me we did the odd gig. Like my trim?' and he brings his moustache close to her, then parts his lips to show his teeth which are a fungused green.

'In case you think that's dirty, it's moss … not a rotten tooth in me head.'

'He's a yucky,' Maddie says beside her now, pulling on her sleeve, asking to be lifted up and as she lifts him she goes to the open door calling Smokey, calling Declan, then goes outside to pull on socks and wellington boots.

Suddenly the visitor is hitting the table, pounding with his fists, no time for coffee, no time for a leak, time to go.

'We're ready we're ready,' she says as she grabs her shoulder bag and their coats.

'He's a robber he's a robber,' Maddie whispers and she pinches him to be quiet.

Crossing the field O'Kane talked back to the birds, shouted at them to belt up. As they arrive at the grassy fork where her car is parked he runs to where he has stashed it and she sees the brown gauntleted handle of dark wood and the barrel covered in different-coloured plastic paper.

'I never let my child near guns,' she says.

'Uncle Rodney … the boys in the north, the balaclava crowd want to recruit me … I'm a crack shot but I'm no one's poodle … a loner … a lone cowboy, that's me.'

'If that thing is loaded, I'd like you to unload it.'

'Drama queen are you … get in the fucking car … we have business, missus.'

Maddie begins to shout and kick, refusing to let the robber into the back seat.

'That's my seat … that's my seat … it's not his seat.'

'Now now, darling … it's only a short journey.'

'Darling,' the stranger says, then grabs the long plait of her hair, runs it over his mouth and nibbles it.

The car starts, stalls, backfires as with loud swift bangs they are off.

'You've got a small gun yourself in your exhaust,' he says jokingly.

His arm is across the back of her seat and he tweaks her hair from time to time.

'I wish you wouldn't do that,' she says.

'Angry are you … you should take a course in anger management … noisy car you've got.'

'Yes … they'll hear us coming.'

'But they won't hear us going baby. Baby. Into the sunset … had breakfast had you?'

As they approach the town he huddles down in the back seat and pulls his jacket over his head and Maddie is howling, trying to undo the straps of his carry cot, yelling to get out because the robber has turned into a monster. She slows down outside the pub only to find it closed, the green blind drawn, nobody about except a woman in the distance, going down the hill walking her dog. Outside the post office, Birdie's van is parked under the palm trees and Birdie is in the passenger seat sorting a bundle of mail. With her whole being she wills the woman to look in her direction. Birdie does look and merely shakes her head to indicate that there are no letters for her.

'This is where we part company,' she says, turning to him.

'Put your foot down … put your dainty foot down,' he shouts from the shelter of his jacket and she feels the cold graze of the gun slide down the side of her neck.

Once out of the village he begins to laugh, loud, gutsy peals of laughter, the laughter of somebody locked inside a barrel and frantic to be let out. They pass the town hall, the hurling field, the funeral parlour with a lit cross, ponies in a field, and clumps of yellow gorse just coming into bloom. A man at a gateway looks in her direction, then looks away as if he has not wanted to see her.

At the crossroads she swerves onto the tarred road toward the next big town, believing that their ordeal will end there. He is shouting at her to reverse, reverse, fucking bitch, fucking cunt. She reverses back to where there are two signs bearing the name of the wood—Cloosh Wood. One is high up and written in black on a white signpost and the other a fish shaped oblong of oak with fancy lettering. At the first entrance to a dirt road there is a red and white barrier and he shouts at her to go on, go the fuck on. At the third entrance there is no barrier and he leans forward and grasps the wheel, steering them towards a dirt road and a grid over which a carpet of young green branches have been laid.

'Where are we?' she asks.

'God's country,' he says boastfully.

To one side is woodland, a sombre-green gloom stretching as far as the eye can see, the village, the showery apple orchards of home far behind them, an emptiness that is ghastly. She listens in vain for the thud of a hammer or the revving of a chainsaw, but there is none, only him starting up a yodel as he runs around coiling and uncoiling an imaginary lasso rope.

'Wayyupwayyupwayyupwayyupwayyupwayyup,' he keeps saying and it takes her seconds to interpret it as 'Way Up'.

'That's how gamesmen lift the birds,' he tells her, except that there are no birds, no birdsong, no evidence of life except a tub shaped black barrel with Poison scrawled on its surface and a wooden tool-shed, the very new wood syrup coloured in the sunlight. Perhaps it meant that workmen came and went and presently she expects to see a forester materialise out of that wilderness of green. On a nearby tree at the entrance to a shaded path is a round mirror with a rubber rim, his spy glass and that along with the strewn branches over the grid tells her that he has planned this escapade. She jumps as a forked twig drops onto her jacket and he flicks it off.

'Is that Kelly green?' he asks fingering the collar.

'It's royal blue actually,' she says tersely.

'OK OK ... wrong script ... erase ... erase ... wipeout.'

'People saw us you know,' she says, the calm of her voice in contrast with the pelting of her heart.

'There's no one out there for you ... or me sunshine,' he says.

'I have friends ... I do community work. I teach ... they'll be on our trail,' she says.

'Lonesome trail,' he says. He is staring at her, his eyes both penetrating and dead looking like worn leather.

'Why don't we have a smoke,' she says.

'Your shout,' he says and they sit on a log, their backs to the wood facing a wasteland of tree stumps and ash heaped earth. He watches her take the brown cigarette paper from its folder, make a trough, then flake some tobacco into it and roll it.

'Lick it … lick it,' he says and watches her moisten it, then tells her to light up.

'Top o' the world ma,' he says grinning then throwing off his jacket and he leans back along a log, smoke wreathing across his young face and his mad chuckling eyes. He is not yet twenty she reckons, his Adam's apple supple, like a yo-yo, his arm muscles thick and corded. The short hairs of his moustache reddish brown in that light, have the bristle of a cornered hedgehog. Maddie has not said a word, his face buried in her lap, peering out at moments through the lattice of his outspread fingers.

'Ever see *White Heat*?' O'Kane asks.

'I don't think so.'

'Top film … Cody's mother thought he was the little lamb of God.'

'Every mother thinks that.'

'Bollocks. Town bicycle every mother.'

'You'd want to watch your language,' she says and as she gets up and crosses to the car he grabs hold of her ankle and squeezes it.

'Yonder,' he says pointing to the wood.

'I don't want to go in there … it's dark … it's dismal,' she says, in a voice a little quiet, a little placatory.

'That's where you're going Goatgirl … that's the deal.'

He waits until they have crossed to the narrow entrance between a line of trees and then he follows, calling 'So long' to the ash heaped wasteland behind them. How engulfing the darkness, how useless their tracks in the rust brown carnage of old dead leaves. Pines and spruces close together, their tall solid trunks like an army going on and on, in unending sequence, furrows of muddy brown water and no birds and no sound other than that of a wind, unceasing, like the sound of a distant sea. But it is not sea, it is Cloosh Wood and they are being marched through it. The ground is soggy under foot, with here and there shelving rock sheathed in slippery moss. Not even an empty cigarette carton or a trodden plastic bottle, nothing: emptiness, him, them, insects like motes of dust suspended in the air, yet crawling onto her and onto Maddie, who is scratching and whimpering to go home. She is carrying him and hums to simulate some normality. She thinks before she turns then asks, 'What is this for?'

'They're after me.'

'Who's after you?'

'Dublin gang … knackers.'

'They'll find you here anyhow.'

'No way … they're afraid of the banshees.'

'Look, I'll drive you wherever you want … I'll drive you to the boat … I'll give you money.'

'You've no money.'

'I'm getting a loan from the bank on my house … we can go there and draw some.'

'To the branch?' he says puzzled, then a flying smile.

'To the branch,' she says matter of factly.

'By the way, that's my house you're in … I dossed there … I left that bracelet in the coal bucket.'

'You can have it back … you can have it all back … the house, the bracelet, the land, the lot.'

'Trying to bamboozle me?'

'I'm not bamboozling you … this child is delicate … he has to have medicines every four hours … he suffers with palpitations … we were to drop you in the village, that was the deal. Now we come to this … forest.'

'Your man stayed all night … under the sheets … did you walk up his leg or down his leg … make any babies?'

'He was a friend … a platonic friend … he's helping me to sort the house out.'

'Fucking prostitute.'

Mick Rafferty is on the phone to his wife, in the shop where she does part-time work. He talks in a hushed urgent voice and she talks back in the same way, not wanting to be heard.

'I think I saw the Kinderschreck.'

'Oh Jesus, was he in our barn again?'

'No … in the back of a car … with the newcomer, the red-head … laughing like mad.'

'Michael are you sure.'

'I'm sixty per cent sure.'

'Oh God protect us.'

'You're going to your mother's tonight … you and the children … you're to come now and pack the bags.'

'And what about you?'

'I can tackle him … I have a gun … but if everyone is here yelling I'm powerless.'

'Why would he be laughing Michael?'

'I don't know … maybe he was telling her a horror story.'

'Maybe he was … maybe she'll fall for him … maybe she'll take him off our hands.'

'I doubt it,' he says and slowly puts down the phone. He recalls the desperate look on the woman's face and the Kinderschreck laughing so bad that his back teeth were showing. He knows that laugh. He and his wife and children have heard it and trembled to it in the nights that the Kinderschreck had slept in their hay shed and he had been too afraid to go out and order him off. The only traces of him in the morning being lavatory paper and empty biscuit packets.

They are standing arguing. O'Kane takes a round tin box from his pocket, a box that held floor polish once and he rattles it jubilantly. Maddie listens with his eyes, with his ears, with all of him as the lid is slowly turned. She jumps several paces back, staggers and gasps at the sight of the cluster of bullets, brass coated, their snouts close together. He picks up the rifle, takes out the magazine, puts the bullet in, closes it, then pushes the catch forward and holds it with his index finger, studying them.

'Please … please don't fire that gun … talk to me.'

'Boom boom boom,' he says and as he pulls the trigger, a sharp brittle clatter breaks the immense silence, the lead slug cutting through the tree tops, the leaves swirling in its aftermath and a burning smell.

'Imagine if you were a child hearing that,' she says.

'Don't touch them … don't touch one of them, they're mine,' he is yelling, bent over Maddie who has crouched by the tray of bullets, studying them.

'Leave him alone … he doesn't know what they are … he's never seen one … he's a child,' she shouts.

'You will behave yourself whilst here,' he says and lifts Maddie by the collar of his jacket and she stands between them, daring him to strike her, brave cowboy that he is.

He seems amused by her flaring up—'Relax … Goatgirl.'

'Look … listen … put yourself in our shoes … our … predicament.'

'You know what your problem is?'

'What?'

'Your problem is you don't trust.'

'And what's your problem?'

'My fucking head isn't right … my heart is right but they fucked my head up.'

'All right then … let's talk to your heart.'

'Give us a snog.'

'Don't be cheeky.'

'We're not talking heart to heart are we … we're talking shit … are you wired?'

'Where are your family?'

'Family … that's funny. They killed my ma … the way they killed Cody's ma.'

'There must be somebody.'

'Only my granny … and my sister.'

'Where are they?'

'Loughrea.'

'I know Loughrea. I have friends there … why don't we go and we can call on your granny?'

'Too risky.'

'What are you wanted for?'

'Larceny, robbery, possession of firearms … devil's work … bastards want to put lead in me.'

'But it's not fair to punish us … we're not your enemy … we don't want to put lead into you.'

'You're the one,' he says and takes a folded brown envelope from his pocket and hands it to her. Her name is scrawled in pencil inside a crude drawing of a pumpkin. 'Read it.' She looks down at the daubed ruled page, the laboured childish handwriting and recognises it from the note that was left on her car seat outside the caravan site. She reads rapidly:

I am asking you to go with me I know you might not understand what
it means but I would like if you say yes please say yes do not show
this letter to anybody or tell anybody because they would tease us

95

don't tell anyone please understand if your answer is yes we will start now please say yes don't be embarrassed signed Michen.

'It's for you,' he says as she hands it back.

'It's an old letter and it says Veronica, Dear Veronica.'

'She fucking pulled back … she's for it … should've given her lead.'

'I'm not Veronica … you know that.'

Furious now he snatches the letter back and shouts, 'Giveusthephone giveusthephone giveusthephone.' He bellows his orders into it—'Reported on sick parade … metal in Vomitus. Released from medical centre. Reunited with family at front gates. Energy level terrific. Chlorophyll feed. C and D not necessary. Proceeding north west as per coda. Over. Over.' He is looking at them but not seeing them, arguing furiously with a host of voices, his answers clotted, indeterminate.

Mick Rafferty is bundling his wife and children into the car. Aoife, the youngest, is crying because the boogie man that slept in their hay shed is back. His father says that he is not in their hay shed now and never will be.

'Are you sure it was the Kinderschreck,' his wife Tilly asks.

'I'm seventy per cent sure.'

'You were only sixty per cent sure an hour ago.'

'I'm sure for definite.'

'Maybe you should go to the guards.'

'If I go to the guards it'll only bring him back on us … the guards are as afraid of him as you or me.'

'You said he was laughing.'

'The girl wasn't laughing. She looked scared … dead scared.'

'Oh God grant someone will tie him up soon.'

They are walking again, Eily's face caked with mud and scratched because twice she has tripped and fallen. At moments her eyes seem to go blurry. Endless line of trees, tree trunks, thin branches jutting out like spikes. Maddie keeps slipping down onto her hip and gently she hauls him back, trying to fold him in sleep, because asleep he is not crying, not fretting, he is dreaming, dreaming of home maybe, of Elmer and his blackthorn stick for thwacking the cows. At moments the needles and branches appear to her to have gone inside her mind and inside her mouth. Tiny insects crawl in the corners of her eyes and nest under her clothes. The air is stifling. 'Hold on … hold on tight,' she whispers to Maddie each time he begins to slip. At moments she is weirdly calm, telling herself there is a particular place, a point they have to reach, for some bizarre reason, which will be the turning point and they will be going back home. She even asks herself why it had to be, why her, some lesson to be learnt, some truth, some indelible truth. Other moments she begins to hallucinate, sees the apple blossom blowing through their garden, sees Declan and Cassandra and Sven, all waving to her, holding up a burned kettle. She remembers the harried drive along the road, the gorse coming into bloom, the postmistress in her van, the tall man at the gate ignoring her. As for the time she has no idea. This is all time and no time. Her twenty odd years condensed into this lunatic present. So it is the next step and the next and the next half step and Maddie beginning to pee and taking him behind a tree, the steam, warm and sweet smelling, his face stark white but his cheeks red as tomatoes.

'Mama.' He has not called her by that name since he was tiny and it has come back to him in this extremity.

'I'm here … I'm here,' she says, smoothing his sweating hair.

'Will Cass and Sven and Declan and everybody come?'

'Yes they will.'

'And tie the robber up.'

'They will,' she says holding him tight, tighter, willing him back into her, into safety. He looks so little, so helpless with his dungarees down around his ankles, both knowing and not knowing what is going on.

'Up up up,' she says hoisting him over her shoulder. She thinks that if they can come through the darkness and out into a clearing that the worst will have transpired. Not yet thinking the unthinkable. She stops all of a sudden, falters, then her legs buckle, refusing to carry her any further. Sunk to the ground and looking up at O'Kane, she pleads with him—'You wouldn't put your granny or your sister through this.'

'I would if I had to … I nearly killed my granny. My voices were telling me, egging me on, "do her do her".'

'What voices?'

'Big tall man with horns … over in England after I got out of jail I went to my cousin's … he wanted me to pick up a carving knife and cut my cousin Anthony up in bits … I went into the toilet to fool him … I counted … I counted to a hundred.'

'Come on … that's what we'll do … we'll count to a hundred,' she says standing again. She starts counting, as if she is on a stage, then Maddie joins in and so does he, a rousing trio, a choir of voices, ringing out in the emptiness of the vast, drowsing, unheeding, noonday wood. When they have reached several hundred they are panting and he stops and leans against a tree, a baleful look on his face. She knows she has broken through to him, to that human kernel in him and as she believes, in all mankind. Even his eyes seem less threatening, bewilderment in them. He is trembling and she thinks that the fear which had run in her blood and run in her thinking runs in him too and that it is a matter now of reaching to the child in him, the child cut off from the outraged youth.

'I was in the fear zone back there,' he says wiping the sweat from his face, from his palms, with a filthy handkerchief.

'We were all in the fear zone back there … but we're better now.'

'I was seeing hazes, I was cracking up,' he says and looking at the sky, laughs, says, 'Doctor cunt rode his horse down the mountain in the snow, got a bag of messages and hung them on the side of the saddle … you don't believe me, do you?'

'I do believe you.'

'He wanted attention. Do you want attention.'

'Sometimes.'

'Near thing with my cousin Anthony …'

'You're fine now,' she says gently.

'Send that kid tobogganing,' he says, the toe of his boot squashing hers.

'There's nothing for him to toboggan on and anyhow he's exhausted.'

He draws her towards him, an urgency in his voice: 'We really didn't know, did we, how good it could be … them times rolling around up here in the leaves and the muck … knackered … stuffing the food into my mouth like a mother … like a mother. I must admit I don't often fall in love but you got under my skin … animal magnetism.'

'Tell you what … let's go back to the town and I'll buy you a pint.'

'What do you teach them kids in that school?'

'Games. Rhymes.'

'Up came the blackbird and bit off her nose,' he says.

'One two three four five, once I caught a fish alive. Six seven eight nine ten, then I let it go again,' Maddie pipes up to surpass him.

'Bogger ... behave yourself whilst here.'

'Darling, tell him the poem you learnt ... go on,' she says, coaxing Maddie, trying to mediate. Maddie mutters it and she repeats it with a studied calm.

> *I went out into the hazel wood*
> *because a fire was in my head*
> *and cut and peeled a hazel wand*
> *and tied a berry to a thread.*

'I'd like to learn that ... the teacher learnt us a story about a princess that pricked her finger on a spinning wheel and was put away and the prince had to come and beat down the brambles to rescue her.'

'We have that story ... we'll loan it to you when we get back.'

'Who says we're going back?'

'I do, because I'm the boss ... I'm the mother.'

'OK ... free kick to you' and he goes into peals of laughter and Maddie stares at him, quite still, still and white like a little snowman.

'That Swedish cow in your school is after me ...said the name of the rowanberries in her lingo ... ever tell you about my first kiss ... she bought me a charm ... raving slut ... hope you're not going to ask me to dance.'

'Not on this rough ground, nobody could dance here.'

'That's one of the things I missed out on, dancing and scuba diving. You go through them jail gates and you're gutted. They drill a hole in you. Take your balls. I bullshitted them. Couldn't unmask me. Extremely attractive nurse on wing said I was malingering. My grimace was not the prodoma of genuine psychosis. They studied my laugh, my grimace. Jack Pallance came by, stole it for Shane ... never paid me a penny.'

'Do you get help now that you're ... free.'

'Help. Horse shit. I was misdiagnosed ... I got my mind back second day after I was released.'

'I worked with disabled children up in Dublin … maybe I could advise you as to where …'

'Who the fuck is talking about disabled children. I'm a man. You wanna watch your language lady, you could be prodomaed for that.'

'I thought we were friends …'

'We are … I have a picture of you on my wall … next to a picture of my gun.'

'What's all this fascination with guns?'

'You want to hear a secret?'

'OK.'

'In the street the men watch you … want you … your honey pot.'

'I'm a mother first and foremost … my little boy is closer to me than anyone in the world. He was born premature … I was on a holiday with my sister Cassandra and the pains began and we thought it was indigestion … there we were walking along one of the canals in Amsterdam and I'm doubled over with pain and my sister starts waving a white handkerchief at the skipper of one of the ships and he stops and takes us in … my little boy came out in a big whoosh on the floor of a big ship, couldn't wait to come into the world, could you?' and she massages Maddie's scalp under the mop of damp sweating hair.

'I get very low and lonely … people leave out bread and milk for me the way they would for a dog.'

'Where do you stay?'

'In the area … mostly up here … I hid here as a kid.'

'What's your real name?'

'Mich … short for Michen.'

'Michen, why don't we drive over to your granny, like we said.'

'Boom boom boom,' he says, pointing the rifle alternately at them, at the latticed leaves, telling some imaginary gang to keep out, verboten, piss off.

'You're all right … you're all right … they're just voices … they're just in your head.'

'Fuck them … you and me will go and take that nanny goat out of her misery … broke her hind leg. I'll let the kid pull the trigger …'

'You will not.'

'It's along here,' he says pointing to a trail. 'I have a pet fox as well … a dog fox, he has balls … he only comes out at dusk.'

'I thought we were going to Loughrea.'

'This is on the way home.'

'Home, Maddie … home on the range …' She is singing snatches of different songs, jumbling them together, knowing it is crazy singing but it is to get through the next minute to the next, to keep O'Kane on the last rafter of sanity.

They come to a disused lime kiln and he stands and whistles. The goat has gone, only a twist of brown frayed rope, evidence of its being there. In a slant of sunshine, a crop of tiny toad-stools, their fawn mantles trembling like little globes and a white flowering weed, a creamy lacework threading through the flaked and broken stone. Idiotically she breaks off a stem, it has a sickly, sweet smell, and puts it in her pocket as a keepsake.

He runs back and forth whistling for his pet fox, ogling it. Ruben … Ruben.

Back at home, Birdie feels that bit uneasy, deciding she should jot down what she saw in case she is ever questioned.

I am a postwoman by occupation and I live alone. I am responsible for delivering the post in a van owned by An Post in an area which includes a radius of approximately one hundred miles. Much of it is very remote and includes a vast area of forest and mountain. I was sitting in the van which I had parked under the palm trees across the road from the post office when I saw a light coloured car come round the corner. It could be called cream or beige but certainly not white. As it passed just beside me I had full view of the interior of the car. The driver was Eileen Ryan and she did not look towards me. It seemed to me that she might be restrained from the side to prevent her looking in my direction. It reminded me of someone having a crick in her neck. I thought it strange that she didn't pull over for post, sometimes she would pull up when she met me and ask if I had post for her. The look on her face was one of anguish, of pain. Her hair seemed to be more tossed than usual. There was something on the front passenger seat, it would seem to be a child. There was a huge bulk in the rear seat. This bulk was a greeny canvas colour. This bulk did not show its face.

101

Her car swerved to my side of the road after passing me and then raced up and seemed to move faster. When the car swerved the person in the rear seat was visible to me. I realised it was Michen O'Kane, him they call the Kinderschreck. He had a tight haircut and a new moustache. I know him since his mother died. From a week after her death until a short time before his father remarried the whole family including his father, himself and his sister came to my house five days a week for an evening meal. I am not related to the family. As a devout Christian it is my duty to look after someone in need. When he got into trouble at first and was later released from some reformatory I heard he was hungry and living rough. I used to leave milk and biscuits on a gate pier. After a few weeks I heard that he was caught again for something and was put away again.

As time went on I had no contact much with him and for the first time in two years saw him last Easter Tuesday. I was going to deliver post when he appeared from behind a tree at Derrygoolin Bridge and waved me down. He told me he was starving and hadn't eaten for two days. I felt pity for him. He said he had a few bob in his pocket and asked if I would get him food. I said I would pay for it myself. He said he would hide there and meet me on my return. I bought biscuits, sweets, buns and oranges. He had asked for these items of food as he had no knife to cut bread or make a sandwich with. He said not to tell anybody that I'd seen him and said, 'I know I can trust you … you were good to me as a child.' Most likely he thumbed a lift from the woman, who may be moving away, as people are always coming and going in this neighbourhood nowadays, not like the old times, the decent times.

He is lying on his belly, the gun cradled to his chest, pressing his nose into the earth, shreds of clay at the end of his nostrils, his eyes black-looking as he stares into the distance.

'Let's go to Loughrea,' she says for the umpteenth time, her voice weak and hoarse.

'Can we?' he says excited like someone just coming awake.

'We must. This little boy is dropping and he's hungry.'

'Hungry' and he looks at Maddie as if he had been oblivious of him all along. From his pocket he pulls out a few loose biscuits. They are chocolate coated with a white putty filling. They taste stale and musty but they eat them out of duty.

'I took rat poison once … I bit my stitches … reason for refusing food, wants to die … denied martyr status … fuck them. Not wired are you?'

'No … I'm not wired … it's just that it's all been a bit of a shock for Maddie.'

'He and me get on fine … I'm OK with him … I'm cool,' he says, scuffing Maddie's hair.

'As I told you he has to take medicine every four hours … and we haven't got it with us.'

'He'll have it.'

'You wouldn't hurt a child,' she says.

'Only an animal would hurt a child,' he says and seeing there is feeling in him, way inside him, she weakens and suddenly she is crying, her head on her lap, tears streaming into her hair, onto her clothes, saying 'sorry sorry' and Maddie patting her in dismay. She had not shown her weakness before, not since morning, since the drive, passing the ponies, the man at the gate, taking the main road and him telling her she was a fuck bitch and a messer and having to reverse. She had trembled but she had not cried, staring out at the wasteland of tree stumps and charred branches and the realisation that something drastic had commenced.

'They're at me again,' he says and he plugs both ears with his fingers and runs around the trees, hitting them and yelling at his assailants.

'I can't hear anything,' she says going up to him.

'He's whispering … so as no one can hear.'

'Whispering what?'

'He's not pleased with me.'

'How do you know?'

'He smiles when he's pleased … but he's not smiling now … he's fuming … he says we can't turn back.'

'Tell him that we will give him a reward … a big reward.'

'Ssh,' he says and shuts his eyes to listen.

She kneels and prays, not the known prayers, an interceding to God, each word plucked, eked, from the pit of her being and then he turns, shakes his head and picks up the gun—'If it was up to me I would turn back.'

'Who is it up to?'

'My master.'

'I beg you … I am at your mercy and I am begging you,' she says as if she is still praying, but he hustles her on.

They are moving again, crawling through a tunnel, dark within dark, scrambling on their knees, her breathing jerky, Maddie's face burning and the rest of him quivering.

'He hasn't a pet fox,' he whispers to her.

'No, but don't let on.'

'Redhead,' O'Kane calls as he emerges and she knows by the suggestiveness in his voice that he wants her alone.

She takes Maddie across to where there is a trough of muddy water, with bits of broken stick and picking them up she says— 'Look you can play boats.'

'They're not boats.'

'Just pretend … just be a champ for a little while more.'

'I want to go home.'

'I know. When we go home I'll make you a big pan of chips.'

'I don't want chips,' he says querulously, vexed with her because she is leaving him alone. 'I don't love you … I don't love you anymore.'

Crossing back she sees O'Kane haul something cumbersome from a grove of young saplings, drag it, then prop it up for her to see. It is a glass casket with the figure of the Virgin Mary, such as she has seen on roadside shrines.

'That's Our Lady,' he says.

'I know.'

'Have you been devoted to Our Lady?'

'When I was young at school.'

'Top woman. Never known to fail. She baked me a fruitcake at Christmas.'

'So you're devoted to her.'

'Oh she's the business' and he runs his hand in the folds of her plastered body and then throws her aside—'Fuck you Our Lady.'

Next he takes out a bunch of withered lilies and scatters them on the ground, then a crumpled green dress, a scarf, an umbrella, a large white comb and a cassette with a tangled tape spilling out of it. He unfolds the dress and holds it up in front of her, the creased sleeves dangling down, as he watches for her approval.

'You like it.'

'It's very nice.'

'When it comes to fashion I know my stuff … put it on.'

'I won't put it on now … I'll do it later.'

'You're getting married in it.'

'Ah no,' she says, over-gently.

'Let your hair down,' he says and hurriedly, she starts to un-plait it, to keep his hands off her.

'To your bum,' he says and runs the comb through it, breaking the teeth in his frenziedness.

'Am I fat? Am I ugly?' he asks. 'No ... you're not.'

'Running around your kitchen naked ... there's man eating maggots in that swamp near there ... gagging for women ... Monaghan fella told me ... nasty customer ... schizo ... high risk ... high high risk ... so how you do feel about the future?'

'Hopeful,' she says. When she sees him take out the wedding ring she almost screams. It is thin with a brassy lustre and she makes a fist as he tries to put it on.

'I have a ring from the father of my child ... I can't have two rings ... that's bigamy ... keep it for your own ... sweetheart.'

'Sweetheart shit. Why do I go to this trouble ... haul this stuff up ... this gear ... flowers ... music ... beef or salmon madam ... you know what I'm saying.'

'Yes.'

'Then say yes.'

'Look I'm not who you think I am ... you're confused ... you're confusing me, with others ... your mind is in a ferment.'

'Are you on my wavelength, are you on my ECG?'

'Not completely.'

'I'm talking to you Goatgirl.'

'I know I know.'

'Tell me what that means, yes or no?'

'I can't,' she says and thinking it might pacify him she takes the bit of flowering weed from her pocket and offers it to him.

'Cunt ... you don't give a shit about me ... didn't even come to my birthday. Go. Just go.'

She picks her steps nervously but unerringly to where Maddie is, lifts his hands out of the muddy water and takes him in her arms. She starts to run. The ground feels light, like it is on springs and her head terrifically calm, as she begins to recall different landmarks, the tunnel, the toadstools, an old sock, the churned-up roots of the fallen tree and the long steep path that led from the entrance.

He has almost caught up with them. He calls furiously, like some demented general egged on by the heat of battle. It could be heard for miles, it must be heard for miles.

She turns, then Maddie turns. 'He's going to shoot Eily,' Maddie says.

'I won't let him and I won't let him shoot you … I know what to do … you just hide here and I'll be back in a minute, minutes.' She tucks him down, covering his head in a camouflage of pine needles, kisses him, says 'Not a peep … not a peep.'

A quiet has come over O'Kane, a deathly quiet that seems like deliberation but is not, his jacket on the ground, the rifle on top of it, his sleeves rolled up, the eyes a molten black, absorbing her.

Motionless, barely breathing, she knows she has come to the rim of horror, but still, still trying to reach the inner crater of his mind she says, 'Spare me … spare me and I will make it up to you.' But he is not hearing, the grand plan had commenced long before, the grand plan evidenced in the bit of mirror hanging from the tree, the strewn branches over the grid, she the instrument of something outside of herself, iconic, picked from a thousand faces for wanton ritual.

'What are you going to do with me?' she says.

'Everything.'

'God is watching you,' she says in a flat, hushed tone.

He pushes her forward towards a raised mound under a horseshoe of pine trees, their branches a young green, softly swaying as if they are saying something to each other. To one side there is a shovel and a furrow newly dug, an inevitability to it all. Her blood freezes, because there is only there and only then, the taller spruces slanting against the slope, the stagnant air itself waiting to scream.

'Will you leave the child outside the shop.' Each word said slowly, over-calmly, with quiet, grinding emphasis. He appears to be heeding it.

In that suspended second, her thinking races ahead and looking through the trees she says, 'I hear someone coming' and as he runs to ensure, she steps on the gun, bounces on it, as on a trampoline, her strength prodigal, her determination supreme. He lunges, appalled that she should have tricked him and now the ultimate flood of rage that has been waiting is loosed from the wrenched and bloodied sockets of his fucked life as he tears at her clothing in an ecstasy of hate, as though tearing limb from limb all womankind.

106

When he flings her down she feels the harmlessness of damp earth, his craziness shutting out all of life, all of light, a tiny pearl button of her blouse skiving off, his mouth, his mucus over her, still begging him, her words being swallowed '*Promisemeyouwill leavethechildoutsidetheshop promisemeyouwillleavethechildout-sidetheshop promisemeyouwillleavethechildoutsidetheshop.*'

All earth, all air, all forest is filled with Maddie's cries calling her, running, kneeling by her, child and warrior in one, throwing fists of clay at her attacker, clay that falls in splotched medallions; a warring triptych, flailing and furious, her yoked body, Maddie clinging to her, their desperate cries as one, going up to the trees and down to the wisps of dew that have outlived the morning, rising and expiring, dying and perpetuated in that catacomb of green, up there at the edge of the world, on the point of sacrifice.

WILD PONIES

Pre-dawn, the grey woozy world, a horn of a moon going back in and rain dripping off the branches.

O'Kane wakens in the back of the car, pulls the blanket down and sits up crumpled, he looks around, feels for the rifle and listens; then he gets out.

His piss against the green lichen of the tree rises in a prolonged and steaming arc and he breathes deep and slow into the neutral greyness, allowing not even a chink of a thought, saying time to move on.

The car bounces over the narrow slash of tarred road, swaying on the bends, uphill and downhill, past the odd bungalow, a gateway, a red letter box, a caravan, cows. Another mile or so and he is on the dirt road and after that on a mountain pass, lurching and bouncing among the ruts. No guards, no lorries, no scumbags, bandit country. He is in his element, whistling, cheering, like he has won a race, a tremendous high, his energy gathered and transferred into the driving, the last drive in that rackety little yoke, soon to pass into another county, a deserted outback, the end of the little yoke, its last hooray in a whoosh of flame. He is untouchable.

When he has to slow down he thinks fuck shit and reaches for the rifle. Crazed ponies everywhere, bucking and leaping and he thinks of finishing them off, pictures their heaped bodies all over the road, then thinks the fucking car will be stuck and the scumbags able to trace it. They are Shortie's ponies, brown and fawn and grey and striped, bouncing in the air, butting the car in ones and in pairs, neighing, wild eyed. He thinks, nothing for it but to drive them off the road and he ploughs through them with a hectic speed and they scatter towards the mountain. He stops the car on the broken bridge near where Shortie lives. His van is gone. The yard a scrap heap of junk and Shortie's jaunting cars for gigs in the summer, hens and two foals at the front door leaving their cards and swishing their chestnut tails.

From the booth he takes some clothes and the yanked off

number plate, smells the clothes, flings them in the back and then stands on the rickety bridge of iron and cement-blocks and looks down at the water that is the colour of porter and frothy like porter too. He is about to pitch it in when a whelp has come up behind him and grabbed the calf of his leg through his trousers. He roars. It is the dog from her place, looking at him with a wolf 's venom, one brown eye and one blue, not growling, not barking, just staring at him.

'You devil,' he says and strikes it on the snout with the metal plate but it crawls away, yelping and each time he tries to catch it it slips from his grasp like it is covered in oil or car grease. Then he tries another tactic which is to coax it, to bring it closer. From his pocket he takes a few biscuit crumbs, holds them in his paw, calling, 'Smokey Smokey.' It doesn't come. It is on its belly now, crouching, the lips lifted over the blackish teeth. He kicks it and it takes the kicking and when he has kicked it unconscious he jumps the bridge, slides down the slope and hurls the number plate into the river. He watches it go, bobbing between the stones, in and out of the froth, swept in the current, turning a corner where there are willows when the fecking dog reappears and jumps in and goes on down river along with it.

Back in the car he is huffed and he is hungry.

To Fiona, the young assistant, he looked crazed, spinning into the shop, his arms flying it and laughing at nothing. She had come in early to unpack stuff, and shouts, 'We're not open, we're not open.' There was muck on his boots, pine needles in his thick crop of brownish curly hair and one sleeve of his anorak rolled up, like he had just been in a fight. A maniac.

'We're not open.'

'You're open now, Pussy,' he said, racing around helping himself to cartons of cigarettes, biscuits, cream cakes, toilet rolls and she keeps staring at the gap in the shelves and imagining how Mrs Morrissey will fume and scold her when she finds that they have been robbed. As he stands by the chilled drinks cabinet he jerked his head for her to come over.

'Fanta,' he said and when she hesitated he shouted, 'Santa Fanta, you stupid cunt.'

She hauled out as many bottles and cartons as she could hold and slung them into a wire basket for him. Lifting a big haunch of ham in its muslin cap he plumped it onto the slicer and chuckled as she almost cut herself with nerves slicing it. He lifted off the slices as fast as they came and gobbled them down.

'What's your name, pudding face?'

'Fiona,' she said. It was the first sound of her voice since he had come in and it was squawky like a chicken's.

'Open the till, Fiona.'

'There's nothing in it,' she said and drew out the steel drawer with steel clips empty of notes and the several cavities empty.

'You're not getting my drift, Fiona.'

'I've nothing for you,' she said shrilly.

'You've plenty for me … open your purse, cunt.' As she tumbled the contents of her handbag onto the counter a tiny blue medal rolled onto the floor and ridiculously she shouted, 'Don't take that … it's for a novena.'

His right hand slid along her throat, that and a foul splutter of obscenities into her ear, yet she did not move and she did not scream but began to feel her legs go under her long tweed skirt.

She was unable to tell Mrs Morrissey the exact time the lunatic had left, as by then she had blacked out and they found her slumped on the tiles just underneath the open till.

He drove out of that county and into the next. Stone walls instead of woods and trees, no cover. He drove for hours and passed through bog-land, in teeming rain and while it was still lashing he drove across roadside streams and much later on into a field, empty of everything, except emptiness. A rotting wooden grid led to another field and another and he was sitting inside the car, waiting for the fucking rain to let up.

It was a slow sulky burn, the flames wouldn't suck, wouldn't hiss, wouldn't boil. They kept stopping and starting in the drizzle. He had to douse it again and again. The wadding didn't want to burn, there was spite in it. The high was not so high now and he was freezing cold.

He sat by the ugly, black burnt out shell of the car saying her name as if she might answer to it. Then when he tried to leave he was stopped. Fog walked into the field and all around the field and he was trapped in it. He tried going through a gap but it was foggy in the next field too and then the voice came—'Cover your tracks, son, cover your tracks, son.' He was a big tall man in a hard hat and he was leering—'Cover your tracks son.'

He ran to gather clothes that he had flung up into trees and into ditches and he brought them back to the embers and made another fire and crouched there and watched them burn. They smelt of chickens' feathers being burnt. He'd covered his tracks, son.

VIGIL

Cassandra is in Eily's kitchen pacing, the front door open, the better to call out when they get back. There is something about the kitchen that is not right. A kettle has been left on the gas ring, a new kettle at that and the after smell of burned rubber. Then there is Eily's purse, the medicine that Maddie has to take every four hours and Elmer propped on the dresser, all evidence of their leaving in a hurry. In a corner his purple Rolls Royce, his 'Vintage' as he calls it and a stack of wooden bricks. She thinks maybe that Eily has had to bring him to the doctor and considers ringing the surgery but stops herself.

To be in Eily's kitchen without Eily is quite unsettling. She misses the laughs, the smokes, the bit of bickering. In the basket are the several stones that Eily collected on her journeys, stones sometimes chosen in the vertigo of love. She picks one up—round, squat, grey, inscrutable, its stony life locked within it, so that it tells nothing of its former whereabouts. She is jittery, stroppy at moments, and in the tiny mirror her eyes are stricken as if someone had tried to scratch them. Then she jumps with relief at the sound of their arriving by the side of the house. It is Smokey, black and slimy as if he'd been dipped in a barrel of oil and letting out short weird whelps.

'Smokey ... Smokey, where were ye?' she says and listens for the footsteps coming across the fields, the pair of them humming and chatting and rehearses her own scolding voice saying, 'You stood me up yesterday ... you bloody stood me up.' Eily and herself had arranged to meet in the town that morning, to go to an auction room and buy a few pieces of furniture.

During those next hours while she waits she invents reasons for Eily's absence, says how wilful she is, often taking off on the spur of the moment, maybe gone to the city, or maybe gone to meet Sven who might be reinstated. She climbs the stairs to see if Eily's Turkish travel bag is in its usual place under the bed and flinches at the sight of it. She telephones three friends, finds only Hildegard at home and voicing her anxiety she feels ridiculous. She has to listen to a homily on Eily being a free spirit, a changeling, probably at that moment walking along some river bank with Maddie and a new admirer paying her court.

She cannot stay indoors a moment longer. Hours have gone by, smoking, scouring the kettle, making cups of tea, some mindless cleaning to this and that. At the fork where the grassy paths join she notices a man's glove, thick and black, like a boxing glove, a menacing purposeful feel to it as if a fist was bunched inside it. She draws back from it, too fearful to touch it or pick it up.

It is getting dusk, big sulky clouds threatening to rain and the new born lambs in Dessie's field bleating. It feels like a maternity ward, mothers bleating too, running around after their idiotic young who can barely stand on their buckled new born legs.

'Shut up shut up,' she shouts but it is to Eily she is really shouting. She remembers when they were young and how they used to play hide and seek in an old fort and Eily was always the one to find the most covert place.

'I can't play this game for a second longer … come back, come back from wherever it is you have absconded to' and saying it she puts her palms up in a gesture of prayer and as the clouds break and she feels the first big spatters she believes they are in answer to those wretched hours, her mind askew, imagining the worst.

In a tender reversal now of her spleen and her impatience she thinks how grateful she will be to see them, how deep that river runs with Eily and herself.

When they had not returned by morning Cassandra drove to the barracks only to find that it was shut. She had to turn an iron handle and speak into a machine, then communicate her desperation to a faceless guard six or seven miles away. He is dismissive, reminding her that a grown lady, ergo her sister had probably gone off for the long weekend and who wouldn't, what with the gorgeous weather that was forecast. She formed a picture of this young man, callow, restless and irritable because of not being out in that promised gorgeous weather.

'She's missing,' she says emphatically.

'A missing person is not a missing person until seven days have elapsed.'

'She's very responsible … she would not disappear without letting me, her sister know.'

'Oh yeah … I stopped her for speeding a few times … arty, isn't she?'

'What's wrong with arty?'

'Next thing you'll be asking me to give her Housewife of the Year award.'

'Oh please … please this is serious,' she says, trying to reach him now, trying to smother her anger and suddenly and pitifully she is kneeling on the gravel, her mouth to the face of the machine begging him to at least drive out and go with her to Eily's cottage to see if there is anything suspicious there.

'I don't have a patrol car … and I can't leave the station … you see we're short staffed on account of the bank holiday.'

'What do I do?'

'Go out searching if you want,' he says and then the connection is cut off and the machine has that terrible deadness of machinery. From behind the barracks she can hear a lawnmower start up and knows that a guard or a sergeant must be there so she calls out, her voice shrill and warbling above the solid whirr of the blade in near and less near precision, someone beyond that fence who hears her cry but is ignoring it. She climbs onto the fence and sees him in his shirt sleeves, impassive as a plank and when he turns he shows no recognition, his eyes empty of seeing as he stoops and empties a scuttle-load of young grass, the lime green specked with bits of chopped daisies.

That night a strange thing happens. Cassandra lay, waiting for sleep, knowing that she would not sleep, her mind in splinters thinking of the machine she spoke into and the guard that met her in a different station who also seemed indifferent to her plight. She is thinking of the moment when she will have to break it to her distraught mother and father, picturing their faces, their disbelief, their shock.

When she hears footsteps in the garden she's not surprised, it is as if she has been waiting for this nameless person to come and take her too. Naked, she pulls the quilt up to her chin, with only her eyes listening, hearing the knocking on the door that is quite timid. The caller has not struck the knocker, merely tapped tentatively on the wooden panel. She waits for a voice, a command.

She is in the kitchen now, the light from the hall shedding only a faint beam so that to the person outside, the kitchen is a sphere of dark. The telephone is over by the fireplace, the green light of the answer machine like a little bead. She believes that she will be shot as she crosses to it. The knocking grows more persistent but is still gentle as if the person on the other side is pleading with her to have trust in it. She kneels by the side of the door and in a strangled voice asks, 'Who is it?'

'Can you open the door.'

'Who is it?'

'Declan.'

'Declan who?'

'I'm a friend of Eily's … I was doing the roof for her … you met me.' As she opens the door she sees a young man, his gaunt face terrified and a cigarette about to drop off from the corner of his lips.

'We think that the Kinderschreck might have taken them.'

'The who?'

'A local … a wild man … he's only out of jail a few weeks … since he got back home he's created mayhem, stole cars, beat up a pensioner … took a gun …'

'Why do you think he would have taken Eily and Maddie?'

'If I tell you, will you promise that you won't say it was me? A man saw them around noon last Friday … the day they went missing … his wife let it out in the shop … the man is demented ever since, he's too afraid to go to the guards in case the Kinderschreck comes back to kill them.'

'Who is the man that saw them?'

'His name is Rafferty … they live a mile outside the village … on the right hand side … a lovely flower garden.'

'And he saw Eily driving with this wild man?'

'Don't say I told you.'

'Why not. Why not Declan … we must all band together.'

'It's my mother … I'm out all day working and she's afraid he will come and take revenge … you see he's sworn to paint the town red …'

She feels cold, forewarned, knowing that the suspendedness of the last three days is a mere prelude to something terrible. She knows. Yet she still thinks of them as alive, Eily's spirit would have spoken to her, sent her a sign of some sort, some premonition as she lay in the coiled darkness anticipating footsteps on the gravel under her window.

'We'll have to get the guards to track down this wild man,' she says.

'We'll have to storm heaven and earth,' he says sheepishly.

He did not leave, he vanished, like a fish darting down into the depths of a river and she stood and watched the sky a tapestry of stars and she could hear seagulls crying, the lonely, icy, almost human shrieks of seagulls who had come sixty or seventy miles in from the sea. And why. They stand as one on Mrs Rafferty's cement path, appealing to her in her doorway. There is Cassandra, Delia, Hildegard and Kim. It is evening as they have had to wait until Delia finished school, Delia round and strong and complacent, a link between the local people and the outsiders. The garden is a shower of colour, tiny blue flowers faint as drizzle, big white daisies and devil's pokers a flame red, with red bonneted gnomes in the flowerbeds, like bucolic guardians. The pebbledash of the house a mosaic of ornamental shells and wedges of deep blue glass holding lakelets of blue light. Mrs Rafferty is vague, uncomprehending, her eyes averted, insisting that she does not know a thing, cannot understand why they have come. All of a sudden she seems animated, says by far the best place for their enquiries are shops, post offices, bars and restaurants. She even recalls the name Celine, the proprietor of a new international bar who would be familiar with the comings and goings of travelling folk.

'Eily Ryan is not a traveller ... she moved here,' Kim says.

'Is that so?' Mrs Rafferty says vaguely.

'Your husband saw someone in her car,' Cassandra says.

'I'm not my husband.'

'I'm her sister ... I'm desperate ... my mother and father are desperate ... put yourself in our position ... help us.'

'I can't,' Mrs Rafferty says, retreating backwards into the house and almost colliding with her husband who has obviously been listening. He salutes them with a stricken look as if their arrival bespeaks doom for him. He speaks rapidly as if in a witness box, speaking a prepared statement: 'I saw her drive past here at approximately twelve noon last Friday. There was a man in the back aged about twenty with dark brown hair and he had on a green jacket' and pointing to the wellingtons Hildegard is wearing he deems them the same green as the man's jacket, an army green, yes, army green.

'Can you name him,' Delia asks, sympathetic.

'No … all I can tell ye is the registration of the car … it's the same as my pick up truck. TZY.'

'Was it O'Kane?' Cassandra asks.

'I couldn't answer that.'

'But you know him, Mick,' Delia says.

'Many people know him … you know him yourself … he's a pest.'

'I taught him for a short while,' she says. She has taught his own children also and somehow she feels that he is better disposed towards her.

'I've told you all I know,' he says and puts his hand out to shake hers in conciliation.

'It was my idea to come to you,' she says, her big brown saucer eyes gazing into his, begging him.

'Unease quickly spreads,' he says in a droning voice like a man talking in his sleep.

'Which direction did the car go, Mick?' she asks.

'Maybe Portumna … or maybe up there,' he says pointing to the swathe of evergreens.

They drove to the forest then, a place of unyielding solitude, vast, quiet and they got out of the car and stared into a hinterland of green, trees stacked close together, the trapped wind like the sob of a sea, stared at it and then at the charred tree stumps on the other side, and throwing up her hands Cassandra asks, 'Where do we begin … where do we begin to search?'

'We begin by getting the goodwill of the guards … the local people, the foresters, people who know these woods, know them backwards,' Delia says.

They stood in silence, reluctant to leave, each thinking it some kind of dishonour to go.

As they drive back down the road they see Mrs Rafferty away from her own gate with a cardboard box over her head. She gestures for them to slow down and in a galloping voice says, 'My husband is seventy per cent sure it was the man you named.'

'Seventy per cent,' Delia says.

'That's how he worded it to me … it's on his conscience,' she says, her sloe eyes darting in every direction.

'Will he go to the guards?'

'I'm trying to get him to go but he's afraid … we're all in fear of our lives,' she says and from deep inside her comes a strange racking cough like a death rattle.

Kim debates aloud to herself whether she should or should not tell them something that only she knows.

'For God's sake, Kim.'

'A year ago last September I was off down near Eily's place, picking blackberries and O'Kane came on me in that sneaky way of his and he made me go across to the house ... he said it was his headquarters and that it would be up for sale soon, but if anyone else bid for it he would shoot them.'

'There we have it,' Hildegard says and blesses herself.

'Can we speak to you in confidence?' Delia says to the tall guard on the other side of the counter.

He knows that they have come concerning the missing people and he is already resistant.

'Go ahead,' he says but he makes no attempt to bring them into the back room marked Private. That he is impatient is evidenced by his clicking the barrel of a biro, rearranging sheets of paper while pretending to listen.

'We want a search in Cloosh Wood,' Cassandra says.

'Cloosh Wood ... you're talking of over a thousand acres ... it takes forty minutes alone to drive there and drive back ... we've only four officers in our entire unit.'

'It's got to be done,' she says.

'Why there?'

'It's O'Kane's area,' Kim says.

'O'Kane fever ... why has everyone got that scoundrel on the brain. We're not treating this case as an abduction ... they are simply a mother and a son who have taken off somewhere.'

'He was seen in her car last Friday,' Delia says very quietly.

'That doesn't mean anything ... he's always thumbing lifts.'

'But he's dangerous.'

'He only does Mickey Mouse crimes.'

'Burning Mrs Slattery's car isn't a Mickey Mouse crime ... kicking a pensioner unconscious isn't a Mickey Mouse crime.'

'Who saw him in her car ... some visionary?' he asks testily.

'No, a farmer outside the village ... Mick Rafferty ... but he's being cautious about it ...his wife broke it to us.'

'Well that might be a link,' he says, pausing, reaching now for a pad to jot down the farmer's name and address and cursing locals twice O'Kane's size for giving him bed and breakfast instead of turning him in.

'Would he be armed?' Kim asks.

'Not a firearm ... maybe an axe or a knife.'

'If he has her, what might he do to her?'

'Not that much ... he's a loner, he'd use her to get him from A to B and then he'd vanish ... women are not his thing,' he says, a little abashed at the necessity to broach such a thing.

'That's not true,' Kim says abruptly.

'Why so?'

'I was in a caravan site two years back and he spent some time there ... we used to all sit outside at a picnic table in the summer evenings and one evening he said a thing I would rather not have heard.'

'About women?'

'About women and what he would like to do to them,' she says and lowers her head with shame.

'Would you come out with us and talk to this Rafferty man ... it's serious,' Delia says.

'I'll go out later on ... I'll have to refer to someone higher up to get the OK and then I'll go out and take a statement from him.'

'That's my sister,' Cassandra says holding up a photograph of Eily, thinking it will melt him, enlist him, those huge trusting eyes, the face pale and moulded under the brim of a straw hat.

'Good-looking woman,' he says.

'We'd like it in the local newspaper.'

'You'll pay dear for that unless you have an in with an editor or a sub-editor.'

'What about television?'

'She'd have to be missing for at least a week for that crowd to cotton on.'

'Guard Tighe,' Delia says putting her hands flat on the counter, her ample body softly feminine, her pleading eyes, staring directly into his, not letting him slip from her—'You see, Eily moved into a house that O'Kane thought was his.'

'His lair,' he says soberly. 'His fox's lair,' she counters. 'And finds Mrs Fox at home.'

'And Baby Fox,' Delia says, her voice tapering out. His voice ceased, but his thinking quickened and his thin, sallow face was a map of tiny creases.

SUSPICION

At first glance Aileen could tell there was something wrong with him, she sensed it the minute he came in, soaking wet, his hair plastered down, his eyes caved in and black as soot. It was back and forth, back and forth, from the kitchen window to the side window, from the back door to the hall door, on edge, listening for the slightest sound, kicking the cupboards open in case there was someone inside them. He wanted clean underpants and wanted them fast. They sparred over that. She said he was not in an English hotel now, meaning an English jail and that his granny was not a laundry girl.

'Where is my granny … this is her house not yours.'

'I come every Tuesday to give her a hand.'

'Where is she?'

'She's down the fields dosing a sick calf … a woman of her age doing things men should be doing. Where have you been?'

'In the woods.'

'What were you doing in the woods?'

'You'd love to know, wouldn't you?'

'I can see you're in one of your hate moods.'

'Hand me the fecking underpants,' he shouts as she roots in a clothes basket and hauls out different garments, socks, pillow slips, rags. He takes off his jeans and wrings the wet out of them onto the floor, jumping at the sound of a passing car and rushing into the back hall shouting at her to lock the fecking doors and keep the pigs out. When he draws the striped underpants on over his dirty white ones she asks him if he is stone mad and tries to pull them, saying that if anything happened to him, like he had an accident, people would think he was kinky. He laughed at that and drew them up above his waist and for a split second she saw the prankster of his youth in him. When she lifted his anorak to dry it before the fire she nearly dropped it on account of its being so heavy.

'Jesus how can you carry it … it's a ton weight,' she said and he grabbed it from her and told her to leave his stuff alone, to mind her own fucking business. 'What in the name of God is at you?'

'They're coming they're coming for me … they're taking me away.'

'There's no one coming for you … there's no one out there … it's only rain dropping out of a gutter.'

He made her open the door and go out and walk around to the gable to see if someone was lurking. It was then she noticed it propped against a pipe, bagged up with different colours of plastic and tied with different twines. She stood looking at it and called to him—'What is this yoke?'

'A fishing rod.'

'A fishing rod … you're not a fisherman.'

'It's the season … the Mayfly … French and German and Dutch people in the hotel … they'll pay me to be a gilly.'

'It's not a fishing rod,' she said studying it.

'It's a curtain rail.'

'What in feck's name would you want with a curtain rail and you sleeping rough in the woods.'

'I got a nice place … I'm doing it up … me and someone.'

'I hope she'll straighten you out … Father rang here and said you nearly ran him over working on the road, him and three others … you tore past them in a car … still whipping cars are you … one of these days you'll be in trouble again.'

'Never … I'm a big player now.'

She pleaded with him not to bring it in the house because she well knew what it was. He laid it on the table with a braggishness and untied the knots slowly, unwrapping it more slowly still, as if it was Christmas and he was opening a toy. His eyes lit, watching her watching it. She screamed when she saw the grey muzzle of a gun. Once he had unwrapped it completely, he put his hand on the trigger and held it, playful, tantalising, and for that interminable minute she stood watching, not daring to speak, merely looking at it, waiting for it to go off. When he was satisfied that he had frightened her, he let go of the trigger and unbreached it and it lay there like a broken ornament, the brownish wood handle with writing on it, stained in black, a silvery pin and the metal barrel like the eye of a telescope taking in her and the contents of the kitchen.

'Gather it up and get it out of here,' she said.

'You want me caught, don't you?'

'I don't want you caught but I want you to talk to me … I want you to tell me if you're getting yourself in deeper into something you won't be able to get out of.'

'I'll never do time again … me or Uncle Rodney,' he said and bent his cheek to it and caressed it and she knew then there was something very wrong, very weird about that.

'Why didn't you bring this girl along?'

'She sleeps all day.'

'Oh, a Sleeping Beauty.'

'A Sleeping Beauty,' he said to the mirror and asked it if it thought he was good-looking, or if he was too fat.

Hearing her grandmother and the dog she told him for feck's sake to get that thing out of sight, to cover it up. The moment his grandmother arrived in the kitchen she ran to hug him, asked why he hadn't been sooner, why hadn't Aileen given him his tea and why a new moustache and a little fledgling beard. She kept looking at him, regretting that he looked older and please God wasn't he out of trouble now and starting a whole new life.

'They fucked my head up bad in England,' he said.

'Don't use bad language, son.'

'But not my heart,' he said, letting her touch the outline of his moustache.

'Your soft heart,' his granny said and recounted that day in the morgue when his poor mother died and it was snowing outside and him sliding down the banister and out into the grounds to bring back a snowball to run over his mother's face, to give her the kiss of life.

'The kiss of life!' Aileen said, watching him watching the doors and the windows.

As a car swung into the yard he shouted at them to lock the door.

'It's only Tom … it's only cousin Tom … he's coming to fetch a lawnmower,' his granny told him and ordered him to sit down.

'What's that thing outside the door with plastic over it?' Tom asks as he comes into the kitchen and sees O'Kane with a mug of tea and apple pie placed before him.

'It's a long gun,' Aileen says tartly.

'A long gun!' his granny exclaims.

'I wouldn't use it to hurt anyone … never.'

'Well you'd better get it out of here ... I passed a patrol car a couple of miles up,' Tom says.

'Where were they going?'

'Looking for you perhaps,' Tom answers and opens and closes the oven door to show his disquiet, then goes to the dresser and takes the news cutting out of a tureen and places it on the table.

'Nice work,' he says holding up the picture of O'Kane, that was caught on video, attacking an old lady.

'A poor woman ... the same age as myself,' his granny says, tears in her eyes.

'I didn't do it ... I was framed ...'

'You've no business coming here,' Tom tells him.

'I came to see my granny.'

'I'm glad you did, love ... we went through a very hard period ... you gave us a fright when you stabbed your sister that time ... scared us all ... and you're always running away.'

'Will I be able to stay until it gets very dark?'

'I don't know ... things are different since you went to England.'

'No one wrote to me ... not even you.'

'I didn't know what to say to you, son ... I realise now I should have written.'

'I'll be gone before daylight.' He looks at his grandmother tenderly, the look that promises to do no wrong and she looks back torn, then reaches into a drawer and takes out money and puts it in his pocket.

'I burnt a car up in a wood a while back.'

'Whose car?' Aileen asks.

'An old banger ... the gears weren't working ... there was a hole in the exhaust.'

'Come outside,' Tom says, taking the heavy jacket from the back of the chair.

He is in the back of Tom's car, the gun on the floor with a sack over it, Tom speeding and the radio on full blast.

'What's that gun for anyhow?'

'Shooting rabbits.'

'How did you come by it?'

'I bought it off a man called Gleeson ... I paid twenty quid for it.'

124

'You mean you stole it.'

'Is this a set up … are you driving me to the barracks?'

'Christ Almighty … I'm giving you a lift to the roundabout.'

'Stop the car … I'm going to do a legger.'

'You're welcome to do a legger' and as Tom slows, the music is stopped abruptly for a news flash. They hear how a woman and a child have gone missing in a district ten miles away. The announcer gives the woman's name, her height, her age, her occupation and the type of car she was last seen driving, along with the age and colouring of the child.

'That's a sacred bond, a mother and a child,' O'Kane says.

'What would you know about a sacred bond,' Tom says and keeps the engine running as he thrusts him out of the car, cursing him for the trouble he brings on them.

O'Kane walks, concealing the gun, jumping as cars whizz by, uncertain as to whether or not he will risk the town, the voices saying, 'Sort this out … sort this out.' When he sees the street lights, he stops and thinks. He remembers a chip shop and the priest's house where he mowed grass.

The priest's house is at the approach to the town with a short avenue leading up to it. The lights are out and the car is not there. He thinks of breaking through the back window but then decides it might get messy so he goes behind a low wall to wait. He kneels there, the rain driving into him, a rush of rain down out of the trees, clean rain, washing him out and he lifts his face and his body to it, allows it to soak into him and through him, making of him an innocent son.

It was a different priest, young, dark haired, wearing a gold watch and a natty suede jacket.

'Will you help me?' he asked.

'Who are you?' the priest asked, a bit tetchy.

'I knew Father Hayes … I did jobs here … I mowed the grass.'

'Father Hayes passed on. What can I do for you?'

'There's someone in a bad way in a wood … you have to bring me there.'

'How do you mean a bad way?'

'He fell and broke his neck.'

'But why come to me, especially at this hour of night?'

'You're a priest … God's brother.'

'But I don't even know you.'

'If we don't go … it will be a black night.'

'What do you mean by that?'

'He needs the last rites.'

'Well if it's that bad … then I expect we have to go,' the priest said and opened the door cautiously to let him in.

FATHER JOHN

I am writing this in an empty house while the young man sleeps beside me. Beyond the shutterless window a lonely quiet and the vast wood, the scene of some awful secret that he won't tell me. At one point he threatened to kill me. I don't believe he will. To ask him why he wants to kill me is quite useless, might as well ask him why his eyes are a dark colour or mine are grey. However he claims to like me, to have got to like me after our little contretemps because I did not show fear. I feel sure that he has broken out of an asylum and is being searched for in some county or another.

He looks so young sleeping there on the floor with the cake crumbs at the side of his lips. It was a sponge cake that Baba Melody gave me when I was leaving her house earlier tonight. A sponge cake and eleven duck eggs. He was waiting for me in the rain when I drove over the grid into my own gateway. I could scarcely believe it. He said he was home from England and that there was someone in trouble over in his own area and needed the last rites. Driving along, I asked him why he was out on such a wet night, he said, 'It was all to do with the devil's work' and suddenly he ordered me to turn the car around. At first I thought he was joking, then he lifted the muzzle of the gun out from under his anorak and I don't know which gave me the worst fright, it or his disjointed talk or the so-called jokes he made. Passing the grounds of a hotel with its tall cedars, he threw the duck eggs out of the window and laughed boisterously. He asked if the sponge cake was a gift from a lady friend. I said I don't have a lady friend, I'm a priest who has taken the vows of chastity. He mocked that and said we were all the same under our habits. Then he asked who won the match and I said there was no match, that it was a weekday and not a Sunday. He said he'd lost a few days, scrunched up in a hole somewhere and that one morning he wakened and there was a young foal licking his face. He said he needed to be in a forest, they were the only safe places.

The first forest we tried had a locked barrier and he said they'd regret that, the keeper would regret that and he would be back to get him. He was talking, talking, talking. The odd thing is I discovered later on I had a connection with him through his sister. I had baptised her child, his nephew and he appeared in one of the photographs in a clean suit, holding the child. He asked me did I consider him good looking. I said very. He said he'd been in a lot of jails since then and picked up a lot of hooliganism. Kept telling me to speed up.

When we came to the track that led into Cloosh Wood he got very agitated and asked if I would help him. He made me promise to help him no matter how terrible the shock. I gave him my word. We walked, or fairer to say we stumbled, through a very dark, very soggy wood, treacherous under foot and seemingly vast. Then he ran to one side and came back with a torch which I presumed he had hidden there. The light from it was sputtery and soon expired. All of a sudden I felt myself go stone-cold. I cannot say what it was because he would not let me any closer. I just had the sensation that I was approaching a scene of calamity and instinctively I began to say some prayers for whoever might be lying there in that loneliest of spots. He went berserk, said that I wanted to frame him like all the other f*****s. I somehow managed to calm him and we found our way through the undergrowth and through the dark to this empty ghost of a house where he claims to have lived as a child. He said it was the happiest time of his life because it bordered on the woods. I believe that he brought me to give the last rites to someone and then bewilderingly changed his mind. He kept saying 'I'm an animal … I'm an animal.' The moment I proposed hearing his confession, he went ballistic, told me to mind my own effing business, said I was part of a ring out to get him. I reminded him of the secrecy of the confessional and said I would not break his trust to anyone. He said then that he had misled me. The person that was in danger was in another wood altogether, held captive by a gang. I felt that he was lying. I told him that the best thing we should do was sit down and talk things over until daylight. I said everything was worse at night, fears were worse and suspicions were worse. I asked him was he hungry and he said yes he was starving. I sent him out to the car for the remainder of the sponge cake and he was eating it as he came in. It was unnatural the way he pawed at the cake and as he ate it he was also sucking it as if it were both food and drink.

We sat on the planked floor and I tried to get him stable, telling him news of the parish, children about to make their first holy communions, a hurling match I had been to on Sunday and a holiday I will be taking in the autumn to the Holy Land. All of a sudden he picked up his gun and put it to his head and I jumped and grabbed at it to wrest it from him. We fought like soldiers all around the room him asking me to shoot him, begging me, said he deserved to die and that he would be better off out of this world. I asked him what he meant by such a remark and unfortunately inflamed his temper again. He grabbed the rifle, cocked the hammer as an expert might and with his hand on the trigger pointed it at me and said 'Happy Christmas … this one is for you Santa.' The crackle of it and the speed of the lead going through the panel of the door, then the tiny hole all happened in an instant. How quickly life can be taken and how thoughtlessly. I asked why such an outburst. He said I had it coming to me, that I was caught up in bad work, associated with the devil, especially some she-devil and that I was about to baptise the devil's children. I pointed out to him that if that had been so, I could have killed him in that vulnerable moment when he asked me to. He thought about that and seemed satisfied but nevertheless he took out a box of bullets and reloaded the gun before my eyes. I hid my fear as I think that would have made him more threatening.

He apologised for choosing me, kept saying there was no one for him, then repeated the names of Christian brothers and prison officers that are supposed to have been brutal to him. He asked me if we could go to his mother's grave in the morning because he wanted to speak to her and to pray, he wanted to unburden everything. Before nodding off to sleep he thanked me and said I was brave when he fired that lead. I don't believe he will kill me, that is why I have stayed. I believe that at the deepest level he needs a friend and that I will become that friend. He did say that a dog would have a better life than him. My whole priesthood, I now believe, was intended for this, for this dark night of the soul, watching over a young boy whose soul is in torment.

SHADOWS

They jump at their shadows' shadows and the thicker shadows of the headstones that seem to collide into one another in the enveloping dusk. It has begun to rain again and the lake has the turbulence of a sea, rough waves pounding in and out and the old bent thorn trees creaking, letting out little squeals like the squeals of field mice.

They are all women, all edgy, tired, footsore; their mistrust has deepened since they commenced their search that morning, scouring vacant houses, caravans, outhouses, horse boxes, unused lime kilns and inlets all along the lake shore where small boats bobbed and sidled in their beds of reed.

They had come to his mother's grave, some approving, some not, they encircled it as though believing there lingered evidence of his having recently been, and expecting from the tall tombstone and the damp mound of earth, something to float upwards, a whispered message from the other world, a deliverance. At the same time they are in fear that O'Kane might be behind one of those headstones about to take a shot at them. Gladys, whose brother is a guard, says how he told her that once a person has shot or maimed, it is quite simple to do it again.

'Who's talking of shooting or maiming anyone? No one,' Lorna says, nettled on account of her being a third cousin of O'Kane's, on his father's side.

'Let's ask his poor dear mother,' Martha says and kneels and gestures that they kneel with her.

'Ask her why she reared him so rotten,' Nancy says.

'Sh sh.'

They are about to start the rosary when Ming suddenly stands up, looks out at the water and in a shrill hysterical voice says, 'Why are we here in a graveyard? It is so negative.'

'It is essential,' Lorna snaps.

'You are all crazy women ... you are all judgemental women,' Ming says then and they are disbelieving, hearing accusations from her who had always been so polite, so reserved, so courteous that if she called to their houses she would not step over the threshold, ever.

'Coming here was stupid,' she says defiantly.

'How can you say that? Some of us gave up our work ... we've left our children with others to mind,' Nancy says.

'You are all doing it for obligation ... for reputation ... you are hypocrites ... you you you,' she says, her face chalk white, her black wet hair streaming, like some tragedienne in a play.

'What is it, Ming?' Martha says offering her a hand.

'She is not anywhere here near water ... I am one hundred per cent sure of it.'

'You're just het up ... you're just a little bit overwrought.'

'She's a foreigner ... they don't feel like we do ... they've no hearts, they've no religion ... they come to our beautiful little country to rip us off,' Lorna says.

'Don't Lorna ... don't ... there's enough anxiety hanging over us.'

'You all walk so fast,' says Ming. 'You know the countryside ... I don't know the countryside ... I was left alone in a wet field facing to the north ... I asked you to wait, one of you said yes but disappeared ... I was frightened ... scared.'

'We don't know north from south ... we are not compasses, we are human beings,' comes Lorna's retort.

'Eily is putting us through this,' Ming says.

'You are angry with her ... you, the one who knew her ... her friend, her confidante!' Gladys says.

'I didn't know her ... no one knew her ... she had secrets that she never talked of.'

'Such as?'

'I can't say ... please excuse me ... my mind is working crazy at this time' and she bows contritely to each one.

'So are our minds working crazy but we cope,' Martha says, a little wearily.

'You stayed with Eily, didn't you?' Nancy asks.

'Yes, that was last year ... there were strange noises in my back garden and I couldn't sleep ... probably foxes ... I mentioned it to Eily and the next day I found a letter on my doormat inviting me to stay in her flat, near here, overlooking the lake. She was very kind ... she made me very welcome ... but then one evening a young man came, a young man with short blond hair

131

and she tried not to introduce me … she didn't want me to know that he was her boyfriend, just as she didn't want him to know that she was a mother … she was very secretive.'

'So … maybe you agree with the guards … maybe they have a point when they say she's just off on a dirty weekend.'

'That is not what I meant at all. She was a secretive person but she is not a harlot.'

Ming is wishing now that her jangled nerves had not betrayed her. She feels that she must say something to redeem Eily's name and almost pompously she says, 'She had a strong spiritual side … there was a sacred book she used to read before she went to sleep.'

'Huh, with a boyfriend in tow.'

'Excuse me but you have no truth,' Ming says to Lorna.

'What do you mean?'

'She was on a quest.'

'What kind of quest?'

'Goodness … spirituality.'

'She liked a good time.'

'That is how you see it … but in the Buddhist teaching, the blank scrolls contain the true meaning.'

'You're nuts.'

'She's nuts.'

Suddenly they are all shouting, rounding on her, each racked by her own fear, imagining their own children spirited out of their beds and buried in some bog hole. At the sight of a figure beyond the lych gate they jump and listen to the scrape of metal over the grazed stone step.

'It's him. It's O'Kane,' Lorna says.

'Keep together,' Martha says, gathering them into a huddle.

'Let's call out,' Nancy says and they stand in a herd as the figure comes slowly towards them, his hat slouched over his face, magnifying their terrors, walking around the gravestones until Lorna recognises that it is her husband Milo and shouts, 'What are you doing here?'

'I'm hungry … the kids are hungry … there's no dinner on the table.'

'Giving us the fright of our lives,' she says.

'Anyhow yer search is called off.'

'Are they found?'

'No, but her car is … burnt out twenty-five miles away in a field.'

'But that shouldn't stop us searching here … in this area.'

'The guards say they have a lead anyhow, and that vital evidence can be interfered with because of footprints and so forth … so the search is off.'

'Who ordered it off?'

'It was on the local radio … although I met a young guard in the town and he didn't know about it … he said the dragnet was in place.'

'Who knows what … who is in charge … who is at the helm?'

'All is unclear.'

'All is a fuck up,' Milo says and they troop out after him with a sense of failure and frustration, not even realising that they have left Ming behind on the grave.

She did not follow. She was afraid of them, afraid of their girth, their hardness, the way they all seemed to swoop down on her. She wanted to cry, because she was crying in her mind but something told her that she must not cry—'If I shed tears, tragedy will happen,' she said aloud to the grave and the moaning trees. If she withheld her tears, Eily would be safe.

Looking up she saw human faces between the tombstones, joking faces that were laughing and she knew that at that moment she too was turning mad. She stood up, looked out at the dark blue of the water that was a Prussian blue and kept telling herself that she must not cry, because if she shed tears tragedy would happen, kept repeating it, staring out at the iron blue of the water.

Searching

Another group of women set out very early the next morning, the mist a cottony white, a presence, so that walking through it was like breaching through net. They were heading towards Cloosh Wood.

In there, whispering, moving quietly, cautiously, sometimes having to crawl under a shelving of fallen and leaning boughs, in fear of every stir, dreading what might be behind the next tree trunk and the next, a little breathless, the air sultry, silent and as a game bird is risen, the speckled feathers in a frantic unnerved flight give them the jitters. Afraid, and yet driven by a kind of blind intuition, certain that their determination will lead them to mother and son, proud of having eluded the guards and the other local volunteers.

They have fanned out, promising each other to call every so often in solidarity. Immense solitude, the trees like pillars, solemn and solid, trees which seemed to have been planted by no man; trenches of brown water scummed with hordes of insects, a suffocating place.

Suddenly Josephine is heard to shout, 'Girls ... girls come quick.' They run through the undergrowth and see her pointing to something on the ground with her umbrella. It is a child's shoe, pink canvas and caked with mud, its lace missing. The sight of it chills them. They form a circle around it, clasped now, and it speaks to them of a child recently there, losing its shoe and not being allowed to stop to put it back on. It speaks of haste and captivity and even violence. They search now in the scrub, they kneel and delve their hands into years and years of packed damp pine needles, they reach into the lower branches of the trees and shake them, hoping to find a second shoe, the cardigan, a coat, any clue indicating that they might have passed that way.

It is Anya who calls first. She says 'Maddie' then she says 'Eily'. Her voice is subdued, nervous, expecting almost to be chastised as she looks at them and then gaining courage she shouts the names boldly and then the others follow and the drowsing wood is wakened from its inertia with the repetition of the two names, Eily and Maddie and hope and fear alternating in those who were chanting them. 'Where are you, where are you?' their shouts carry from tree to tree, from furrow to furrow, up and beyond and their echoes came back to them in a wan, despairing mimicry.

They decide to bring the shoe back to the barracks, carrying it on the umbrella as if carrying a trophy and they arrive in the town and make their way slowly and a little triumphant towards the barracks.

Dread, hysteria and mounting speculation. The shoe rests on the sergeant's desk, absurdly small and muddy and does not constitute a clue of any kind because he has established that it is a shoe for a child of six or seven and moreover the missing child wore blue wellingtons.

The woman's belongings, the few bits of jewellery, garments and undergarments are in a cardboard box on the floor and tucked far inside his desk is her diary which he has read and which at times induced in him a moral repugnance because of certain confidings, hinging on men and desire.

'She played with fire,' he says to himself, looking down at the garments and out at the crowd around the gate, craning inquisitive and soon to start haranguing because enough was not being done to find the missing people. They stand out there, some of them in their Sunday best as if they are waiting for a miracle. He recalls once being on a holiday in Italy with his wife and how by chance they had formed part of a crowd that waited in a church for the solidified blood of a saint to start flowing again. It happened once a year in the month of August. He remembers the dark nave of the church and coming upon a huge painting of the Virgin and Child, so lifelike that the Virgin's blue cloak seemed to stir from her breath, flowers in vases, fresh roses and withered roses not thrown out, all kept in preparation for the miracle of the flowing blood of a Madonna. His wife Ellen with the help of the dictionary had gleaned this from the expectant crowd and so they waited too and at dusk as candles were lit, all eyes were fixed on that cube of blood, solid sealing wax in an oblong glass case. Then the air went cold, a shiver ran through the atmosphere and people started to tremble and break free from behind a tasselled rope, pressing forward to weep and gnash at the impending revelation.

He did not hear the footsteps, simply saw his wife standing above him in a dither.

'There's a priest gone missing now.'

'Where?'

'Over in Eyre Court ... a young priest ... Father John Fitzgerald.'

'Who told you this?'

'He didn't show up for mass ... he was supposed to rehearse the little children soon to take their Holy Communion ... and when he didn't show, his housekeeper went across and got suspicious because the eleven duck eggs and a sponge cake she'd given him weren't in his fridge ... so she alerted the parish priest and he called in the guards.'

'Who told you this?'

'A young guard from there come over to liaise with the guards here.'

'I should have been briefed first.'

'There's something else.'

'What?'

'The rumour is that Father John knew Eily Ryan ... that they were lovers ... he was seen going into an empty house in Tipperary with a red haired woman ... that they had planned their disappearance ... and maybe now they're in Berlin or Paris or Amsterdam' and as she is saying it he sees the excitement mounting in her, that strange, giddy, prurient, unwifely grin and tells her to go out and bring in that skittish guard, bring him in to account for himself.

He opened the drawer again and took out the diary, innocent seeming with its flowered paper cover, in contrast with the warblings within. He resolved that in due course he would burn it. He felt he would be doing the right thing by burning it. Woman's filth, Eve, taken from the rib of Adam, to wreak unchastity upon the world.

An auction room has been converted into an incident room for the search parties to foregather. They have come with sticks and food and water and dogs, the dogs mostly setters, yelping and whining to be let loose, to be let into the woods. To one side of the room a little classroom has been set up, crayons and copy books and boxes of puzzles, as Vanessa, a student, has been appointed to mind young children while their mothers join in the search. All around, the wardrobes, sofas, mirrors, hall stands and ornaments add to the surreal feeling as people mill around impatient to get moving. They are annoyed with the guards, yet Bobby, the American woman, is the only one to vent her fury. She has been the bane of the sergeant's life since she first set foot in the county. First it was to complain of the pollution from the factory, then it was an objection to a new street light as not being in keeping with the quaint mode of the others and now it is why he hadn't got his act together sooner. She stands close up to him, wagging her index finger to smite him.

'We're getting our act together … well over a hundred guards are being recruited in … army infantry, helicopter back up, house to house enquiry, underwater unit, sniffer dogs … what more do you want?'

'Three and a half days since Eily went missing … twenty-four hours since you learnt that O'Kane was seen at close range in the back of her car …'

'I have heard she looked very relaxed when she was seen with him in her car.'

'Bullshit … she was scared to death but she was simply not a priority for you.'

'We treat every case with the same degree of importance.'

'But you did nothing.'

'Look, we have no evidence of any abduction … none …'

'So where do you think she is … by a hotel pool? And where do you think he is?'

'Bobby … I run this show, not you.'

'One of your officers told her sister that next thing we would be asking to name her Housewife of the Year.'

'That does not reflect gardai policy.'

'Only when the priest went missing did you sit up …'

'As I said on the local radio and I will say it again, any case that involves boundaries makes things more complicated … gardai in one station or another having to liaise with their colleagues.'

'So where is O'Kane?' she asks.

'There are two or three woods that he frequents … he's in one of them.'

'Get him,' she says with a vengeance.

He turns away from her and defers to Joseph, one of the foresters, who has his back to the crowd and is bent over a series of maps, marking out particularly dense areas with a red pen.

'Why did you call off our search yesterday?' Vera asks him, a little nervous and a little piqued.

'Because you were all going criss-cross up there ... it was useless, you were getting nowhere ... no organisation, no strategy ... today we have a strategy and Joseph is best suited to mastermind it ... he knows those woods, he planted those trees, he patrols there, and turning to Joseph he asks him to brief them.

Joseph is a little shy and coughs a few times and begins: 'What we do is this ... we form lines about one foot apart ... ten to a line ... now the person in front of his or her line takes the lead and goes into the forest and after about fifty yards shouts ALL CLEAR ... the second person picks that up and follows and repeats the coda and so on to the third and fourth and fifth ...'

'Might she have jewellery on?' someone asks.

'That's a good point,' the sergeant says and asks those who knew her to recall things they'd seen her wear. Vera remembers a leather thong with a wooden pendant and Madge starts to speak but succumbing to emotion, keeps saying, 'I'm a blatherer ... I know I'm a blatherer ... but I am her friend.'

'Are we talking a doomsday scenario here?' Declan, a little drunk, asks as he staggers to where maps of the forestries are spread out on a desk.

'No ... bad as he is, O'Kane would not kill,' a young guard says and turns to the sergeant for confirmation who is already counting and herding them into groups of ten. At that moment a stranger rushes into the room in a thrall of excitement, waving a sheet of paper and carrying a rowan branch as if it is a wand. He is tall and sallow, with a long white robe under his raincoat and his hair tied in a pony tail.

'She is there,' he says pointing to a star on a drawing which he has made, a perfect depiction of a country area with green colouring for the forest, brown for the humped bridges and an outline of an empty house with creeper hanging from the eaves.

'Where is there?' Vera calls out.

'I am not familiar with the place names ... I've never been to these parts ... I was guided here.'

'It's been in every paper ... a woman and a child and a priest are missing … it's on every radio station,' he is told.

'I don't listen to radios … I listen to my dreams …I meditated and the answer came to me.'

'What answer?'

'A woman in a swathe of woodland who is prevented from screaming.'

'Who are you?' the sergeant asks, irritated by his arrogance, his sandals, his John the Baptist robe.

'I am a link in the chain … a bond of connection between the missing woman and yourselves,' he says unruffled and goes out with the same smiling rapture as when he came in, propelled by some inner calling.

DONNAGH

It's like we are looking for a wolfman who leaves his traces and then vanishes. The question now is, will we ever catch him? Has he powers beyond the natural? That is what is being said. The truth is, we're all feeding on our fears, men and women both, retreating into blindness like into a dark cave. When Liam Purcell and myself came on an empty cigarette carton and banana skins, on the cow walk, our antennae were out.

We stopped first at Glebe House, which has not been occupied for years. There was a good, newish caravan cushion on the floor. It was brown corduroy with leather buttons. Liam said it was not there two days ago when he looked in that window. He has cattle up that way and fodders them morning and night so he notices anything unusual. On the side of the track into the wood there was a lady's black sweater and I picked it up with a stick and put it in the back of the car to bring to the guards. Then two hundred feet into the forest we came on the remains of a lunch—an empty biscuit packet and a tin that had sardines. I also picked them up for evidence. Further on I found a blue torch with a red battery submerged in a pool of water. When I switched it on the light was weak. Nearby was a fertiliser bag. Things.

My wife, her friend Josie and myself visited our cousin Mary Kate down at the shore as she feels in real danger down there because Eily Ryan lived in that very same apartment for a short while. The whole conversation hinged on the disappearance of Eily and her child and a priest and the possible connection with O'Kane.

'I wonder will he come for me,' Mary Kate said looking towards the window.

'Don't say that … in God's name don't say that,' my wife said.

'I know he will,' Mary Kate said and went up the stairs for the umpteenth time to look to see if her child was safe.

We sat there smoking, drinking cup after cup of coffee, turning on the wireless at news time, expecting some bulletin. At one point I just sensed that O'Kane was nearby. I don't know how or why I felt it but I just knew. I opened the window in her living room and heard movement to the right and told them to shush.

'Is he there?' Mary Kate asked.

'There's someone there,' I said and I called out and we switched on the outside light and we went out with sticks, the four of us shouting, but he had disappeared. We stayed an hour longer to give Mary Kate courage but finally we had to leave because of work in the morning.

When we passed Tuohey's milk parlour, their security light was on and I said I found that odd as it was worked by sensor and no vehicle had passed up or down the road while we were in Mary Kate's.

'That's not normal,' I said.

'Nothing is normal now,' my wife said and Josie and she huddled together in the back, screaming, as if they were going to be shot.

At Houlihan's pier we saw a blue flame, about twenty foot high off the ground and I thought at first it was a lifebuoy on fire and I wanted to swing to the right and investigate but the women wouldn't let me, they said, 'Drive on drive on.' They kept insisting then that it was a crowd of drunks who had lit a fire on the harbour and that it would be awful to call the guards at that hour of night.

Deep down we believe he has been sent by God, as punishment upon us.

'Cripes … a dancing girl,' Frank says as he slows down the car to look.

'A mermaid,' Paddy says as they stare at the ball of lit blue that seems to be above the water, skimming it.

'It's a gas explosion on that houseboat … we better call the fire brigade,' Frank says, a little less skittishly.

'I'm one of the fire brigade,' Paddy says and splutters. They are both half drunk and they are enthralled by it. It is well after midnight and each had promised the other that they would leave the pub after the next drink and on and on it went, Frank's uncle looking at his watch and begging them to bring him home to his bed.

'We better get out and investigate.'

'We had not … we better be going back to Lawler's Pub and ring the brigade … the funny thing is it wasn't there five minutes ago when we were driving down …'

'That's the thing with fire … it's a phenomenon,' Paddy says, his tongue tripping on the big word.

On their way back to the village they come on Charlie who is carrying a pregnant sheep into his yard and they shout out to him about a boat being on fire and how they're going up to Lawler's to ring.

'Ring from here … it's faster,' he calls back.

While they are waiting for the fire brigade to arrive, the three men decide to go back and getting there, walking in a closed knot, trampling their lit-up shadows, they find a car halfway in over the pier as if someone has tried to push it but failed. They are drawn to it, closer and closer, like men seeing fire for the first time, the lick of the flames dancing across their faces, their hands blackened by going too close to it and already they guess the worst.

'It's O'Kane's style,' Paddy says and as they gape at it the sharp and brittle crack and clatter of a gunshot is heard and a bullet lands somewhere in the ornamental bushes around the ruin of an old house.

'He's around ...'

'Let's get the hell out of here.'

They waited in Charlie's house until the guards came and when they returned, the fire had almost ceased, the car, a black shell with nothing to show of itself, no windows, no seats, no number plates, just a cavity in which rosary beads dangled inside from a charred dashboard.

The fire engine arrived soon after, but without its siren on and the firemen jumped out, still half asleep but fully togged, ready to do their gallant work and a little crestfallen at finding they had come as the last puttery flames were ebbing, dying out. They walked around it saying the same commiserating things and the fire engine itself, its silent bells, its roped ladder and its coils of hosing looked like a big toy, faintly ridiculous in that scene of dread.

One of the guards found a registration branded into the glass of the rear window and they took turns to peer at it with a torch, then with the naked eye, to read the letters and the numbers, with collars of soot around them. With infinitesimal care he removed the soot with some sticky tape and the other men watched in a strained, admiring raptness. They deliberated, then each man called out the lettering and the numbering as he believed it to be and their guesses matched.

Charlie's house was suddenly like a canteen. Neighbours had gathered because of hearing the cars and the fire engine and Charlie's wife, her hair loose and flying as if she belonged in some ancient drama, kept plying them with warm scones, repeating the miracle that had happened while the men were gone, that a sick sheep that they were sure was going to die, had given birth to twins. She marvelled that it was twins and that the sheep, poor creature, had had a dropped womb and wasn't it a good omen. It was only when the guard came back in from the hallway where he had been ringing the station that she seemed to take in the gravity of what was really happening.

'It's the priest's car,' the guard said.

'Father John's car ... Father John's car.' The evocation of his name sent shivers through them and one who knew him spoke of his kindness, his down to earthness, the way he mixed with the people and played hurley like any ordinary bloke. She was pressed for more information and all she could think to say was that he had a good dress sense and wore a beautiful gold watch.

'It doesn't look good,' Charlie said.

'We've dragged our feet too long over them missing people,' the men said, eager now to go on a reckless search in the dead of night.

Around the cold jetty in the sad dawn, twenty or so people converged to see it and what they saw was a crinkled plastic sheet covering a shell of a car like a shroud. They knew it was the priest's car, just as they knew of the rosary beads that had not been burned out and the shot that had been fired a few feet away after midnight. With a terrible constraint they kept looking towards the lake, believing that Father John was down there among the ghosts of others who had drowned, fishermen caught in a squall, drunk youths coming home from a disco and Fidelma that had left her husband after the first night of marriage. No one said so but each felt he was down there, and standing in the cold they looked up at the first sight of the helicopter, rackety, invasive, a big threatening bird, bringing unease to fields and meadows, to lanes with gorse bushes all in bloom, to the soft-seeming haze of the sheltering mountain.

CAPTURE

'*The fox is invisible.*' He keeps shouting it from the depths of a ditch where he has hidden all night, shouting it and emptying the rainwater out of his boots.

The heat is on. They are searching boats, harbour front, fields and sheds, shitting themselves because they can't find him. He has seen his picture in the newspaper next to the woman, like they are a bridal couple. She has both her eyes, gazing. There is a picture of the fecking dog with the number plate in its mouth. A picture of the priest, a lock of hair down over his forehead, holding a hurley stick.

In that ditch before the dawn, he has his first fill of the chopper coming in to get him. He can feel their desperation in the way they tear over the fields, zoom up and down, in and out, skimming the tree tops, trying to sniff him.

'You could get me but you're afraid of me … scumbags,' he shouts up to it as it skims off over to the lake and the island where the butcher grazes his cattle. He gets out of his hole and walks across to a gateway, leans on it, waiting for someone to pass. A creamery lorry drives by and the driver gapes at him with fear and semi-recognition and drives on. He leaves an old bucket upside down in a field, another trick to confound them.

'The fox is flying it,' he says to the bushes, to the hawthorn and across to the house that he has already targeted. He is merely waiting for the man or the woman to come out, to walk up the road, to open a gate and let the cows make their own way on down to the milking parlour. He has watched them do it each morning, either one of them going up to open the gate and the other going down to the milking parlour to get the machines ready, and Kitty the daughter asleep. She is a redhead too but not golden like the woman, raw, foxy. He bursts out laughing at the thought of her scream.

At the sound of something breaking Kitty sits up startled and thinks *Jesus, the dishes, I didn't stack them right in the press, my mother will eat me.* Her younger sister Deirdre and her grandmother in the far wing of the house and her parents gone milking, same as always, then not the same.

The door is kicked in and she screams, she screams at a face masked with black nylon tights, shouting at her to get up, fast. Behind the gauze of the nylon she recognises O'Kane, his eyes like coal, spittle along his lips and every other word fuck, fuck. To save her grandmother a heart attack she gets out of bed and says pluckily, 'There's nothing for you in this house, O'Kane.'

There are splinters of glass all over the kitchen floor where he has broken a panel and she has to pick her steps to get the car keys that he has asked for out of the drawer.

'Take them,' she says and flings them across a worktop.

'You're coming too, Ginger,' he says.

'I've an exam today … it's a very important day for me,' she says, that little bit less insolent.

'It'll happen without you.'

'At least let me get some clothes on,' she says, pulling the lapels of her pyjamas across her front.

'Get the fuck out the door and stop messing.'

He sits beside her, the gun across his sprawled legs and a couple of minutes beyond the gateway she sees her own mother seeing her and flinging her hands up aghast. He has already mapped a route in his mind.

'Go left.

'Go right.

'Go along the pier.

'Go up to the ash tree.

'Go to Dick's Cross.'

'You think my mother didn't know you … you think that mask disguises you … well, it doesn't,' she tells him.

'You're a fecking useless driver …'

'You were only a class ahead of me at school … such a shy little lad … you wouldn't come in the playground … waiting for your mother … and look at you now … having the country at gunpoint.'

'Stop the fecking car,' he orders her and as he gets out she thinks she will have a few seconds to bolt, but he has already anticipated that and levelling the muzzle on her forehead, he backs out, opens the back door and lobs the gun above her head as he settles into the back seat and pulls the tights off. He allows the legs to dangle on his shoulder and gives them a little mocking toss from time to time. He nuzzles them and she thinks *I know who they belong to*. He looks less of an ogre without the tights and she tries talking to him, as if she is not afraid.

'You've made a bit of an impression, haven't you?'

'Is that what they're saying?'

'You're wanted … your picture in the papers … where did you sleep last night?'

'In a hole.'

'And why did you come to us?'

'That fecking chopper.'

'Everyone is asking about the missing people.'

'What missing people?'

'A woman and a child and a priest.'

'I know nothing about a priest.'

'So you do know about the woman and the child.'

'She gave me a lift a week back … I got out at a shop … that's all I know.'

'That's not what people are saying.' Suddenly he is shouting at her to go left, go left and she is on a dust road, pouches of it splashing the windscreen as if it had not been trodden in centuries.

'People must have lived here once,' she says, pointing to gable walls of fallen cottages, mere attempts at normality.

'It's my area now.'

'And that's why we're here?'

'I want to get to France.'

'What the hell happened to you to turn you into such a raving lunatic?'

'They put acid into my brain. They doped me first with sleeping pills and poured melted plastic over my feet so as I couldn't move.'

'You better have that head of yours seen to.'

'I don't want to. I'm in with the top man now.'

'Who's he when he's at home!'

'Man with the horns. He'd suck your titties any night … or that sister of yours or your old dopey granny.'

'You've seen too many horror movies, O'Kane.'

'My arse is bleeding. I cut it going into your place.'

'That's because you hadn't the manners to knock.'

'You're funny. How are you feeling anyhow?' and he nudges

her in the back.

'Freezing. Could I have my jacket?' she says and as he passes it to her, her hand comes off the wheel and in that instant the car swerves to one side and slides into loamy ground, the wheels slurping, then sinking down into a swamp.

'You done it on purpose, you bitch.'

'If I done it on purpose … I would have done it on the main road.'

'Reverse.'

'I can't reverse. It's stuck' and they get out to push it and he tries raising it onto a ridge of stones, all to no avail and finally he gets newspaper out of the boot, rolls it furiously into twists and as he opens the nozzle to dip them in the petrol she lets out a cry. 'Don't. My father loves his little car … his little Minny.'

'He'll get another little Minny,' he says and as they walk away from it she can see by the haltingness of the flames, the way they hesitate, that Minny will not catch fire. She will stay put and be a clue when her parents and the guards come on their trail.

Nothing, only emptiness, no cattle, a round rusted empty cattle feeder in the middle of nowhere and they walking over boggy ground, the stones and the thorns cutting her bare feet. There are telegraph poles to one side of the bog, the wires sagging down, wires onto which birds fly and perch for a few moments and her whispering to them, 'Tell them, tell them where I am.'

'My fucking feet,' he said.

'My fucking feet,' she said back. She tried to stop but he pushes her on and way way down below they come to a view of lake water rippling and glinting.

'You can see the Shannon,' he said.

'I don't need to see the Shannon … I live beside it … how long more do you intend to keep me?'

'For as long as I want.'

'If you're thinking of killing me, you better know that I'm not ready to die.'

'Are you afraid?'

'Everyone's afraid of death, sonny boy … even you … acting the big fella with Jeremiah Keogh's gun.'

'Who told you about Jeremiah Keogh's gun?'

'His sister did. He's too chicken to go to the guards.'

'What else are they saying about me?'

'They're saying you'd be as well off to give yourself up.'

'Never … I'll never do time again.'

'The priest's car was found burnt out on the pier … people saw it for miles … they knew it was your work …'

'They'll never get my dabs on it,' he says with triumph. She stops and grips his arm to hold up one of her feet to show him how it is bleeding. He goes berserk, telling her to wash it wash it or the fecking dogs will smell them out.

'I can't wash it … there's no water … anywhere … we might as well be on the moon,' she says.

'You're a cheeky bitch.'

'You're not going to kill me, Michen, are you?' she says almost comradely.

'If I have to I will … it'll be a fast end … you won't feel any pain.'

'Jesus. Them that love me will feel pain … anyhow if you kill me you'll have no cover … I'm your cover.'

'Bitch.'

They walk and walk. Bronze bracken, tough tawny grasses and furze bushes cutting her feet. Bouts of talk and bouts of silence. All of a sudden he stops, thinks, a storm going on inside his head and decides that they will turn back, they will take a different route. She realises that he is starting to panic.

'Look … we're going around in circles.'

'Shut up.'

'You won't get away with it, you won't.'

'Shut the fuck up.'

He starts to shake his head then, shakes it violently, cursing at some sudden apparition, and then he staggers, like he is drunk or blind as he blunders towards her.

'I can't see you … I can't see you,' he is shouting.

'What's wrong with you.'

'I've gone blind.'

'I'm here.'

'Lead the way,' he says gripping her arm and she thinks as she leads him along in that wasteland, what a deceptive picture, what a tableau, pilgrims, tired, foot-sore, making their way to the Inn.

'There's a rain barrel here … I want to drink,' she says, stroppy.

'Where … where.'

'Put your hand out' and she guides him towards it and he plunges his head into it and drinks at the same time, like a caveman, then tells her to wash her fucking feet and keep them sniffer dogs away. She cups the dirty water in her hands and drinks it. It tastes of iron. Then she pours some over her feet. His sight restored, he watches her, grinning.

The sound of the helicopter, abrupt and thundery, comes from beyond, scoring the sky, a giant bird, the engine roaring, the rotor scissoring the air and her eyes drinking it in, following it as it comes up from the rim of the horizon, coasts over Cloosh Wood and veers across the range of bracken ground towards them. Unable to suppress her joy she waves a white sleeved arm and hollers, 'Here, here.'

'Get the fuck down.'

'I won't get the fuck down' and he pushes her down with a violence and strikes her across the cheek and they lie in the wet hammocky ground, O'Kane slouches over her, believing his green jacket to be a camouflage, their hearts, their warring hearts like the hearts of lovers, beating violently. It dances above them coming down, closer, closer so that the crew are within calling distance and she is thinking *They'll pick us up … they'll pick up our heat* and it hovers and dips, undulates and all of a sudden it roars away happy with itself. In the wake of its passing the most awful silence, only the shivery vibrations of the telegraph wires.

'Thank fuck,' he shouts.

She closes her eyes not wanting him to see that she is in tears. Finally he eases his chest away from hers and she staggers up, disconsolate.

They go on down, limping, no longer arguing, the sun beating down, the odd house in the distance, ponies in a field sparring over sops of hay, life as it should be. He needs a car. Fast.

'You'll have the drive of your life,' he tells her.

Coming to a two storey house he warns about not doing or saying anything stupid. She sees his finger in the trigger, sees the roof of a hay shed, him kicking open the double wooden doors and dogs barking from inside. The dogs are chained. In the courtyard next to a tub of flowers is a big new Jeep with a sheen to it, a readiness, a yen to go. He shouts for the keys to be handed out. Above the baying dogs comes the voice of a man whom they cannot see, ordering them to get off his property. His accent is foreign.

'Throw out the keys,' O'Kane shouts up.

'I do not have the keys.'

'Throw out your fucking keys' and now they swear obscenities at one another, the self same words sounding different in either tongue and then the barrel of a gun juts through the upstairs window and as shots are fired, two orange cartridge shells land on the gravel near her and the dogs go berserk. O'Kane grasps her, his anger unabatable now and holds her as a shield as they back away towards the gate which is swinging open and shut.

'Tell him we will be back for him and his wife and his kids.'

'We will be back for you and your wife and your kids,' she says, her voice high pitched. She is like a puppet, no, a robot, she is witnessing everything as if it is not happening, as if it is outside of her, their going down the drive, him making her jump over barbed wire, his eyes now bulged and rolling.

The birds are busy, flocks of them darting in and out of the hedges, foraging, one with a very yellow beak carrying a worm back into a nest, to its young, birdsong so gay, so spry, soon to be silenced in the ensuing pandemonium, a fleet of patrol cars coming up the road, an older man emerging from a small cottage, refixing his cap as if it is just another morning and he going a few miles to fodder his cattle and she thinks *Oh, you poor man, you are for it in a matter of a minute and you don't even know.* They crawl under more wire, down a steep slope onto a cattle grid. Everything is eerily clear, the older man getting into his car and reversing, blue string with an assortment of white carrier bags to keep animals out and underneath the grid a pool of rainwater with cress growing in it, a fleet of cars coming up the road and guards jumping out, more than thirty armed guards on the road, on the wall, calling in loud, brisk, but still reasonable voices, 'Let the girl go, let the little girl go' and O'Kane answering that if they come an inch closer he will blow her fucking head off. 'I've seen your face on television ... you're wanted,' the older man says from his car, dazed, disbelieving.

She is pushed into the back of the car, O'Kane lurched over her as the guards yell, 'Throw out your keys, Pat.'

'I can't ... you see, I can't,' Pat answers, helpless.

They drive over the grid and away from the convoy of cars

and men, O'Kane, Kitty and the driver all shouting, mad tossing shapes beyond the window and then a crunch as the car veers towards a drain, comes to a halt and Pat exclaiming, 'We've been shot at ... we've been shot at.'

The back door is opened and a body thrusts itself over them, a multiple scream as the gun explodes inside the car and she opens her eyes to see Pat grasping the raised barrel, clinging to it, the cloth roof dropping down in shreds and a smell of gunsmoke. 'We have him ... we have him.' The guards' shouts go up as though from one throat, passing through their ranks, in glory and disbelief and he is pulled out of the car, his wild scoriated face, his wild unspent voice, shouting in a brief and fading burst—'I know nothing about the woman and the child.'

He moves with a staggering and undefeated bravado, this, for him, just an interim until he is loose again, a free man, them hunting him down, this never ending chase of them and him, hunted and hunters, the victory he had dreamed and re-enacted down the butchered years.

As he is put to the ground and his pockets searched, other guards rush on him exultant; anger and frustration wiped out now in this melee of jubilation, vindication; in triumph, in pride, in honour, his cursing, kicking frame there on the ground, being reined in, his rampaging at an end. But where are the missing people. Where are the missing people. Where ... are ... the ... missing ... people. They ask from different heights, different vantage points, different degrees of desperation, each thinking he will be the one to worm it out of the bastard. Guard Garvey is already a hero, being punched and congratulated for having had the presence of mind to jump forward from behind that wall and immobilise the back wheel of the car and bring the chase to a close.

'Good work, Michael.'

'Pure luck,' Garvey says, his face scalding with pride.

'Where are the missing people?'

She comes, the mercy woman, from some hidden dwelling, loose grey hair, in night gown and wellingtons, cuts her way through the swathe of men and kneels by him, placing her hand along his forehead, motherkind.

'Where are they, son?'

'I can't tell you ... with these fuckers around.'

'That child is in nappies … his bottom will be sore … his poor mother at her wits' end … you can tell me … I'm your friend … I knew your people.'

'They'll be left outside the shop tomorrow night.'

'Are they safe?'

'They have food for two more days.'

'Are they alive?'

'They're in a house … they have television.'

'They're safe … they're safe,' she says, her hands clasped in gratitude.

'Listen, my dear woman … I have to ask you to move out of here,' a detective tells her.

'Don't take him … give me a few more minutes … he wants to tell me … he needs to tell me,' she says and as they move him forward her voice goes on begging, like the long sighing sound of the banshee, up there on a road where nothing had ever happened, just the seasons, branches choking each other in summer and reaching out wanly in the wet winters.

He is cuffed to two detectives and in a lather of curses is led away, the bunched arm muscles with the crazed and supple fury of a python and even as they hold him they fear that he will in some way elude them still, some phenomenal ingredient will transport him back to the empty woods and his murdering haunts.

He jerked fiercely on the cuffs and stood above Kitty who was sitting on a wall with a blanket around her.

'The fox is finished,' he said, his last utterance to the landscape he had violated.

RECKONING

Superintendent McBride stirs the white stomach medicine in the beaker, keeps stirring it in order to delay drinking it because the taste disgusts him. He is a big man with a bit of flab, his hair grey before its time, but his eyebrows thick and sleek and black where he puts a lick of boot polish on them, something his favourite daughter Sile jeers at. He can scarcely believe what has hit him. Five days of searching, five days of pillory and criticism from press and public and finally O'Kane captured in the early hours on a mountain roadway, with not a drop of blood shed. The hero-ism and euphoria of the capture are short-lived because now all eyes are on him and his team to find the three missing people, before they die of exposure or starvation. Rumours abound. Tip-offs abound. They are near the lake, they are in the woods, they are in the midlands, they have been seen driving around togeth-er, the woman, the child and the priest. He has thirty-six hours to find them, thirty-six hours with the eyes of the world beamed in on him, thirty-six hours of scalding pain in his gut and probably no sleep. He is lucky to have got O'Grady and Wilson, whiz-kids at their job, the two most experienced interrogators in the land, famous for their strategy, their softly softly and then wham-bam. Never known to fail. A moment of respite as he imagines reading over the confession when his attention is alerted to the commo-tion in the street outside. Beyond the grimed window pane he sees a guard pushing back spectators as they try to surge forward over the metal barrier. He has given instructions that there be no ugly scenes, no booing, no weeping women with rosary beads, beseeching O'Kane to confess. Journalists jump on windows and roof tops to catch a glimpse of the infamous figure and in the corridor he hears doors banging and footsteps flying. The 'Fox' has arrived. He does not go out to have a look. He waits until Francis, a young, conscientious guard puts his head through the door and then indulges his curiosity—'What does he look like, Flann?'

He smiles at the pragmatism of the answer—'He looks like

any other young lout in an anorak and five days of dirty growth on his chin.'

The superintendent broods, winds his watch, listens to the lisp of the little tick, examines the sleek black hands, like sewing thread, as they meet over the digit eleven. In three days himself and his team should be congratulating one another on having a confession and he will celebrate with yet another glass of his milky medicine.

INTERROGATION

They are on first names, Gerry and Frank and Michen. Easy does it, as Gerry says, he being the smooth-talking one. He is younger, informal, pulling his shirt sleeves up to show that they are all mates together.

'Bit of a rough ride over, had you?' he asks and knowing there will be no answer he says to understand that the boys get a bit hyper once there's press and cameras around. They sit across a varnished brown table, their three sets of elbows leaning on it, the castors wobbling this way and that. As Gerry explains in a soft reasonable voice, all they want is to make things as painless as possible for everybody.

'How long will I be kept here?' O'Kane snarls.

'That's up to you,' Frank snarls back.

'We'll help you if you help us,' Gerry adds.

'I'm entitled to a solicitor,' O'Kane says, then holds up his wrists, pink and ridged from the way they had handcuffed him on the drive over. He licks them.

'Of course you're entitled to a solicitor … no one's stopping you … but if you take my advice we'll work it out here between the three of us … a solicitor will complicate matters at this juncture. Look, we have no papers, no pens, no note taking … it's a nice easy friendly atmosphere … you and Frank and me,' Gerry says.

'Where's Father John?' Frank asks.

'Precisely, we start with Father John … the whole diocese has gone hysterical … masses offered for him every morning … very popular man,' Gerry says.

'What the fuck are you talking about.'

'We're talking about three missing people, a woman and a child and a priest.'

'They must be joyriding,' O'Kane says and sneers.

'Don't give us that shit,' Frank says.

'Easy now, Frank … Michen here has had a tough life … packed off to a home at ten or eleven … your poor mother dying. Do you want to talk about your poor mother? It'll help. They say

156

a grief like that, bottled up, is a bad thing for a child … what age were you?'

'She was smothered in her coffin and I know who did it.'

'Where's the priest?' Frank asks, leaning in close to him.

'You have the wrong man,' O'Kane tells him.

'But you know they're missing.'

'You fuckers set me up … I've never heard of these people.'

'A gun was taken off you at approximately nine thirty-five this morning … it had been fired a few times … what were you shooting?'

'A hit from a bullet doesn't always mean that people die … it can be a shot in the air.'

'Mich … what's the story? The sooner you get it off your chest, the sooner you will be out of here … the superintendent in this unit is as decent a man as you could find … a family man … if you co-operate so will he … he's no sadist,' Gerry says.

'I was shooting vermin.'

'What kind of vermin?' Frank, at his most sarcastic.

'So you were in the woods … maybe you came across people in the woods … or you might have heard them … crying out for help,' Gerry, still solicitous.

'I want cigarettes.'

'You'll get your fucking cigarettes when you answer these questions … where are the missing people?'

'You won't get my dabs on them and you can't keep me here much longer. I know the law … I'm here under Section Thirty.'

'Section Thirty my arse … where are they … either you tell us or we'll drag it out of you.'

'Now now Frank … we're all a bit het up. You see, Michen, there's a fierce responsibility on our heads. The whole country is asking, not just two men in uniform. These people have to be somewhere in this locality and you're the one that knows it … you were seen with the woman and the child … people saw you in the back of her car, crouched down.'

'She gave me a lift a few miles up the road … then I got out because I don't go near towns.'

'Where did she go?'

'Ask the assholes in the town. She was a mover and shaker … ye should have found her by now … get me my fucking cigarettes.'

'Look if you don't level with us, the boys from Dublin will handle this and they'll put the squeeze on you ... up in the upstairs room, if you get my drift.'

'Knackers have them.'

'What knackers?'

'I'm not telling you. If I tell I'll be framed.'

'Are they alive?'

'The woman and the child are alive ... I saw them Wednesday ... they had food, they were watching TV.'

'So they're in a house.'

'I'm not saying.'

'Are they in this locality?'

'No ... they're hundreds of miles away.'

'And they're hostages?'

'I told you all I'm fucking going to tell you.'

'Is the priest alive?'

'It was a robbery that went wrong. The bathroom window was open and Joe and I waited inside ... Joe conked him with an iron bar ...'

'Who's Joe?'

'I can't tell you.'

'Cunt. You'll go down one way or another ... you saw that crowd waiting outside when you were brought in ... there are men that will be more than happy to take you for a ride.'

'I'll get your wife and your kids, scumbag.'

'You'll be behind bars for thirty years, scumbag.'

'Look, Frank, why don't you go and get a cup of coffee and Michen and myself will sort this out ... oh and ask one of the lads to go get cigarettes.'

'Bastard,' O'Kane says.

'He's a tough man, Frank, but don't get on the wrong side of him. Anyhow, to get back to business ... if Joe conked the priest, does it mean that he killed him?'

'I saw the blood pouring out of his head ... he was not afraid to die ...'

'So he's dead?'

'He didn't die straight away ... they put him in a laneway in a wood and shone the lights of the car on him ... he tried to run away but he couldn't ... God's brother.'

'Who shot God's brother?'

'The knackers … if she's not dropped outside a shop by mid-night tomorrow I'll grass them up.'

'In the name of Jesus, grass them now.'

'Off the wall … off the wall,' Gerry says as he flings his jacket down in frustration.

'We know he's off the wall but what have we got?' the super-intendent asks him.

'He shot the priest … he turned the car lights on in a lane in the wood and made him kneel down …'

'We have him … he's admitted to it.'

'He won't sign it … he won't fecking sign it.'

'He will sign it.'

'He won't … sign … it.'

'Go back in … bring Kinsella with you, all twenty-two stone of him, hold the pen in the fecker's hand and tell him it's us or the Dublin crowd … the rat pack. No, on second thoughts, this is country business … we're running this. He's a country boy, he needs country muscle.'

ABSOLUTION

The elderly priest and O'Kane shake hands and stand in the little visiting parlour, each waiting for the other to take a seat. There is a tray with cups, saucers and a plate of biscuits. He is an old priest, Father Christopher, kind, quiet spoken, happiest when reading his missal, spring cleaning his soul for eternity.

'How are you Michen ... how are you doing?'

'Bad ... they're bastards ... I met you in Killarney...'

'I don't think so.'

'You were at the tote window ... you didn't have your collar on.'

'Well, I'm glad to see you now, to see you're bearing up.'

'I have things on my mind ... a lot of things.'

'Yes, Superintendent McBride said you asked for a priest.'

'I did ... I do.'

'Is it in a confessional sense, Michen, that you asked for a priest?'

'What else.'

'Now ... before we continue, I want you to understand something. It would be a very onerous position for me to be put in ... a position I would prefer not to be in ... if ... if for instance you had something of import to tell me.'

'Is God like you?'

'Oh no ... God is God. He is above everything ... everyone.'

'Is he understanding?'

'He is ... he is also all knowing and all seeing ... omnipotent ... omniscient.'

'I don't like the Pope ... he's a bastard, I wrote to tell him.'

'Do you pray, Michen?'

'I said a prayer for them missing people ... did God see what I done?'

'He'd see what you done and whatever you done he'd understand it.'

'Will I be forgiven?'

'I believe you will ... remember Jesus in his agony in the

160

Garden of Gethsemane … how he asked forgiveness for his exe-
cutioners—Father forgive them for they know not what they do.'

'I'm not a psychopath … I'm not mad … it's them fuckers
that's making me mad.'

'Tell me, Michen, did you know Father John?'

'Not well.'

'But you called on him.'

'He was wearing a gold watch that had writing on the back of
it … it was given to him as a present … I thought of fecking it off
him but then I didn't because I knew they'd frame me … he was
a good man.'

'As a lay person would you like me to act as a mediator between the guards and the detectives and yourself?'

'They're assholes … I want you to hear my confession.'

'I would rather not.'

But O'Kane is already kneeling, blessing himself, saying the
prayer that he said as a child when he went into the confessional—'Bless me Father because I have sinned.' The priest takes the
purple stole that he carries in case of coming on an accident and
puts it around his neck and kneels and closes his eyes, dreading
what will be revealed.

'It was last Thursday … it was a gang doing a house and it
went wrong … pissing rain … we found the top of the bathroom
window open and the curtain pulled back … The priest drove the
car into the garage and came around the side of the house … Joe
hit him with an iron bar … we tied him up and put him in the
back seat … I drove him to a car park … Joe followed in his car
because he wanted no shit … I had to drive the priest to my own
area … we spent the night in a house … I had a sleep … the birds
wakened me in the morning and I brought him out.'

'Did he take long to die?'

'No, he went fast.'

'Did he say anything?'

'He asked me to spare his life … the woman is dead too.'

'And the child, is the child dead or alive?'

'I don't know … with the knackers you can never assume …'

'Where are their bodies?'

'I won't tell you.'

'You can tell God … it's God you're talking to through me.'

'You're not to tell them out there … you can't break the confessional oath.'

'They must be told.'

'You can't … I confessed before God … I'm not confessing to them … I'm not I'm not I'm not.'

'There's a child, maybe alive … just think of God's rejoicing at this eleventh hour if you save a little lamb from the slaughter … just think.'

'I don't remember shooting him … maybe he ran away.'

'Why did you kill the priest?'

'I had to … he was going to baptise the devil's child … the woman was a devil too, a she-devil … a sinner.'

As the priest intones the words of the absolution they seem hollow, they seem a blasphemy to God and having finished he gets up shakily and goes out, torn between his duty to God and his duty to mankind.

The superintendent and the others know that the priest knows something but that he cannot tell them, so shaken was he when he came out that a guard was sent to the public house to fetch a large brandy and ginger ale. He is sipping it slowly, twirling the glass, looking out the window at people passing by and all he seems to see are young mothers with children and all he can think of is a child screaming over a dead mother, trying to bring her back to life. He can see the guards looking at him and respecting his plight.

'So it's bad,' the Superintendent says.

'It's a shocker,' he says quietly.

'I have only ten more hours … then I'll have to let him go.'

'I'd tell you everything if I could.'

'I know that Father. I know that … can you tell us if you think he would take a life …'

'I think he would but then again it could be just fantasy … he comes out with strange remarks … for instance he said he saw me down in Killarney at the tote window with my collar off … I've never been to a race meeting.'

'That's baloney,' Frank says. 'That's to put you off the scent … our little twister O'Kane knows his stuff … he's been juggling the authorities since he was eleven years … in one of the homes he was shown a piece of paper that said "My future", and asked to finish the sentence he wrote "is very bad". Send him out to the street corners of any slum in any city and he'll see kids whose future is very bad and they haven't turned criminal.'

'What is it that warps a child ... what is it that changes a child from being a child?' the priest asks.

'I can't answer that Father. But if somebody had taken that pup ... his father or an uncle and given him the hammering of a lifetime ... we wouldn't be crawling on our knees begging him to tell us where missing people are. The state spoils them ... all this pussyfooting, all this hand wringing ... his childhood, his loneliness, his mother ... lots of kids with no mothers who don't steal cars and don't burn cars and don't take women at gunpoint ... little creep, little coward.'

'Time, gentlemen, time,' the superintendent says, holding up the watch he has had to remove from his wrist on account of a rash he has developed. His insides are scalding.

'There's something I feel I want to say,' the priest says, rising, lifting his hands helplessly—'The day I was ordained, there were five of us and afterwards we were all told to hold hands and so we did. We held hands and then there was a white linen cloth wound around each of our hands, like a bandage and we were told to take it and keep it and give it to someone very special when the need arose ... my mother died last autumn and I put that cloth in her hands in the coffin. If I had it now I would put it into that boy's hands, but I don't have it, I don't have it ... and I am telling you in the only language that is permitted to me.'

'I see ... I do see,' the superintendent says grimly.

Then laughter started up, loud peals, a baying and their heads turned to the door.

'It's your man ... it's one of his stunts,' Frank says and they wait expecting it to stop, except that it doesn't, it mounts, it magnifies, growing more macabre, more threatening with each bout and they look from one to the other in dismay.

'He has been laughing now seventeen minutes,' the superintendent says holding up his watch.

'I make it eighteen sir.'

'Eighteen minutes of animal laughter.'

'Bizarre.'

The laughter went on unabated and there was something terrible, something eerie in it, as if it would never end and they would never stop hearing it, and even when it did die down, it would be like a poltergeist along those corridors, O'Kane's curse on them.

A PLEA

He is with his grandmother. Through the observation hole they see them kissing, embracing, crying and then sitting close as the grandmother takes clean socks and underpants from a pillow slip and lays them tenderly on his lap as if they are gifts.

'How are you, son?'

'Not so bad,' he says and suddenly starts to laugh and the laugh frightens her because it is as if his insides are being laughed out of him. She holds him to contain it, to calm him in some way and eventually does.

'Why do you laugh Michen … is it because you haven't slept?'

'I fucked up bad with that gun … it wasn't worth a fuck.'

'You'll tell me, won't you … you'll tell me what you've done.'

'I've done nothing.'

'Don't lie to me. It's known that you took the woman and the child in a car.'

'There's another man involved … why don't they find him.'

'Look, you can deny it to them but not to me … it's written all over your face …'

'They're cunts … if I go down I'll bring them down with me.'

'But where are the people?'

'I don't want to talk about them people …'

'You don't have to talk about them. You just have to say, they're in Meelic … they're in Mohara, they're in Derrygoolin or in Derrycon … Clonoila, Clonrush, Coose, Allendara.…'

'They would be places where they might be.'

'Are they alive, son?'

'Oh yes.'

'How do you know?'

'Because a gang have them and they've put a price on their heads.'

'What gang?'

'A hardened gang … Dublin, England …'

'Tell me more … if you can't talk to me … you can't talk to anyone …'

'I've no one in the world.'

'You have me, son, and your sister and your poor mother looking down from heaven on her little boy.'

'My mind is gone, Gran.'

'In what way? Like, can you see me? Can you tell the colour of my eyes? Can you tell the day of the week?'

'Why didn't you come sooner?'

'I did come sooner … I came the moment I heard … I wanted to be near you … I asked them to put a bed in here beside you in the night but they wouldn't … I was awake all night with the bells ringing … did you hear them?'

'I did.'

'They're from the Abbey … the poor nuns get up two and three times a night to pray … three hundred years of prayers and penance … they're praying for you now, love and I'm asking you as your truest friend.

Where are the three people?'

'I can't tell you what I don't know.'

'You can tell me, you can. Get it off your chest … I know you're in pain … I see it in your eyes, in the way you're smoking, in the way you're fiddling, in the way you eat the cigarettes …'

'They think they'll break me … they'll never break me.'

'We're all broken, son … we're all of us broken by this and we won't mend … we won't ever mend.'

'Fuck you … they've twisted you against me,' and jumping up he pulls open the door that is already ajar and flings her out, telling her to fuck off home, traitor that she is. She shakes her head at the two guards that have been standing outside. She doesn't have to tell them what they already overheard.

165

Old Times

The town was dark and dormant, the drawn blinds smack up against the tiny window panes above the shops and public houses. The limestone fortress of the convent solid as a mountain range. Dogs slept and snarled under the gates of the side yards and little streams came rushing down out of nowhere.

A long cylindrical globe of cold blue light shone above the barracks door and inside a team of guards and detectives from across the country paced and mulled and argued, waiting for O'Kane to break. Thirty of the thirty-six hours have passed and nerves are beginning to feel rattled. They took turns to go in pairs, even twice going into the cell to waken him with just that one question—'Where are the missing people ... just tell us where they are.' At times he has roared back at them, other times threatened them and still others laughed, those bouts that sent shivers through them and made them fear for their wives and children at home alone. Their hopes now are pinned on O'Mara, one of the guards that tried to help him in his young days.

'You must excuse my attire,' Guard O'Mara says, shaking hands with several of them who welcome him like a prophet. His pyjamas dip down under his trousers and he is wearing no collar or tie. He is excited. He'd been retired for a few years, his days spent looking at television, looking into the fire, eating too much, especially cream buns and now he is wanted again, intermediary and hero. Superintendent McBride briefs him on the events so far, the priest's visit, the grand-mother's visit, admissions, countered a minute later with no admission, with 'yer all bullshit' threats.

'I can handle him, sure I know him since he was a child, a gorsoun.'

'One of the lads will go in with you.'

'Christ no.'

'Christ yes ... he could knock you out in a split second.'

'Let me do it my way ... me and him go way back,' and he drinks a mug of coffee before he goes in.

'You remember me?' he says to O'Kane who is on the floor

hunched, talking to himself. Getting no reply, Guard O'Mara sits, rocks his body back and forth and commences on the reverie that he has told to himself in the twenty-five mile drive along the dark roads, past houses with frightened people, their lights left on. He talks in a soft fatherly drawl. 'You remember you took a bicycle from the doctor's shed, a lady's bicycle, you didn't do it for gain, you never did anything for gain, I'll say that for you; it was more like a game, a prank. Next thing you broke into a holiday home of a Dutch woman and you found tins of paint and poured them onto the floor and onto the chairs and the sofa. That's how I got your first fingerprint. It was on the bottom of a tin and I lifted it off with a bit of sellotape and sent it up to Dublin to headquarters. You broke into houses and took cushions and pillows that you hid up in the woods. You were going to live there, that's what you said. Your father asked me to talk to you, to caution you and I did but you went on with your blackguarding.

'There was no holding you. I could have arrested you the time you broke windows but I didn't, I let you off, I said there would be no summons if you agreed to stop running wild and to go back home, back to your father. I drove you down there and I watched you go up the path and you were a grand little lad with your curls, a bit afraid but a grand little lad. I drove on back home and it was pouring rain and a fierce gale. There were trees down. 'Twas one of them stormy nights. I can see it now, every second of it, the wipers getting stuck on the windscreen of the car.

'I declare to God I'm at home in my own kitchen in front of the stove drying myself when my wife Mary goes to let the dog out and there you are under our ash tree like a drowned cat, not saying anything, not asking anything, just looking into our lit house. She comes back in and says, "That youngster is out there and he'll catch pneumonia" and I give her the nod and she brings you in. She sends into the bathroom and hands you a bath towel. Later she dries your hair and stands you in front of the stove next to me, the two of us with towels around us like Roman senators, like Nero, my wife Mary not able to do enough for you, making you cocoa, heating scones and imploring you to speak. You wouldn't speak. You wouldn't tell us why you came to us. Maybe you thought you could stay with us, my wife and I. Is that it Michen, is that it, is that what you thought then?'

'They're bastards, they're pigs, they're jumping on me.'

'They're not bastards … they're just doing their job … they're very anxious to find these people.'

'Their time is up … I won't be long more here … they can't keep me …'

'You know me … and if you trust me, I'll make a deal with you. You and I will go back out into the woods and we'll find the three people and we'll restore them to their poor heartbroken families. It's days now and these people are gasping with hunger and thirst … hostages as I presume … the young priest trying to give them whatever comfort he can, the child yelling … you've proved you can scare us now it's time to unscare us, Mich.'

'They'll never be found … never … none of them.'

'Why not, son?'

'I can't tell you. I'm not going down for what I didn't do.'

'But if you didn't do it, you won't be going down at all. Your only crime will be the unlawful possession of firearms and abducting that Boland girl … they're not heinous crimes …you'll be out on bail…local people will go bail for you.'

'Bullshit.'

'You've built up a lot of rage since you were a youngster but just think—that woman, that child and that priest never did you any wrong …'

'I know that.'

'I'm glad to hear you say so. How 'bout me arranging for you to get boots and clothes and the two of us go out?'

'I'll go if it's only us.'

'Jesus, Mich, it can't be only us … there's forty men on this case.'

'You fucker … it's only a stunt.'

'It's not a stunt … I'll see to it that you're sitting in my car next to me and you're not cuffed.'

'I'll come tomorrow not tonight.'

'Tomorrow could be too late.'

'The priest is dead … he's buried three feet down … I took a leather jacket out of his car …'

'Oh God Almighty, where is he buried?'

'I can't tell you … they'll link me to the killing … will the ballistics show that the bullet came from the same gun as I had?'

'Where is he buried?'

'Awful thing to see blood flowing from a man's neck …

spouting.'

'Are the woman and the child alive?'

'They should be.'

'I'll put it to you hypothetically.'

'What's that?'

'Say you're not you, you're an observer, if a person was going to dump a body in that wood, give me a clue where would be the best place ...'

O'Kane thought about the question and for the first time seemed to show some interest, then asked for the door to be closed.

He whispers it—'You go up from the crossroads, towards Derrygoolin, you pass the first two barriers and you come to a third one and in a bit there's an old hut that had a dead goat in it ... there's drains there ... that would be a good place to dump a body.'

EVIL

They have set out early, to pre-empt the crowds, five men squeezed into a small unmarked police car, the air stifling because the windows have to be kept shut, the two detectives on either side of O'Kane recoiling from him.

'Feeling better ... feeling a bit more relaxed,' Detective Morgan says, turning from time to time but O'Kane does not answer. Solon, the young driver, keeps looking in his mirror at the weirdo, slumped, his paws on his lap, like someone in a daze. Morgan has agreed not to cuff him. At unexpected moments he comes awake and taking note of a shop front, or a tin sign flapping over a filling station, or a field with gorse bushes he says, 'I bought sardines there ... I bought buns there ... I had a good shit there' and then reverts to his torpor.

'You were a great hurley player ... won the O'Donohoe shield for your school ... scored the two goals ... great stuff,' Morgan says and again O'Kane is listless.

Passing a glass shrine with a statue of the virgin and a crown of artificial red roses, Detective Lahiffe, attempting to diffuse the tension says, 'Who puts them up I wonder ... is it the state?'

'Not the state ... the locals ... that spot is where there was a terrible accident ... five people killed ... tragic altogether,' Brophy says, proud of his knowledge of the area and familiar with every house, every hay shed, every car or tractor.

'Is it the Blessed Virgin that's always in the glass case?' Lahiffe asks.

'Oh no ... if you go towards Mayo you'll find they have St Patrick,' Solon says.

'Is that a fact Joe?'

'Beautiful ... especially at night ... lights around him like a halo.'

'Of all the vandalism that's around, these shrines are never harmed ... isn't that a marvellous thing?' Detective Morgan says.

'Marvellous.'

'I want to go to my mother's grave,' O'Kane says sharply.

'You can go later … we have our bit of business first,' Morgan says, over friendly.

'I want to go now … I have to talk to her up in heaven … she whispered to me, she has a message for me.'

'Listen … we go to the wood first and then we go to the grave.'

They drive on, in a taut silence until they come to the cross-roads with a sign that leads to Cloosh Wood and Morgan lets loose a stream of heated curses at the sight of so many cars, cameras, droves of people and a helicopter landing in a nearby field.

'Ye bastards … ye fucking bastards … ye said no press no cameras,' O'Kane shouts.

'They won't see you … I'll go up and talk to the Super on duty and have the area closed off. You lie low here with the men,' Morgan tells him.

'Cunts … I'll bring ye down … I'll bring the whole fucking lot of ye down with me,' and he whirls and punches Lahiffe, knocking him sideways, then kicks on the door to make his escape. Brophy pulls him back by the coat, then by the torso and while O'Kane is head-butting him with quick rolling thrusts, the shrill pips preceding the morning news, then a woman's voice, strangled, emotional, says, 'Word has just come in that a body of a female has been found in a shallow grave in …' Then the reception is gone because they have entered the wooded region and Solon searches frantically, twiddling the knobs, the others craning, hearing only static and their own shocked exhalations. O'Kane begins to cry, quiet at first, then less quiet, sobbing, a seepage of tears, as if now he is only his tears; his flesh, his fury, his bellowing, all gone, only tears as he puts his hand out for one of them to hold it. No one does.

'We'd better go back, lads,' Morgan says and as Solon starts to turn the car, a guard on a motorbike comes rushing down, flashing them to wait.

'What is it, Pakie?' Morgan says, winding the window down.

'They're after finding the girl in a furrow between the trees with twigs and brush over her,' he says, his voice hasty and breathless.

'Oh Jesus Christ,' Brophy says in a choked cry, recalling his brother telling him about delivering her stones from a quarry and her getting upset because of the way the ground swallowed them up.

'Who found her? One of our lads?'

'No, a forester … he went up a few hundred yards and jumped the security wire … by himself.'

'And the child?'

'No sign … they're intensifying the search,' Pakie says.

'Take me to my mother's grave,' O'Kane shouts.

'You sonofabitch … you thought you'd get away with it …you thought a couple of months and animals and insects would have eaten her … missing for ever.'

'Let me out … let me out … I want to go to my mother … she knows I'm innocent.'

'Cuff him,' Morgan says, sharp.

'We can't cuff him unless we get him on the ground … and if we open that door he's gone … he's back in them woods, period,' Lahiffe tells him.

'Put your foot down, Joe,' Morgan says to Solon and as the car is turned, Cleary, a second guard, has arrived at the other window, his face streaming and red—'They just found the child, it was under the woman when they lifted her back.'

'A fucking animal,' Solon says.

'You're looking into the personification of Evil.'

'Get him out of the area fast … there's people up there baying for him … people that knew him … that fed him,' Cleary says.

'I'd like to throw him to them … to the gladiators … it's what should be done,' Pakie says.

'Now, lads … we keep the cool … we play this by the book … otherwise it could affect the trial,' Morgan reminds them.

'You realise what he's done … a woman, a child,' Lahiffe says.

'I do and I shrink from him … "Touch not the murderer lest thou too be touched",' Morgan says solemnly.

'Unreal … unreal,' Brophy keeps saying.

'Fecking not unreal … real,' Cleary says, mangling the handles of the motorcycle, shouting to include the warm day, the soft countryside, young buds, hawthorn blossom and a few hundred yards away, a scene so gruesome that he vomited.

'You saw her,' Solon says helplessly.

'I saw her.'

'What state are they in?' Morgan asks.

'They smell. They smell.'

'Picture it ... and picture him ... he killed the girl, he reloaded the chamber and he shot the child ... an animal...'

'No animal would do such a thing ... an animal kills for survival ... this is bloodlust ...'

'I want my mother,' O'Kane says, throwing himself across Lahiffe.

'You sonofabitch ... your mother won't help you now or never ... you're zeroed.'

'Take a back road Joe ... the word will be out,' Morgan says and thanks the two messengers with a grim nod.

It is a narrow road, rutted and grassy from disuse, the drive so frantic it is like hallucination—dust spattering up, the fleeing countryside, the occasional cottage garden, horses, a television mast, O'Kane immersed in himself, in some bottomless cavity, like a grieving animal. Soon now they would enter bedlam but they did not know it and perhaps he did not know it either because he was sitting with his head down, sobs reaching up out of his gut when suddenly the car starts to veer from one side of the road to the other, Solon not yet realising what it is and then feeling that he is being choked as O'Kane has caught his tie and is jerking it violently. The car comes to a skidding halt and lurches up onto a bank where there are geese and goslings, grazing. The cramped car filled now with shouts, urgent, harried, afraid, the two detectives in the back locked in a clinch with him, like wrestlers in a pit, his strength prodigal, their fists not even denting him as if they are hitting leather.

'Lie on him.'

'Restrain him.'

'Get him to the floor.'

'Cuff him.'

'We can't cuff him.'

'Get him off me ... he's biting my ear,' Brophy roars.

'Jesus, as if one madman isn't enough,' Morgan says, hoists himself over the front seat, grips O'Kane by the hair, pulling it with a long practised traction until the mouth and teeth are loosed from the bloodied ear and O'Kane's face getting whiter and whiter—'You're breaking my fucking neck.'

'No one cares if we break every bone in your body,' Morgan tells him as Lahiffe pulls his arms behind his back and handcuffs him, still butting, still vowing that he will bring them down.

The car rocks from side to side with Solon struggling to get a grip on the wheels as they slurp on the mossy bank and beyond the geese in a wild consternation because their young have been slaughtered, bits of yellow, lifeless, furry rag, slung there.

O'Kane sits between them, a lethal presence, the only weapon left to him is his fingers, his thumb tearing the opposite thumb, dragging the flesh away and then each finger picking the flesh of its opposite finger, the shredded flesh, the drawn blood and the chafing of the cuffs as if they are about to spring open of their own accord.

As they near the town the two detectives in the back look from one to the other, comparing their slashed jackets, their bruises, their cut lips.

'Longest eighteen miles I've ever driven.'

'How's the ear?'

'Deadly ... I can't tell my wife he bit me.'

'Cover him up lads ... they'll be looking for his horns here,' Morgan says and they throw a blanket over him to hide him from the throng.

They have gathered outside the station, milled, grave, appalled, but when he is bundled out, the voices break into an instantaneous wail of repugnance and revenge, the same words again and again—'Murderer ... Child murderer ... Butcher.'

The likeness of the dead woman stares back at him from raised posters, stares from several points, her face with an unwonted calmness, the eyes soft as cloud, a long rope of hair under the upturned brim of a straw hat, gazing, at them, at him, at the summer day. He is not seeing it, not hearing their heckles, he has gone back into himself, into a hulking frozenness.

A legion of guards converge around him and he is pushed forward, a bunched and damned silhouette passing into the gloom of the hallway. Then in some monstrous and antic aftermath he turns, head-butts the blanket off and begins to laugh, a mad, mocking laugh and they draw back, a shaft of terror passing through them, witnesses to some medieval grotesquerie, his grinning face, his loathsome eyes with dead yet murderous glare.

They are afraid of him now, the Kinderschreck, one of their own sons, come out of their own soil, their own flesh and blood, gone amok.

BART GLYNN

It was like I dreamed it. It was like I'll dream it all my life. I seemed to have known where I was going, my steps led me there in an orderly, unfussy motion. I didn't salute any of the mob around the crossroads, they were as invisible to me as I to them. I was a phantom in search of a phantom and I would find it. To call it weird is to belittle it. I even think I envisaged how the woman would be. I'd seen her once playing pool in Boyce's bar and sensing this glow around her, amberish, possibly because of the red gold hair. She played like a pro and the men riled her. I had known it before I wakened. To my wife I said, 'Leave the dinner till evening time' and she didn't question me. She never does which possibly accounts for our being together. I am described as a loner. My favourite place is a mobile home thirty miles away by the seaside. I walk and I walk and I need no one. I've never been one to believe in signs or portents or dreaming. I am a rationalist. Having passed the two barriers and little knots of guards stationed here and there it seemed to me that everyone was running in different directions, somewhat clueless. Strangers to the wood. It was a warm day and in the breeze there was the smell of spring itself, a tender smell. The wood was fairly dark and I had to crawl along under the low branches and under the trees that had fallen athwart. Strands of dead moss dipped from their branches. I sensed something in the instant before I saw it. Then that rapid contraction in the chest, that onrush of adrenaline. The exposed calf of one leg was the whitest white, the coat was black and she had thick purplish socks. She was in a furrow, face down, and the pine needles had fallen on her like decoration, fine, thin needles; rust colour. I knew she was dead, the smell alone told me that. She looked so remarkably lifelike that a person might be forgiven for thinking she could be brought back to life with a touch. There were flies on her hair, moving in and out of it and lodging on the crusts of dried blood. They were merciless. Nothing else moved. Not her. Not I. It was her repose that I found the most unbearable, the wisdom of it, as if in those last moments she saw what was coming and somehow she met death. The picture just kept going in and in, a gruesome canvas inside my head, forever.

'Up here … up here.' I went out shouting it. I shouted like a madman but Cornelius said that when he came towards me, my face and my beard had the pallor of a ghost.

GRIEF

'Why didn't he overpower the bastard? Why didn't he take the gun off him? Why didn't he run into the woods? Why did he die like a lamb to the slaughter?'

It is Jack, a second woodsman, asking the detective who has just been winched down. Asking it relentlessly as he has asked it from the moment at dusk when, after the searches were called off until the morrow, he came on him alone, Father John, with his head placed over a limestone slab, his hands folded for prayer, his priest's collar unstained.

'Why, just tell me why, he didn't fight back?'

'No use in whys … because the creatures are all gone,' the detective replies and then genuflects for a moment in lieu of a prayer and then it is the cold grim task of identifying the body and noting every detail for his report.

The same woods, that filtered green, the constant leafy murmur and yet not the same, no longer the harmless place it once was, marked now as a human can be marked by its violation, its wood memory, the habitation of their frightful pilgrimage, their hapless cries; three bodies soon to be wrapped in plastic and brought down to the waiting hearses.

BLUEBELLS

The small country chapel has the smell and leafiness of field and woodland. Garlands of fern and ivy, bluebells in jugs, their bells a clouded violet blue, so close together as if they might just accidentally tinkle; carpets of flowers along the aisle and by the altar steps where the two coffins are placed on either side, the larger brown coffin for Eily and the smaller white one for Maddie. The chapel is filled to overflowing, the sermons, eulogies and songs drift out along with the smell of bluebells and woodbine, out to the grounds and the adjoining fields where hundreds of mourners stand, stunned and teary.

Cassandra spoke for her entire family when she said that their spirits should now be allowed to go free and looked at the coffins as if she was talking to the bodies beneath, bodies that had been cut and sawn and scalped and weighed and swabbed and pieced together again, dressed now in garments of eternal glory.

'Free them,' she said and cupped her hands and as she raised them, people looked up to the rafters believing they were witnessing the transmigration of the two souls.

An estranged father stood apart. That was his child inside the small white coffin, his feelings locked inside his own brusque and taciturn nature. Herself and the child were one, indivisible, and O'Kane, the outcast, had seen that and had wanted it and had had to destroy it in his hunger to belong. The ultimate loser. An estranged father who wanted to cry but did not cry, then. There were tears to be shed but they would be shed elsewhere, him imagining them forever in the woods, their true resting place. He thought *What can I do to prove to myself that I am that bit bigger than I was, before this struck. I can't bring them back. I can think of those last mad minutes until thinking is empty of thought, but I can't bring them back, ever.*

What he did then was to search out O'Kane's father and shake his hand and the man looked at him, perplexed, uncomprehending, his sunken eyes like holes in his face, two fathers, outside that boundary of mother and child, their hands briefly touching, touching on things that could never be said.

BLOOD

'Tell me that you didn't rape her, Mich … just tell me that.' It is
Aileen, teary and unslept and waiting since dawn to be allowed
in, travelling almost a hundred miles since he has been moved
to a prison half way between home and the city. She has brought
him clean clothes, a bar of soap and bananas that he asked for.
The guard outside has explained to her that he has refused to give
blood and asked her to tell him, as they have told him, that it can
be taken forcibly. He looks at her as if he might kill her.

'Tell me,' she says, beseeching.

'They set you up … they want to blacken me with every crime
in the book.'

'Then tell me that you did not rape the woman, simple, simple,
Mich.'

'Fucking voices … won't shut the fuck up … get me a radio …
get me anything … get me a gun … get me out of here.'

'Mich … Michen.'

'She loved me … she was my girlfriend … she sucked my
cock in the woods … we had a tent up there … mad for me.'

'She was not your girlfriend. It's all in your mind and there's
only you and your mind for the rest of your fucked life … Jesus.'

It is as they are arguing that a young prison officer with pale,
almost albino colouring comes in; clean shaven, a crew cut, his
eyes the washed blue of cornflowers, dangling a syringe and making imaginary stabs in the air as he dances around O'Kane.

'We don't need your blood, scumbag … we have it. You cut
your bollocks on the glass door when you broke into that house
… we have your DNA on our files … they flushed you out of her,
above in the mortuary … she's dead but she's clean and you're
unclean and you stink.'

'Is that the woman on the shore,' he asks.

'No, it's not the woman on the shore, scumbag … it's the
woman you brought to the woods. How come you forget the most
important data? You don't forget to ask for bananas or a change
of underpants but how come you forget that, you're a monster,

but you can't hide behind the devil's apron strings any longer ... do you want to know why. Because you are him, hooves and horns and all ... it's been a farce, a roadshow down the country ... everyone willing to help you ... a bishop no less, priests, dignitaries, VIPs, wringing their hands ... poor you ... you never had a chance ... the system failed you ... we failed you ... St Michael's, St Joseph's, St Bridget's, St Patrick's, St Finian's, St Teresa's, St Anne's, Spike Island, Clonmel, Rugby, Featherstone, Wolverhampton all failed the little coward who so loved his mother that he had to take an innocent woman and fuck her and kill her and then kill her child to complete the tableau and kill the priest that was brought to give the last rites. It's all a blur inside that football of a head ... it slipped your memory somehow ... well, I'll tell you something, the bishops and priests and the VIPs will run like rats from you now, repulsed ... your visitors from now on are Us ... state visitors ... state plate ... state blanket ... state funeral ... welcome to hell, O'Kane ... it's been waiting for you.'

'He's a fucking liar, a fucking liar,' he says when they are alone. 'I think you did rape her Mich ... I think you did.'

'Do you want them to lock me up?'

'It's the only thing ... after what you done.'

'Your own brother.'

'You're not the brother I knew ... you're an alien,' she says, fearless, despairing.

'Don't leave me,' he says running to her, grasping her.

'I have to ... I can't stay here a minute more.'

And he did not try to stop her, he just backed away in frozen immobility seeing the shame that welled up in her eyes.

It was after I had sex with her I came downstairs to the kitchen. She had the kettle on. I heard the voice of the devil saying *kill her kill her*. I said we have to go to the woods. She tried to defy me. The gun was hid outside behind a tree. She didn't like it, she didn't want a gun around the child. I said I'm only after getting it. I intend to raid a post office. I didn't think of killing her before that. I had no reason to. She used to come up to my tent in the wood every other day and bring me food and we had loads of sex there. She sucked my cock. She wouldn't let me go to Tullamore.

I made her drive to Cloosh Wood and when we got there she said where's your tent. I said I burnt it, I had no more use for it. I said then I'm going to have to kill you. She said don't be raving. I brought her way in from the road at gunpoint. She was nervous, panicky. She was holding the child's hand. I told her if she tried running away I'd shoot them both. She let go of the child's hand and sent it to play. I brought her up into the horseshoe of trees and she said you're frightening me, you're scaring me, give me that gun. She took it off me. She unloaded it. We were struggling. She hit the bolt and that automatically unloaded it. I tripped her. She fell on the ground and I loaded the gun. She tried to get back up. I shot her in the face. It was messy. I had a problem with the child. What was I going to do with him. He was screaming. He had no mother. I couldn't bear to look at him. I shot him in the side of the head or somewhere around there. I forget. My mind was gone.

I came out of the wood and sat in her car. The keys were missing. I went back to the wood to get the keys from her pocket. She'd gone green. The colour frightened me. I covered her with pine needles and left the wood. I slept in the car a long time, maybe a day. I burned the car somewhere and went to my grandmother's. I was sweating. I threw up. I was hearing the devil's voice. He said burn your grandmother's iron gate, burn her hay shed. I don't remember going out from there but I did, I was walking along the road with the gun. I heard a voice say burn the lockkeeper's house. He wasn't there. I took a blanket. It got dark so I went on up towards the lights in the village and saw the church. The priest's house was beside the church. There was no light in it and I waited. When he came I kidnapped him at gunpoint. He said oh my God. He asked me what I wanted. I said I was in a mood to kill. He said relax and don't kill me, I'll drive you anywhere you want. I brought him to a house in the wood where I lived as a kid. I'd hid in a closet there, pissed in it. My mother thought that very funny. Someone had sunk a well there since we lived in it. The priest said what are you going to do to me. I said I was waiting for orders. He said I was a sick man. He said that he knew my grandmother, that he went to see her sometimes, heard her confession. He had a wallet in his inside pocket. He went into the toilet and hid it in his trouser pocket. I ate cake with sugar on top. I went to sleep.

It was six in the morning and the birds were singing. I said to him come on, time to get up. I took his wristwatch. I gave it to some fucker in Limerick for hash. I laughed at the blood coming out of his head like a water pump. I got a great buzz, a great kick out of that. I liked the jump. I'm possessed.

CHRISTMAS

He lay in his own shit. He lay in his own dark, cursing and conspiring. He hated the screws. The screws hated him. He made their lives hell, refused to use the bucket that they passed in and shat on the floor to spite them. Threw his arms out like they were oars or javelins and told the fuckers he'd be leaving very shortly, going through the roof. The 'Jumping Jesus show' they called it. They were afraid of him. He roared and harangued and they believed that even if his head came off from roaring his lopped head would go on persecuting them. He called them Ambrose. They called him Fattie. 'No hamburgers for Mr Fattie.' 'No radio for Mr Fattie.' 'No walkies for Mr Fattie.' He'd hold four fingers up in rotation, and they knew what it meant. He'd killed three people and there would be a fourth. Sometimes he sat like he was in a trance, sucking his thumb, staring. His laughing was a kind of roaring also. He could keep it up for hours.

The staff shot the pheasant that kept him company because they were jealous of it. He got his revenge. He had birds coming in the window whistling tunes and he whistled back. Then one day six or seven red hens from home came and he talked to them and asked them if they were laying well. He had great times with them. He learned the chookchookchookchookchookchook that they did after they laid. Then one day they didn't come and he cried. Pigs came but they got stuck, they got wedged between the bars, their pink hairy rumps not able to get in and not able to get out. They taught him grunts and the screws listened outside the cell and looked through the spy hole, made bets whether he was or was not a pig. Instead of Fattie they called him Piggy and he called them Ambrose.

He was brought for a walk each day, around a closed yard with a high wall and one tree with dead, papery leaves. There was a lavatory bowl in the corner with no chain and no handle and he shat in it even though he was not supposed to. He saved his shit for there so that they would come with bucket and broom cursing him and making him clean it up. One day there was a new nurse that gave him a funny look and he struck at him in a long lunge, got him to the ground and then started hitting his skull on the edge of the bowl, his face mired in the shit. It was the padded cell after that. He'd hurl himself against the leather walls and be thrown back and rehurl himself, because nothing would convince him that it was not going to give in to him.

That's when Dr Macready was called. Dr Macready had the distinction of being the only one that was not afraid of these nutters, afraid of no one. He agreed with the governor to see him but only on one condition, face to face. He did not want to be in one room and looking at O'Kane through glass in an adjoining room—'I want to get to the real person,' he said and the governor smiled the smile of the disenchanted. It took five visits to break the ice. He was late for his visit and sat down, took out his handkerchief, began to clean his spectacles and said, 'There was a drunk Scotsman on the bus and he kept saying "No sweat John no sweat John" and he walked up and down the aisle and looked into people's faces and said "Peasants" and then he came and sat beside me and studied me and said "Peasant".'

'Are you in America a lot?'

'No … why?'

'I don't want a trial here. They'll be laughing at me … they'll make fun of me and fun of my mother. Could you get me out of here? Could you get me out a back door? I'll harm no one … I won't get a gun …'

'Not a chance in hell, Michen. The only way I can help you is to come in here and see you.'

'Bullshit.'

'Yes and let you bullshit me.'

'I throw food on the floor … I go to the toilet on the floor.'

'I know … I've seen it.'

'I'm a sick man, aren't I?'

'Yes, you're a sick man.'

'And what will you do for me?'

'Not much … but, something … we'll try … together.'

Dr Macready is with him in the hospital; he has been sitting for well over an hour, listening to him as he dozed and rambled—'There's a little gun in your exhaust, I was a colicky baby, I smiled at three months … I twitched at six'—his sighs getting fainter and fainter, a film over the eyes and sudden jerking as his brain seems to fuse out, then another little garbled sentence, then a smile.

The light from the corridor is mellow and in contrast with the harsher light in the hospital ward, O'Kane's face gaunt, his skin yellow, his head lifted back against the iron rungs, his wrists no longer chafing, slack inside the handcuffs, the guard cuffed to him dozing with tedium. Two other guards stand at the end of the bed and one at the door, their squat revolvers slightly obscene looking, their hips waddling as they walk around, to kill time.

Dr Macready is holding in his hand the gift he has brought him because it is Christmas. O'Kane has been on a hunger strike for over twenty days, no longer warring, quiet, shivery, talking of being lifted up into the sky, and at other times seeing orange men dancing on his bed. He is saying that he wants his sins on his tombstone, wants the world to know he is sorry. He insists that it was when the box of Holy Communion wafers were found in Father John's car that his luck changed, and that it was a good thing because it meant he got captured. He said she was a beautiful woman, his dream woman in his dream world and that was why he fell in love with her. He asked the doctor to say goodbye to home for him because home was the most important place in a boy's life, a boy carried the woods into the world. He said his father should have come and forgiven him and he should have forgiven his father because a son had to be a father too. But always back to the woman, still alive in some part of him, still alive in Cloosh Wood, animals attacking her and him trying to save her and turning her over and picking her up. And picking her up.

'Aren't you going to open your present?' the doctor says.

'I can't,' he says and holds up the cuffed hand and smiles. Quiet, dreamlike, as if someone lulled by a potion that has not come from outside, not been administered, but from inside himself, his own metabolism altered making him remote, serene, his demons gone. Dr Macready unwraps the crepe paper and holds up the cigar box with the beige-coloured picture of a South American potentate.

'Who's the man and who's the women?' O'Kane says, staring at it.

'There's only a man there ... can you not see?'

'Is it chocolate?'

'No it's cigars ... I thought it was time for a cigar.'

'I won't come off the fast ... so don't try asking me,' he says very gently.

'I won't let you die ... what do you think happens when you die?'

'You go to the other place.'

'What if you don't like it in the other place?'

'I'll ask the way back.'

'Michen, listen to me.'

'You listen to me ... I'm not mad now and I've no temper and isn't that a good way to die?'

As the door is pushed in Matron calls in a falsetto voice—'A visitor, a VIP' and Dr Macready gets up and says to wait for a moment until he clears it, then leans in over O'Kane: 'I think I told you ... I asked my friend Bishop Cormac to come by ... he's a lovely man, a sympathetic man.'

'Is he an Orangeman?'

The Bishop stands by the bed and puts his hands alternately on O'Kane's shivering forehead.

'Can we take off the handcuffs, Matron ... so as he can talk in private to Bishop Cormac?' Dr Macready asks.

'No.'

'No?'

'I can't take responsibility for that ... if he attacks and kills I will get the blame.'

'He can't hurt a fly ... he's a dying man.'

'I'll have to phone the Governor of the jail ... he may not even be there ... it is Christmas after all' and she points glaringly to a strip of tinsel looped above O'Kane's bed rung.

'Oh Jesus, where are the courageous people,' Dr Macready says, looking from her to the guards and back again.

'You've no idea, Doctor, how obstreperous, how dangerous this man can be.'

'I have.'

'Then you're lucky you're not in a morgue.'

'I'll answer to the Governor and so will Bishop Cormac ... this boy must be persuaded to take a sip of something ... or he'll be in the morgue.'

She nods reluctantly and the handcuff is undone, then the guards file out, somewhat sheepish at the presence of a bishop.

Dr Macready and Miriam, a young auxiliary nurse, are in the pantry waiting. A plate of sandwiches covered with a cloth are on a tray along with tea things.

'It's an awful thing to say but I'm starving,' the doctor says.

'Me too … it's the thought of people stuffing themselves at this very minute with turkey and roast potatoes and little sprouts … and then the plum pudding and the brandy butter and a dollop of whipped cream …'

'Don't,' he says and lifts the corner of the cloth to see what kind of sandwiches they have been brought.

From time to time, Miriam goes to the door that is still closed and comes back with her index finger to her lip.

The Bishop takes them by surprise because of his crepe sole shoes and comes in smiling, his cupped hands raised in a little triumph—'He'll take a sip … he'll take a sip of sugar and water.'

'Fantastic. What did you do?' Macready asks.

'I didn't have to do much … he's a broken man, a broken boy I should say, we talked of what happened … you see it's always coming back to him … the place, the woman screaming, the child screaming … all jumbled … so we made a kind of pact. I said that I'd take his thoughts for one hour every day … I'd pray and meditate and he could have a rest from them … that's how I reached him.'

'So we're to feed him?' Miriam says petulantly.

'Only sips you understand … little by little … that will revive him.'

'My father says he'd shoot the bastard … and we're about to save him … it doesn't make sense,' she says.

'It does Miriam … it makes sense of some kind … you wouldn't have volunteered to be a nurse if you didn't have sympathy …' Dr Macready says quietly.

'OK … I'll give him the sips but I won't tell anyone outside … and I won't tell it at home because his crime is the worst ever committed and it'll never be forgotten…'

'Why is that do you think?' the Bishop asks.

'We'll never know the ordeal these people went through … and that's why we keep reliving it.'

'And he'll never know either.'

'He knows,' she says tartly.

'You're wrong there, Miriam ... he makes no distinction between life and death ... between you and me ... between inside and outside ... it's all the same ... it's all dreamtime.'

'Dreamtime,' the Bishop says and looks at the evening sky, a marvel of pale violet, God's creation, just as the young man in the bed about to take a sip of something, is God's creation as well.

A year has gone by and O'Kane has been moved from prison cell to hospital bed, back to prison again, sometimes in isolation, sometimes not, by turn abusive or opaque, while down at home his spectre haunts the place and those who are obliged to give statements to the guards live in fear of his return, of his coming back to avenge them.

Then it is the time for the hearing and a crowd stand outside as they will day after day to look and to harangue him as he is brought, handcuffed, from the back of the van, sometimes cursing, other times shouting out that he is being persecuted in the prison, that he is being made senile.

On the opening day, his counsel asked the judge to go back with him to those early years, O'Kane the child, withdrawn, timid, flung in with city delinquents, institutionalised for most of his life, assessed but never helped, because no one, no one in the entire world wanted to help him. He described the abyss O'Kane lived in, was still living in, the tortured mind, worms crawling in and out of his skull, voices dogging him, a sense not just of alienation but of living hell. He was at pains to remind the judge and the crowded gallery of the Blitzkrieg that surrounded this very emotional case and turning to the jury tells them that theirs is a sacred task. He said the young man did not deserve to stand there alone because the country itself was on trial, it had failed him, the system had failed him as from the age of ten he was shuttled from one institution to another, motherless, fatherless, never with them and never without them. There were stares and looks of indignation as O'Kane sat handcuffed, bloated, with a blank expression, sleeping the hours away like he was already dead.

Counsel on the opposite side painted a different picture, a picture of an untruthful, cunning, self-interested liar with a blood lust, a man who took pleasure in killing, a man fully aware of what he had done, who now feigned madness to have his sentence mitigated. He said they would hear of voices which the defendant was plagued with, but to make no mistake but that these were gimmicks, *Alice In Wonderland* ploys, tall stories of devils spiking his food or voodoo priests governing his actions or so-called maggots crawling out of his brain. And so endlessly his mental state was batted back and forth between quick jousting surgical minds and mostly O'Kane registered nothing except for the times when he laughed uncontrollably and some in the crowd tittered with nerves.

Day after day, a re-enactment of the scene, the woods, the track, the twigs, the small branches, the brush, the partially covered bodies, the blowflies, the eggs of blowflies, the left foot, the right foot, the flexed knees, the black anorak, the blue anorak, the mother splayed over the child, listeners at once riveted and appalled.

There were tears when exhibits were held up, the priest's elasticated gold watch, a wooden pendant that the woman had worn and the child's sweatshirt with a motorbike pattern on the front. A neighbour of Father John spoke of his last tête-à-tête in her house, the half measure of brandy she had given him and diluted with twice as much water, the slice of sponge cake filled with cream which he ate and the sacred box of communion wafers that he was carrying for children's first Holy Communion three days hence. A cry of pathos was let out at hearing how he had removed his wallet from his jacket pocket and tucked it into the back pocket of his trousers as if he feared being robbed by his captor.

When the time came for O'Kane to be cross examined he seemed to emerge from a long coma, burning to tell how he got great with Eily, their first kiss on a couch in her house, the hashish they smoked, the times in his tent in the wood and of those last minutes when she defied him. He said how she grabbed the gun off him and he grabbed it back and pulled the trigger and shot her in the eye and blood started squirting out and the child ran shouting, 'Mammy Mammy.' On being cross examined, he denied that shooting the child was a vicious deed. He said no. He said that he did not want the child to grow up without its mother, the way he had done. He described and enacted how he hid the child under the mother and put the pine needles over them to keep off the rain.

Cassandra did not know that she was about to do it, did not even remember herself standing up and walking towards the witness stand to where he stood. 'The last picture my sister was painting was called Grief. It was a woman and a child ... with a man at the edge of the canvas looking in.'

O'Kane stared at her, baffled, vacuous and then asked if the typist would read out to him what had been said. He heard it and shook his head repeatedly as if to recapture something that had gone astray in him, then: 'I watched only one woman.'

'Why did you watch her?'

'I was in love with her—that's the truth.'

There were gasps and hisses of outrage.

'You don't believe me ... do you?' he asked.

She paused, the pain, the horror, the sorrow, the anger, the loss all compressed into this definitive moment.

'God help us all, you included,' she said, her voice cold and unemotional and she stood frail and unfrail, outside time and place, outside the shocked staring faces, not knowing if he had heard her.

VISITING HOUR

He is holding two soup spoons that are his friends. They have names. He is beating them hard. That steady hollow clang of metal upon metal, getting louder and louder and queerly hysterical in the austerity of the small dining room. Aileen is sitting opposite him. He has not said a word to her, he is in one of his blankety blank moods as she remarks. Others have got up as soon as they came in, shunned by all, even a black retriever who comes over to sniff them and goes off again. He has put on weight and only his eyes bear resemblance to the youth that he was, just a year before.

'So how are you?'

'In hell.'

'You're not in hell. You're in a mental hospital and you prefer it to the jail. You prefer the food, the walks, the exercise.'

'The chef is poisoning me ... they're all out to get me, tormenting me.'

'Do you want me to talk to the doctor?'

'You're thick ... a thick head.'

'Look, it's a three-hour journey ... the trains are woeful ... I had to get a babysitter for Ben ... you don't even ask how he's doing ... well, he's first in his class and his best subject is English ... so there.'

'I want a...'

'A what?'

'A medal.'

'Oh, are you religious now, is that what they done to you?'

'St Christopher. I want it in gold. It's for a journey.'

'Where are you thinking of going?'

'Tullamore ... I'll build a small bungalow ...get the balance back.'

'I never know whether you're mad or acting mad.'

'Does your heart break?'

'Sometimes.'

He is crying then, his teeth eating his tears; pitiful sounds coming from deep within, a child's despair imprisoned in the bloated being he has become. She leans over and takes the spoons from him, then very gently—'What is it, Mich? If you don't tell me, I can't know and I can't help you.'

'No one will double up with me … they're all afraid of me.'

'You attacked nurses … twice.'

'Why did I kill them people?' he asks vacantly.

'That's between you and God.'

'She's there,' he says and jumps back terrified.

'She's not there … there's only me here.'

'God isn't talking to me … he says I'm an animal … am I an animal?'

'I brought something to cheer you up … a poem you wrote to me … you wrote it in the first place that you went to. It was in a jug all these years … Ben found it:

> '*Each night before I go to sleep*
> *I hope that you my heart will keep*'

'Bullshit,' he says and snatches it and tears it up.

'It wasn't bullshit … it was before bad got into you…'

'I want to die.'

'You can't die until you die … no one can.'

'Would you help me if I asked?'

'You know I would … I love you no matter what. I'm your sister and nothing can change that.'

'Get me back out into the woods … I'll bother no one … I'll live on berries.'

'That's daft talk.'

'Who hunts there now?'

'I don't know … I've never been in them woods and I never intend to and don't think that I don't blame myself for that night in Granny's … you unwrapping and wrapping that gun … up in Mars you were and I did nothing.'

'She was dead then and so was the child …'

'You can't keep going over it.'

'Will you do it for me … ask the knackers?'

'Look … there isn't a hope in hell … there's gates, there's locks, there's a sentry tower, there's dogs, there's guards …'

'You want me locked up for life, you're one of them … you

gave evidence to the scumbags.'

'I only told them that you sometimes flipped … they had me plagued, coming to the house.'

It happened quicker than thought, the mug flying and the tea and the tea bag running down the white wall, a sugar bowl smashed and two nurses coming in quietly and cautiously so that they can see him—'Come on now, Michen … cool it … let's go for a walk' and each one takes an arm and she gets up to follow.

'Keep back now miss … keep a distance … this could be dangerous' and that was the loneliest moment of all, to see him gone into himself, dead to the world around him.

HEAVEN

They had put him down for the night. He had had his quota of pills, the blue, the yellow, the purple and the white. The nurse wished him sweet dreams.

It came down like hail and he sat up excited, thinking the gang had come to rescue him. He'd prayed to them and now at last they'd come. But it wasn't them. It was a big television, so big that it filled the cell. He sat up and the picture came on, first there was a snowstorm and then there was trees and low bushes. It was the school and the Eamonn fellow shovelling shit and the woman carrying a tray with the little loaves of bread on it. People came from behind the trees and the prefab houses, people that he knew and he wanted to shake hands with them but his fingers had turned to dough, his fingers were all glued together. Nobody recognised him.

Then the picture changed to heaven. It was heaven. He knew it was heaven because of gold walls and lamps. Jesus was there and his pet fox was there too. There were angels flying around with trays of biscuits and orange. There was music. It was play time in heaven and they were all there, the woman and the child and the priest and his mother. The child picked up a bucket and spade and began to play on a bit of sand by the edge of a lake. He wanted them to talk to him but they wouldn't. The priest was in shorts and he had a tan. His mother was on a deck chair knitting, keeping an eye on the child. He tried to break into the screen but it wasn't glass, it wouldn't break, it was gooey like putty. Then the woman came out of a doorway and looked straight ahead and then turned her back on him. Her hair was loose and it had grown, it was down to her ankles. There were animals and there were birds, thrushes and a load of blackbirds. His fox trotted across to where the child was playing and he called to it 'Ruben Ruben' and it spat at him.

When it got to be dusk in heaven, the sky became navy-blue, people started yawning and white garments floated out for his mother, the child and the woman, a pyjamas for the priest. Beds were wheeled in, wooden beds with acorns on the headboards.

The child got into a little bed and the woman leant over it and kissed it and then rubbed its tummy the way she used to down at home. He knew that she'd talk to him once his mother and the priest had gone down to sleep. He moved closer and closer so that she could hear.

'Will I go to heaven?' he asked. He asked three times. She turned and looked at him. He thought she was going to say something nice. Her eyes were a fruity green like the lights in a slot machine. She screamed suddenly and one eye slid back into her head and an angel that must have been a surgeon, squeezed the two lids together and began stitching them with fawn thread. Tears began to run down her face and then they were not tears, they were drops of blood and she wiped them with her hair. She got into bed next to the child and the music finished and there was nobody in the room, only him and he was wide awake now.

He began to bite bits of the mattress, tore minute strips and began to plait them together, his eye on the peephole, and he was happy because he was moving on, away from there.

The court was told of it first thing the following morning. Dr Macready stood before the judge and said he had unpleasant news to relate, the defendant had made a serious suicide attempt the night before, had tried to strangle himself with bed covering in the hospital after Eily Ryan had appeared to him crying. He said he had examined the neck and that the marks of the strangulation could be seen very clearly as they extended three quarters of the way round his neck and were blistering. He said it was why the defendant was not wearing a collar and tie as he usually did and was asking permission to have the defendant excused from the court because of finding the trial so stressful, hearing people talking about him, and about his mother and her attempted suicide. As he was saying all this O'Kane began to laugh and now he was in a full spate of laughter at the people looking at him, curious, appalled, while Dr Macready tried to point out that it was not laughing laughter, that it did not mean that the young man was feeling good, far from it, that instead of being repulsed by it, they should look on it as the laughter of the damned.

'He is not fit to plead, your honour,' he said and the judge deliberated and called for an adjournment to give him time to consider the matter.

Crossing the floor the judge stopped and said that he hoped in his heart that the case would not drag on as it had done, it had opened wounds that were too deep, too shocking, too hurtful, it had been a human haemorrhaging and the country was depleted from it.

He appeared in court one last time as his life sentence was read out but he sat, dead to it, dead to the woman in the jury who sobbed openly at the verdicts, dead to the mother who for fifty-two days had sat with the stillness of an archetype, in her brown clothes, her brown hair tied back in a bun, and who simply said to those comforting her, 'I can go home now and be alone.'

AILEEN

Sure it was a Thursday on account of my being late going to bed after the bingo night. Ben was playing with his Lego when the doorbell rings and Queenie the landlady called up, 'The guards are down here in the hall for you.' I knew she was raging at having the guards around again, thinking all that was over and done with and that we were nice respectable people now. I jump up and put a few clothes on and Ben follows me out onto the landing.

'Has that child toys to play with?' the guard calls out. He's sheepish looking, a new recruit.

'Of course he has toys to play with,' I say.

'You might want to give them to him,' he says and I take the hint and push Ben back into the bedroom and close the door.

He is wringing his hands to get it out—'I have bad news for you. We heard it over the nine o'clock news but we thought it was a hoax … they found your brother, dead, in the early hours of the morning … you have to come down to the sergeant.'

'Don't be raving … I saw him less than a week ago and he looked okay except that he had gone from a size sixteen to a size twenty-two …'

'It was a peaceful death.'

'Did he get his hand on tablets or did he cut his arms trying to get out a window?'

'He died in his sleep … they changed his medication and it seems he reacted to it … it was one chance in a million.'

'So he's out of their way now,' I said.

'It seems, it was a very rare phenomenon,' he droned on.

'They doped him up, that's what.'

'His heart stopped … Miss … they tried resuscitation.'

Crossing the green, the busybodies began peering out from between their curtains, the two terriers that spar all day were at it and the Minnie one on her new bicycle scooting up close to us so as to hear what he was saying. Him repeating the same rubbish about a peaceful death and the very rare phenomenon of my brother's heart.

When I got to the hospital they didn't want me to see him in the morgue. I insisted. A warder held my arm—'Let go of me … let go of me,' I said. My brother's hands and everything else was tucked in and all I could see was his bloated face. I leant in over him and talked to him. 'Have you legs, have you arms, did they dope you up?' The warder was right behind me in case I did anything extreme.

When I came out I told the doctor that my brother's last wishes was to be cremated. The doctor said cremation was okay by them. I waited and waited for the ashes and when they didn't come I rang up and was told that there was some confusion. I rang and I rang and eventually I was told that our father wanted the ashes. I shouted down the phone, I said, 'I'm the one that was close to him, him and his father were daggers drawn for years.' They said they'd have to think about it. In the end I had to go up there again to get them. They were in a little box. They'd halved them. That was my brother's lot, halved in life and halved in death.

GROTTO

The sun broke into the showers and lit them with a rainbowed radiance and the showers carried on, festive, larky, bluing the road and spattering watery diamonds on the plastic bags around the silage and on the top bars of iron gateways. The sky was pink and lilac and powder blue; stone walls and patchwork fields, then more ragged undulating country, hazels, poplars, forts of oak, hilly mounds. O'Kane country.

Dr Macready had been thinking of him since he came west a week before for a court hearing, O'Kane, the lost prodigal son that he believed he could have saved if he had been given time. He thought of him often, the ravelled mind that hopped around like it was on a hot spit, running from hate to love, to murder to repentance, fantasy and truth all one. Once, in a moment of searing clarity, asking for his brain to be taken out and washed and then buried thousands of feet in some bog where neither man nor machine could dislodge it.

'But you'd have nothing then,' he had said to him.

'I'd rather nothing … I want to be out of my skull … I want to be empty,' he had said and repeated during those endless hours when they tried to pick out the pieces of his life, the milestones large and small that culminated in the abyss. In less furious moments he would talk of the places with their funny little names and the piers where local people who didn't hate him but feared to let him indoors, would leave tea and bread for him. Dr Macready remembers him re-enacting walking backwards in his cell, remembering the winds he walked in, backwards, on account of their being so strong, so cutting. Now he was in that territory that he knew only from O'Kane's lips and reams of evidence.

It was Friday and he was heading home. He realised that he had taken a wrong turning but didn't bother to turn around, believing that eventually he would come onto the dual carriageway and the city.

Coming up to a crossroads, the name sprang out at him— Cloosh Wood. His absentmindedness had brought him there.

Parking the car by the entrance barrier, he felt not fear but a city man's confoundedness at the stoicism of those living and trothed to such a friendless place. The path was easy to follow, mementos all along the way like stations to a sepulchre. There were bits of mirror, ribbon, broken rosaries, sea shells all whispering their whisper—'This way, this way, ladies and gentlemen.'

When he got there he found to his surprise that he was not alone. A woman knelt in prayer, her body bent over, then at moments stooping to kiss the earth. He coughed so as not to frighten her and waved his hand in a reassuring gesture. It was obviously where the woman and child were slain, quite different to the rest of the forest and the sight of it moved him. A garden had been planted, rose bushes, dwarf trees, wild flowers and their little belongings—a gnome, a tortoiseshell comb, a vintage toy car and a nail brush with the likeness of a frog on its handle. Two tiny white crosses with their names painted on them seemed so child-like and belonged not to death but to moonlight and enchantment. On a lintel of stone a bog oak carving. Pine trees in a half circle, their branches soft and empathising in a semi sway. From one branch there hung a set of chimes.

Eventually the woman turned and looked in his direction and he whispered if by any chance she was a relative. She shook her head. She was wearing a head scarf which she had drawn over her face and a country coat, like a man's coat. Her eyes had that startled, highly strung look that he had often seen in patients.

'A sad place,' he said.

'The women of Ireland want his blood,' she said quite quickly and repeated it with such force, such emphasis that he thought, as she stood, that she was about to strike him.

'And what will they do with his blood ... baptise it ... bottle it ... sprinkle it ... put it in the tabernacle?' he asked over-calm.

'Who are you? Some do gooder?'

'No ... I treated O'Kane ... I was one of the doctors during his trial ... I was one of the few people at his funeral.'

'His death was too good for him ... he should have been hanged from these trees.'

'You will not believe me but I heard him once express great sorrow ... great guilt, over everything that happened here.'

'Sorrow!' she shrieks and she is above him now, her arms dangling, her blue piercing eyes, asking him to recall the woman's bruised limbs, her torn undergarments, her defilement before death, before meeting her God and a hundred yards away a priest, his head on a stone slab, a butcher's block.

'I do recall … but I want you to know that he did repent at that time … he had had no food or liquid for over twenty days … he was a changed man.'

'Tripe!' She shrieks it.

'Madam, is it not better that he showed repentance than that he never showed it at all? Better to atone for one minute than live in a vortex of despair?'

She turned away and muttered, her breath rapid and rasping. It was in that taut silence that a breeze started up and dislodged a piece of paper from the wedge of the joined crosses. It blew this way and that as if deciding where it might land. Eventually it fell close to him and he unfolded it and read it. Then he offered it to her to read but she refused. He read it aloud, he wanted her to hear it—'Darkness is drawn to light but light does not know it, light must absorb the darkness and therefore meet its own extinguishment.'

He looked to see if there was any softening in her features, in her stance, but there was none. The silence was killing. He could feel it magnifying and confirming itself in their separate beings, their irreconcilable natures. Suddenly she put her hand out and she was swaying and he thought that she was about to fall—'I picture her when I come up here as if she is still alive … as if she is within calling distance,' she says, her voice muted.

'I know … I do know that,' he said and reached to steady her but without touching, knowing that she was aching for some kind of consolation, like desert earth empty for rain. Then the chimes started up, brazen, arbitrary, their strikes hitting and grazing one another, sudden jubilance in that hallowed place.

He led the way down, splotches of light and shadow from a harvest moon that seemed to follow them. It would be winter soon, that ground far too soggy, the steep track sheer with ice and snows and no mourners would venture up there for months to come.

After that it would be spring.

SCALLYWAG

There was a boy and he was around four and he made a plan that he told no one, not even his friend Elmer. A big adventure. He was an only child and played by himself with sticks. He went that bit further from home each day and then one day he could only see just the slates and then the next day the copper beech tree brushing them and then he came on a fort and there were purple flowers nearly as tall as himself and he picked them and played wars with them, but they broke because they were not that strong.

The night he stole out there were thousands of stars and he crossed the fields and climbed over the town gate and walked and walked until he came to a big wood where there was all sorts of activity. It was buzzing. There was bats and game birds and badgers all doing the things they could do only at night; scaring each other and fighting and eating their suppers and rolling around in the leaves, basking and having fun. Hi Ho, Hi Ho, it's off to play we go.

When it was time to sleep he got into a big bed of pine needles and thought I'll be a potato, I'll be a spud and snooze down here. He slept a beautiful sleep and there was no telling how long he slept and it didn't matter.

Meanwhile there was major commotion at home, his mother, his father, the guards, the whole country out looking for him. They called in water divers because he loved going to the lake for picnics but he could only swim with arm bands. They were demented.

He came out of the wood, his clothes all crumpled and pine needles in his thick mop of brown hair. He could see the house with the roof gone, nettles and cows in the front garden grazing between the broken statues. Fawn cows and spotted cows. They just went on grazing, they didn't pay any attention to him. Sometimes cows look cross and have glum faces, but these didn't. He walked in and out between them. They were far taller than he was, their coats were silky and they had big soft pink diddies. It was amazing the amount of grass they could take in their mouths, but of course they spilt a lot of it. Their tongues were rubbery. A farmer came and said, 'Are you the boy that's missing?'

'I dunno.'

'Yes, you are, you scallywag.'

When his mother and father arrived with a guard and a man there was a big reunion, kissing and crying and his mother wrapping a tartan rug around him in case he caught cold. 'Where were you?' 'Brazil.' 'Weren't you afraid?' 'No.' 'Did you miss us?' 'No.' 'Just say you missed us a teeny little bit.' 'A teeny bit.'

They'd never know, they'd never get to the bottom of it and they shouldn't.

Magic follows only the few.

Author's Note

In April 1994, Imelda Riney, aged twenty-nine, and her son Liam, aged three, went missing from her isolated cottage in Co. Clare. Father Joe Walshe, a curate in Co. Galway, disappeared a few days later, and when their burnt-out cars were found, suspicion pointed to Brendan O'Donnell, a local youth, home from England, on remand from prison. O'Donnell was captured after six days, having abducted another young girl, Fiona Sampson. Later, the bodies of the three missing people were found in nearby Cregg Wood; all had been shot at close range. Brendan O'Donnell was charged with their murders and in 1996 tried in the Central Criminal Court in Dublin. He was jailed for life. In July 1997, he was found dead by nursing staff, in the Central Mental Hospital in Dublin.

Best
FRIENDS
Together

Rosie Rushton lives in Northampton. She took up writing because it gave her a wonderful excuse not to do the dusting and because the word processor was the only thing in the house that didn't answer back. Her three daughters managed to attain adulthood despite having the most embarrassing mother in Northamptonshire. She is passionately interested in family and relationship issues. In addition to writing teenage fiction and running workshops in schools around the country, Rosie writes a weekly column for her local paper, contributes to a variety of national and local radio stations and writes travel features for national magazines, a somewhat remarkable feat for one who gets lost in a multi-storey carpark. Her two greatest ambitions are to write children's drama for television and see her first adult novel published before she is too old to look good in the publicity photographs.

Other books by Rosie Rushton, published by Piccadilly Press:

Poppy

Olivia

Sophie

Melissa

Just Don't Make a Scene, Mum!

I Think I'll Just Curl Up and Die

How Could You Do This to Me, Mum?

Where Do We Go From Here?

Speak for Yourself

Staying Cool, Surviving School

You're My Best Friend, I Hate You

Best
FRIENDS
Together

ROSIE RUSHTON

Piccadilly Press • London

Text copyright © Rosie Rushton, 1998
Cover photographs © Ute Klaphake, 1998

Printed and bound by Creative Print and Design (Wales), Ebbw Vale for the publishers Piccadilly Press Ltd., 5 Castle Road, London NW1 8PR

A catalogue record for this book is available from the British Library

3 5 7 9 10 8 6 4 2

ISBN: 1 85340 459 4 (trade paperback)

Designed by Judith Robertson
Cover design by Mandy Sherliker

CHAPTER 1

An
UNEASY
Start

Nick Bowen pulled back the net curtain and stared out at the row of identically boring red-brick houses on Talbot Street. God, how he hated this place! His mum kept saying it was only temporary, somewhere to live while they sorted out the mess that their lives had become – but after just three weeks in his grandmother's house he felt as if he was suffocating. The place was so cramped after the spacious farmhouse in Tuscany, his grandmother so – grandmotherly. If she ruffled his hair just one more time, or told him to "let it all out", he thought he might explode.

"Nick! What's taking you so long? You don't want to be late on your first day!" his mother's voice called up the stairs.

"OK, OK, I'm coming." Nick turned away from the window, irritated by the false cheeriness in his mother's tone. She had been like that ever since they arrived here, telling him that they had to be brave, and that Dad would have wanted them to get on with their lives and make the best of things. Sometimes he thought she was actually excited by all the awful changes they were having to make.

Like this school business. She went on and on about how Lockbridge High was top of the league tables for comprehensives in Yorkshire; how good it would be for him to go to a mixed school and how he was sure to make heaps of new friends. But he didn't want new friends: he wanted his old ones. He wanted to be back at Benham Grange, his old public school, captaining the cross-country team, leading the early morning training across the fields, not stuck in some dire comprehensive in this dreary city where he didn't know a soul. But most of all, he wanted his dad.

"Nick!" The door flew open and his mother burst in. "Darling, have you got everything? Bag? Pens? I've done you a lunch box, it's in the kitchen, and . . ."

"Oh, Mum, stop fussing!" Nick didn't mean to sound off at her, but just thinking about the day ahead was making him feel about eight years old, with a churning stomach and sweaty palms. It wasn't just the thought of walking into a classroom full of strangers, it was the knowledge that, sooner or later, people would ask where he lived and what his parents did, and then he would either have to lie or tell them the whole, horrible truth.

"Sorry, love – it's just that I do so want this to work out for you." Jenny Bowen opened her arms to hug him, but he side-stepped and walked past her on to the landing. He couldn't let her see him cry and if she was nice to him, he just might.

"I know you miss your dad," she added softly, chewing her bottom lip. "I do too, you know."

6

"Do you?" Nick turned and stared at her. "Are you sure?"

"Of course I'm sure!" his mother gasped. "I can't get used to not having him around to . . ."

"What, to yell at? And nag?" Nick shouted. "You didn't exactly make life easy for him while he was alive, did you?"

"Nick! I . . ."

"Well, it's true – if you hadn't gone on and on at him about . . ."

"Enough, Nicholas!" His grandmother appeared, panting slightly, at the bend in the stairs. "I know you're hurting, love, but there's no need to take it out on your poor mother."

"It's OK, Mum." Jenny held up a hand. "You'd better get going, Nick – are you sure you don't want me to run you there in the car?"

"No, thanks." It wasn't that he relished the idea of the school bus, more that he couldn't face fifteen minutes more of his mother trying her hardest to be jolly. Or worse, run the risk of her launching into yet another account of how the mess they were in now was all down to his father's mismanagement of their affairs. Being alone would be preferable to that.

"See you later." He stomped down the stairs and through the front door, slamming it behind him. There was already an autumnal chill in the air, even though it was only the first week of September. Further down the street, small clusters of Lockbridge High kids chattered and laughed their way to the bus stop, jostling one another and kicking the odd drinks can into the gutter. At Benham Grange, Nick thought disdainfully, they would have been in detention for looking the way they looked, shirts hanging out, trainer laces flapping. Not that

Benham boys were allowed to wear trainers except for games. Benham was a decent school. Benham was where his father had been educated. Dad would have a fit if he knew what was going on.

Nick lashed out a foot and kicked the bottom of a lamppost. Across the road a couple of girls, arms linked, eyed him for a minute and then turned away, nudging one another and giggling behind their hands.

He was going to hate this school. He knew he was.

"Nick!" He turned to see his mother running down the road behind him, waving his lunch box. "You forgot this."

He snatched the plastic box and shoved it into his kit-bag. "Thanks," he muttered.

"You will be OK, won't you, darling?" his mum asked, brushing a strand of sandy-coloured hair from her face.

Nick looked at her. There were dark lines under her eyes and her forehead was wrinkled in concern. She seemed very small and very vulnerable. He suddenly remembered how his dad used to look over her shoulder and wink at him whenever Mum got into what he called one of her fusses.

"Just agree and keep her happy, old chap, that's what I do!"

It was as though his dad was standing beside him, whispering in his ear.

"I'll be fine, Mum," Nick said, trying to smile. "Just fine."

He only wished he could believe it.

CHAPTER 2

DASHED
hopes

Chloë Sanderson leaned out of her bedroom window and gazed hopefully up and down the busy waterfront below. Where was he? He should have been here ages ago. If he didn't hurry, she would have to leave for school and she simply couldn't face another day of not knowing.

"Chloë! Nearly ready?" Her father stuck his head round the bedroom door. "It's almost eight o'clock."

"I'm just waiting . . ." She hesitated, fiddling with a long strand of crinkly auburn hair. If she told her father the truth, she would get the whole spiel about this being the start of her GCSE year and not the time to be filling her head with a load of romantic nonsense.

". . . for Mum," she finished lamely. In a way, it was true. She knew Mum was into another one of her early-morning jogging phases, but whenever Chloë woke up to find her gone, her mind went back to that awful time when she . . . But that was over. In the past. Forgotten. That would never happen again.

"Oh, she could be pounding the pavements for ages," her dad replied with a wry grin. "If you want a lift, you'll have to come now – I've got this production presentation at nine."

He tapped his foot impatiently. Chloë knew that today meant a lot to her father; his last series for Channel Four had flopped and a great deal was riding on this new idea. For days now he had been morose and silent, hunched over his desk in his study or spending hours on the telephone.

She flicked her hair over her shoulder and chewed her lip. A lift would save the hassle of the school bus. But then, what if he came and she missed him? She couldn't risk it. "No, it's OK, Dad, you go," she said. "I'll get the bus – catch up with my friends."

Such as they are, she thought, as her father gave a quick wave and clattered down the spiral staircase that separated the two bedrooms from the rest of their spacious duplex apartment. Now that Emma had gone, school was going to be dire.

"Oh, darling, that's a bit dramatic!" Chloë's mum had protested the evening before, when Chloë confessed that she was dreading school without her best mate. "I know you'll miss Emma dreadfully, but you've plenty of other friends. What about Natalie and Becky?"

But Mum didn't understand. Natalie and Becky were good fun and fine to hang out with, but Emma had been her soul mate. They had been joined at the hip ever since Chloë had started at Lockbridge High School, halfway through Year Eight. In those early days in Leeds, before she had learned to disguise her plummy Home Counties accent, she had been teased, not just for the way she spoke, but because she lived at The Wharfside, which was the city's most up-market address, and got dropped off at school in her father's blue BMW coupé. Emma had been the first person to talk to her without taking the mickey, and they hadn't stopped talking since. For three years, they had done homework together, shopped together, consoled one another over broken romances and stood up for one another when parents flew into unreasonable outbursts over dyed hair or broken curfews. They had shared clothes, CDs and all their innermost secrets. Well, maybe not all. There were some things which Chloë had known from an early age she must never share with anyone.

Her thoughts were interrupted by a clattering at the front door. He was here! Suddenly her mouth went dry and her heart began racing in her chest. It would be today, wouldn't it? It had to be.

She rammed a barrette through her hair, flew across the landing and sped down the stairs.

"Darling! All ready for school! Brilliant!" The front door burst open to reveal Chloë's mother, dressed in jogging pants and a bright pink T-shirt, and gasping for breath.

Chloë's heart sank. She looked over her mother's shoulder but there was no one else there. He hadn't come.

"Oh, it's you," Chloë mumbled.

"Of course it's me, darling – who else were you expecting?" she grinned broadly. "Lovely morning, you really should come running with me. Wonderful way to start the day! Makes one feel good to be alive!"

As Pennine TV's most successful presenter, Suzy Sanderson was prone to talking at high speed, peppering her conversation with exclamations and sounding enthusiastic about everything from the state of world politics to the price of tinned tuna at Sainsbury's.

"Have you eaten? No? Oh, Chloë, I keep telling you that breakfast is the most important meal of the day."

How can I think about food when my heart is breaking? thought Chloë, but knew there was no point in saying anything.

"Are you OK, Mum?" Despite her preoccupation, Chloë was relieved to see that her mother appeared to be in high spirits. But it was always worth checking.

"Fine, darling, never better," said Suzy brightly, pulling on a sweatshirt and crossing through to the kitchen. "And we've got such a fun programme this afternoon."

I'll probably never have fun ever again, thought Chloë.

". . . and then I'm interviewing Marika Fennimore, such a lovely lady. Should I wear my pink suit, do you think? Or the green? Now, darling, you must eat. What about some toast?"

Her outburst of verbal diarrhoea was interrupted by the unmistakeable clanking of the letterbox.

"I'll get it!" Chloë called, dashing to the front door. At last! He'd come! Please, God, let it be there. If you let it be there, I will never ask you for anything else ever again.

She grabbed the pile of post almost before it hit the ground and flicked through the envelopes.

Bill. Bill. Fashion catalogue addressed to her mother.

And that was it.

Nothing for her.

Nothing.

No letter from Jack. Well, thank you, God.

She flounced back into the kitchen and flung the mail on the table, biting her lip in a desperate attempt not to cry.

"Darling, it was just a holiday romance," said her mother, guessing the situation and giving her a quick hug. "You mustn't read too much into it."

She dumped a yoghurt and a banana in front of Chloë and gestured to her to eat.

"You don't understand!" It never ceased to amaze Chloë that a woman who had won a BAFTA award for Television Presenter of the Year and who was known for her incisive and perceptive interviewing style, could be so stupid when it came to anything relating to her own daughter. Although, thought Chloë, ripping the top off her yoghurt pot, it was probably just as well that her mum didn't know the full story – about the secret meetings late at night, the long, lingering kisses, the sudden, exciting realisation that she was feeling things she had never felt before – the sort of things Natalie bragged about but Chloë had never imagined would happen to her.

He had said he loved her. He had said that the rest of the summer would be hollow and meaningless without her. So why hadn't he written? Perhaps he was ill. Maybe there had been a yachting accident. Maybe he was lying on a bed of pain, weakly calling her name.

"Darling, there'll be others," said her mother soothingly, plugging in the new cappuccino machine and slumping down into one of the Shaker style kitchen chairs. "You're still very young."

"I'm practically sixteen!" retorted Chloë. "I'm not a kid any more – I'm a woman!"

A stunning, sensual woman. That's what Jack had called her. She couldn't live without him. What was she going to do?

Her mother chewed her lip. "Darling, you and this Jack – I mean, well . . ."

"What?"

"You didn't . . ."

"Mum! That is such an intrusive thing to ask!" Chloë hurled her empty yoghurt pot into the bin and stood up. "As it happens, no."

Actually, she didn't like to admit it even to herself, but a small part of her had been quite relieved when the holiday was over, because Jack was getting more demanding and Chloë was finding it harder and harder to stick at the hand holding, lip brushing, hair caressing stage of things. Of course, Jack was nineteen and an instructor at the Skiathos Sailing Club, and knew about such things – but Chloë hadn't been at all sure that she wanted to know much more just yet. But now she was home, she realised that she was hopelessly, passionately, irrevocably in love with Jack. She had written to tell him so. She had said that she wanted to spend the rest of her life with him. That was two whole weeks ago. So why hadn't he written back? Maybe there was a postal strike in Skiathos.

"Well, I've got a piece of news that will cheer you up," said her mother, kicking off her trainers and wriggling her toes in relief. "There I was, leaping up the stairs two at a time, all red in the face and breathless, when what do you think happened?"

"I can't imagine," commented Chloë dryly.

"This rather large woman burst out of the door of number four – you know, the apartment at the back that's been empty for ages – and crashed straight into me!"

"Mum, is there a point to this story?" sighed Chloë. "Only I do have a bus to catch, you know."

"I'm coming to that, darling," her mother gabbled, leaping up and switching off the coffee machine. "Well, of course, I said I was sorry and she said so was she, but she was dashing to the phone box – their phone hasn't been connected yet . . ."

Phone. I could phone him. How much does a call to Greece cost?

". . . and then she looked up and saw who I was."

Here we go, thought Chloë with a sigh. Here comes the "I do so hate being recognised" bit.

"Well, you know how I hate being recognised," her mother went on, "but, bless her, she did seem thrilled. She came over all flustered and said how she loved the programme and how they had just moved in and was it really me?"

"And you said that you did hope so because if it wasn't, some stranger had just learned this afternoon's script," chanted Chloë, who knew her mother's repertoire of witty ripostes off by heart.

"What has all this got to do with me?"

"Well, when she backed away into their flat, I couldn't resist a peek over her shoulder – darling, they have the most extraordinary taste in curtains – and there, standing in the hall, was this girl."

"Oh, shock horror!" teased Chloë. "*Girl seen in flat number four. Police alerted.* Mum, what are you on about?"

Her mother tilted her chin and inclined her head in the manner she adopted when about to make a pertinent point to the viewers of her 'Penny Wise' programme. "She was wearing Lockbridge High uniform."

Chloë's eyes widened. "Really? Who was it?"

"Well, I don't know, do I?" her mother reasoned. "Certainly not anyone you've ever brought home here, that's for sure – not that you bring your friends round often enough, which is a pity because . . ."

"OK, OK!" Chloë was not about to get into that discussion again. "What was she like?"

Her mother shrugged. "About your age, pretty, dark blonde shoulder-length hair, tacky sort of hairband thing, chubby legs, skirt far too short . . . I didn't really get time to see much. One can't very well stare, can one?"

Chloë raised her eyes heavenwards. "You don't seem to have done too badly," she said dryly.

Suzy laughed, ripping open an envelope. "Well, I was fascinated by them. To be honest, they didn't seem quite the type one would expect to find living here. The hall table was definitely self-assembly flat pack, and that woman was wearing furry slippers."

"Mum! You are such a snob!" protested Chloë. "Well, it can't be anyone I know or they'd have said they were moving here. Must be a new kid."

"So why don't you pop downstairs and suggest you both go to school together? That way, you'd get a new friend."

"Oh Mum, please!" Chloë jumped up, grabbed her jacket and headed for the door. "I'm not some dippy toddler trotting off to playgroup."

"Sorry!" Her mum held up a conciliatory hand. "I just thought . . ."

"You thought that I'd find out all the gossip about them and save you the trouble," finished Chloë.

Abruptly she fixed a sweet smile on her face, moved back and kissed the top of her mother's head for good measure. "Mum," she said pleadingly, "can you lend me some money?"

Her mother frowned. "How much? What for? What did you do with last month's allowance?"

"Oh sorr-eee!" snapped Chloë, all hopes of an international phone call disappearing with her mother's words. "I didn't realise I had to present a set of accounts."

"Hang on, hang on!" said her mother, taking her purse from the counter top. "Five pounds – sorry it's coins, I haven't got any notes left."

Better and better, thought Chloë.

"And I want it back when you get your next allowance. It's high time you learned a bit of money sense before . . ."

"OK, OK. Is five pounds enough for . . . ?"

"For what?"

"It's fine," said Chloë hastily. "Thanks, Mum. Must dash or I won't have time to . . ."

"To what?"

"Oh – check out the new girl."

Her mother beamed. "Great idea, darling," she said. "You have a nice chat."

"Oh, I will," said Chloë. And it won't be with her. Whoever she may be.

CHAPTER 3

A
DIFFERENCE
of opinion

"**M**um! If you say 'Oh, fancy that' once more, I shall go mad!" Sinead Flaherty hurled her cereal bowl into the sink and then remembered with relief that they had just bought a swish new dishwasher.

"But I mean to say, Suzy Sanderson!" sighed her mother, buttering a slice of toast. "Living in the same block as us! Isn't that wonderful?"

"Considering that it means her daughter also lives here, no it's not!" retorted Sinead, hooking a strand of dark blonde hair behind her ear. "Of all the places in Leeds we could have moved to, you have to go and choose the very same apartment block as Chloë Sanderson!"

"Oh, come along now, Sinead love," protested her father, glancing up from his perusal of *Which Car?*. "You should be chuffed. It's a wonderful opportunity for you to get in with them."

"What makes you think I want to get in with her?" retorted

Sinead. "After what she did to me . . ."

She stopped. Perhaps the events of the previous term were best not mentioned to her parents. What they didn't know couldn't hurt them.

"Well, I think it would do you a lot of good to make some new friends," declared her mother, biting into her toast. "You know, a nicer type of girl . . ."

"I've got perfectly nice old friends, thank you!" retorted Sinead, shrugging her arms into her new Kookai jacket. "Although, thanks to you, we now live miles away from any of them!"

"Hardly miles," replied her mother mildly. "Only the other side of town."

"Anyway, Mum says some of your friends are a really bad influence," intoned Erin, who was twelve and had recently decided to become a missionary. "She says . . ."

"Oh shut up, you sanctimonious little prig!" retorted Sinead, who knew only too well what her mother thought of her mates.

"Sinead! Don't speak to your sister like that!" Her mother glared at her across the table.

"Oh, that's right, take her side!" Sinead headed for the kitchen door. "I'm going."

"I'm not ready!" protested Erin, scowling at her sister.

"So?"

"Mum said you had to walk to the bus with me."

"*Mum said you had to walk to the bus with me,*" mimicked Sinead. "Honestly, you're so wet we could wash windows with you."

"Now, now," said their father placatingly, pouring himself a second cup of tea. "Just stop it, you two. Look, Sinead love, you can ask your friends over whenever you like. I guess they'll be gobsmacked when they see all this." He gestured through the open kitchen door to the wide expanse of sitting-room and the canopied balcony beyond.

That, thought Sinead, heading into the hallway and grabbing her schoolbag, is precisely what is worrying me. It had been OK at first. When she had told Abby and Bianca and the others that her mum's ancient third cousin in America had died and left her some money, they had joked about how Sinead could take her new-found wealth and get herself kitted out at Apparition, the newest up-market clothes shop in Leeds, and go somewhere exotic on holiday and fall passionately in love with a man on a yacht. Sinead had imagined it would be a few thousand pounds at the very most. It had all been a big laugh.

But then Mum had found out just how much she had inherited. Like zillions. Well, not zillions exactly, but hundreds of thousands, the sort of figure that makes you get all muddled over how many noughts there should be.

"Holy Mary Mother of God!" her father had said when Mum had read out the solicitor's letter, the paper shaking in her stubby fingers.

"Shaun!" her mother had admonished him. "Will you mind your language in front of the children?"

Becoming rich overnight was no excuse, in Kathleen Flaherty's opinion, for taking the Good Lord's name in vain.

"Oh, I'm sorry, love, but, well – it fair takes your breath away!"

Kathleen had shaken her head. "I just can't believe it," she had gasped. "It's all too much!"

"We'll move!" her father had shouted, throwing his arms round Kathleen. "Get off this council estate, go somewhere really smart!"

Sinead had assumed that they would buy one of the cool new executive homes round in Cooper's Lane where some of her mates lived. But they hadn't. For reasons best known to themselves, her parents had chosen this apartment in Lockbridge, on the other side of the city, down by the canal. Her father remembered the building when it had been a corn mill and he had gone all sentimental and soppy because his grandfather had once worked there. At first, Sinead had thought it would be quite cool; there were loads of new clubs opening up nearby and some neat shops under the railway arches. But she had reckoned without her mates' reaction.

"The Wharfside?" Abby had gasped when Sinead told her. "It costs a bomb to live over there!"

"Well, get you!" Bianca had jibed, tossing her head and linking arms with Abby. "Swank city or what?"

"It won't make any difference to us," Sinead had assured them hastily. "I mean, we'll still hang out together and everything."

"Oh yeah?" Bianca hadn't sounded convinced.

"I guess we won't be good enough for you, mixing with the smart set," Abby concluded. "You'll have better things to do, now you're rich."

Sinead noticed the longing and the envy in her voice.

Admittedly, she thought, tapping her foot impatiently while her sister dithered over packing her schoolbag, she hadn't seen much of her friends during the holidays, what with the family going to Majorca for a holiday and moving into the new flat. But it would be all right, Sinead told herself now; she'd bought them loads of presents, and as soon as her mates saw that she hadn't changed, that she was still the same Sinead who thought up all their scams and was good for a laugh, they'd stop noticing where she lived. She just had to prove that she was still one of them.

"Come on if you're coming," urged Sinead, nudging her sister. "We'll miss the bus."

"Hang on," said her father, grabbing his jacket from the coat peg. "I'll give you a lift. I've got to visit a site over that side of town."

"You mean the car is actually mobile?" Sinead asked. Her father's ancient Cavalier spent more time at the repair shop than on the road.

"For once," grinned her dad. "But you wait till next week when I get the new one – then you can arrive at school in real style."

"Now don't you go getting anything flashy," Sinead's mother interjected sternly. "Just a nice reliable little runabout, that's all we need!"

"Runabout? No way, sweetheart!" cried Sinead's father, wrapping his arms round Kathleen's waist. "We're going to have something that makes a statement. I'm thinking about a Mercedes . . ."

"Mercedes? Us? Oh, get away with you!" cried Kathleen, pushing Shaun through the front door and stuffing a lunch box into

Erin's schoolbag. "Now I was thinking, Sinead – since this Zoë . . ."

"Chloë," corrected Sinead.

"Whoever," said her mother. "Since she's in your class . . ."

"My *year*, not my class," sighed Sinead, blotting her lips on a tissue and picking up her schoolbag.

"Oh, stop splitting hairs!" retorted her mother. "I just thought you might like to invite her back for tea, and then . . ."

"Mum! Get real! Tea? Here? With her?"

"What's wrong with that?"

Sinead raised her eyes heavenwards and opened the front door. "You want a list? Because she's the pits; because tea parties are for kids; because . . ."

"OK, OK!" Her mother held up her hands.

And because, thought Sinead, shoving her sister through the door and waving a brief goodbye to her mother, my main aim is to keep in with Abby and Bianca. And getting all matey with Chloë Sanderson is the fastest way to ensure that never happens.

CHAPTER 4

WISHFUL
thinking

Sanjay Fraser rested his elbows on the parapet of the footbridge and gazed down at the murky waters below. A solitary swan glided downstream, her unseen paddling disturbing the sweet wrappers and empty drinks bottles floating on the surface. The much-hyped regeneration of the waterside had not quite reached Cutler's Cutting; derelict warehouses still stood, weeds growing out of long disused windows, waiting for the developers to transform them into up-market apartments that bore little, if any, resemblance to their humble origins. Further up the canal, he knew, this transformation had already taken place; apartment blocks with names like Quay Court and The Wharfside boasted wrought-iron balconies crowded with terracotta pots filled with flowers, and in what had once been unloading bays for barges expensive cars with personalised number plates waited for their affluent owners. By comparison, Cutler's Cutting was dreary and deserted, which was why Sanjay chose to cycle to school that way from Avenue Mansions, the far less elegant block of flats on the far side of the canal where he lived with his parents and twelve-year-old sister Rani. This way took a lot longer than the clearly marked City Cycle Path, and he hardly ever saw anyone he knew. And both those factors suited him just fine.

Sometimes Sanjay would daydream that he was like the other guys in his year. He'd imagine what it would be like to be tall and broad-shouldered, instead of the smallest guy in the year who looked about thirteen. He'd picture himself with a bunch of mates, hanging out under the railway arches or chatting up girls down at Ritzy's. As if! He had all the right words in his head, but the moment he opened his mouth he got tongue-tied and flustered and ended up sounding a right idiot. It was best not to start in the first place.

He picked up his bike and wandered to the end of the footbridge and down on to the towpath. Two ancient narrowboats, their paint faded and peeling, knocked rhythmically against the stone quay. On the roof of one a ginger cat mewed pitifully, pacing to the edge and crouching as if to risk a leap on to dry land, and then, at the last minute, losing its nerve.

"Hey, cat, it's OK – jump!" Sanjay stoppped walking and held out his hand. The cat eyed him with disdain and resumed its pacing.

He's like me, thought Sanjay suddenly; trapped in a world where he doesn't belong and yet too scared to do anything about it.

"Come on, you can do it!" he called encouragingly to the cat. "It's not far."

The cat was not convinced.

"Oh, all right," said Sanjay, "I'll come and get you." He dumped his bike on the ground and made to step on to the boat.

"That's private property!"

Sanjay turned to see a large woman in a voluminous, tent-like garment the colour of candyfloss glowering down at him.

"I was just – the cat – mewing – thought I could . . ."

Sanjay cursed himself. Why did he always sound such a dolt whenever he was faced with a stranger?

"Oh, that's Delilah!" exclaimed the woman, waving a beringed hand in the air. "She loves the boat."

No she doesn't, thought Sanjay, she hates it. Any idiot can see that. She wants to be free to wander about, catch mice and do cat-like things in the long grass.

"OK, then," he muttered, picked up his bike and cycled furiously down the towpath. Why he felt angry, he didn't really know; after all, it was no skin off his nose if the cat stayed there all day. Except that he knew what it was like to have everyone making assumptions about you; to have your life stretching ahead of you, every year mapped out to someone else's plan and to know that you couldn't do a single thing about it.

Stop it, you idiot, he told himself firmly, swinging the bike off the quayside and into Churchgate Hill. It was a cat, for heaven's sake, it's no big deal. But even as he tried to dismiss the animal from his mind, the pictures began swimming before his eyes. And not just pictures, but words too. The cat in his head began chatting to him. And, as he pedalled with increasing effort up the steep hill, he found himself talking back to it.

All of which was just further proof of what he knew already.

There was something seriously wrong with him. What other fifteen-year-old guy held lengthy conversations with imaginary animals but couldn't manage a single sparkling sentence with human beings? Who else found pretending a whole heap easier than living in reality? It wasn't even as if his life was that bad, not by some people's standards. He had a comfortable, if somewhat cluttered home, parents who thought he was the bee's knees and a sister he adored. Not, of course, that he admitted to anyone that he loved her so much; he might be stupid, but he wasn't that dumb. At Lockbridge High, doting on your kid sister was considered seriously uncool. But then, when it came to cool, Sanjay knew he was a total non-starter. He was like that stupid cat – a coward, a wimp and a misfit.

Sometimes, he mused, joining the cycle path for the last kilometre to the school gates, he felt as if he didn't know who he was. It wasn't that his dad was a white Canadian and his mum was a high-caste Hindu from Bombay. It was that the Sanjay Fraser that everyone – parents, teachers and classmates – thought they knew bore very little resemblance to the Sanjay who lived inside his head.

"Sanjay's just like me," his father would declaim to his university friends. "Destined for the academic life."

"Like me, Sanjay is happiest with his head in a book," his mother would declare when being interviewed by enthusiastic journalists following the publication of yet another of her books on Indian social history.

"Sanjay is a hardworking, self-disciplined boy who sets himself high standards and consistently achieves them," the headmaster had intoned in his last school report. But it was all untrue. Sure, he got good grades, but only because he spent all his energy on work because that way he didn't have so much time to acknowledge that he was peculiar.

"Sanjay Fraser? He's a boff and an anorak."

"Sanjay? Weird or what?"

That was what his schoolmates said behind his back. But they never bothered to drop their voices. And he always pretended not to hear.

He wished people were like computers. He wished you could design a programme to make them react to you just the way you wanted. With computers you were safe; what you put in was what you got out. It was all so logical. But people weren't logical. No matter how hard you tried to supply them with the right information, they only heard what they wanted to hear, only saw what they chose to see. He'd got used to the fact that his mates were all like that. What he was beginning to realise with increasing irritation was that his parents were just the same.

He was nearly there. Far too early, as usual, but then it had been one of those mornings when he had simply had to get out of the flat. His father had launched into one of his question-and-answer sessions on the latest political furore to hit the newspapers and when Sanjay said he wasn't interested, he began his usual lecture about needing to keep his finger on the pulse of world affairs if he was going to make it to Cambridge. No one ever thought to ask Sanjay whether he was remotely interested in going to some swanky university. They just assumed they knew.

If only Rani had been clever, maybe they could have pinned all their hopes on her. But for Rani even everyday tasks were a challenge; Sanjay was the only one who would fulfil his parents' dreams. And he knew he mustn't let them down.

He swung his bicycle through the school gates and jumped off. Now he was here, he didn't know what to do. The first day of term was always the worst; people all around going on about where they had been and what they had done and who they had done it with. Any other day he could lock up his bike and head straight for the computer room until registration, but until he had been given his new Year Eleven password the computers were out of bounds. There wasn't even any homework he could pretend to be checking. He just hoped that everyone would leave him alone.

He guessed they would.

They usually did.

It was only the Sanjay inside his head who had proper friends.

CHAPTER 5

Chance
ENCOUNTER

THE CANAL CAFÉ

The Eatery with Attitude!

OPEN NOW

Early-bird Breakfast,
Shoppers' Brunch, Laptop Lunches,
and Saliva Stirring Suppers!

THERE'S NOWHERE ELSE IN LEEDS LIKE US!
A Family-run Restorant with Meal Appeal!

"Dad!" Jasmin Johnson paused in mid-dash out of the café door and eyed the new poster critically. "There's something wrong here."

"There's a whole heap of things wrong here," muttered her mother who was wiping tables with all the enthusiasm of a condemned woman cleaning up the patch round the electric chair. "What did you have in mind – the stuck-up neighbours, the lack of customers, my twelve hour working day . . . ?"

"This poster," interrupted Jasmin, jerking her head towards the luminous pink sign propped up in the café window. "Dad's spelt restaurant wrong."

"Wrongly," corrected her mother, who was very hot on adverbs. "Let's see."

She straightened, peered at the lettering and ran a weary hand through her coarse black hair. "Harr-eeee!" The resonant tones which had made Josephine Johnson one of the Brixton Gospel Choir's most powerful soloists reverberated through the empty café.

"I'm coming, I'm coming!" Jasmin's father, a stockily built black man with charcoal-grey curly hair and huge liquid-brown eyes bustled through from the rear kitchen.

"What's up?" he asked, turning his head to face his wife. As he did so, Jasmin averted her eyes. Eighteen months on from that terrible day, she still hadn't got used to the livid scars that made a trellis across the left side of her father's face, puckering the skin into a little knot at the corner of his mouth. She hadn't told anyone how it made her feel – you couldn't admit that the sight of your own dad made you want to cry.

32

"You've spelt restaurant incorrectly," said Josephine. "It won't give a very good impression of the food if you can't even take care over the poster."

Jasmin noticed her dad's shoulders droop and glared at her mother.

"Silly of me," he said. "Still, it's easily corrected – it's only temporary, till we get a proper sign done."

"Temporary or not, it's got to be right," insisted his wife. "I can't be expected to do everything round here."

Harry sighed. "OK, OK, I'll see to it later."

"Why not do it now? We're not exactly inundated with customers, are we?"

She gestured round the café in exasperation. "Early-bird breakfasts, indeed! I said it wouldn't work," she muttered. "This isn't Brixton, you know. I bet the posh lot round here eat their muesli in their designer kitchens. Why I have to get up at six in the morning just to hang around an empty café and . . ."

"Mum!" Jasmin hissed a warning at her mother.

"It's early days, love." Harry Johnson touched his wife's shoulder.

"I know, I know," Josephine said with a tired smile. "I'm sorry – it's just . . ."

"What, love?"

"Nothing. Just me being silly. I'll be fine once we get the vacancy filled." She gestured to the window where another notice announced that The Canal Café required an Assistant Manager to start immediately.

"I put an ad in the local paper," Harry affirmed. "We're bound to get replies soon."

"And I'll help when I get back," added Jasmin, scooping her ebony hair into a scrunchie. "Must dash or I'll miss the bus."

"Well, at least Jassy seems happy," she heard her father say, as she pulled the door closed. "Settled in really well, hasn't she?"

Oh right, thought Jasmin, hitching her schoolbag on to her bony shoulder and breaking into a run along Millers Lane. Believe that, and you'll believe anything. Not that she could tell her parents what it was really like for her; her dad had had enough aggro to last him a lifetime and her mum – well, to be truthful, she didn't know her mum any more. She had changed since the attack, happy one moment and grumpy the next, backing her dad's new venture one day and moaning on about the boredom of her life the next. But then, she thought, swerving to avoid an old lady walking an even more elderly spaniel, everything had changed. And all because of a couple of thugs who'd had too much to drink.

She threw an anxious glance to left and right, the way she always did when the memory of that awful day flooded back into her mind. Don't be daft, she admonished herself, trying to ignore the stitch in her side. Nothing's going to happen to you. It's eight o'clock in the morning and broad daylight, not a dark February afternoon in a London sidestreet. If only he hadn't come to fetch her.

She swung round the corner into Sparrow Street and slackened her pace to a brisk walk. She felt better now. There were more people in this street, which led up from the waterside to the town centre, and besides it was only another couple of hundred metres to the bus stop. Even from this distance she could make out the patches of maroon and grey which signified huddles of Lockbridge High students gathering outside the newsagent. She glanced back down the street. No sign of the bus yet. She slowed to an amble. If she timed it right, she could reach the stop at the same moment as the bus pulled up. That way, she wouldn't have to stand around feeling a right idiot while everyone treated her as if she was invisible.

She sighed, pausing by a bank of telephone kiosks and trying to look as if she was about to make a call. It hadn't always been like this; back in London she'd had a whole bunch of friends and she'd felt as if she really belonged. But then at her old school at least half the pupils had been black; at Lockbridge High she was the only Afro-Caribbean in her class and one of only three in the entire year.

Don't kid yourself, she thought. You know perfectly well it's got nothing to do with being black. When she had started at the school the previous term, most people had been really friendly. Faith and Shelley still tried to be; three times during the holidays they had phoned to ask her out for the evening, and each time she had said yes, only to back out at the last moment. Was it surprising that they were beginning to lose interest? Who in their right mind wanted a total wimp for a mate?

If only she could go back to being like she used to be. She never used to be such a drip. Not until . . .

"Hateful thing! Stupid, wretched – oh sugar!"

Jasmin's bout of self-analysis was rudely and somewhat

surprisingly interrupted by the door of the nearest kiosk pushing open and a cascade of coins falling at her feet.

"What's the point of having public telephones if they don't . . . oh gosh, sorry!"

"It's OK," said Jasmin, squatting down and scooping up the money. "There – I think that's the lot."

She looked up as a faint smile of recognition crossed the other girl's face. "Oh hi, Jasmin, I didn't realise it was you!" Chloë Sanderson tipped the money into her purse and stuffed it into her jacket pocket.

"Is something wrong?" Jasmin didn't really know Chloë all that well; Faith and Shelley reckoned that rich white kids like her were best avoided, and besides, all last term Chloë had hung out with Emma, Natalie and Becky, who were all as super confident as she seemed to be. In fact, Jasmin had never seen Chloë look anything but cool and laid-back. Until now.

"No, not really. Well, yes, sort of." She sighed and ran her hand through her hair. "It's just that I need to . . . oh, here comes the bus."

Jasmin fully expected Chloë to go off and sit with one of her mates but instead she clomped down to the first spare pair of seats and gestured to Jasmin to sit beside her.

"You might know what to do," she said, pulling her bus pass from her jacket pocket.

"About what?"

"Phoning abroad," said Chloë. "I mean, you must phone Trinidad or Jamaica, or wherever it is your relatives all live."

Jasmin burst out laughing. "London, actually," she grinned as the bus lurched round a sharp bend. "And a whole clutch of uncles and cousins up here, over in Chapeltown."

"Oh gosh, sorry!" Chloë clamped a hand to her mouth. "That must have sounded awful – I didn't mean it like that, I just thought . . ."

Jasmin shook her head. "It's OK. So what's the problem? Phoning abroad is no different from phoning round the corner. You just do it."

"Not if all the public phones in Leeds are either broken or refusing to take your money, you don't," sighed Chloë. "It is so annoying."

"Why can't you phone from home?" asked Jasmin with a frown. "It's cheaper and much less hassle."

"Not when you've got neurotic parents, it isn't!" retorted Chloë, as the bus pulled up at the next stop. "Honestly, whoever thought of itemised phone bills had an exceedingly sick mind. My dad would go ape if he found out that I was even thinking of calling . . . oh hi, Nat – had a good holiday?"

Chloë turned as a plump girl with ash-blonde hair and big blue eyes circled with black eyeliner pushed past and gave her a friendly punch.

"Ace!" said Natalie. "You wait till I tell you what happened in Ibiza. You'll just die!" She pushed on down the aisle.

"Hang on!" Chloë jumped up and pushed past Jasmin. "So your mum let you go? How did you manage that? Did Sam . . . ?"

Her voice faded and was swallowed up in the general chatter from the busload of kids.

Jasmin turned and stared out of the window. She felt somehow cheated that Chloë had dashed off and abandoned her, which was silly really because it wasn't as if they were mates or anything. She didn't seem stuck-up, whatever Faith might think. Still, she was hardly the sort of girl who would want Jasmin for a friend. She obviously had her life well and truly sussed.

Except for that phone call business. Jasmin guessed it must involve a guy; most things that parents disapproved of did. But it was surprising that Chloë was letting it get to her like that. It was hardly a problem; there had to be plenty of phone boxes that did work, or she could always . . .

That was it! A grin spread over Jasmin's face as the bus gathered speed on the bypass. There was a perfectly simple answer to Chloë Sanderson's problem. And Jasmin held the key to it.

CHAPTER 6

NEW BOY
on the block

Nick stared out of the window at the hordes of kids piling off the three school buses and heading for the school entrance. He felt such an idiot standing there in the entrance hall, waiting for his new year tutor to come and fetch him. The whole place felt so alien after the four hundred-year-old Great House of Benham Grange, with its sweeping gravel drive and acres of rolling playing-fields. Lockbridge High was hideous, a green and grey monstrosity built in the mid-Sixties with an apparent total disregard for aesthetics. He hated it already.

Crowds of students were jostling past, some arm-in-arm, others having mock punch-ups, all of them knowing exactly where they were going and who everyone was. A few of them glanced at him, and turned away the moment they made eye contact. The rest pushed past as though he was invisible.

The noise was unbelievable. It would never have been allowed at Benham Grange. But then, at Benham, new pupils were welcomed in the head's study and given coffee and biscuits. Benham would never leave you standing on your own like a total nerd.

Why didn't someone come? That secretary woman had buzzed through ages ago and assured him that Mrs Braithwaite was coming.

"Just wait over there, dear, and she'll be along with your minder," she had cooed.

"Minder?" Nick had been puzzled.

"Oh, everyone new gets someone in their class to show them the ropes for the first few days," the secretary had said, grinning broadly as if the idea had been her very own. "You know, a friend to make you feel at home."

That, thought Nick now, is all I need. Day after day being shadowed by one of those awful, eager types who never stopped talking and kept bombarding you with questions about your personal life. Well, they would be out of luck, after what had happened to him in the last three months, he wasn't going to open up to anyone.

The sudden, ear-splitting shrilling of a bell shattered his thoughts. The clusters of kids chatting in the corridor broke up and everyone headed off in different directions. How much longer were they going to leave him standing there? Honestly, this place was so incompetent. He might as well find his classroom on his own; surely they had a plan of this building on one of the noticeboards. Whatever, he wasn't prepared to hang around any longer and be stared at.

He picked up his bag and strode across to the display board, his eyes scanning the mass of posters and leaflets pinned to the sludge-coloured hessian.

Ecstasy kills! Be Drug Aware! screamed one.

Work hard, play hard simpered another.

Run For Your Life! Join Year Eleven's sponsored sprint and raise money to help beat heart disease!

To his horror, Nick felt his eyes fill with tears.

"*It was his heart, Nick.*" His mother's words on that awful evening echoed in his head. "*There was nothing they could do.*"

His clenched fist had slammed against the noticeboard before he knew it. At least the pain that shot up his arm was something positive in a world which had turned totally negative. No money left, no home, no boarding-school. No Dad.

"Are you OK?" A tall, slender girl with a freckled nose and long auburn hair slowed as she passed him, her eyes resting on the hand he was rubbing surreptitiously.

"Yeah, fine thanks." Nick felt himself colouring and looked away, trying to look sorted. What a complete idiot! The last thing he wanted to do was draw attention to himself, particularly in front of a girl. At Benham they had only taken girls in the Sixth Form; the head said they were a distraction to academic progress. He wasn't used to being surrounded by them, much less having them asking awkward questions.

"You're new, aren't you?" the girl asked affably. "What year?"

"Eleven," he muttered.

"Same as me," she said. "I'm Chloë, by the way."

She waited. Nick said nothing.

"And you are . . . ?"

"Nick Bowen," he muttered reluctantly.

"Is someone coming for you?"

"So rumour has it," Nick replied loftily, wishing she would just go away and leave him alone. "Not that there seems to be much organisation round here."

Chloë grinned. "Don't you believe it," she said, totally unfazed. "A week in this place and you'll realise that even your breathing has to be timetabled."

Despite the way he was feeling, Nick couldn't help smiling. The girl chuckled.

"And if you want proof, it's on its way," she said, glancing over his left shoulder. Nick followed her gaze. A large, florid-faced woman in a totally unsuitable blue floral dress was striding towards the double doors, accompanied by a short, thin boy with coffee-coloured skin and huge dark eyes, whose expression suggested he was being marched to the guillotine.

"Mrs Braithwaite – that's our year tutor – is rather deficient in the sense of humour department. I'm off – see you around, I guess."

Nick nodded and smiled weakly.

"See you," he said.

"And I hope you feel better soon," said Chloë.

"I'm fine . . ." Nick began but she had already sprinted off down the corridor. How could he have been so dumb? Now she'd be sure to tell everyone that she'd seen the new guy lose his cool, and if this place was anything like Benham, he knew he'd be in for a week of hell.

"Ah, Nicholas, there you are!" A voice that would not have been out of place in the percussion department of a symphony orchestra boomed along the corridor.

Nick took a deep breath and turned, fixing a polite smile on his face. This was it. There was no turning back. What was it Dad used to say?

"Look cool, son, and they'll think you are cool."

His eyes rested, not on Mrs Braithwaite's broad, lipstick-smudged grin, but on the scowling frown of the boy with her.

He looked pretty much like Nick felt.

"But, miss, I can't!" Sanjay had protested when Mrs Braithwaite had collared him in the locker room and informed him that he was to be minder to the new boy.

"Oh, don't be so ridiculous, Sanjay!" his teacher had expostulated. "Of course you can – I'm hardly asking you to negotiate for world peace at the United Nations, am I? All you have to do is take him to lessons, show him where the dining-room is, that sort of thing. It's not brain surgery."

It might as well be, thought Sanjay now, as Mrs Braithwaite bustled ahead to welcome the new guy. Nick was tall and broad-shouldered, with dark brown wavy hair and the athletic stance of a seasoned sportsman. As he shook hands with Mrs Braithwaite he smiled broadly, clearly perfectly at ease with the whole situation.

Mrs Braithwaite had told Sanjay that Nick had had family problems, but he certainly didn't look weighed down by them now.

"What problems, miss?" he had asked.

"No need to ask too many questions," the teacher had suggested. "Let him settle in at his own pace."

"OK," Sanjay had agreed, relieved to have an excuse to keep his mouth shut.

"And this," boomed Mrs Braithwaite now, extending an arm towards Sanjay, "is Sanjay Fraser. He's going to be looking out for you for the next few days. Sanjay, this is Nick Bowen."

"Hi, Sanjay, good to meet you!" Nick stretched out a hand.

"Hi," grunted Sanjay, dropping his eyes and examining the cord carpet in some detail.

"Well, I'll leave you two to get acquainted. You'll need to hurry, Sanjay, the registration bell went three minutes ago."

And with that Mrs Braithwaite strode off in the direction of the staffroom.

"We go this way," muttered Sanjay heading along the corridor towards the classrooms. "You're in my class, 11T – Mr Tompkins."

"Right." Nick fell into step beside him. Sanjay felt a weed; he hardly came up to Nick's shoulder and had to hurry to keep up with his long strides.

"What's he like?" Nick asked suddenly.

"Who?"

"Mr Tompkins."

Sanjay shrugged. "He's OK, I guess," he said. "Teaches maths."

He tried to think of something really witty to say about Tommo but failed miserably.

"You been at Lockbridge High long?" Nick asked, without looking at him.

"Since Year Seven," muttered Sanjay and lapsed once more into silence.

He had to ask the guy something. He couldn't just mooch along like some gormless kid. "So where do you live?" he gabbled.

"What?"

Nick was staring at him as though he had asked for guidelines on splitting the atom.

"Where do you live?" repeated Sanjay.

"Oh – nowhere, really."

"Nowhere?"

"Well, er – we're house hunting," said Nick, quickening his pace.

"Oh right – so are you in a hotel or something?"

Nick turned, his lips parted in an eager smile to reveal a set of perfectly white, perfectly even teeth. "Yes, that's right," he said. "A hotel – say, is that the library?" He gestured towards a pair of double doors.

Sanjay nodded. Since the word LIBRARY was displayed in bold capitals on the door frame, he thought it a pretty dumb question, but he guessed the guy was nervous, what with it being his first day.

"And this is our classroom," he said, pushing open a hideously green painted door. There was a brief pause in the cacophony of sound that hit their ears, as several people turned to eye the newcomer. Sanjay noted how suddenly the girls in the room stopped what they were doing and began flicking hair behind their ears and tilting chins provocatively.

"Settle down, 11T!" The door slammed and a squat man in ill-fitting cord trousers and a shapeless sweater that appeared to have been knitted from faded string strode into the room.

"Right, everyone, welcome to Year Eleven! And welcome also to Nicholas Bowen. Nicholas has recently moved to Leeds from . . ."

At that point, the door of the classroom flew open and a pretty, curvy girl with dark blonde hair and a flushed face dashed through.

"Sinead Flaherty! Hardly the most promising start to a new school year!" Mr Tompkins eyed her with disdain.

"Sorry, sir – my dad's car broke down," she gasped. "I had to run all the way from the roundabout." She hurled her bag on to the table next to Nick. It shot across the polished surface and fell to the floor, spilling books and pens everywhere.

"It's OK, let me!" Nick squatted down and picked up her scattered belongings, handing them back to her with a smile.

"Way-hey!" some wag from the back of the room jeered.

Sanjay watched as Sinead caught Nick's eye, blushed and began stuffing her things back into the bag. Conquest number one, he thought wryly. That guy has cool down to a fine art.

"Is it conceivable, Sinead, that you could manage to execute the simplest activity without disrupting the entire class?" Mr Tompkins said with a sneer in his voice.

"Sorry, sir," she muttered.

"If you don't get your act together soon, you will be. Now, as I was saying," the teacher went on, "Nicholas is new to Leeds, new to all this, in fact." He waved a hand airily round the room. "Why don't you tell us a bit about yourself, Nicholas?"

"Nothing much to tell, sir," he muttered. "Except I'd rather be called Nick."

"Nick? Right, fine."

A bell shrilled urgently, interrupting Mr Tompkins in mid-flow. He glanced at his watch. "Right – first period. Get to your lessons."

Sanjay noticed Nick's shoulders drop in obvious relief. He could identify with that – there was nothing worse than having the whole class look at you as if you were some specimen in a museum showcase. He guessed teachers only asked you to talk about yourself so that they didn't have to bother reading the head's brief on new kids.

"So where now?" Nick was at Sanjay's elbow, looking as if he wanted to be as far away from here as possible.

"It's history first," replied Sanjay. "Follow me."

They pushed their way down the crowded corridor in silence. As usual, Sanjay couldn't think of anything to talk about. But somehow that didn't worry him as much as usual. He got the feeling that Nick wasn't too keen on talking right now either.

CHAPTER 7

Mood
SWINGS

Chloë 4 Jack
Chloë loves Jack
Mrs Chloë Kempton

Chloë doodled a couple more love hearts and sighed. It just didn't feel right being here, stuck in this boring history lesson with the rain beating down on the classroom window and Mrs Braithwaite droning on about the Vietnam war. As if it mattered. She didn't belong here any more; she belonged with Jack.

She glanced at the clock on the classroom wall. Nine thirty. Jack would be rigging the Lazers and Toppers ready for the morning sailing lessons. She closed her eyes and conjured up a very satisfying image of his tanned, muscular legs, the long fingers that had run through her hair, his generous mouth that had kissed . . .

"Chloë Sanderson!" Mrs Braithwaite's voice shattered her dreams. "You may feel that your grasp of twentieth-century history is such that you can afford to nod off during my lessons but your results last term would suggest otherwise."

A muffled titter rippled round the room.

"Sorry, Mrs Braithwaite," said Chloë, endeavouring to look suitably remorseful.

Silly old bat. She was as bad as Dad, going on and on about how GCSEs were vital to her ongoing survival on the planet, and how the world didn't owe her a living and it was time she realised that there was more to life than shopping, boys and discos.

"You can't expect to have this sort of lifestyle handed to you on a silver plate for ever, you know," her father had declared the previous evening, as she sat with her parents in their elegant dining-room. "There will come a time . . ."

". . . when I have to make my own way in the world," Chloë had chanted, ripping a ciabatta roll in half and stuffing a piece into her mouth. "I know, I know."

It wouldn't have done to have told him her real plans, she thought now, peering unseeingly at her history textbook. Her father might well have a reputation for making wacky, off-the-wall TV programmes, but when it came to his attitude to his only daughter, he was as strait-laced as they came. Until this summer she had been happy to go along with the idea that she would do her A levels, go to uni and get a good job like both her parents. But now she thought differently. Jack had made her see sense.

Jack said that academic achievements were grossly overrated; he said that learning about the Real World was far more important than sticking your nose into a pile of books, and that some of the world's greatest entrepreneurs had managed very well without a string of exam successes behind them.

"It's a crime that someone as lovely and as vibrant as you should be shut up in school slogging over exams," he had said, nibbling her ear-lobe. "I was thinking . . ."

"What?"

"Well," he had said, taking her hand and kissing her fingers one by one. "I'm going to do another season here and then I'm off travelling. If you weren't going to be stuck in school . . ."

The sentence had hovered unfinished in the balmy air. And that was when Chloë had decided. Her parents would go ballistic, but then there was no need to tell them. Not yet. But she had made up her mind. She'd do her GCSEs and then she was going to chuck school and see the world. With wonderful, sexy, gorgeous Jack. After all, whatever her parents might think, she wasn't a kid any longer; in a few weeks' time she would be sixteen and she could do what she liked.

Not that being sixteen was without its complications, she thought, idly copying Mrs Braithwaite's notes from the board. She'd only been back at school for an hour and already three people had asked the inevitable question.

"When's the party, Chloë?" Natalie had asked on the bus. "Will we get to come to your place at long last?"

"Where's the celebration, Clo?" Becky had said in the locker room. "Can't wait."

It was a sort of unspoken rule that everyone had a bash for their sixteenth birthday, and it was worrying Chloë a lot. Not that she didn't like parties, she adored them. As long as they were other people's. It was the thought of having one of her own that bothered her.

"Darling, what nonsense!" her mother had trilled the week before when the subject of her birthday had come up over breakfast. "I keep telling you to invite your friends round more often; we'll throw a party here for as many as you like."

"Not here, Mum," pleaded Chloë. "People will make a mess."

She had expected her mother, who had recently lashed out a serious sum on a new cream carpet, to back off, but she persisted. "So? We can clean up! It'll be such fun."

But it wouldn't. Chloë knew that if she had a party, she wouldn't enjoy one single minute of it. She would spend the whole time remembering what had happened the previous Christmas when her mum gave that swish dinner party for her TV friends, or trying to forget that awful night after her thirteenth birthday when . . . No. She wouldn't think about it. She was sure that sort of thing would never happen again, but she wasn't about to take any chances. She'd just forget it.

Besides, what was the point of a party without Jack? What was the point of anything without Jack? She glanced at the clock. In five and a half hours she could try phoning him again. She wasn't going home until she had spoken to him. If she didn't hear his voice soon, she would die.

She fingered the plaited friendship bracelet that Jack had given her on the last day of the holiday.

"Every time you look at it, think of me," he had whispered, ignoring the thunderous glances of Chloë's father, who was eyeing them from the side of the swimming pool.

As if she could think of anything else.

"I'll treasure it for ever," she had told him.

"One day I'll buy you something much better," Jack had promised.

Perhaps he was thinking about her birthday. Perhaps he would send her a present. Maybe that was why a letter hadn't arrived. Parcels took ages, after all. That would be it.

She sighed and smiled to herself. The new guy on the next table turned and raised a quizzical eyebrow. She ignored him. She was too busy imagining just what it was that Jack would send her.

"And this is for you!" Sinead handed Bianca a small package wrapped in shiny red paper. She had been counting the minutes until breaktime, desperate to see her friends' faces when she handed out her presents.

"Go on, open it!" she urged.

Bianca dumped her drinks can beside her on the grassy bank above the playground and ripped open the parcel.

Lying on a bed of cotton wool was a pearl pendant on a silver chain, and a pair of matching earrings with tiny diamanté drops.

Bianca gasped, her mouth dropping open in amazement.

"They're real pearls," Sinead said eagerly. "From Majorca – they specialise in pearls out there."

"But they must have cost a fortune!" Bianca exclaimed. "I don't believe it, you . . ."

"Don't you like them?" Sinead looked worried.

"Course I do," said Bianca, chewing her lip. "But . . ."

"And you like yours?" Sinead turned to Abby, who was still staring at the twisted gold rope bracelet with the heart-shaped lock.

Abby nodded. "It's mega," she said. "I've never ever had anything this posh."

Sinead beamed, a warm glow enveloping her whole body. It was so good having money to spend on her friends, even if it had caused something of a row between her mum and dad.

"You can't keep giving the kids money!" her mother had protested on holiday when her dad handed out another fistful of pesetas. "It's not going to do them any good, thinking that everything's going to be handed to them on a plate."

"Oh, Kathleen, love, come off it!" her father had retorted. "They've hardly had it easy up to now, have they? A bit of a spend won't do them any harm."

"Well, I'm not having this inheritance changing them into

spoiled brats," Kathleen had insisted. "That's the first step down a slippery slope, so it is."

"I know, love, but . . ."

"And just you remember whose money it is!"

That had been the worst moment. Sinead's dad had stared at her mum, and her mother had jutted out her chin, the way she always did when she was determined to get her own way. For a moment, neither of them had spoken.

Then, just as suddenly, her mother had grinned, raised her eyebrows and shaken her head. "Oh, go on with you, then," she laughed. "But just while we are on holiday, mind. Once we get home it's back to normal."

But of course, it hadn't been. They bought the flat and loads of new furniture because their old stuff looked completely lost in the huge rooms of the apartment. They'd got an enormous flat screen TV for the sitting-room as well as portables for the kitchen and bedrooms, and a bright blue fridge that made crushed ice for your drinks.

"So, did you meet any cool guys in Majorca?" demanded Bianca now, fastening her pendant round her neck.

"Some," said Sinead, casually ripping open a bag of crisps in an attempt to look enigmatic.

"And?" Abby leaned forward eagerly. "Did you pull?"

"Fat chance," sighed Sinead. "You know what my mum's like – I don't know why she doesn't tie me to a chair leg and have done with it. Every time these guys even looked at me, there she was, grabbing my arm and marching me off on some boring excursion."

She didn't add that the only boy who had taken any interest in her during the entire fortnight had been thirteen with the body of a stick insect and the intellect of a small earthworm. Or that when Juan, the waiter at the beach bar, had asked her to dance at the weekly barbecue she had dashed off and hidden in the loo because she didn't know any chat-up lines. In some ways it was convenient having an Irish Catholic mother who expected her daughters to live like nuns, at least it gave Sinead someone to blame for her lack of success with boys without totally losing her credibility.

"You didn't just go along with it, did you?" Bianca asked jeeringly, peeling the wrapper off a piece of chewing gum. "Parents have no right telling you who you can and can't hang out with. Mine would never dare."

"Mine neither," agreed Abby. "Next time you really fancy a guy, go for it. Don't ask Mummy's permission."

"I don't, I . . ."

"Perhaps," ventured Bianca, watching Sinead's face closely, "she's never fancied anyone enough."

"Of course I have!" retorted Sinead, glancing across the playground.

Her two friends followed her gaze.

"You don't!"

"Him? Really?"

Sinead turned back to them. "What? Who? I don't know what you mean."

"Come off it," cried Bianca. "You fancy the new guy. Nick whatever-it-is. Admit it."

"I thought you went all coy when he picked up your books," added Abby.

"So what are you going to do about it?"

"Nothing – I mean, I don't fancy him, I just . . ."

She was saved from further explanations by the insistent jangling of the end of break bell.

"Well," said Bianca, nodding her head in the direction of the double doors, where Nick was pushing his way through the crowd, "if you are keen, you'll have to get a move on. Look who's barging her way in now."

Sinead looked. And felt her blood begin to boil. Pushing open the door and chatting nineteen to the dozen, was Chloë Sanderson. Not content with landing Sinead in it last term, now she was after the very guy Sinead fancied. Not, of course, that she would admit to fancying him, but when he had smiled at her that morning, she had felt as if tiny electric shocks were shooting through her body.

"See?" Bianca grinned. "You've gone all gooey. Go for it, why don't you? You've nothing to lose."

Which, thought Sinead, was a pretty dumb thing to say. As if she was about to risk making a total idiot of herself in front of her mates and this Nick guy. Not to mention Chloë – she'd love to see Sinead messing up. Besides, with the oh-so-elegant Chloë on the case Sinead knew she didn't stand a chance.

"For the last time, I'm not interested," she announced firmly, standing up and brushing grass from her skirt.

"So why," asked Bianca meekly, "haven't you taken your eyes off him for the last three minutes?"

"Hi, Nick – you're looking confused." Chloë pushed open the double doors and smiled at him. "Haven't you got someone looking after you?"

Nick nodded. "Sanjay Fraser," he said. "But he had to dash off to the computer room for something."

"Oh, that's Sanjay for you," grinned Chloë. "He's a techno whizz kid."

Nick smiled. "I guessed that – when I said that I wasn't interested in computers, he looked at me as if I'd confessed to not knowing my alphabet!"

Chloë laughed. "I swear Sanjay doesn't live on our planet – he's in a virtual reality world all of his own! Anyway, where are you headed?"

Nick pulled a timetable from his pocket. "Maths – set one," he said.

"Oh, great, same as me," said Chloë. "We go this way." She pointed down the corridor. "So you've done maths for GCSE already, then?"

Nick nodded. "Last year," he said. "Everyone at Benham . . ." He faltered.

"Benham?"

"My old school," Nick concluded reluctantly.

"Oh right," said Chloë easily. "Where was that, then? Oh, this way – it's miles, I'm afraid."

She gestured up a flight of stairs and began pushing through a throng of Year Eights clattering in the opposite direction.

"So where was this school, then?"

"Sussex," said Nick shortly.

"And that's where you lived, was it? Sussex?"

"Italy."

"Italy! Mega! We went there once – Florence was to die for. So, you were in boarding-school? So how come you're here, then?"

"Look, what is this? The Spanish Inquisition?" Nick rounded on her, his kit-bag swinging on his shoulder and nearly decapitating a small child with a worried expression. "Shall I just hand you a CV and be done with it?"

Chloë pulled back, her eyes widening. "Sorry," she muttered. "I was just trying to be friendly."

She glanced at Nick, who was biting his lip and staring straight ahead of him. "In here," she said curtly, turning into a large, airy classroom overlooking the games field. "I'll leave you in peace, then."

She walked deliberately to the far side of the classroom and began talking cheerfully to Natalie and Becky.

But while Nat held forth about Sam's expertise at high diving and how his thigh muscles rippled in the sunlight, and Becky assured her that he couldn't be as cool as her Dave, Chloë was musing about Nick.

There was something about that guy. Something he wasn't saying. One minute he was making jokes about Sanjay, the next he was biting her head off. She liked a mystery; she liked getting to the bottom of things. Not, of course, that she was remotely interested in Nick. She couldn't stand surly guys, and besides, there was no way he could compare with Jack. But still, it was fascinating. Why would he be so jumpy about his past? It sounded pretty glamorous to her; swish school, living abroad. So why was he so cagey?

She glanced out of the corner of her eye to where Nick was sitting, moodily flicking through a maths textbook. He was a dish, there was no doubt about it. His dark brown hair flopped over his forehead and his deep-set blue eyes flashed when he laughed. But right now, his head bowed and mouth slack, he looked a lot younger than sixteen. And very – what was it? Sad? Angry?

No. Lost. That was it. He looked utterly and completely lost. Of course, it was bewildering, the first day in a new school, especially one as big as Lockbridge High. But still.

Chloë got the firm impression that school was only part of Nick's problem. And for some reason that she couldn't explain, she was determined to find out just what the rest of it was all about.

Why did I explode at her like that? How could I have done that? Nick stood up, his chair scraping against the floorboards, as Mr Tompkins came into the room.

The whole class tittered.

Nick glanced round the room. No one else had stood up. He

couldn't believe it. At Benham it was automatic that you stood up when a member of staff came into the room.

He sat down.

"Charmed as I am by your elegant manners, Nick, we don't stand on ceremony here at Lockbridge," drawled Mr Tompkins. "You've left the rarefied echelons of public school now, you know."

Another ripple of laughter.

Nick said nothing. What was the point? Things were going from bad to worse. First, Chloë had seen him slamming his fist into the wall, then Sanjay had disappeared and left him on his own. He'd turned on Chloë when all she was doing was being friendly and now he had drawn attention to himself in front of the whole maths set and Mr Tompkins had made a big thing about him coming from a public school. That was all he needed. He could kill him.

What is it with me these days? he thought, praying that the burning in his cheeks would subside. Why do I feel so angry with the whole world all the time?

"Anger," his old housemaster at Benham used to say, when disciplining warring First Formers, "is a kind of temporary madness."

That's how I feel, thought Nick. Mad. Like the whole world has gone crazy and there's not a single thing I can do about it.

"You will now all attempt question eight on page fifty-four," announced Mr Tompkins.

Nick turned to the page and gazed at the close print. But, as he began punching numbers into his calculator with unnecessary vigour, his mind was on other things.

None of it made any sense. Life had been getting so much better; ever since his dad had taken voluntary redundancy and his parents had set up business in Tuscany, buying up derelict farmhouses and converting them into holiday homes, Dad had been really happy – over the moon, in fact.

"This business is a licence to print money," his father had told him when he flew out to Italy for the school Easter holidays. "Give me a couple of years and we'll be seriously rich."

Only he hadn't been given a couple of years, which was why they were in this mess now. Whatever his mum might say, Nick knew that his dad had been right. After all, he wouldn't have mortgaged their house and borrowed all that money and run up huge debts if he hadn't been absolutely certain that he was on to a winner. His dad was no fool.

But Dad was dead. The house in Tuscany had been repossessed by the bank. Everything was gone.

What would happen? What would they do? He couldn't get a straight answer out of anyone. Gran just said that Mum had everything under control, but when his mum wasn't treating him like some dumb kid and promising that something would turn up, that she'd work things out, she was slagging off his father, saying that he obviously hadn't cared about them or he couldn't have cheated them the way he did. That was what made Nick angriest of all, the way she made it sound like it was all Dad's fault. And Dad wasn't here to defend himself, so Nick had to do it for him.

"Nick?" Mr Tompkins was standing at the whiteboard, marker

pen poised. "Do you have an answer to the question?"

Suddenly, it was all too much. This place. These people. These eyes watching him.

He pushed back his chair. "Excuse me, sir," he said automatically, his inbred good manners taking over even at this moment of crisis.

With that, he strode to the door, yanked it open and stepped into the corridor.

"Nicholas!"

He turned and ran down the corridor. He didn't know where he was going and he didn't care.

"Sanjay! What's this you're up to?" Mr Buckley peered over his shoulder at the computer screen.

"Oh, it's just a bit of fun, sir. Just killing time in break."

Why do I always say that? Sanjay asked himself angrily. Why can't I just come out with it and say that this is the kind of stuff I want to do for the rest of my life?

"It's great – I didn't know you had a wacky streak in you!" smiled Mr Buckley, as Sanjay began shutting down the programme. "And this new software the governors gave us is pretty neat, isn't it?"

Sanjay nodded.

"Play around with graphics and suchlike a lot, do you?"

"A bit, sir."

A bit! Get real! He'd done little else all summer holidays –

sitting in his tiny bedroom, shutting out the real world and creating his own.

"Sanjay can't get enough of studying," his father had proudly told their neighbours. But he hadn't been studying at all, he had been doing the one thing that really fired him up. The Internet helped; there were so many people out there keen on the same sort of thing. But the more he found out, the more he realised how much there was to learn. He needed a better software package, a more powerful computer. But most of all he needed courage. The courage to tell his parents that what they thought Sanjay was going to do next year wasn't exactly what he had in mind.

"Well, well, I'm seeing another side to you, Sanjay Fraser!" chuckled Mr Buckley, pushing his wire-framed spectacles further up his nose and beaming all over his rather spotty little face. "I never realised you were . . ."

The door crashed open and a horde of Year Eight pupils clattered in, chattering like a barrel-load of recently released monkeys.

"Must dash, sir. Sorry, sir. Got to look out for a new boy," Sanjay gabbled, grabbing his bag and heading for the door.

"Come and chat to me some time," called Mr Buckley. "We must develop this talent of yours. You could go far."

Could he really? Maybe Mr Buckley would be able to tell him how to sell it to his parents . . .

Get real. They were hardly going to ditch their ideas about Cambridge and Harvard and Masters degrees and PhDs in favour of what Sanjay's father would call trivia and tripe.

It was nice that Mr Buckley liked his stuff. But nothing would come of it. Nothing could.

At last. Jasmin had been waiting all morning for the right moment to collar Chloë and now she was just behind her in the queue for the cafeteria.

She tapped her on the shoulder.

"Oh hi, Jasmin," Chloë smiled. "How's it going?"

"You know this guy you want to phone?" Jasmin asked, without any preamble.

Chloë gasped. "What . . . ? How did you know it was a guy?" she demanded, casting a quick glance over her shoulder.

Jasmin grinned. "Common sense," she said. "You'd hardly be in such a state if you were calling up your granny."

Chloë bit her lip. "What about it?" she asked.

"I have the solution," said Jasmin, peering at a dish of lasagne and rejecting it on the grounds of inedibility.

"You have?" Chloë looked doubtful.

"The café," said Jasmin, grabbing a salad. "You can make the call from there."

Chloë frowned. "What café?" she asked.

"Ours, silly," said Jasmin. "The Canal Café on Millers Lane."

"That new place? Is that yours?" exclaimed Chloë, plonking a cheese roll on to her tray.

Jasmin nodded. "We opened last week," she replied. "Anyway,

it's got a payphone for customers, so you can use that. I know it works because it's brand new."

Chloë's face broke into a broad grin. "Ace!" she said. "And your parents won't mind?"

"Not if you buy a coffee, they won't!" Jasmin laughed. "Customers are still something of a novelty. Come back after school, why don't you?"

"Great! I will, thanks." Chloë glanced round the cafeteria, looking for somewhere to sit.

"There's a space," commented Jasmin, jerking her head towards the door.

"Mmm . . ." Chloë hesitated, still scanning the room. Jasmin guessed she was looking for her mates.

"I'll see you later, then," she said reluctantly.

"No, hang on – I'm coming," replied Chloë. "I was just looking for Nick."

"Nick?" Jasmin frowned as they made their way across the room.

"New guy in our class," explained Chloë.

"Oh, I get it," teased Jasmin. "One abroad, one at home . . ."

Chloë laughed. "No, it's not like that!" she protested. "It's just that Nick – well, he was in a really weird mood earlier, like he had something mega on his mind. And then in the middle of maths he just upped and left. No explanation or anything. You should have seen old Tommo's face!"

"I can imagine," grinned Jasmin. "I guess this Nick doesn't

realise what Tommo can be like when he's crossed. Shall we sit there?"

Chloë followed her gaze. There was a table with only one person sitting at it, his head buried in a magazine.

Sanjay Fraser.

"I think," said Chloë, "that would be a great idea."

"I don't know where he is." Sanjay averted his eyes from Chloë's penetrating gaze. "I looked for him when the lunch bell rang but no one had seen him."

Chloë sighed. "He dashed out of class in the middle of maths," she said.

"Why?"

"Well I don't know, do I?" said Chloë. "Anyway, what do you know about him?"

"Not a lot," shrugged Sanjay. "Except he's new to Leeds and he's living in a hotel. His family are house-hunting."

"Really?" Chloë was thoughtful. "Which hotel?"

"How should I know?" retorted Sanjay. "He's not very forthcoming with details."

"Tell me about it," muttered Chloë.

The bell shrilled urgently and Sanjay stood up. "I'd better go and find him, then," he said. "Cheers."

"Find out where he's staying!" Chloë called after him.

"I must go too," said Jasmin. "I'll meet you at the bus after school, Chloë. Assuming you still want to make this call?"

"Of course I do!" affirmed Chloë. "Why wouldn't I?"

"No reason," grinned Jasmin. "See you at four."

With a bit of luck no one would spot him here, tucked round the corner behind the gym. Now that he had thought up an excuse for his stupid behaviour in maths, he was ready to eat his packed lunch and then get back to lessons. He knew he was supposed to go to the cafeteria, but he needed just a bit longer on his own, to get his head together and clear his mind.

He pulled the lid off the blue plastic box and stared at the contents. A ciabatta roll, some vine tomatoes still on the stem, three slices of mortadella and a wedge of Dolcelatte cheese. The exact lunch his mum always gave him on the first day of the holidays.

He bit into the cheese. Immediately his memory winged back to the terrace of the villa, his dad balancing on the stepladder doing battle with the rampant hibiscus.

"I'll tame this thing if it kills me," he had called to Nick, that great grin of his creasing his tanned cheeks. And then . . .

"Ah, Nick! Here you are!"

He looked up in horror to see Mrs Braithwaite bearing down on him. Now he'd be for it.

"Mr Tompkins tells me you left his lesson in something of a hurry." She sat down on the bench beside him and beamed. Despite the resonant tones of her voice, she didn't sound at all angry. "Is something wrong?"

"I am so sorry, Mrs Braithwaite," he said in the apologetic, well-modulated tones that he'd always used at Benham when in a tight corner. "It was very rude of me, I know – but you see, I suddenly felt rather nauseous and . . ."

"But you should have said!" exclaimed Mrs Braithwaite. "Someone would have taken you to the school nurse. Let me show you the way now."

"No, no, I'm fine now," he said, jumping up and ramming his lunch box back into his bag. "I'll get along to lessons."

"You're sure?"

"Positive." Nick smiled in what he hoped was a confident manner and began walking towards the science block, Mrs Braithwaite hard on his heels.

As he turned the corner, a speeding body lurched into him.

"Oh! Oh, it's you. Thank goodness, I . . ."

"And just where, Sanjay Fraser, have you been?" Mrs Braithwaite demanded. "You are supposed to be looking after Nick, not abandoning him to a solitary lunch-hour. It's not good enough, you know."

"I, er – well, I . . ."

"It's OK, Mrs Braithwaite. Sanjay told me he had things to do and I said to go ahead. I'm fine on my own."

Mrs Braithwaite nodded. "Well, I am sure, in view of everything, there are times when you just want to be left alone," she said conversationally.

Nick swallowed. He didn't know what to say. But Mrs Braithwaite didn't appear to require a reply. "Off you both go to chemistry, then," she said and bustled off in the opposite direction, her ancient brown sandals making squelching noises on the tarmac of the path.

"Thanks for saying that," breathed Sanjay as they crossed to the science block. "And I'm really sorry I lost you – I didn't mean to, but . . ."

"Look, it's OK," said Nick.

"Chloë said you bunked off maths."

Oh cheers, Chloë. "I felt sick."

"Chloë was worried. She was all for sending out a search party."

Nick raised an eyebrow.

"Chloë's like that," Sanjay said. "She likes to get everyone sorted. By the way, she asked me which hotel you're staying in."

"Hotel? Oh, hotel."

Sugar, sugar, sugar. Why had he said that? He hadn't a clue about hotels in Leeds. Think, for heaven's sake. Think.

Sanjay pushed open the door to the science block and looked at Nick questioningly.

"Well," said Nick, with what he hoped was an enigmatic smile, "if she really wants to know, she'll have to ask me, won't she?"

Sanjay grinned. "You fancy her," he said.

"What? Oh please. I hardly know the girl. Besides, she's not my type. So you can get that idea out of your head right now."

"OK," said Sanjay with a slight shrug. "Want to share a Bunsen burner?"

Nick let out a sigh of relief. He wasn't going to ask more dumb questions. He'd got away with it. For now. Only a couple more hours and he could go home. No. He didn't have a home. Villa Flavia was gone, and his grandmother's end-of-terrace would never feel like home.

Surely Mum would find them somewhere decent to live soon? There must be some money kicking around – an insurance policy, surely?

That was it. Dad would have had insurances.

Nick smiled to himself.

He'd tell her this evening. She must have forgotten in her grief. Such as it was.

Don't.

Don't think like that.

Just light your burner.

Just get on with it.

CHAPTER 8

Parental
PROBLEMS

While Nick was busy clutching at straws, his mother was sitting in the kitchen of thirty-three Talbot Street doing sums and wishing she could turn back the clock.

"It's hopeless," she sighed, running her hands wearily through her unruly, sandy coloured curls. "There isn't even enough for a deposit on a flat. What are we going to do, Mum?"

A tear spilled over and trickled down her cheek as she turned to face her mother.

"Well, we're not going to cry over spilt milk, for a start!" Joan Andrews retorted briskly, patting her on the shoulder and heaving herself out of the chair. "You know you can both stay here for as long as you need."

"But, Mum, it's not suitable!" protested Jenny Bowen.

"Oh well, of course, if it's not good enough for you . . ." began her mother, turning on the tap and filling the kettle.

"Mum, you know that's not what I mean," said Jenny. "It's just that Nick – well, he needs space of his own, a place to invite his friends. It's hard enough for him changing schools without . . ."

". . . without having to move downmarket, you mean? I'm sorry if my home doesn't match up to your swanky Italian villa."

"Mum, don't!" Jenny burst into tears.

"Oh, love, I'm sorry, take no notice of me," her mother said, switching on the kettle and enfolding Jenny's tiny frame in her chubby arms. "It's just that – well, I'm so furious with that son-in-law of mine, for what he did to you both. I mean, I know you shouldn't speak ill of the dead but . . ."

"That's right, so let's drop the subject, shall we?" Jenny wiped her eyes furiously, sniffed and picked up the sheets of paper over which she had been poring. "I've worked it out. I'm going to get a job – that way, I can rent somewhere for me and Nick . . ."

"And what is the point of paying rent when you can live here for free, tell me that!" demanded Joan. "I know it's not a palace, but I love having you."

"Listen, Mum," said Jenny. "I'm really grateful to you for taking us in, but I have to make my own way. You see that, don't you? I have to prove I can go it alone."

Her mother nodded. "I know, love," she sighed. "And don't get me wrong – I'm really proud of you, the way you're handling all this. I know how hard Greg's death has hit you."

Jenny smiled wanly and turned away. Yes, it was hard. But what was harder still was knowing that Nick blamed her, at least in part, for his father's death. Sometimes Jenny thought he might be right.

Perhaps she should have been more supportive, not gone on at him so much. But she hadn't been able to just sit by and watch while Greg squandered money and bragged about becoming a millionaire. She had told him that he was overstretching himself and taking stupid risks. She had begged him not to borrow so much money. They'd argued over it more than once.

"Nag, nag, nag, that's all you do!" he had shouted at her just the day before he died. "You'll be happy enough to spend it once I've made it, though, won't you?"

Only he didn't make it, thought Jenny now with a sigh, and spending was something she wouldn't be doing for a long time to come.

I've overspent, thought Suzy Sanderson, dumping a clutch of designer carrier bags on to the studio floor and sinking into a chair.

She had only meant to buy a scarf but the sales had just started and it was all so tempting. But still, if she put half the stuff at the back of the wardrobe and threw the carrier bags away, Edward need never know. Not that he'd mind, of course; he knew that being in the public eye meant looking good all the time. But still, money had been a bit tighter lately, what with his last project biting the dust and this new one being so slow to get off the ground. She just prayed that his meeting today would bear fruit; if only this new sitcom of his was taken up by the BBC, he'd be back in the mainstream of TV comedy again, and then he might start relaxing.

"Suzy! Karl wants to see you pronto!"

Jemima, Suzy's production assistant, bounded up to her, ample bottom bouncing in extraordinary fluorescent pink Lycra.

Suzy frowned. Karl Dempster, Pennine TV's dynamic head, never saw anyone before lunch. Unless he was about to carpet them.

"What's it about?"

Jemima shrugged. "Search me," she said. "But he was smiling."

"*Smiling*?" The idea of Karl smiling was about as hard to take on board as news of a heatwave in the Antarctic.

"I'd better go in," said Suzy, doing a quick repair job with a lipliner pencil. "We don't want to miss the moment."

"But, Kathleen, love, don't you see? There'll never be a better moment than this, ever!"

Shaun Flaherty put his arms round his wife's shoulders and gave her a hug. "It's something I've always wanted to do," he said. "And I'd be good at it, I know I would."

His wife sighed. "Oh, love, I don't doubt you would," she said. "You've always had a streak of the artist in you, and you've the patience of a saint, so you have. But . . ."

"But what?"

"Well, isn't it all a bit too much too soon?" she asked. "I mean, to throw in your job at Dennings and Rigby – you've been there for years!"

"Precisely!" asserted Shaun, thumping his fist on the kitchen table. "Thirty-two years, man and boy – but if I don't give this a go, I know I am going to regret it for the rest of my life. I'm not asking for much, love, just a little lock-up shop somewhere handy and a bit of cash for advertising. I can see it now: 'Shaun Flaherty – Furniture Restorer and Decorator, No Job Too Small'." He waved his arms to indicate his shop sign.

Kathleen chewed her lip. "But Kieran's still got two more years at university, and then the girls . . ."

"Kathleen, we have money now! You have to get your head round the fact that we're no longer counting the pennies. Five hundred thousand pounds, we've been left!"

"I've been left." Kathleen's voice was soft but firm.

Shaun's shoulders dropped. "Sorry. I keep forgetting. When we had nothing, we shared it all. Now we've got heaps, it seems sharing is a whole lot harder."

Kathleen flung her arms round his neck. "I don't mean it like that, Shaun. I'm sorry, love. Really. I just get scared, that's all."

"Scared?"

"That this money will change us. I mean, you setting up in business, us going abroad for holidays, this apartment. It's all like a dream. And I keep thinking it will all go horribly wrong."

Her husband squeezed her hand. "Nothing's going to go wrong, Kath love. Trust me. Heaven knows, we've had enough bad times, so let's just enjoy the good ones, shall we?"

Kathleen smiled and nodded. "I guess," she said.

"And this idea of mine?"

"Do it," she said in a rush. "Get your shop and paint your tables. Go for it."

As her husband wrapped his arms round her and swung her off her feet, she laughed out loud at his pleasure.

But the little niggle of anxiety deep inside her chest very stubbornly refused to go away.

She'd have to be getting back. Jasmin would be home from school soon, and besides, with Harry's brother being there, it would look bad if she wasn't around to cope with the teatime rush.

Rush! That was something of an exaggeration. Josephine Johnson threw the last handful of crumbs at the family of greedy moorhens on the canal bank and began walking reluctantly back to the café. In the week since they had opened, the place had hardly been swamped with customers. A steady trickle in the evenings, admittedly, but during the day hardly a soul. What if it never got off the ground? All Harry's insurance money had been ploughed into it, not to mention a loan from his brother until the compensation was paid. They'd sold their house in London. There was no going back.

"Why would we want to go back?" Harry had asked her when she had voiced her fears. "After what happened, I never want to see those streets again."

And then, of course, she had felt guilty. Guilty for being homesick for Brixton, guilty for feeling that, just at the very moment she had decided what she wanted to do with the rest of her life, the chance to do it had been snatched away.

Of course she had to support Harry in this new venture; after what he had been through it was the least she could do. It was just that she hadn't thought that so much of it would be down to her.

And it wouldn't have been in the past. The old Harry would have been out there, hauling in the punters from the streets, cracking jokes, talking nineteen to the dozen. It was his easy way with people that had made him so popular as a cab driver; people would ring up and ask for him by name, just because he brought a smile to their faces.

Ironic really, thought Josephine now, turning into Water Lane. Harry's own smile was lopsided now, the muscles on the left side of his face damaged irrevocably when that young thug had slammed a broken bottle into his cheek. Why had he stopped? Why hadn't he just driven past and let them get on with it?

But Harry wasn't like that. When he had spotted those two louts laying into the smaller lad, pushing him up against the school wall and kicking him with their great booted feet, he had pulled over into a lay-by, jumped out of the cab and confronted them.

Courageous Cabby Wounded By Mindless Thugs! the headline of the local paper had screamed the following evening.

The Price of Heroism! cried the *Evening Standard* underneath a picture of Harry's swollen and disfigured features.

But the wounding had done more than scar his face. It had broken his nerve. The streets he had known since he was a boy suddenly became threatening, the idea of letting strangers into his cab too much to contemplate. He had begun talking more and more of getting right away.

Sometimes Josephine felt as if she would never forgive Louis, Harry's brother, for suggesting that they move up to Leeds.

There's this great place up for sale, he had written. *Make a wonderful restaurant – and you know you've always been a whizz with the old wooden spoon. I'll help with the capital, we'll split the profits – it can't fail!*

And here they were. Sure, Harry was ensconced out the back, whipping up all sorts of gastronomic delights to tempt the customers, but it was she who had to stand out front, lay up tables, stick a smile on her face even when she felt like screaming to be set free. The bell on the door only had to jangle once for Harry to retreat into the security of the steamy kitchen; she had nowhere to run to.

It hadn't been so bad for the first few days; she'd had some help. But then she had caught that Kelly with her hand in the till, and now she was on her own. It wasn't fair; she had had it out with Harry at the very start. She would support him, but she wouldn't run the place. And what had happened? She was running the place.

"Oh pull yourself together, woman!" she admonished herself out loud, to the astonishment of a passing cyclist. "Get back there and get stuck in!"

They'd make a go of it; of course they would. They'd get more help and then she could join another choir, get involved in a new church, maybe even put her other plans into practice. It just needed a few money-spinning ideas and a bit more razzmatazz to get the thing going.

The trouble was that right now, the one thing Josie Johnson felt short of was even the merest hint of razzmatazz.

"You did *what?*" Dipti Fraser switched the telephone to her other hand and pushed her ebony hair behind her ear. "Oh, Duncan, not today! Not here! And certainly not them!"

She closed her eyes and counted rapidly to ten while her husband gave her a dozen reasons for his self-centred behaviour.

"How could you? I mean, it's the kids' first day back at school – I thought we could have a nice quiet evening. Well, you'll just have to un-invite them."

She winced as her husband's voice rose two octaves.

"I don't care if they're Yale's top professors, I don't care if they are world authorities on the meaning of life, I don't want them to dinner and I don't expect to be told at four o'clock in the afternoon that they are arriving at six!"

She slammed the phone down and clamped a hand to her forehead. Calm down. Breathe deeply. Think beautiful thoughts.

"Damn! damn! and double damn!"

She glanced round the untidy study and began picking up the sheets of paper strewn haphazardly over the floor. She had just got to a crucial part of chapter eleven, things were just beginning to hang together. And now she would have to stop, and tidy up and buy food and arrange flowers because, despite her protests, she knew full well that Duncan wouldn't say no to his precious professors.

She sighed. Another evening of intellectual conversation, when all she wanted to do was get on with her secret project.

Of course, it wasn't altogether Duncan's fault. He didn't realise how much of a chore she had found all this academic entertaining of late. She hadn't even told him exactly what it was she was working on. Provided he saw her settle down at the word processor every morning, with her obligatory mug of camomile tea on one side and her ylang-ylang candle burning on the windowsill beside her, he assumed she was ready for another day researching her next book on Indian mythology. It was best that way. If he knew what it really was she was doing these days, she could imagine what he would say. And while her mastery of the written word was such that it won her glowing reviews in all the literary magazines, when confronted with her husband in full flood, she was usually rendered speechless.

She scooped up her papers, slipped them into the top drawer of her desk and locked it firmly, putting the key in its secret hiding place. Clicking the computer mouse on Save, she filed her work and switched off. Then, as the finishing touch, she placed copies of the *Bhagavad-Gîta*, the *Gîta Govinda* and the *Râmayana* in prominent positions on the desk.

Very suitable. The well organised working space of one of the country's leading experts on Hindu culture. If only they knew.

Which, of course, they mustn't. She would make sure of that. If she was careful, there was no reason why anyone should ever find out what Dipti Fraser was really up to.

CHAPTER 9

FIBS
and fantasies

"**S**o are you coming down town with us?" Abby asked Sinead as they piled out of school. "There's this wicked new clothes stall opened up in the Corn Exchange – really way out and cheap too."

"I can't . . ." began Sinead.

"You forget, Abby," Bianca interjected. "Sinead doesn't do cheap any more. She probably wears designer knickers these days."

"It's not that, silly," Sinead protested. "It's just that Mum's expecting me back and . . ."

"So phone her!"

Sinead hesitated. "I could, I suppose," she said. She could hardly tell them that confessing to her mother that she was with Bianca and Abby would only bring forth a lecture on unsuitable companions and the importance of homework.

"Well, if it's such an effort, don't bother!" Bianca retorted. "Come on, Abby, there's the bus."

Sinead watched as they ran off, whispering behind their hands. Now they'd think she was being off with them, and they'd start shutting her out and . . .

"Hang on! I'm coming!"

She swung her schoolbag on to her shoulder and belted after them. It was as she jumped up on to the platform of the bus that the shoulder strap broke and books went flying everywhere.

"Make a habit of this sort of thing, do you?"

She turned to see Nick Bowen eyeing her quizzically and scooping up her homework diary and history textbook.

She felt her cheeks burn, partly because she felt such a clumsy nerd and partly because of the strange effect that his smile was having on her heart-rate. "Sorry," she gulped. Bianca would have been ready with a witty retort; she couldn't think of anything clever to say.

"No problem," he said. "Hang on, there's something under the seat."

"Hi, Nick! How was your first day? Down on your knees yet again, are you?"

Sinead looked up.

"Hi, Sinead – you OK?" It was Miss Clever-clogs Chloë muscling in again. Sinead, from her squatting position on the bus floor, took in Chloë's long, slender legs in their completely unblemished tights and funky leather clogs, and her hair that looked as if someone had just polished it to a perfect shine, and felt lumpy, boring and a mess.

"Oh, Chloë!" Nick scrambled to his feet, leaving three of Sinead's books and a tin of pencils under the seat. "Hang on – I need to talk to you!"

I bet you do, thought Sinead, grabbing the rest of her things and stuffing them back into her bag. "Thanks, Nick," she called hopefully to his disappearing back but he didn't hear. His mind was quite obviously on other things.

Well, stuff him. Stuff Chloë. Stuff everyone, Sinead thought, clomping upstairs after her friends.

"I'm coming shopping," she panted as she flopped down in the seat behind Abby and Bianca.

"Cool," said Abby. "Have you got cash?"

Sinead nodded. "Plenty," she affirmed.

"Oh good," grinned Bianca. "Let's retail."

"Say, Chloë, hang on a minute!" Nick grabbed the overhead rail as the bus lurched round a sharp corner.

He took a deep breath, swallowed and looked at a spot somewhere over Chloë's head. "I'm really sorry that I sounded off at you this morning," he said. "It was dumb of me."

Chloë's face broke into a broad grin, showing two rows of perfectly symmetrical, pure white teeth. "That's OK, don't worry about it," she said. "I have days when I could cheerfully kill anything that moves on the face of the planet. Oh, this is Jasmin, by the way – Jasmin, this is Nick."

Nick smiled at the petite black girl with huge dark eyes.

"So – I hear you're living in a hotel right now," chattered Chloë conversationally. "Which one?"

Nick's heart sank, his brain racing to think of the name of one local hotel that would do. "The Hilton," he muttered, praying that the city had one.

"Wow!" breathed Jasmin. "Very nice too."

"Great!" echoed Chloë. "Right next door to Granary Wharf – aren't the shops just to die for?"

Nick made a non-committal sort of noise deep down in his throat and made to move away up the bus.

"So is it your dad's job?"

"What?" He wheeled back round to face Chloë.

"Your dad's job – is that why you've moved to Leeds?"

Nick felt his features freeze. He stared at her. At Jasmin, whose eyes were fixed enquiringly on his face. Just say it. My dad's dead. Just tell them.

"Yeah, that's right."

"So what does he do?"

He couldn't stand it. He knew it was crazy but he was overcome by the same urge to run that had propelled him from Tommo's maths lesson that morning.

"This is my stop," he gabbled, grabbing his bag and beginning to shove his way to the front of the bus.

"Hey, Nick, not this one!" Chloë's voice followed him down the bus. "The Hilton's two more stops yet."

He ignored her shouts, jumped off the bus, kept his head down and started walking purposefully down the first sidestreet he saw.

He had already had more than he could take for one day.

"Ta-ra!" Jasmin threw open the café door. "This is it!"

"Wow! It's brilliant!" Chloë's gaze took in the snazzy decor, the figure-of-eight bar and the wrought iron balcony entwined with creeping ivy. From the ceiling hung wooden pallets loaded with all sorts of weird objects, from an ancient cricket bat to an antique doll's pram, and round the edge of the room, high-backed wooden alcoves hid discreet scrubbed tables adorned with funky candle-holders shaped like musical instruments.

"And there's the phone," added Jasmin, pointing to a small booth in the corner by the till. "I'll let you get on . . ."

"No, wait! I think perhaps . . ."

"Can I help . . . ? Oh, Jasmin, it's you!" An elegant black woman wearing a scarlet wrap-around skirt, black crochet tunic and a vast quantity of brightly coloured bangles emerged from a door at the far end of the room. As the door swung open, the sound of deep voices raised in heated debate echoed into the room.

"Hi, Mum! This is Chloë – she's in my class."

"How nice!" Jasmin's mother beamed at Chloë.

"Hi, Mrs Johnson – this place is so cool!"

"Cool it may be, full it certainly isn't!" grinned Josie with a shrug. "Want something to eat, girls?"

"Chloë's got this phone call to make," explained Jasmin. "That's why she's come. The phone box at the end of the road is broken."

"So make your call, and then we'll have cake," Josie cried expansively. "Dad's been experimenting with coconut and chocolate muffins."

"Scrummy!" said Chloë. "That'd be really nice, Mrs Johnson."

Jasmin's mother nodded and marched off in the direction of the kitchen.

"Shall we have the cake first?" suggested Chloë.

Jasmin eyed her closely. "You're chickening out!" she said accusingly.

"No, I'm not, it's just . . ."

"Just what? Oh, sorry – I get it, you want to whisper sweet nothings down the line. I'll disappear." Jasmin turned and headed towards the kitchen door.

"No, don't go!" Chloë pleaded. "I need moral support. Hang on, let me get the number."

She scrabbled in her bag and pulled out her purse. Opening it, she took out a sliver of paper the size of a fingernail.

"What is *that*?" asked Jasmin.

"His phone number," replied Chloë. "Well, not his exactly. I tore it out of a holiday brochure."

Jasmin frowned and cocked her head to one side. "A holiday brochure? Chloë, just who is this guy?"

Chloë sighed. "I met him on holiday," she explained. "We stayed at this apartment in Skiathos – it's part of this really swish sailing club . . ."

"Are you rich, then?" The question was completely matter-of-fact, as if Jasmin was asking whether Chloë ate cabbage.

Chloë shook her head. "Mum had to do a bit of work out there so we got the rest of the holiday pretty cheap," she said. "Anyway, Jack's an instructor there. Honestly, Jasmin, it was just like you read about: he looked at me and I looked at him and it was like there was no one else on the whole beach."

"And?" urged Jasmin.

"We just spent every spare moment we could with one another. We even had a whole night together . . ."

"Chloë!"

"Not that sort of whole night, silly, my mother would have gone ballistic!" exclaimed Chloë. "There was this all-night party, but we just sat out on the rocks and talked and held hands and watched the sun come up and . . ."

"Kissed?"

Chloë nodded. "I miss him so much," she sighed. "Only – well, he hasn't written and . . ."

"So get phoning," ordered Jasmin, picking up the receiver and handing it to Chloë. "You dial, I'll feed the coins in."

Chloë punched in the digits for the Skiathos Sailing Club and waited. And waited. And waited.

"They're not answering – yes, they are! Oh my God! What do I say? Jasmin!"

"How about 'Hello, may I speak to Jack, please?' "

"Hello? Hello?" Chloë glanced at Jasmin, pulling a face. "They're speaking Greek."

"You don't say?" teased Jasmin, ramming coins in the slot. "Funny that, considering they're in Greece."

"Hello? Please may I speak to Jack Kempton? Jack Kempton. K-E-M-P-T-O-N. Oh right. Thanks.

"They're getting someone who speaks English," she mouthed to Jasmin. "Oh, hi. May I speak to Jack Kempton, please? Out sailing? Oh. Well, can I leave a message? Thanks."

She covered the receiver again. "She's getting a pencil," she beamed at Jasmin.

"Oh hi. Yes, can you tell him Chloë phoned?" she shouted down the phone. "Chloë. His sister? Oh no, no, I'm not family. I'm his girlfriend."

Jasmin watched as Chloë's eyes suddenly narrowed and her mouth dropped open. "What do you mean?" she heard her gasp. "But, I don't understand . . ."

Jasmin could hear the voice at the other end of the phone rising to a crescendo and noticed Chloë's cheek flush a dull shade of red.

"But . . ."

There was the sound of a distant click, as Chloë stared open-mouthed at the phone.

"What happened?" Jasmin asked. "What did she say?"

Chloë blinked rapidly. "She said," she whispered, with a catch in her voice.

"Yes?"

"She said that I couldn't be his girlfriend."

"Why, for heaven's sake?"

"Because," she gulped, "she said that she is."

She didn't really want cake. She wanted to run away and hide, to burst into tears and shout and scream. To be anywhere but here, being introduced to Jasmin's family when her heart was breaking into a zillion little pieces.

"I really ought to be going," she ventured as Mrs Johnson shepherded the two of them out of the café and into the vast, steamy kitchen. In one corner a television was blaring and in another a huge dishwasher chugged away, making it necessary for Chloë to shout to make herself heard.

"Will your mother worry, dear?" enquired Mrs Johnson solicitously. "You could always phone her."

"It's OK, she's working," said Chloë before she realised she had just dispensed with her best excuse for escaping. "But I think . . ."

"No one leaves here with an empty stomach!" boomed a deep voice and a burly man in a scarlet waistcoat and pin-stripe trousers emerged from the walk-in larder carrying a huge platter of cakes.

Chloë prayed that no one had heard her gasp.

"This is Dad," Jasmin said, as Chloë willed herself not to stare at the pattern of pale, shiny scars on his glistening black skin.

"Hi, Mr Johnson," she said, fixing her eyes on the mound of cakes. "They look good." Keep talking, don't stare.

"Worth staying for, eh?" he laughed, his eyes not meeting her face. "Have a muffin."

Chloë smiled wanly. She didn't think she would ever eat again.

But she felt so sorry for him that she took one anyway.

"Harry Johnson's cooking is worth crossing continents for," interjected another equally stocky man wearing an even louder waistcoat and sporting at least four wobbling chins.

"And this," said Jasmin, "is Uncle Lou."

Chloë smiled weakly. She didn't frankly care who it was. Jack had got another girlfriend. Jack didn't love her any more.

"Now let's ask these two young things," grinned Jasmin's uncle. "We're trying to come up with some ideas to make this place the talk of the town, something to get the folks flocking in and spending big-time!"

"Even little time would be an improvement," muttered Jasmin's mother. "Maybe we've got it all wrong."

"But it's ace!" exclaimed Chloë, surfacing from her misery for a second and then plunging straight back into the slough of despond. "I mean, it would be great for parties and stuff."

For anyone who had a life worth celebrating, that is, she thought miserably.

"That's it!" exclaimed Jasmin's father. "Louis, I do believe she's cracked it!"

"How do you mean?"

"We throw a party – a huge, opening night party!" enthused Harry.

"But we're already open," protested Jasmin.

"That doesn't matter," her uncle replied. "That's the swanky way. Hotels do it all the time – they open for a few weeks and then have the celebration."

"It might work," said Jasmin's mother tentatively. "If we got the press to come and take pictures . . ."

". . . and I did lots of exotic food . . ."

". . . and we decorated the whole place with a theme . . ."

". . . like what?"

"I can't hear myself think!" protested Jasmin's dad. "Turn that wretched thing off." He gestured to the TV.

"No!" Jasmin's mother held up her hand. "I'm waiting to see that 'Penny Wise' programme in a bit – that Suzy Sanderson's one of the few people on TV worth watching – so down-to-earth and sensible."

"You should try living with her," muttered Chloë, whose stomach was tying itself in double reef-knots just thinking about what that girl had said, and how her mum had told her over and over again that holiday romances never lasted.

"What do you mean?" Jasmin stared at her. "You don't – Suzy *Sanderson*? It's not – is she . . . ?"

"Yes," sighed Chloë, "that's my mum."

The next five minutes went pretty much as they always did. After all the "well, fancy that"s and the protestations of undying loyalty to every programme her mother had ever made (and quite a few she had had no part in), she had to endure everyone telling her how like her mother she was and how silly they had all been not to realise sooner.

"So how come you're at a comprehensive school when your mum's a superstar?" asked Jasmin bluntly.

"Dad doesn't approve of private schools," said Chloë. "He says they don't teach you anything about the real world. And talking of Dad, he'll be home – I really must go. Thanks for the tea, Mrs Johnson."

She guessed afterwards that they must all have thought her rather rude, dashing off like that. But there was only so long that you could hold back tears and no way was she going to let any of them see her cry.

But once the front door had banged behind her and she was running, head down, towards The Wharfside, she let the tears fall. And once she had started, she couldn't stop.

"He wouldn't do a thing like that! He just wouldn't!" Nick slumped down on to a kitchen chair and put his head in his hands.

"Darling, I know it's painful but you did ask the question," sighed his mother. "Dad didn't leave any insurance. Or a pension. Or anything else, for that matter. He cashed the whole lot in when he was trying to make a go of the business."

"So why didn't you stop him? Why didn't you tell him it was crazy?"

"Oh, so it's my fault, is it?" Jenny Bowen gripped the edge of the kitchen sink until her knuckles turned white. "This morning you were accusing me of spending my whole life nagging your father, now you're complaining because I didn't. Well, I tell you why I didn't say anything. Because he did it all behind my back. He didn't have the guts to admit what was going on."

"Dad was the gutsiest person I know!" stormed Nick. "Dad built up that business from nothing and . . ."

"Dad built that business on a tissue of lies and deceit! He pretended that he was making money, when all the time he was losing it hand over fist!"

Nick's shoulders sagged. He didn't believe his mum; she was exaggerating, she had to be. She and Dad had argued a lot over the last few months. Now she was carrying it on even though he was dead.

"So what are we going to do?" he asked dully, knowing that if he carried on shouting he would burst into tears, and that would be unforgivable.

"Well," said his mother brightly, "I'm going to get a job and then we'll both start looking for a flat."

"A decent one?"

"Nick, it won't be Buckingham Palace, that's for sure," said his mother reasonably. "I can't imagine that I'm going to walk into the sort of job that pays for luxury. But it'll be a start."

She ruffled his hair and he jerked away.

"Now, tell me all about your first day at Lockbridge High," she said.

"There's nothing to tell," he shrugged.

"Oh, come on – you must have . . ."

"Mum!" Nick jumped up and headed for the door. "I went to school, I did lessons, I came home. OK?"

And I lied and I shouted at people and I made a complete mess of everything, he added silently in his head. I'm not normally like that. I just feel so angry, like I want to lash out at everything and everybody. Even Mum. Especially Mum.

He clomped up the narrow stairs, pushed open the door of his poky little bedroom with its Sixties floral wallpaper and ghastly green candlewick bedspread and threw himself face down on the bed.

"What did you have to go and die for, Dad?" he muttered, beating the pillow with his fist. "How could you? How could leave me?"

And then, because it was the end of a very long day and because he had never felt more alone in his life, Nick stopped trying to be strong and began to cry like a very small boy.

"I'm wiped out!" Sinead tipped her purse upside-down to prove her depleted financial state to her friends. "I must go."

"Thanks for lending me the tenner," said Abby. "I will pay you back, honestly."

"Me, too," added Bianca. "Seven pounds fifty, wasn't it?"

"Don't worry about it," replied Sinead airily. "Call it a present."

"Really?" Abby and Bianca's eyes widened in unison.

"Of course," affirmed Sinead. "Must dash. See you tomorrow."

Had she not been in such a rush to catch the bus, she might have turned round and seen her two friends giving one another the thumbs-up sign.

In the five minutes it had taken Chloë to walk from The Canal Café to The Wharfside she had gone over and over in her mind every word the girl on the end of the telephone had uttered. There hadn't been many.

"I don't think so!" and "I'm his girlfriend!"

And then the sound of muffled giggles.

It couldn't be true. Jack had told her that he'd had other girls in the past and, of course, she knew he must have done – he was nineteen, for heaven's sake. But he had sworn that none of them had meant a thing compared to her, and that now he knew what real love was he wouldn't look at anyone else. What was she going to tell Nat and Becky? She'd spent half of history sending them notes, telling them that she and Jack were an item, that this was the real thing.

"Does he phone every day?" Nat had asked during PE. "Sam can't leave me alone."

"Not every day," Chloë had replied. "Greece is a long way away. But most days."

"Is he really fit?" Becky had demanded.

"Amazing," Chloë had concurred. "I'll bring my photographs."

And now – but then again, she didn't have to tell them. She could pretend that everything was hunky-dory, not let on that her whole life was in ruins.

She turned the corner into the forecourt of The Wharfside and brushed a hand across her eyes. Her dad's BMW was standing in its designated parking space which meant his meeting was over and he would be up in the flat. If he saw that she had been crying, he'd start asking questions and all she wanted was to shut herself in her bedroom and never talk to anyone ever again.

"Oh, excuse me, you must be Zoë!" A large woman with short,

brown, bobbed hair and an old-fashioned fringe bustled up to her, wringing her hands.

"Chloë," said Chloë, looking straight ahead and not slackening her pace.

"Oh yes, dear, sorry. Look, I don't suppose you know where she is, do you?"

What is this woman on? thought Chloë, eyeing with some amazement her bright blue jumper across which galloped three Lurex panthers, and wondering why she had chosen to team it with a red pleated skirt and fur-trimmed bedroom slippers.

"Er – who?"

"Sinead, dear," said the woman.

"*Sinead*?" gasped Chloë, stopping still in surprise.

"Oh dear, I haven't introduced myself, have I? I've met your dear mother, of course, such a thrill – lovely lady, isn't she? I'm Kathleen Flaherty, Sinead's mother. We've just moved into flat four, so lovely for you and Sinead, isn't it?"

Chloë's mouth dropped open. She couldn't believe it. It was Sinead that her mum had seen that morning. Sinead Flaherty living here. One floor below them. As nightmares went, this one ranked X-certificate. After that little misunderstanding the term before, she knew that Sinead really had it in for her.

"Only I'm a bit worried, you see – Erin, that's my youngest, she's been home for ages, and Sinead should have been with her. But then – I say, dear, are you all right?"

"Fine," replied Chloë, rather more abruptly than she meant to.

"I saw Sinead with this new boy . . ."

"Boy?" Mrs Flaherty looked as worried as if Chloë had announced that Sinead was last seen being airlifted into a spaceship by a group of aliens.

"Yes, Nick . . ."

"Nick? Where? When?"

"On the bus. Coming home."

"Doing what exactly?"

"Just talking," Chloë said hastily, staggered to find that there was someone even more neurotic about the opposite sex than her own mother. "Oh, and then she got off at the Corn Exchange with Abby and Bianca."

"Abby and Bianca?"

"Yes." Why, wondered Chloë in exasperation, does she need to repeat every word I say? What does it matter anyway? What does anything matter now Jack has deserted me?

Mrs Flaherty pulled back her shoulders and pursed her lips. "Oh, she did, did she? And never a thought to telephone me. I'll be having words with that young lady. As I was saying to Sinead this morning, never mind that Bianca, it's people like Chloë that you should be spending time with, now we are coming up in the world."

Oh terrific, thought Chloë. Make Sinead hate me all the more, why don't you? And what was all this about coming up in the world? She didn't mean to be a snob, but frankly the Flahertys weren't the type of people you associated with The Wharfside; Chloë knew that they used to live on the Burnthedge estate, which was hardly the most affluent area of Leeds. Perhaps they had won the Lottery.

She began edging nearer to the door, but Mrs Flaherty was now in full flood. "You must come and have supper one evening, dear," she enthused. "Sinead would love that."

Any need to comment on such a ridiculous suggestion was prevented by the sight of Sinead hurtling round the corner, carrier bags banging against her legs.

"There she is!" said Chloë. "I must go . . ."

"And just where, young lady, have you been?" demanded Mrs Flaherty. "And don't try lying because Chloë here has already told me. You've been with those no-good friends of yours, haven't you?"

Sinead threw Chloë the sort of look that kills at twenty paces.

"Well?" Mrs Flaherty placed her hands firmly on her hips. And in that moment, seeing her cheeks flush with embarrassment, Chloë knew that Sinead would never cope with this alone.

"Oh gosh, Mrs Flaherty, I am *so* sorry!" Chloë fixed a look of abject despair on her face. "I completely forgot – Sinead asked me to tell you that she would be late, only I had to go somewhere on the way home and it totally slipped my mind!"

Sinead's eyes widened in astonishment.

Mrs Flaherty's forehead creased in a frown. "But why didn't you say, dear, when I first asked you about . . . ?"

Chloë's mind went into overdrive. Then she remembered Mrs Flaherty asking her if everything was OK. She dropped her eyes and bit her lip in what she hoped was a heart-rending manner.

"I'm sorry," she whispered. "I've got a few things on my mind and . . ." She paused, remembering her mother's phrase about timing being everything in the creation of dramatic effect.

"That's all right, dear," said Mrs Flaherty soothingly. "Sinead should have phoned me herself, not imposed on your good nature. Still, no harm done, I suppose."

Sinead and Chloë exhaled in relief at precisely the same moment.

"What I want to know is this," began Mrs Flaherty.

"I must dash," said Chloë firmly, pushing open the double doors and heading for the stairs. She was not about to get embroiled in another interrogation. She had done her bit.

"Such a nice girl," she heard Sinead's mother croon as she rounded the bend in the stairs. "And now we're living here, I am sure that you two will become the very best of friends."

There was, thought Chloë, as she reached her front door, no limit to some people's optimism.

"Do I *have* to be there?"

Sanjay looked up from his computer screen in annoyance. He was just getting this graphic right, another half-hour and he'd have cracked it.

"Of course you have to be there!" retorted his father as Sanjay turned the screen out of his field of vision. "It's a wonderful opportunity for you to meet two of America's leading academics. I'm sure you'll find them most stimulating."

"I've got loads of homework, Dad." Sanjay tried the studious son approach in the hope of getting out of this tedious dinner party.

"Well, I suppose if you really *are* hard-pressed . . ." His father walked round behind Sanjay and peered at the screen.

And frowned.

"What is this?"

"Just stuff."

"Stuff?"

"I was just messing around." Sanjay began closing down the programme.

His father eyed him severely. "So much for loads of homework," he intoned. "Sanjay, this is your GCSE year. You don't 'mess around' as you put it, in your GCSE year."

Or in any other year in this family, thought Sanjay as his father disappeared on to the landing. Sometimes he wished he was like Rani – which was a terrible thing to think, and he knew he didn't mean it. But no one expected anything of Rani; her smallest achievement made them happy. They let her be herself. And she was happy.

He wasn't. He paused, his hand hovering on the mouse. It was true. He wasn't happy. He felt alone. It wasn't a new feeling but somehow it bothered him more than it ever had before. He was quite sure that no one else at Lockbridge High would be spending the evening talking to a pair of dry and dusty professors; no one else would pass the next few hours pretending to be something they weren't.

Except Nick, he thought suddenly and with some surprise.

Sanjay was sure Nick was pretending. He wasn't quite sure what about – but one thing was clear, Nick wasn't happy and it wasn't just first-day nerves. He smiled at everyone and said all the right things, but it was as if his real self was locked deep inside him and all you got to see was a kind of plastic image. Bit like me, really, thought Sanjay.

Which was stupid. Of course Nick Bowen was nothing like him. Nick was tall and athletic and sophisticated. Nick probably knew exactly where he was going in life and how to get there. Nick would have a whole clutch of friends by the end of the week.

And, for some extraordinary reason, Sanjay wished more than anything that he could be one of them.

"Sanjay! Come and help Rani lay the table, there's a love!" His mother's voice echoed from the kitchen. Pushing all thoughts of Nick from his mind, Sanjay switched off the computer and crossed the hallway to the dining-room.

"Where do the spoons go?" Rani's round, smiling face looked adoringly across at him. "I'm muddled. Again."

Sanjay grinned. "You're doing fine," he said. "Let me show you."

"You're very clever," stated Rani with conviction. "I wish I was like you."

"No," said Sanjay. "You're just lovely as you are."

CHAPTER 10

CLOUDS
gather

"**A**re you all right, Dad?"

Chloë realised even as she said it that it was a pretty dumb question. Clearly her father was far from all right. When she had arrived home from school he had been in the study talking – no, shouting – on the telephone and for the last half-hour he had been slumped in an armchair, chin resting on his hand, staring into space.

"What? Yes, I'm fine. Fine."

"Meeting go well?"

"As it happens, no. Any more questions?"

"Sorry. I'll make some tea."

"Yes, that would be nice. Sorry, darling – just had a tough day. Take no notice of your moody old dad."

Chloë smiled and sighed with relief. It was OK. He'd be fine.

She was heading for the kitchen when she heard a key in the front door.

"Darlings! I'm back!"

On a cloud of Allure perfume, Suzy swept into the sitting-room, carrier bags rustling.

"I just have to tell you both what's happened. I can't believe it myself. I keep thinking I'm dreaming!"

Chloë's glance went from her mother's animated face to her father, still sitting motionless in the chair, hardly responding to Suzy's obvious excitement.

"Tea, Mum?" She tried to catch her mother's eye, to give her some kind of non-verbal warning about her dad's mood.

"Tea? Good gracious, after what I've got to tell you it'll be champagne all round."

Suzy flung her shoulder bag on to the sofa and perched on the arm. "Just listen to this. They've given me 'The Breakfast Break'! Me! Karl called me in and told me this afternoon. I'm going to be doing the breakfast show!"

Chloë's eyes widened. 'The Breakfast Break' went out five days a week; it was one of Pennine TV's highest profile shows. "Wow, Mum! That's amazing!" Chloë gave her a bear hug. "Dad, isn't that great news?"

Edward Sanderson turned and looked at his wife. Slowly he stood up.

"Bloody wonderful!" he said. And walked out of the room.

"How could I have forgotten? How could I have been so selfish?"

Suzy Sanderson ran her fingers despairingly through her hair. "I'd been thinking about that meeting of his all morning, but then when Karl told me the news, it just went out of my mind."

"I don't think it went very well." Chloë poured out a cup of tea and handed it to her mother. "He's hardly said a word since I got home."

"I'll go up to him," said Suzy, pushing back her chair and taking a gulp of tea.

"No, don't!" Chloë caught her mother's eye and then looked away. "I mean, why don't you leave him be? He'll calm down and then you can talk about it."

"I can't just leave it," protested Suzy. "I'll take him a cup of tea."

"No need – I'll have it here." Edward appeared at the kitchen door, his jacket slung loosely over his left shoulder.

"Darling, I'm so sorry!" Suzy crossed to the door and planted a kiss on his cheek. "How did it go? Was it too awful? Didn't they buy?"

"No, they didn't buy. They didn't even take an option on it. But still, what does it matter? We have one successful superstar in the house – who needs two?"

Chloë swallowed. Her father was smiling but his voice had a bitter edge to it and the knuckles of his right hand were white as he gripped the mug of tea.

"Edward, dear, I'm sure someone else will want it – the scripts are brilliant. So funny. And I don't remember anyone ever doing a sitcom about skiing instructors before."

She patted his arm. "Tell you what, I'll have a word with Dickon Leadbetter. He's the new Head of Comedy at the Beeb, you know.

Nice guy – he owes me a favour or two and . . ."

"Terrific!" Edward slammed the mug of tea on to the table with such force that brown liquid splashed all over the checked tablecloth. "So now I'm dependent on my oh-so-famous wife's cronies for work, am I? Well forget it!"

He shrugged his arms into his jacket and turned away.

"Darling, I didn't mean it like that, I was just trying to . . . where are you going?"

"Out," said Edward.

As the front door slammed, Chloë and her mother stared at one another.

They said nothing.

There was nothing to say.

Sanjay was bored stiff. He had sat through this interminable meal, listening to his father droning on about the latest research into linguistic development in the Amazon basin, wishing he could be at his computer doing something interesting. Rani had been excused hours ago, because her attention span was limited and besides, she had been half asleep. Even his mum looked weary and distracted, as if her mind was miles away from the intellectual repartee at the opposite end of the table.

Sanjay was just about to plead pressure of homework and flee to his bedroom, when his father turned to him. "Now, Sanjay, tell our visitors of your plans for the future," he said, dabbing his mouth with his napkin and leaning back in his chair.

"What?"

His father's face clouded slightly. "Your plans, Sanjay."

To create fantasies, wonderful animated cartoons, virtual reality games, learning aids for special needs children . . .

"Cambridge to read law, I guess," he said dully.

"Great stuff!" exclaimed one of the visitors.

"Yes indeed!" agreed the other.

"And then we thought Harvard," added Duncan.

"Or Yale," corrected his mother, ever mindful that their guests were from that university.

"And what branch of the law are you most interested in, Sanjay?" enquired the older of the two professors.

"I haven't thought," replied Sanjay, without meeting his gaze. "If you'll excuse me, I have homework."

"But Sanjay, the cheese . . ."

Stuff the cheese, thought Sanjay. Stuff law. Stuff everything.

CHAPTER 11

Lows and
HIGHS

Chloë yawned and jammed the top back on her pen. That would have to do. It wasn't the best essay she had ever written but she was too tired to care.

From downstairs she could hear the low murmur of her parents' voices. Her father had been out all evening, but an hour before the front door had slammed and she'd heard him calling out to her mother.

"For pity's sake, don't you think I need a bit of peace!"

Chloë was pulling her nightshirt over her head as the sound of her father's raised voice caused her to start.

And then there was a crash. And a stifled cry.

Chloë's heart began to race. Another crash. She pulled open the bedroom door and stood, frozen, at the top of the stairs.

"Don't! Edward, please!"

Her mother's voice this time, high and brittle.

Chloë ran down the spiral staircase, her legs shaking and her mouth dry of saliva.

A chair lay on its side in the middle of the room. Books were strewn all over the floor.

Her father was standing over the sofa; her mother lying, eyes wide with fear, cowering under his shadow against the cushions.

"For the last time," her father was shouting, "I don't want journalists telephoning at all hours and cameramen draping you over the sofas to take Suzy-At-Home pictures – get it?"

"Fine, darling, I'll tell them . . ."

Edward gripped Suzy's wrists in his hands and pressed his face almost on top of hers. "Just remember that this is my home too, will you? Of course, I realise that you *pay* for most of it, seeing as you are the high-earning superstar . . ."

He pushed her head against the back of the sofa.

Chloë had cried out before she realised it. At the sound of her voice, her father wheeled round.

"Leave her!" Chloë's voice was a broken sob. "Leave her alone!"

Her father stared at her. Chloë stared back. It was her father who dropped his eyes first.

"I'm leaving," he said and stormed out of the room and through the hall.

The front door slammed shut.

"Mum, are you OK? He didn't . . . ?"

Suzy stood up, held her hands to her face for a moment and then smiled. "It's OK, darling, it's absolutely fine," she said, her voice wavering slightly. "Just a silly disagreement – and really, all my fault. So silly of me."

She smoothed her skirt and took a deep breath. "Now, how about a nice cup of tea before bed?"

Chloë nodded. "OK," she said. "That would be nice."

But she knew that all the cups of tea in the world were not going to sort out the problem her mother still refused to face.

Nick lay in bed, hands clasped behind his head, staring at the ceiling. What was he going to do? He couldn't go on evading questions for ever; sooner or later everyone would find out that he'd been lying and then they would all think he was a complete jerk.

He rolled over on to his stomach and pummelled the pillow. Why couldn't he just say it like it was? "My dad's dead." It wasn't as if he had to tell them his father had cheated and deceived them and . . .

"Stop it!" He was just so shocked by his own thoughts that he spoke aloud. How could he even think that? How could he be so disloyal to his own father? Mum might try to make him believe that Dad had messed up big-time, but he knew differently.

But the money had all gone. And letters were still arriving from people who said that Greg Bowen owed them money.

But then, that sort of thing happened in business all the time, didn't it? Speculate to accumulate, that's what Dad used to say you had to do.

Dad had just died at the wrong moment. It would all have worked out fine if only he had lived.

But he hadn't.

And one day, Nick was going to have to tell the truth.

But not yet.

Please. Not yet.

Jasmin switched off her bedside light and smiled into the darkness. She was pretty sure her plan would work. What she wasn't quite so sure about was whether it was really fair. But if it meant that she and Chloë could get to be real friends, it was worth it.

When Faith had challenged her about being friends with Chloë she'd said they were just talking about homework. She knew Faith and Shelley had a problem with Chloë. But Jasmin really liked her. She would never have dreamed that someone as sophisticated and cool as Chloë would get talking to someone like Jasmin. Which, of course, she wouldn't have done had it not been for the drama over the phone call. She just needed a bit more time, so that they could get to know one another really properly and then she was sure they could be mates.

And she thought she knew just how to make that happen. She couldn't wait for the morning. Then she could put the first part of her plan into action.

The second part might take just a little longer.

It didn't make any sense. Sinead kicked off her duvet and stifled a yawn. Only last term Chloë Sanderson had dropped her right in it with Mrs Braithwaite and here she was today, lying to get her out of a fix. What was more, it had worked. By the time her mum had gone on and on about what a lovely girl Chloë was and wouldn't it be nice to invite the Sandersons in for a sherry, she seemed to have forgotten all about Sinead's shopping expedition.

But why would Chloë suddenly start caring whether Sinead got into trouble? She had been pretty cool, spinning that story about forgetting the message. But then cool was Chloë's middle name, which was why Sinead had envied her for so long. She was everything that Sinead wanted to be – tall, slim, clever, sophisticated, the sort of person who never spilled drinks down themselves at parties or dropped bags of books all over the bus. There had been a time, back in Year Eight, when she had thought it would be nice if they could be friends. But she had soon realised what a dumb idea that was – Chloë's mum was famous, her family were rich . . .

But we're rich now, thought Sinead with a start. We're living in exactly the same sort of apartment as the Sandersons. Dad's giving me a big allowance every month. There's no difference any more between me and Chloë.

But there was. She knew there was. And she was very much afraid that there always would be.

CHAPTER 12

BUILDING
bridges

"Darling, you must get going – you'll miss the bus!" Suzy Sanderson bundled Chloë towards the front door and gave her a quick hug.

"Will you be all right? What about Dad?"

Chloë's father was still asleep upstairs. It had been two in the morning when she had heard him plodding up the stairs but thankfully, even though she had lain awake straining her ears for another half-hour, there hadn't been a sound from her parents' bedroom.

"I'll be fine, sweetheart!" Her mother smiled confidently and gave her hand a squeeze. "You worry too much."

There was, thought Chloë, as she clattered down the stairs and through the foyer, plenty to worry about. She knew the warning signs; she had seen them enough times not to ignore them. Her mother was making light of things, but that was what she always did. Until it was too late.

"OK, so don't talk to me, then!"

Chloë turned with a start to find a breathless Sinead at her elbow. She was wearing purple eyeliner which gave her a very surprised expression and had all her school books in a wicked silver crochet bag which would have been more suited to a ballroom than a city pavement.

"Sorry – I was miles away."

"I gathered," said Sinead, as they turned the corner on to the waterfront. "I called you three times. Anyway, I just wanted to say – well, why did you do it?"

"Do what?" Chloë's mind was still on her parents.

"Cover up for me last night – pretend I'd given you a message," persisted Sinead. "I mean, we don't even speak to one another."

"Well, we are now," said Chloë reasonably. "Besides, I know what parents can be like. I thought that if I said it was my fault, you'd be off the hook with your mum. She was hardly likely to blow her top with me, was she?"

Sinead shook her head and frowned. "But I thought you'd be pleased to see me in trouble. After all, last term . . ."

"Look," said Chloë with a sigh. "Can't we settle this once and for all? I never meant to land you in it. We had fire drill, Mrs Braithwaite got her knickers in a twist because you and Bianca were missing and I said – without thinking, I admit – that I'd seen you both heading out of the school gates half an hour before."

"And we got hauled up before the headmaster and threatened with suspension," continued Sinead, as they turned into Millers

Lane. "If my mum had ever found out, she would have killed me."

Sinead eyed Chloë carefully. "And don't you go telling her!"

"Oh come off it," protested Chloë. "I'm hardly likely to, am I? Look, I never meant to get you into trouble, honestly I didn't."

Sinead smiled and the dimple in her chin deepened. "I guess not," she agreed. "I suppose I asked for it anyway – but Bianca had been going on and on about how she reckoned I would turn all stuffy and stuck-up just because we had come into money . . ."

"I thought you must have," said Chloë conversationally as they crossed into Sparrow Street and headed for the bus stop. "You used to live in Burnthedge, didn't you?"

"So what if I did?" snapped Sinead, her blue eyes flashing with indignation. "I suppose you think that just because we got money from someone dying and aren't all grand like your family, we don't have the right to live somewhere posh?"

"Hang on, I never said that," protested Chloë.

"Yes, well, just because your family are so stuck-up . . ."

"Oh thanks!"

"Well, it's true – when my dad said hello to yours on the stairs last night, he didn't even get a reply."

Chloë's mind raced. "Oh, that would be because he'd – er, just had some really bad news about a colleague of his. He was going to the hospital to see him."

"Really? Oh, gosh, sorry."

Chloë didn't like to lie, but there were times when there was simply no alternative.

At least I'll keep fit this way, thought Nick, panting slightly as he rounded the corner and saw the Hilton hotel loom into view. This way, he wouldn't have to face up to any more questions for a bit. He had told his mum that he was missing his cross-country running and needed some early-morning exercise. By jogging to the hotel and catching the bus from there, his alibi was safe for a little longer.

He knew it was crazy, but he couldn't help it. The longer he could keep people at arm's length, the better he would like it.

"Chloë! Hey, wait!"

At the sound of pounding footsteps Chloë turned to find Jasmin running up the road behind her.

"Listen, I've been thinking," Jasmin gabbled at once, clasping her chest and panting for breath. "You know what that girl said on the telephone?"

Chloë glanced at Sinead and hurriedly pulled a face at Jasmin. She didn't want her disastrous love life to become common knowledge throughout the whole of Year Eleven. Jasmin, it appeared, was not in the business of taking hints.

"Well, I reckon that she could have made the whole thing up. She probably isn't his girlfriend at all."

"What? Who?" Sinead's face had brightened with interest.

"Oh, hi Sinead," said Jasmin, dumping her bag on the pavement as they reached the bus stop. "Well, you see, Chloë's got this guy she really fancies . . ."

"What guy?" Sinead demanded instantly.

"Here comes the bus," gabbled Chloë.

". . . only Chloë thinks he's got someone else because when she telephoned him, this girl answered and when Chloë said she was his girlfriend, this girl said that she couldn't be because she was."

"Is it me or are you talking gibberish?" demanded Sinead, pushing her way on to the bus.

"No, listen, there's this to-die-for guy . . ."

"I don't want to listen," said Sinead. "Have your girly-girly talks on your own." And with that she stomped up the stairs, leaving Jasmin and Chloë looking after her in amazement.

"What's up with her?" asked Chloë.

Jasmin shrugged. "Search me," she said. "Now, about your love life . . ."

Chloë fancies Nick, thought Sinead, staring miserably out of the bus window. It has to be him, the way she was hanging around him yesterday. And of course, he's bound to fancy her back, all the guys do.

I wish I could get a boyfriend.

Everyone else manages it.

I wish it was me Nick chased after.

What's wrong with me?

Chloë had four different lessons that morning, but she couldn't remember one word from any of them. Could Jasmin have been right? Could that girl have just been pretending to be Jack's girlfriend, putting off Chloë in order to clear the way for herself?

And if so, what should she do about it?

"Phone again," declared Jasmin at lunch-time. "Only this time pretend to be some aged aunt or something."

"What if he doesn't have an aunt?" reasoned Chloë.

"Don't make difficulties," said Jasmin. "Think positive. We'll try again tonight."

CHAPTER 13

SCHEMES
and strategies

They tried every night that week. The first time the line was constantly engaged, the second time no one answered. The third time they got a Greek man who sounded as if he had been partying on retsina all night and didn't understand a word they were saying, and the fourth time they were told that Jack Kempton was away flotilla sailing and wouldn't be back for ten days. Before Chloë had time to leave a message, the line had gone dead.

It would have been bad enough if that had been the only thing she had to worry about but it wasn't. Her dad was in one of his really black moods. They could last for days, weeks sometimes, and she knew that more often than not they ended the same way.

But it would be all right this time. Her mum said they had talked and talked and Dad was fine really, just overworked and stressed and in need of a lot of understanding. So Chloë had been extra polite, and kept her music really quiet and even vacuumed her bedroom without being asked because the one thing her father couldn't stand was a mess.

And every morning she waited for the post and every evening she hurtled home in the hope that a letter had arrived by second delivery.

It never had.

She wondered how long it took to die of a broken heart.

Nick had a rather better week. He had timed his morning jog so that he reached the Hilton bus stop within a minute of the bus arriving, and in the evenings he simply got off at the hotel, walked into the foyer in case anyone was watching, turned round and jogged home. It was very time-consuming and utterly boring, but it had the desired effect and kept everyone off his back.

By Friday, Nick had lost four pounds and Sinead was grounded.

"It's not fair!" she ranted at her mother. "Just because I was ten minutes late home . . ."

"Thirty minutes, and at ten o'clock at night!" retorted her mother. "I won't have you hanging round street corners with that Abby girl – it's dangerous, it's not seemly . . ."

"You don't want me to have a life!" stormed Sinead. "Abby's mum doesn't mind!"

"That says it all," began her mother.

"Oh typical! And we weren't hanging around, we were . . ."

She paused. Telling her mother that they'd talked their way into Ritzy's even though it was an over-eighteen disco might not be wise.

"Can't I have a second chance?" she pleaded.

"No," said her mother.

"I hate you," said Sinead.

"I dare say," said her mother.

If the thunderstorm on Monday had never happened, Nick might have got away with lying for a whole lot longer.

But when school finished the rain was pouring down in stair rods, lightning was flashing every few minutes and the thunder crashed overhead. Everyone tore to the buses, raincoats over their heads, feet splashing through the puddles in the school yard.

"I'm leaving my bike and getting the bus," Sanjay told Nick as they peered out at the indigo sky. "I'll get soaked if I try to cycle."

Even then, Nick didn't worry. He would just carry out his usual routine and no one would be any the wiser.

But when the bus pulled up at the Hilton and he stood up to grab his bag, Sanjay got up too.

"This isn't your stop, is it?" Nick sounded anxious. "You don't live round here."

"Over the bridge, in Avenue Mansions," said Sanjay, gesturing across the canal to a 1930s block of flats with green balconies and mock shutters at the windows. "I can cut across the footbridge and along the towpath. It'll save time."

As the bus pulled away from the stop, the rain seemed to be lessening slightly. Nick hovered at Sanjay's side. "Well, see you then," he said, not moving.

"Right. See you then, and don't forget . . ."

"Nick! Darling! Over here!"

Nick and Sanjay turned. Dodging the traffic in the middle of the road and waving her arms excitedly was Nick's mum.

"There you are! Thank goodness!" she panted as she stepped up on to the kerb. "I thought you couldn't possibly jog in this weather but then I thought, knowing Nick, he'll keep at it, so I brought a waterproof for you to jog in and . . ."

"*Mum!*"

"I know, fussy mother – oh, and you're with a friend. And this is . . . ?"

"Sanjay, and he's just leaving," grunted Nick.

"Nice to meet you, Sanjay," smiled Jenny. "What a day! Would you like to come back for a cup of tea? It's only a ten-minute walk, down past the . . ."

"Sanjay's in a terrible rush," interrupted Nick, conscious of the boy's wide-eyed expression of surprise.

"Me? Oh yes. Right. Fine. See you, Nick!"

With relief Nick watched as Sanjay slung his schoolbag over his shoulder and strode off down the road. "What did you have to go and do that for, Mum!" he exploded. "Making me look a right idiot like that?"

"Nick! What did I do?"

Blew my cover, that's what you did, thought Nick in despair. Now everyone is going to know that I lied. I'll be a complete laughing-stock.

"Nick?"

"Nothing. It doesn't matter."

Nothing mattered any more.

"Hi, honeybunch!" Jasmin's dad grinned at her as she shook her umbrella and slammed the café door. "You wait till you see what I've got!"

"Let me guess," said Jasmin. "A new deep-fat fryer, a waffle maker, some weird gadget for making patterns on puddings?"

Her dad laughed. "Much more exciting. Come and see."

And what Jasmin saw gave her the best idea she had had in ages.

An idea she felt certain would solve Chloë's problems once and for all.

Nick stood at the window, staring out at the darkness. He couldn't sleep. All he could think of was Sanjay's astonished expression when Nick's mum invited him home for tea. What was he going to do? How was he going to face everyone tomorrow?

It was pretty obvious that Sanjay would tell them all that he had lied about the hotel, and they would think he was a complete jerk. He would have to face more questions and admit that it wasn't true that they had moved to Leeds because of his father's job. He could just imagine the sniggering that would go on behind his back.

Why had his mum been such an idiot? But even as he thought it, he knew he was being unfair. He was the idiot, no one else. An idiot for pretending, for supposing that he could keep this farce going.

He'd have to tell the truth. Tomorrow. Just thinking about it made him feel sick.

"Only three more stops!" Sanjay turned and grinned at Rani as the bus swung round a sharp bend the following morning. Usually one of his parents dropped her off at school, but as Sanjay's bike was still at school and his dad was engrossed in writing a speech for the faculty dinner, he had offered to take her. He didn't mind; it meant getting off the bus one stop early and walking the rest of the way to Lockbridge High, which gave him time to think.

"Sanjay? Is this seat free?"

Nick tapped him on the shoulder and gestured to the vacant space next to them.

"Yes, sure." Sanjay thought that Nick looked even more ill-at-ease than he had done the afternoon before. "You OK?"

"Fine," said Nick dully.

"Who's that?" Rani, inquisitive as ever, demanded.

"This is a friend of mine, Rani. His name is Nick."

Rani's face broke into a broad grin.

"This is my sister," began Sanjay nervously and then cringed as Rani opened her arms and enveloped Nick in a hug.

"Hi, Rani," replied Nick with a smile. "It's good to meet you. That's a great necklace you are wearing."

"Mine," nodded Rani, fingering the plastic beads with pride.

"Very smart," grinned Nick.

Sanjay looked at him gratefully. "Sorry," he said. "She gets a bit eager at times. Oh, we get off here – I'm dropping her at her school."

Nick stood up to let them pass. "Can I walk the rest of the way with you?" he asked suddenly. "Do you mind?"

Sanjay opened his mouth to make some excuse. "Sure," he heard himself say, "that would be cool."

"That was really nice of you," said Sanjay, as they watched Rani running over to her teacher. "You know, the way you chatted to her. Some people try to ignore her – Down's syndrome scares them. She'll be your friend for life now," he added with a chuckle.

Nick sighed. "Which is more than most people will be," he said. "I've been a total idiot."

"The hotel?" queried Sanjay, as they began walking along the road towards school.

"You guessed." It was a statement, not a question. "I shouldn't have said that I was staying there – it was so stupid. What are people going to think?"

"Oh, don't worry, I'll tell them I made a mistake. They'll believe that," Sanjay said with a wry grin.

"That's really nice," said Nick, "but it won't help because I said the same thing to Chloë. And I said that we had moved because of my dad's job, which wasn't true either . . ."

"It wasn't?"

"No." Nick looked straight ahead of him and swallowed. "My dad's dead."

For a moment, Sanjay said nothing. He glanced at Nick and

realised that his eyes were full of tears.

"That's hard," he said finally. "No wonder you didn't want to put it into words."

Nick turned and looked at Sanjay with something bordering on respect. "That was it," he said slowly, as they turned the corner by the school playing-field. "Thinking about it is bad enough, but to have to talk about it, answer people's questions – that just freaks me out."

"I'll tell Chloë if you like and say that you want to be left alone."

"No, it's OK," said Nick hurriedly. "I'll tell her."

"You do fancy her," smiled Sanjay. "I thought as much."

Nick shrugged. "I guess normally I might," he admitted. "Right now, though, getting through each day is enough without bothering about chat-up lines."

Sanjay nodded sympathetically. "So where *do* you live?" he began, and then pulled a face. "Sorry, I'm doing it now – bombarding you with questions."

"It's OK, I don't mind you asking things."

"You don't?"

Nick shook his head. "No, you're a mate. It's different."

Sanjay fell silent, not because there weren't a thousand questions he wanted to ask but because it had been so long since anyone had told him he was their mate. And he didn't want to do anything to make Nick change his mind.

"I can't believe we're doing this!" Chloë exclaimed that afternoon, as she followed Jasmin up the stairs and into the cramped little office at the back of the Johnsons' apartment. "Are you sure it will work?"

"We won't know until we try," replied Jasmin philosophically. "Now just sit there while I log on to the server."

Chloë perched on a stool. It had been a weird day. She'd been feeling miserable and lonely – she was avoiding Natalie and Becky because she just couldn't bear listening to them talking about their wonderful boyfriends. And she'd thought that Jasmin wasn't that interested – when Chloë had suggested going out one evening Jasmin had been really off with her. But then today Jasmin had come up with the idea that no one was giving Jack her messages, and she had also worked out a solution to the problem.

"E-mail," she had said that morning on the bus. "That's what you need."

Chloë had frowned. "We haven't got it," she had said. "We're not very technologically aware in our family."

"But we are," Jasmin had grinned. "Dad got wired up with all the gear yesterday, and that's when I got the idea. E-mail, Internet, you name it, we've got it. I was up till one o'clock this morning, playing round – it's really addictive, that stuff."

Chloë had been impressed.

"Come round after school and I'll show you how," Jasmin had urged her. "You have got an e-mail address for this club place, haven't you?"

Which, of course, she hadn't. But Jasmin was not easily put off. The very instant the afternoon bell had rung, she had dragged Chloë off into town, marched into the first travel agency they came across and hunted through all the brochures on Greece.

"Got it!" she had cried ecstatically, causing several heads to turn, "reserv@sailclub.skiathos.co.gr." She scribbled the address on a piece of paper.

"Right! Let's go."

As they had hurried through the streets and past the Hilton hotel on their way to The Canal Café, Jasmin had nudged Chloë. "Nick's family must have oodles of money to be able to stay somewhere as plush as that, mustn't they?"

Chloë had hesitated. "Look, don't go telling everyone, but they're not staying there. Nick made it up."

"What on earth for?"

"His dad died recently and they're living with his grandmother – he told me today," Chloë had said. "I get the feeling there's more to it than that, but I didn't like to ask too much."

"Poor guy," Jasmin had sighed. "When my dad got attacked we thought, just for a bit, that he might die. It was awful."

"Is that where his scars come from?" Chloë had asked.

Jasmin had nodded. "That's why we moved, London had too many awful memories. But you don't forget just by moving. Something like that stays in your mind."

Tell me about it, thought Chloë now, watching with admiration as Jasmin expertly logged on to the computer. Every day, whatever she was doing, her thoughts kept winging back to her mum and dad, wondering if Dad was in a better mood, praying that Mum would have a long day at the TV studio and not get home before

Chloë was there to keep an eye on things.

"OK," Jasmin cried in triumph. "Now type your message."

"What shall I put?"

"Something romantic yet intriguing. Not too slushy, though; anyone over there can read it."

"Oh great," sighed Chloë. "Here goes."

"Do you think he'll reply? How long does it take to get there? You are sure it sounded OK?"

Jasmin giggled. "It was fine – and I'll keep checking for replies. Now, what about your part of the bargain? You haven't forgotten?"

Chloë shook her head. "I'll get it sorted this evening," she said.

"Do you think she'll say yes?"

"Of course she will," affirmed Chloë. "It's just the sort of thing my mother adores."

"Darling, what a splendid idea!" Suzy Sanderson clapped her hands in delight. "Of course I'll do it."

"Thanks, Mum!" Chloë gave her a hug. "They'll be really chuffed."

She bit her lip. "By the way, was there any post for me?"

"No, angel, sorry – nothing at all."

It had been nearly a month. What had happened to him? He couldn't just have forgotten her. How long did it take to get a reply to an e-mail? Perhaps it was there already.

"Can I ring Jasmin and tell her you'll do the opening?"

"I've got a better idea," said her mother. "Dad's eating out tonight so why don't you and I pop round there for supper?"

"Cool!" agreed Chloë. "Now?"

"No," said her mother. "When you've done your homework."

Typical, thought Chloë.

"Mr Johnson, that was wonderful!" Suzy dabbed her mouth with her napkin. "I've never tasted monkfish like it."

"And the chilli was gorgeous," added Chloë. "You're so lucky being able to eat here every day, Jasmin!"

"She gets tired of it," laughed Josie, clearing the plates. "All she wants is burgers and chips."

Suzy laughed. "To business," she said. "Mr Johnson . . ."

"Please, call me Harry."

"All right, Harry – now I understand you're planning a grand opening."

Harry nodded.

"And you would like me to do the honours?"

Harry's mouth dropped open.

"He doesn't know yet," interrupted Jasmin. "It's our surprise. Dad, if Chloë's mum was at the opening party the press would come and then you could put her picture on the wall and say she ate here, and the place would be full every night."

"True," agreed Suzy without a hint of embarrassment. "I do seem to carry a bit of kudos, you know. Now, my fee – one thousand pounds usually, but for you, eight hundred."

There was a stunned silence. Josie dropped her eyes, Harry shuffled his feet. Jasmin gasped out loud.

It was Chloë who broke the silence.

"Mum! Jasmin's my friend! You can't charge money!"

"Well, of course she must," began Harry. "She's a famous lady, after all. But I'm afraid we can't really run to that just now and . . ."

Suzy held up her hand. "Then I think I have the very solution," she beamed. "Chloë's sixteenth."

The assembled company looked bemused.

"Chloë's birthday is coming up," she explained. "The silly child has been dithering for ages about what to do, and I said from the start that a party would be the thing. So that's what we'll do. I'll do the speech and ribbon-cutting bit for free, if you'll let Chloë invite a few friends along as well. How would that be?"

"Cool!" agreed Jasmin.

"Thank you so much," said Josie.

"Chloë?"

It would be nice to have a party. And this way, it wouldn't be at home, so she wouldn't have to worry about anything. And she'd get more pressies that way.

"Great," she said with a grin. "Thanks, Mum."

"Mum, what about this?" Jenny Bowen tapped the evening paper with her finger and began reading. "*Waterfront café requires assistant manager. Must be numerate, fun-loving and prepared to work shifts.*"

"Looks interesting, dear," said her mother, peering over her shoulder.

"You can't take a job like that, Mum!" Nick looked up from his French translation. "That's so common! It's probably nothing more than a glorified waitress."

"Oh, Nick!" His mother sighed. "I'm hardly going to land a job as chairman of ICI, am I? It's years since I had a proper job. Besides, I like being with people. It helps me to forget . . ."

"Dad? I'm glad you find it so easy!"

His grandmother shook her head. "It's because she doesn't find it easy, love, that she needs something to take her mind off things. You wait – when you've made some new friends, you'll start feeling better."

Nick sighed. "I suppose so," he admitted. He had felt better for talking to Sanjay, and even telling Chloë about his lies hadn't been as bad as he had expected. She had been really nice, not asking lots of questions or telling him that he'd been a jerk.

She was really ever so nice.

I wonder, he thought, whether she's got a boyfriend. Maybe I could ask her out one evening, just to . . .

What am I thinking of? My dad died just three months ago and I'm sitting here thinking about some dumb girl. That's awful.

"What are you thinking, Nick?" asked his mother, eyeing his scowling expression.

"Nothing," he grunted.

He bent his head back down to his work and concentrated on

conjuring up his dad's face in his mind. For a few awful, agonising seconds he couldn't remember what he looked like. Then, just as suddenly, his father's face swam before his eyes. And that was even worse.

CHAPTER 14

PARTY POOPERS
not allowed!

Ten days later, Jasmin slipped a card into Chloë's hand.

FUNKY FOOD, TRENDY TOONS, COOL DUDES –

BE WHERE IT'S AT!

WITH CHLOË
FOR THE WILDEST BIRTHDAY PARTY EVER

AT THE OH-SO-COOL CANAL CAFÉ

EIGHT TILL LATE (well, Midnight)
SATURDAY OCTOBER 19th

"So what do you think?" Jasmin jigged from one foot to the other while Chloë read the invitation.

"Neat," grinned Chloë. "It's really nice of you to have done these for me – I'm useless at arty stuff."

"Can we be friends?"

Jasmin had blurted it out before she knew it. What a nerd! Now she'd blown it – anyone with a smidgen of cool would know that you never asked to be someone's mate; it was the wettest thing out.

"What do you mean, can we be friends?" Chloë queried.

That does it, thought Jasmin.

"We already are, aren't we?"

Jasmin sighed audibly and a great grin spread across her face. "I guess we are," she said.

"So will you come?"

Chloë hovered by Nick's side as he scanned his eyes over the invitation while they waited for registration.

"I, er – I don't know."

Chloë's heart sank.

"It'll be cool, really it will," she urged. "And it will be a great way for you to get to know other people from school."

Nick nibbled a fingernail. "I don't know," he repeated. "It doesn't seem right, well, that's to say . . ."

Chloë touched his arm lightly. "It must be really hard for you, thinking about having fun after losing your dad so recently," she said. "But I guess he'd want you to make friends, wouldn't he? I mean, he'd want to feel that there were people looking out for you."

Nick turned and for a long moment, he said nothing at all.

Then his face broke into a smile. It was the sort of smile that would have done very nicely as the centrefold of *Heaven Sent* magazine, and it had a rather unexpected effect on Chloë's heart-rate.

"And you'd look out for me?" he said, a hint of teasing in his voice.

"Of course," she said, ever so slightly flirtatiously. "Isn't that what friends are for?"

"I'll come," agreed Nick.

"Brill," said Chloë. And immediately felt guilty. For about two minutes and ten seconds she hadn't had a single thought about Jack.

"Me?" Sanjay leaned against the railings round the school playground and stared at the invitation. "You want me to come to your party?"

Chloë laughed. "Anyone would think," she said, "that I was asking you to open Parliament. It's only a party, for heaven's sake."

"But why me?"

"Because I want you to be there, silly," said Chloë. "Nick's coming, and you're his mate and . . ."

Sanjay nodded. "I know," he said. "But I'm not awfully good at parties."

Chloë grinned. "Why? What do you do? Run amok? Fall down drunk?"

"No way, of course I don't!" Sanjay gasped.

"I was teasing, silly!" interjected Chloë. "I just wondered what you meant."

Sanjay shrugged and stared intently at the gravel. "I'm no good at chatting to people," he muttered.

"You're chatting to me," reasoned Chloë.

Sanjay's eyes widened and he looked at her in surprise. "Yes," he said. "I am, aren't I?"

His face broke into a grin. "I'd love to come. Thanks."

"Have you asked Bianca and Abby?" Sinead's face puckered into a frown as she leaned across Chloë to grab the salt.

Chloë shook her head. "I don't really know them that well," she said, sticking her fork into the solidifying mass that the school called macaroni cheese. "And besides, to be honest, they're not my type."

"Oh, get you! Too good for everyone else, are you?"

"OH SINEAD! What is it with you? Can't I say anything without you taking it the wrong way?"

Sinead bit her lip.

"Look," continued Chloë reasonably. "I can't ask the entire school, can I? Mum said thirty max, so I can only ask the people I really want."

She gave up on the macaroni cheese and bit into her apple. "So are you coming or not?"

Sinead hesitated. "I don't think I can," she said. "Me and Abby and Bianca – we go down town on Saturdays. I can't very well let them down."

"They've got each other," reasoned Chloë. "But, of course, if you don't want to come . . ."

Sinead sighed. She did want to go, especially now Chloë had said that she really wanted her. But then again, she knew how Bianca would react.

"Shove up!" Sinead turned as someone tapped her on the shoulder. "Can I squeeze in?"

She felt her cheek burn scarlet. "Course," she said, desperately trying to sound cool and casual as Nick slid on to the end of the bench.

"So, Chloë," Nick said, slicing his jumbo sausage in half, "tell me more about this party."

"Are *you* going?" Sinead almost choked on her chips.

Nick nodded. "Sure," he said easily. "Are you?"

"Yes," said Sinead. "Yes, as a matter of fact I am."

"You fancy him!"

Chloë grabbed Sinead's arm as they headed out of the canteen on the way to geography.

"No I don't!" Sinead shrugged her arm away. "You don't have to worry, we all know that it's you who's after him."

"ME? Get real. I've got Jack." It was out before she realised it.

Sinead's face softened as she turned to face Chloë.

"Jack?" she enquired hopefully.

Chloë sighed. "This guy I met on holiday – he's got a body to die for and he's . . ."

"So you and Nick aren't getting it together?"

Chloë raised her eyebrows and shook her head. "No way," she said. "I hardly know him, and besides, I guess he's got so much on his mind right now . . ."

"Like what?"

Chloë stopped and pulled Sinead to one side of the corridor. "Nick's dad died recently," began Chloë.

"That's so sad!" gasped Sinead.

Chloë nodded. "He's really cut up about it – and I've got this feeling there's something else going on. I don't know what it is but I think things are really hard for him."

Sinead nodded thoughtfully.

"He's had to leave his old school," continued Chloë. "I guess maybe it's money worries – he's really cagey about where they're going to live and stuff like that."

"Poor guy!" Sinead looked really concerned. "I can't imagine life without my dad, can you?"

Chloë could. But the emotions that fought for supremacy in her mind just made her feel guilty and she pushed the thoughts away as fast as they came. Luckily Sinead was too preoccupied to notice.

"Actually," Sinead confided, "I do quite like him."

"NO!" Chloë teased. "I'd never have guessed. So – get glammed up on Saturday and go for it!"

"Do you really think I'd stand a chance?"

"If you don't try, you'll never know," declared Chloë. "Besides, what have you got to lose?"

CHAPTER 15

SHOCKS
and surprises

"**M**um! I'm back!"

At the sound of Nick's voice Jenny Bowen threw her black skirt on to the bed and shrugged her arms into her housecoat. This was promising: her son sounded almost cheerful.

She ran down the stairs to find him kicking off his trainers at the door.

"Why aren't you dressed?" he demanded urgently. "Are you ill?" A shadow crossed his face.

"I'm fine, darling," Jenny laughed. "Just trying on clothes – I've got some news."

"Me too," said Nick. "I'll be out next Saturday night."

Jenny's heart lifted. Don't sound too interested, she reminded herself. Don't ask too many questions.

"Somewhere nice?"

"A party," he said. "This girl I know from school invited me; it's at some posh new café place."

"Which one?" Jenny's voice was sharper than she had intended.

"The Canal Café, or something. Why?"

"Ah."

"What's the matter? What's wrong with it?" Nick frowned. "Oh I get it – no, Mum, I won't take drugs, no, Mum, I won't get drunk . . ."

Jenny shook her head. "It's not that, Nick – I trust you, you know I do. I just thought I should mention that . . ."

"What?"

"Well, I – the thing is, that's the place I showed you in the advert. The one with the vacancy, remember?"

Nick nodded. "Yes, I remember. So I suppose I could suss it out for you, see if it really is an up-market job . . . oh no. Mum? You didn't? You haven't?"

Jenny nodded. "I applied. I got the job."

Nick looked appalled. "You're not going to be there? Not on Saturday?"

Jenny nodded apologetically. "I start tomorrow."

"You sound cheerful, Mum." Jasmin flung her schoolbag on the nearest table as her mother came to the end of a particularly lively rendition of 'When The Saints Come Marching In'.

"I am," grinned Josie. "I've found someone to fill the vacancy."

"Cool," said Jasmin, slipping behind the bar and reaching into the cool cabinet for a can of cola. "Hopefully someone with a few more brain cells than that Kelly girl?"

Josie nodded. "Actually," she said, "it's something of a coincidence. She's got a son at your school."

140

"Mum," said Jasmin pityingly. "There are one thousand, one hundred kids at Lockbridge High and most of them come from this side of town. It's hardly the eighth wonder of the modern world."

"Ah," said Josie smugly, "but this lad is in Year Eleven. Now what did she say his name was? Dick? Rick?"

"Not Nick?"

"That's it. Nick. Nick Bowen."

Jasmin's eyes almost shot out of her head. "His mum is going to be working here? Are you sure?"

"Of course I'm sure, I've just appointed her," laughed her mother. "So handy – she only lives a few minutes away, in Talbot Street."

Josie held a glass up to the light and polished it vigorously. "She's starting tomorrow – I thought that would give her time to get used to things before the party next Saturday."

"She's going to be here for the party? But she can't!" gasped Jasmin. "Nick's coming to it!"

"Really? That is nice, isn't it?"

"I have a feeling," murmured Jasmin, "that Nick won't think so."

"You didn't actually say that? Not in so many words?" Nick stared at his mother.

"Darling, I had to be honest . . ."

"You said that you needed the money? You told perfect strangers that we'd lost our home and business?"

Jenny drew herself up to her full height. "Yes, I did," she said firmly.

"But how could you? Now all my friends will find out and . . ."

"And if they do, does it matter?" asked his mum. "Look, Nick, if I'm going to be working for these people, I owe them the courtesy of telling them the truth."

"Besides," interrupted Nick's gran, pausing in her stirring of a pan of home-made soup, "she had to explain the lack of references, didn't she? I think your mum's done really well, don't you?"

Nick caught his gran's eye. He looked from her to his mother, her cheeks flushed and eyes pleading. His shoulders dropped and he moved across the room. "Yes, I do," he said, giving her a hug. "But promise me just one thing?"

"What's that?" asked Jenny.

"On Saturday, you will keep a low profile, won't you? You won't talk to me, will you? Or to my friends? Just make like you're not interested?"

Jenny pressed her lips together in an attempt not to laugh. "I promise," she said. "I'll be the very soul of discretion."

Chloë slid her key into the lock and opened the front door.

"Mum?"

She knew her mother should be at the TV studio, rehearsing for the new show which was due to start in a week's time. But her VW Polo was still in its parking space. Maybe Dad had run her to work.

No reply. That's what had happened then.

Chloë headed for the kitchen and food, and that was when she saw it.

On the carpet.

A bloodstain.

And another.

"Mum? MUM!" Her voice rose in panic as she galloped two at a time up the stairs. There were drops of blood on the landing carpet too.

"MUM!"

She pushed open the bedroom door.

Her mother was sitting on the bed, her back to the door. At the sound of Chloë's cries, she turned slowly.

Her arms were wrapped tightly round her stomach. Her nose was swollen and bloody. On her neck there was a huge purple bruise.

Tears slowly, silently coursed down Suzy's cheeks.

"Mum!" Chloë enveloped her in her arms. "He didn't . . . ?"

Slowly Suzy Sanderson nodded, wincing in pain as she moved her head. "Yes," she said dully. "Yes, he did it again. He hit me."

"It's all my fault! I should never have gone to school and left you! He's been in a mood for ages. I should have realised!"

Chloë bit her lip and struggled not to cry as she held an icepack against her mother's nose.

"Darling, you mustn't think like that," said her mother, holding her hand tightly. "If it was anyone's fault it was mine; going on and on about the new job."

"The job?"

"That's what started it all. It's been brewing for ages – and then this morning, I was showing him the scripts and set designs . . . so stupid of me. I should have realised how your poor dad would feel about it."

"Poor DAD?" Chloë exploded. "He hit you, Mum! He attacked you – and you start sympathising with him?"

"You have to realise, darling, that your dad doesn't mean to do it – it's just that things get on top of him and then he gets depressed and . . ."

"Oh right!" Grief and fear were making Chloë angry. "So everyone who has a couple of bad weeks starts lashing out, do they?"

"I was thoughtless, Chloë. I didn't think how he would be feeling, especially since his show has been rejected yet again. He won't do it again, I know he won't."

"Oh, Mum, get real! How many times have I heard you say that? Ten? Twenty? I remember you saying that kind of stuff when I was about six. And he always does do it again, doesn't he? I can't . . ."

The loud shrilling of the doorbell interrupted her outburst.

"If that's Dad . . ."

"It won't be," her mother said quietly. "Just get rid of whoever it is."

Chloë dragged herself downstairs and opened the door.

"Hi, Chloë!" Sinead was standing outside wearing a gold Lurex miniskirt and an emerald-green halter-necked top. "What do you reckon? This top – or this one?" She waved a black net tank top in Chloë's face.

"What?" Chloë stared uncomprehendingly at her. "Oh look, please go away. I can't talk to you now."

"Why? What's wrong?" Sinead stared at her. "It won't take long . . ."

In her head Chloë could hear all the warnings she had received from her mother in the past. Don't let anyone know what's happened. We don't talk about it, it's over. It wouldn't do for people to find out, I'm in the public eye. We don't wash our dirty linen in public.

"Chloë? What's the matter?" Sinead was pressing her. "What's that on your – oh my God, it's blood!"

"Just go, can't you!" Chloë choked out the words and slammed the door in Sinead's face. As she did so she heard ominous sounds from the top of the stairs. Sprinting up them, she crashed into the bathroom.

Her mother was leaning over the loo, being very sick.

Chloë sank to the floor. "Mum, tell me what to do! I don't know how to make you better!"

"Now look," said Kathleen Flaherty, pulling up a chair to the kitchen table, "before we all go rushing into things, let's get this straight. You're sure it was blood?"

"I'm certain, Mum," reiterated Sinead. "It was on Chloë's hands, and on her shirt, and she was in an awful state . . ."

"Perhaps she has murdered someone," intervened Erin, hardly pausing in her systematic demolition of a jam doughnut.

"Oh, grow up, Erin!" retorted her mother, much to Sinead's satisfaction. "This could be serious."

"I still say that I should go up and investigate," said her father. "You read such awful things in the papers about neighbours who ignore one another's troubles."

"Well, we don't want to go poking in our noses where we are not wanted," said Kathleen. "The child probably cut herself; it's hardly going to be anything awful, not in a classy family like that."

Shaun stood up decisively. "I'm going up," he said. "I'll think of some excuse."

"But what if it's nothing?" protested his wife.

"Then we'll all be very happy, won't we?" said Sinead's father.

"I'm fine now, darling, really I am."

Suzy was sitting at the kitchen table, sipping the tea that Chloë had made. "And now, tell me, what exactly did you say to Sinead?"

Chloë took a gulp of tea. "I just told her to go away," she confessed. "I was crying – I didn't know what to do, I . . ."

"It's all right," said her mother calmly, unscrewing a tube of concealing make-up. "But if any of them ask any questions, this is what you say."

"And you're quite sure everything is all right?"

Mr Flaherty sat perched awkwardly on the very edge of one of the white leather sofas. "There's nothing I can do?"

Chloë shook her head. "No, honestly," she reassured him for the third time. "Mum gets these migraines from time to time, only this time she fainted and gave herself a nosebleed. I'm sorry I made a fuss; blood freaks me out a bit."

Mr Flaherty nodded and stood up. "Well, I'll be leaving you in peace, then," he said. "I see you've a broken chair over there."

Oh my God, thought Chloë.

"Perhaps you'd ask your parents if they'd like me to mend it for them," he said a little nervously.

"Oh no, I'm sure . . ."

"To be honest with you, it would be doing me a favour," said Mr Flaherty. "I'm setting up a furniture making and restoration business, you see, and as I was saying to Kathleen only yesterday . . ."

What he was saying to Kathleen, Chloë never did discover. At that moment the front door opened and her father walked in.

He looked at Shaun uncertainly.

Shaun held out a hand. "Shaun Flaherty," he said. "We're your new neighbours."

"Pleased to meet you," said Edward nervously. "Where's your mother, Chloë?"

"Out."

Shaun looked at Chloë. He looked at her wide, frightened eyes, opened his mouth and shut it again.

"No – I mean, she's . . ." Her voice trailed off.

"I'll be on my way, then," said Mr Flaherty evenly. "Now remember, Chloë, we're just downstairs, and should you be needing a single thing at all, you must let us know, so you must."

He caught Edward's eye. "By the way of chair mending or whatever," he added for good measure. "Cheerio, then."

The front door shut.

Chloë exhaled with relief.

"Edward?"

She wheeled round. Her mother was coming slowly down the stairs, her face tight with fear.

"Oh, Suzy, Suzy, forgive me," Edward Sanderson said, opening his arms and then letting them fall at his side as his wife walked past.

He slumped into a chair, his eyes filling with tears. "I love you, Suzy," he sobbed. "I'll never, ever do it again – I swear to you."

Neither his wife nor Chloë said a word.

They had both heard it all before.

CHAPTER 16

CONFESSIONS
and cover-ups

She had done quite well so far. She had managed to avoid everyone. She had been so reluctant to leave her mum that she had missed the school bus and had to take a taxi, and the first two lessons had been Spanish, which none of her close friends took, and theatre studies, during which she had to pretend to be a locust which rather eliminated any risk of conversation.

But now it was break and she could see Sinead heading purposefully in her direction. She tried to dodge behind the gym but it was too late.

"Look, I'm sorry about last night," Sinead began, linking her arm through Chloë's. This gesture was sufficiently uncharacteristic as to prevent Chloë from thinking of an excuse to rush away.

"Only I wanted your advice about what to wear to the party," she said. "I mean, I've got loads of new gear, but somehow nothing seems quite right. I can't wait for Saturday, can you?"

A sharp stab of anxiety shot through Chloë's mind. The party!

There was no way her mum could do the opening now. In the past, when her father had lost it and lashed out at Suzy he had been careful not to leave any marks that showed, but this time it was different. No way would those bruises have faded in five days.

"So what are you wearing?" Sinead persisted.

Chloë thought fast. "I'm not actually sure that the party can go ahead," she said. "What with mum not being well and . . ."

"Oh, it'll be fine!" Sinead interjected airily. "Migraines don't last that long – my mum gets them and she's usually fine in a day or so."

Chloë knew that to argue any further would just make everything worse; anyway, she guessed that the Johnsons would still let the party go ahead even if her mum didn't cut the ribbon and make a fancy speech.

"Oh sugar," sighed Sinead, "there's the bell. Look, what if I come up to your flat tonight and we have a trying-on session – that way . . ."

"NO!" retorted Chloë. "That is – why don't I come down to you? I mean, all your clothes are there and we can find something really cool for you to stun Nick with."

Sinead beamed. "OK," she said, throwing her drinks can into the bin. "And Chloë?"

"Yes?"

"You are all right, aren't you?"

Chloë smiled brightly and nodded. "Of course I am," she assured her. "Never better."

*   *   *

"You'll never guess what!" enthused Jasmin to Chloë as they queued with Sinead for lunch. "Uncle Louis's booked this funky new band for the party on Saturday – they're called Fruit Juice and they are so cool!"

"Neat!" exclaimed Sinead. "I heard them at Fat Harry's last week and they're amazing."

"That's great," replied Chloë half-heartedly, dumping a cheese roll on her tray. Somehow, with her whole mind swamped by thoughts of her mum, she couldn't get excited about anything.

"You still pining over Jack?" demanded Jasmin.

"Yes, I guess," said Chloë. She couldn't admit that even Jack had disappeared from her thoughts after what had happened to her mum. She wouldn't care if she never heard from him at all, as long as things at home could be all right.

"He'll reply soon – perhaps on your birthday," said Jasmin brightly, and then sighed. "I wish I could afford something new to wear but I've spent all my allowance and Mum's really stuffy about subbing me."

"No probs," said Sinead instantly, trying to resist a plateful of chips and failing. "I've got loads of stuff – really good labels, too. You can borrow something."

"Really?" Jasmin's eyes lit up.

"Sure – Chloë and I are having a trying-on session tonight; come over, why don't you?"

"Well, I . . ."

"Only make it after eight thirty – Mum's one of those 'no fun till homework's done' types."

"I can't, actually," said Jasmin hurriedly, thinking how dark it would be by then. "I've got to help out in the café."

"Pity," said Sinead. "Perhaps tomorrow?"

"Perhaps," said Jasmin.

"Go on," Sanjay urged Nick. "She's over there with her mates; wave or something."

Nick hesitated.

"Leave it to me," said Sanjay, waving his arm in the air. "Hi, Chloë – these seats are free!"

Chloë, Jasmin and Sinead threaded their way through the surging mass of hungry pupils and dumped their trays on the chipped Formica table.

"Say, Nick, isn't it cool about your mum and the job?" Jasmin said, launching into conversation with her usual lack of reserve.

"Mmm," said Nick, surveying his burger with intense interest.

"Nick's mum is going to be working for my parents," continued Jasmin, turning to Sinead and Chloë.

"*With* them," Nick corrected sharply. "She's the assistant manager."

"Is that what she did before – when you lived in Italy?" asked Chloë.

"You lived in Italy?" Jasmin gasped before Nick had the chance to answer. "So how come you're here?"

She winced as Chloë's ankle-boot met her shin with rather more force than was necessary.

"It's none of your business," began Sanjay, rising to his friend's defence.

"No, wait," said Nick. "I've got to tell you some time." He took a long swig from his carton of apple juice.

"My parents ran this company, buying up old houses in Italy and turning them into holiday homes," he said. "Then Dad died."

He paused for a moment. Involuntarily, Sinead touched his arm and then pulled her hand away in embarrassment when she caught sight of the others looking at her.

"We found out that he had lots of debts," gabbled Nick. "Not his fault, honestly – it was just that he'd entered into all these amazing deals and had died before he had time to make them work."

"That's so sad," breathed Jasmin.

"I mean," continued Nick, as if talking to himself, "the guys who lent him all that money – banks and companies and everything – they really had faith in him, or they wouldn't have done it."

"He must have been a brilliant businessman," said Sinead.

"He was," nodded Nick with a grateful smile. "It's not his fault there's no money left."

"And so you had to come back to England?" queried Chloë.

Nick nodded again.

"And you bought your house in Talbot Street?" Jasmin concluded.

"Oh, it's not ours!" exclaimed Nick hastily. "It's my gran's – we'll be moving to our own place really soon."

"Not too soon, I hope," laughed Jasmin. "My mum's over the

moon at having your mum round the corner – she'll go into a decline if you leave."

"Oh, we won't leave Leeds," said Nick, "but we wouldn't want to live in a place like Talbot Street for long."

Sanjay frowned. "What's wrong with it?"

"It's just so different from the house in Italy," he said. "That had loads of space, and vines growing up the walls and a pool in the garden and . . ."

"Ah," said Sinead. "But there was one thing Italy didn't have."

"What?" asked Nick with a puzzled frown.

"Us," said Sinead.

Nick grinned. "That," he said, "is very true."

"So where shall we go on Saturday night? Fat Harry's or Ritzy's?"

Bianca blotted her lips on a tissue and peered in the mirror of the girls' locker room.

"I don't think I can manage Saturday," said Sinead tentatively. "I've got something on."

"Like what?" demanded Abby.

"Family party," stammered Sinead. "Boring or what?"

"So can't you get out of it?" asked Bianca.

Sinead shook her head. "My mum would kill me . . ." she began.

"And you forget, Bee, that Sinead is such a good little girl that she always does what Mummy says," sneered Abby, linking her arm through Bianca's.

Sinead chewed her lip. If she didn't go, they probably wouldn't ask her again and then she'd have no one. But then again, she really wanted to be at the party. Not that Nick would take any notice of her, of course.

"I suppose I could come . . ."

"Forget it," retorted Bianca, turning her back and calling over her shoulder. "Who needs you?"

Chloë slammed the front door behind her and hurried through to the kitchen. There was time for a quick raid on the fridge before her mother got back from work.

But the kitchen wasn't empty as Chloë had expected. Her mother was sitting at the scrubbed pine table, her head in her hands.

"Mum! What is it?"

Suzy looked up. Her face was streaked with tears, great blotches of mascara smudged under her eyes.

"What's happened?" demanded Chloë, her voice rising in panic. "Has Dad . . . ?"

Suzy shook her head. "Sit down, darling," she said wearily, "We need to talk."

"Hi, Gran, where's Mum?" Nick pulled open the fridge and took out a carton of milk.

"In town, buying clothes for the new job," grinned his grandmother. "Want a piece of fruitcake?"

Nick nodded. His grandmother cooked with a total disregard for cholesterol or calories and it was wonderful.

"And I thought you might like to cast your eye over these," she said, pushing a pile of colour charts under his nose.

Nick frowned. "What for?"

"Well," said his grandmother, cutting a wedge of cake and putting it in front of him, "I thought we'd get that spare room redecorated for you. I know it's a bit dowdy – I haven't touched it since Bill, bless him, died."

Nick smiled. "That's really kind, Gran," he said, "but we won't be here long enough. Mum's going to get us a place of our own just as soon as she can."

"Oh, I know, dear," replied his grandmother calmly. "But that won't be quite as soon as she thought. She's not going to be earning a fortune at this café, you know."

"So why did she take the job?" demanded Nick, his heart sinking.

"Because it's a start, because she's a brave lady, because she knows she can't go on living in the past," said his gran softly, taking his hand. "Look, Nick, I know how hard it is for you, believe me I do. You miss your dad, your schoolmates, your house – but the hard reality is that life has to go on."

Nick swallowed but said nothing.

"Oh, I agree," his gran continued, "you could spend every day yearning for what you had, going over and over it all in your mind, wishing it hadn't happened. But that won't bring Dad back; it won't put money in the bank. And it won't make you happy."

"I know," said Nick. "But I guess being happy is just something that's not going to happen."

"Nick, darling, if you don't let it, it won't happen," said his gran, squeezing his hand. "But believe me, as soon as you decide to start moving on, you'll find that all sorts of people are waiting to help you."

Nick thought for a moment. About Sanjay. And Sinead and Jasmin. And Chloë.

Chloë.

"I guess you may be right," he said. "I'll try."

"That's my boy," said his gran, ruffling his hair.

And although he pulled a face and jerked his head away, he was rather surprised to discover that for once, he didn't mind her being grandmotherly one little bit.

"What do you mean, he's gone away?" gasped Chloë. "You're telling me he's just upped and done a runner, left . . ."

"No, darling, that's not what I mean," said her mother. "I told him to leave."

Chloë's mouth dropped open.

"Not for good, sweetheart," said her mother. "Just to give me time to sort my head out, think things through."

"But where's he gone?"

"To that hotel in Holmfirth that he likes. We'll just tell people he's away researching a new programme."

Suzy ran her fingers through her hair and winced as she touched a bruise. "I've been living in a no-exit nightmare for years," she said dully. "Telling myself that if I just tried that little bit harder, was that tiny bit more understanding, it wouldn't happen again. It always does happen again."

Chloë took her mother's hand. "Do you want – I mean, are you going to split?"

Suzy sighed. "I don't know, and that's the honest answer," she said. "I don't want to break the family up – he's your father. You love him."

"I hate him!" spat Chloë, her eyes filling with tears.

Suzy shook her head. "No, sweetheart, you hate what he did, not him. It's OK to love him. I do."

"Still?"

"Still," said her mum. "That's why there's no easy answer."

Chloë put an arm round her mother's shoulder. "Mum?"

"Yes?"

"I just want you to know that I shall always love you, whatever you decide to do."

They didn't say any more. They just sat with their arms round one another, and cried silently together.

"Why do people always drink tea in times of crisis?" mused Suzy, pouring Chloë another mugful. "Still, I suppose it's better than turning to alcohol."

Chloë tried a weak smile.

"Which reminds me," said Suzy briskly. "What about a fruit punch for your party? Josie rang and suggested it. We adults get champagne, of course!"

Chloë frowned. "But, Mum, you can't do the opening now!"

"Why on earth not?" said her mother.

"You know why!" snapped Chloë. "Your neck – it's all bruised."

"So I'll wear my Nehru jacket, that will cover it up," declared Suzy. "I have to carry on, darling. If I stop, if I begin cancelling things, I'll crumple. Really go under. You and my work are what keep me going."

"But . . ."

"Chloë, trust me. I've lived with this for eighteen years. I know what I have to do."

"You can't wear that, it looks horrendous!" Chloë had been feeling like a piece of taut string ever since she had arrived at Sinead's apartment and the sight of her friend in a bright orange bustier and lilac crochet miniskirt was more than she could stand.

"Oh, well, great, thanks a bundle!" stormed Sinead. "I'll have you know this top cost forty-five pounds and the skirt's from Apparition!"

"So?" Chloë asked wearily. "It doesn't matter if they cost thousands if they don't look right together. Try this." She hurled a pair of cranberry hipsters and a silver shirt on the bed.

"But they were really cheap, from Crazy Kiddo," protested Sinead.

"Try them!" ordered Chloë.

Sinead pulled them on and peered into the mirror. "Actually . . ." she began.

"Now put these on," ordered Chloë, thrusting a pair of sequin trim sandals into her hand.

"Neat," said Sinead with a grin. "Does it make me look fat?"

"No way," declared Chloë. "You look discreetly sexy and very alluring."

"I do?"

"Definitely," affirmed Chloë. "Happy now?"

Sinead nodded and gave Chloë a hug. "You know," she said, "you're all right."

"Well, thanks," said Chloë dryly. "You're not that bad yourself."

CHAPTER 17

SHOCKS
for Sinead

"So are you coming tomorrow night or not?" Bianca whispered to Sinead in the middle of the world's most boring maths lesson.

"I'll try," Sinead replied. "But if I'm not outside the Corn Exchange by eight o'clock go on without me."

"OK," shrugged Bianca, looking slightly mollified. "But do try – it won't be the same without you."

Sinead glowed inside. They wanted her. They needed her. Perhaps, after all, she should go with them and give the party a miss.

"Abby was saying what fun you . . ."

"Bianca Clarke! Is it too much to hope that you might apply yourself to the work in hand rather than exercise your already overworked vocal chords!" Mr Tompkins marched to her table and glowered at her. "Not that I assume your brain cell is producing much of interest today."

"It was my fault, sir," said Sinead immediately. "Sorry, sir."

Bianca threw her a grateful grin. The glow inside Sinead grew.

I'll go to Fat Harry's, she decided. My old mates need me.

If she hadn't needed the loo before PE, she would never have found out. She was sitting there, examining her fingernails and wondering who it was considered that fifteen-year-olds needed to leap over hurdles in order to further their education, when the outside door slammed.

"I think I might have persuaded her to come." It was Bianca, rifling through her make-up bag.

"Thank goodness for that," she heard Abby reply. "There's no way I can go unless she does."

Sinead smiled to herself.

"I mean, if she doesn't turn up, what will we do?" continued Abby. "I haven't got any money."

"Me neither. But she will. I made her think that we loved and adored her."

Sinead's smile faded.

"Well, we love and adore her money," giggled Abby. "As long as she keeps chucking that around she can hang out with me, no problem."

Her voice faded as the two of them drifted out of the cloakroom.

Sinead sat motionless.

She wouldn't cry. There was no way she was going to be the biggest fool in the school and a crybaby with it.

But sometimes the best resolutions bite the dust.

*   *   *

She had tried to avoid Bianca and Abby all day, but as everyone piled into the school forecourt and on to the buses, Abby tapped her on the shoulder.

"See you tomorrow, then?"

"Probably not," said Sinead, in what she hoped was a calm but aloof manner.

"What? You said that . . ."

"Bye, Sinead!" Nick brushed past them and grinned. "See you at the party!"

"Party?" demanded Abby. "What party?"

Sinead turned and fixed her with a steely gaze. "Now wouldn't you like to know?" she said.

CHAPTER 18

Many
H A P P Y
returns

"**S**o how's your birthday been so far?" Jasmin asked Chloë as they balanced on chairs, stringing banners across the café.

"Brilliant!" replied Chloë brightly, because she knew it was the answer her friend would expect to hear. "Mum and Dad gave me this wicked camera with a zoom lens and everything."

Only Dad hadn't been there to give it to her. She felt so guilty; she should have been pleased that he was out of the way, that her mum could breathe easily for a few days and sort things out. But part of Chloë felt like a little kid who had been abandoned in the playground; she felt as if her family was disintegrating around her and there was nothing she could do to stop it happening.

"Bring it tonight," urged Jasmin. "It would be a laugh – you could snap people snogging and stuff."

"OK," said Chloë with a sigh. "Not that I'll be getting a share of that sort of action. I wish Jack was here. I don't suppose . . ."

Jasmin shook her head. "Nothing yet," she said. "But you mustn't give up hope."

Chloë said nothing. With everything else that was going on at home, she had even forgotten to watch the post for the last few days. But she had hoped that he would send her a present, a card, something to show he cared. She missed him such a lot – so much that she'd given up going out with Nat and Becky at weekends, because watching them drooling all over Sam and Dave was more than she could bear.

At least, that's what she told herself. She knew deep down that the real reason was that she didn't want to leave Mum on her own.

Just in case Dad came back and was angry.

"How do I look?"

Chloë's mum gave a little twirl. She was wearing a calf-length emerald-green skirt with a matching high-collared jacket, on which she had pinned a diamond brooch in the shape of an elephant.

"You look great," replied Chloë.

"Now remember, darling, if anyone asks – and I don't think they will because this concealing make-up is pretty hot stuff – just remember that I fainted and hit my face on the washbasin as I fell."

Chloë nodded.

"And that will account for any stiffness when I walk," added her mother.

"You are sure you want to do this?"

"Darling, I can't hide away – I have a new TV series to present on Monday. Besides, life goes on."

She gave Chloë a hug. "You look sensational," she said, eyeing Chloë's scarlet slip dress admiringly. "So what are we waiting for? Let's party!"

"Happy birthday!"

"Love the dress!"

"This is for you!"

Chloë received all the hugs and kisses and began tearing the wrapping paper off of Sinead's parcel. And gasped.

Inside was one of those huge, plush boxes of cosmetics that you see in swish department stores. It had cleanser and body lotion, lipstick and eyeliner and a massive bottle of perfume.

"Wow!" Jasmin gasped over Chloë's left shoulder.

"Cripes!" breathed Natalie.

"It's lovely," said Chloë. "But you shouldn't have."

"Why not?" said Sinead. "You're my friend."

There was a brief, rather uncomfortable silence.

"This is for you," said Jasmin. "But it's not much. Sorry."

Chloë unwrapped a leather thong with a pewter heart hanging from it. "Oh, Jasmin, that's so pretty!" she cried.

"It's not grand or anything," said Jasmin. "It's only from the market."

"But it's lovely," insisted Chloë, fastening it round her neck and hugging her.

"Go on, Sanjay, give her yours!" urged Nick. "This," he added, turning to Chloë, "is mega."

Sanjay handed Chloë a large white envelope. She ripped it open and pulled out a sheet of pink card.

It was a cartoon, with a huge figure 16 in the middle and all their faces peeping round.

"Sanjay! Did you do this?"

He nodded. "It's not very good . . ." he began.

"It's amazing!" cried Chloë. "I'm going to frame it and hang it over my bed."

"Really?"

"Really."

Then Nick gave her a pair of socks which played Happy Birthday and Chloë insisted on putting them on there and then.

She put the box of cosmetics on a side table out of the way.

"I'll save those for a special occasion," she said to Sinead.

She thought it had gone all right. Her mum's speech had been a riot and everyone had cheered and clapped when she cut the ribbon and declared The Canal Café officially open. Only Chloë noticed the slightly awkward way she stood and how she carefully turned the left side of her face to the camera when the local paper began taking pictures. Nick's mum seemed a bit subdued, hardly speaking to anyone, but then, thought Chloë, she's probably still too grief stricken to socialise.

At ten o'clock her mother had gone home and the rest of the

adults had drifted off and the party had really started to rave.

Everyone seemed to be enjoying themselves. She had been, too, until suddenly, a few minutes before, it had all washed over her again. The sight of her dad standing over her mother, gripping her wrists. The memory of her mother's bruised and battered face, of her tears and her determination. Don't think about it, she told herself firmly, flopping down into the nearest vacant chair. Just concentrate on the party.

"I blew it, didn't I?" Sinead sank down in the chair next to her.

"Blew what?" Chloë frowned. "Nick's danced with you loads of times."

"Not that," sighed Sinead. "That present I bought you. It was totally over the top, wasn't it?"

Chloë began to shake her head and then stopped. If she and Sinead were really going to be friends, there was no point pretending. "A bit," she nodded.

Sinead looked crestfallen.

"You don't have to buy me things," insisted Chloë. "I mean, it's lovely and I shall feel a million dollars using all that stuff, but I invited you because I wanted you here, not because I wanted a present."

Sinead smiled. "I used to dream of having money to spend," she admitted. "I thought everyone would like me if I bought them loads of stuff."

"I like you," said Chloë. "Stuff or no stuff. Promise me: no more lavish spending. Because I can't keep up."

"OK," grinned Sinead. "I promise."

"Chloë?"

"Yes?"

"I was wondering . . ." Nick paused and took a deep breath. "There's this film and I thought we could go but then again, you probably aren't into cinema, and I can easily go on my own because . . ."

"I'd love to," said Chloë. "When?"

Quite how it started no one really knew. One minute they were all doing the last dance, the smoochy bit, and then the band switched tempos, and suddenly some bright spark was suggesting a conga along the waterfront.

"Come on, Jasmin!" called Chloë. "Hold on to me."

Jasmin hesitated and then wrapped her hands round Chloë's waist. But they were only halfway down the cobbled path when she broke free. "I'm going back inside," she said. "Catch you later."

"Are you cold?"

"Yes," said Jasmin hurriedly. "That's right. I'm freezing."

"I'm fine, honestly – you get back to the others." Jasmin gave Sanjay a watery smile.

"I don't want to," said Sanjay. "I'm useless at dancing and besides, you're not fine."

Jasmin bit her lip.

"Jassy! What are you doing skulking in here?" Mr Johnson,

169

striped apron wrapped round his not insubstantial waist, paused in his clearing of dirty glasses. "Go and join the others."

"I came to help, Dad," she said.

"Don't you worry about that," he said. "Now off you go!" He bustled out of the room with a tray of glasses.

"You don't want to, do you?" Sanjay said.

Jasmin shook her head. "Why am I such a wimp?"

"What's wimpish about not liking dancing?" asked Sanjay.

"It's not the dancing I don't like," confessed Jasmin. "It's the dark."

"And I'm terrified of wasps and heights and talking to people . . ."

"Talking to people?" Jasmin looked at Sanjay in astonishment. "But you're so easy to talk to."

"I am?"

Jasmin nodded. "I've never told anyone else that every time I'm out in the dark I think of those thugs that attacked Dad – that I see him lying there with all the blood and . . ."

She shuddered. "He was coming to fetch me, you see, and someone told me he was hurt, and I ran round the corner and there he was . . ."

Her voice trailed off. Sanjay squeezed her hand. "It's OK," he said. And then saw his hand lying in hers.

And decided to leave it there.

"Thanks a lot, Mrs Johnson – it's been so cool!" Chloë beamed at Jasmin's mother.

"You must come round whenever you like, all of you!" declared Josie, waving her arms expansively. "I'll even give you reductions – crowds of young people milling around will make us look as if we are the – what do you call it? Hippy cool place?"

Everyone laughed.

"Mum?" Jasmin took her mother's arm.

"Yes, dear?"

"Kitchen," said Jasmin. "Now."

It was midnight by the time everyone had been fetched by their parents, and only Sanjay, Chloë, Jasmin, Nick and Sinead were left. Sanjay's father was talking intently to Jasmin's mum and Nick's mother was giving the bar a final wipe.

"Chloë, love, I told your mother I'd see you home, seeing as how I'm here for Sinead," said Mr Flaherty who had spent the previous fifteen minutes extolling the virtues of Gaelic football with Harry Johnson.

"Is she OK?" Chloë tried not to sound panicky.

"Right as rain," said Mr Flaherty with a gentle smile. "But she'll have my guts for garters if I don't get you home soon."

"Dad, just go and wait in the car," ordered Sinead. "We won't be long."

"Two minutes," said her father sternly, "and no more."

"Nick and me are going to see *Icy Encounters* at the cinema tomorrow afternoon," Chloë said as they all drifted out the door.

"Who's coming with us?"

"Me," said Sinead immediately, eyeing Chloë with a slightly less than friendly look.

"Evening or afternoon?" asked Jasmin, trying to sound casual.

"Afternoon," said Chloë.

"Can I go to the cinema tomorrow, Mum?" Jasmin yelled over her shoulder. "Yes," she said without waiting for a reply.

"Sanjay?"

"Me?"

Chloë sighed. "Yes, Sanj, you," she said teasingly.

"Tomorrow?"

She sighed again. "Yes. Tomorrow. Friends do things together at weekends, you know. Unless of course, you don't want to be friends with us."

He looked alarmed and then saw her broad grin. "I think," he said, "that I can just about hack it."

Chloë lay in bed staring at the ceiling. She wondered whether her dad was lying awake too. Would her mum have him back? And if he came, would it all start again?

She was sixteen now. Old enough to know that life wasn't one long series of happy endings. The problem wouldn't go away overnight. Whatever her mum decided to do, Chloë knew she'd have to come to terms with it and face it.

But somehow, it might be easier now. Now she had some real friends. Not, of course, that she would ever tell them the whole story.

*   *   *

Nick lay on his back, thinking. But for the first time in ages, it wasn't his dad he was thinking about. It wasn't the sound of ambulance sirens that reverberated in his memory or the image of the For Sale board being hammered into the lawn of their villa. He was thinking about his mates.

Not the ones from Benham. His new ones.

And Chloë.

He was so cute. He was so understanding. Of course, he was only a friend. Nothing more. Yet.

Jasmin turned off her bedside light and pulled the duvet round her neck. "Sanjay," she whispered and smiled in the dark.

"Where did you go this evening?" muttered Erin sleepily as Sinead slipped into bed.

"To a party with my mates," she whispered.

"Bee and Abby?"

"No," said Sinead. "My real mates."

"Right, straight to bed, Sanjay." Duncan Fraser unlocked the front door. "You have a lot of homework to finish tomorrow."

"OK." Sanjay couldn't remember when he had felt happier. He had done it. He had been to a party, he had talked to people, he had held a girl's hand. And what's more, they had talked to him.

And he hadn't been totally useless, not like he imagined he

would be. Nick had thanked him for being so understanding about his dad, Jasmin had confided in him and made him promise that it would be their secret. Even Chloë, who didn't have a care in the world, had said that it wouldn't have been the same if he had refused to come.

"These young people you were with tonight," his father continued.

Here we go, thought Sanjay. Here come the criticisms: too loud, too flashy, not studious enough.

"Nice crowd," said Duncan. "Good friends, are you?"

Sanjay suddenly realised the truth. "Yes, Dad, we are," he said with conviction. "Really good friends."

If you would like more information about books available from Piccadilly Press and how to order them, please contact us at:

Piccadilly Press Ltd.
5 Castle Road
London
NW1 8PR

Tel: 020 7267 4492
Fax: 020 7267 4493